Praise for *New York Times* bestselling author B.J. Daniels

"Daniels is truly an expert at Western romantic suspense."

—*RT Book Reviews* on *Atonement*

"B.J. Daniels is a sharpshooter; her books hit the target every time."

—#1 *New York Times* bestselling author Linda Lael Miller

"Daniels is a perennial favorite on the romantic suspense front, and I might go as far as to label her the cowboy whisperer."

—*BookPage*

Praise for author Nicole Helm

"An intimate, rewarding romance with a hot hero whose emotional growth is as sexy as his moves in the bedroom."

—*Kirkus Reviews* on *Want You More*

"Nicole Helm has done a great job of writing three-dimensional characters.... A super beginning to this series. I look forward to the next book in the series, *Wyoming Cowboy Protection*."

—*Harlequin Junkie* on *Wyoming Cowboy Justice*

DEADLY SECRET

B.J. DANIELS

Previously published as *Rustled*
and *Stone Cold Undercover Agent*

ISBN-13: 978-1-335-40641-5

Deadly Secret
First published as Rustled in 2011.
This edition published in 2021.
Copyright © 2011 by Barbara Heinlein

Stone Cold Undercover Agent
First published in 2017. This edition published in 2021.
Copyright © 2017 by Nicole Helm

This edition published by arrangement with Harlequin Books S.A.

For questions and comments about the quality of this book,
please contact us at CustomerService@Harlequin.com.

Harlequin Enterprises ULC
22 Adelaide St. West, 40th Floor
Toronto, Ontario M5H 4E3, Canada
www.Harlequin.com

Printed in U.S.A.

CONTENTS

RUSTLED   7
B.J. Daniels

STONE COLD UNDERCOVER AGENT   191
Nicole Helm

B.J. Daniels is a *New York Times* and *USA TODAY* bestselling author. She wrote her first book after a career as an award-winning newspaper journalist and author of thirty-seven published short stories. She lives in Montana with her husband, Parker, and three springer spaniels. When not writing, she quilts, boats and plays tennis. Contact her at bjdaniels.com, on Facebook or on Twitter, @bjdanielsauthor.

Books by B.J. Daniels

Harlequin Intrigue

Whitehorse, Montana: The Clementine Sisters

Hard Rustler
Rogue Gunslinger
Rugged Defender

The Montana Cahills

Cowboy's Redemption

HQN

Sterling's Montana

Stroke of Luck
Luck of the Draw

The Montana Cahills

Renegade's Pride
Outlaw's Honor
Hero's Return
Rancher's Dream

Visit the Author Profile page at
Harlequin.com for more titles.

RUSTLED

B.J. Daniels

This book is for a good friend
and fellow writer who is a huge fan of cowboys.
My hat's off to Joanna Wayne, the woman who
keeps those cowboys down in Texas
finding the loves of their lives.

Chapter 1

Dawson Chisholm reined in his horse to look back at the ranch buildings in the distance. This was his favorite view of the Chisholm Cattle Company. He'd always felt a sense of pride and respect for the ranching empire his father had built.

Today, though, he felt the weight of responsibility on his shoulders for the ranch and feared for his father—and the future. Someone wanted to destroy not only what Hoyt Chisholm had built, but Hoyt himself.

"I'm going to ride up into the high country and check the cattle on summer range," he'd told his five brothers. They knew him well enough to realize that as the oldest brother he needed some time alone after everything that had happened.

They'd been at the main house sitting around the kitchen table this morning, avoiding the dining room since their father had been arrested for murder and their stepmother, Emma, had taken off to parts unknown.

The house had felt too empty, so they had all moved back in even though they had their own houses on the huge ranch. When their father's new bride, Emma, had come to the house two months ago, she'd required them all to show up freshly showered and changed for supper every evening.

No one questioned Emma's new rules, which included no swearing in the house and bowing their heads in prayer before supper. In the weeks since she and Hoyt had wed, she'd made a lot of changes at Chisholm Cattle Company.

That was until the body of Hoyt's third wife turned up and he'd been arrested.

Dawson still couldn't believe it. There was no way his father was a murderer. Unfortunately, given the evidence against him and his wealth, the judge had denied bail and Hoyt was now sitting in jail in Whitehorse awaiting trial.

Emma... Well, she'd packed up and skipped town with only a short note saying she couldn't do this. It had broken their father's heart. Hoyt Chisholm had looked older than his fifty-six years when Dawson had visited him yesterday evening. He'd taken the news about Emma even worse than Dawson had thought he would.

"Emma wouldn't just leave," his father had argued. Emma had been nothing like his father's other wives. Redheaded with a fiery temper, plump and annoyingly cheerful. Her stepsons hadn't wanted to like her. But she'd won them all over and their father clearly adored her.

"She left a note, said she couldn't do this and packed

up all her stuff and was gone when we got home," Dawson said, unable to hide his own anger—and not just at Emma. His father had gone off to a cattleman's meeting in Denver two months ago and, after a quick stop in Vegas, had come back with a wife. Why was his father surprised the woman would leave, under the circumstances?

"Listen to me," Hoyt said, leaning forward behind the thick piece of bulletproof glass as he spoke into the phone provided for inmates to talk to visitors. "Emma wouldn't leave. You have to find her."

Dawson didn't need this. He and his brothers were having a hard enough time running the ranch without their father. He had a lot more important things to do than find his father's fourth wife.

But, he had to admit grudgingly, he'd liked Emma and maybe that was why he was so angry with her for bailing on their father.

"Where would you suggest I look? Is there family I can call? Friends? Is she even from Denver?" When his father didn't answer any of the questions, he said, "You really don't know anything about her, do you?"

"I know she wouldn't leave me," Hoyt had snapped.

Dawson sighed now, took one last look at the ranch and spurred his horse into the thick cool darkness of the pines. The ride up from the main house had taken most of the day. The big blue sky overhead was tinted pink to the west where the sun had dipped behind the Bear Paw Mountains.

He breathed in the sweet scent of pine. Since he was a boy, he'd always come to the high country when life got to be too much down on the prairie. Having five brothers, all of them adopted by Hoyt years ago, not even a ranch as large as this one felt big enough sometimes.

"I need one of you to see if you can find Emma," he'd told his brothers before he'd ridden out.

"Dad just doesn't want to believe that she deserted him," Marshall had said. "What's the point in finding her? She won't come back."

"I'll go," Zane had said, speaking up. When they all looked at him as if he was crazy, he said, "Dad loves her. He has enough problems without worrying about Emma. I'll see if I can find her. Did he give you any place to start?"

"All we know is that he met her in Denver," Dawson had said. "I suppose you could start there."

None of them had any hope that Zane would find her. Even less hope that if he did, she would come back and stand by their father's side during his trial.

Dawson couldn't really blame Emma when he thought about it. Rumors had circled around Chisholm Cattle Company for years after Hoyt's first wife, Laura, had drowned on a Fork Peck Reservoir boating trip.

The rumors only got worse after his second wife, Tasha, had been killed on a runaway horse. When his third wife, Krystal, had disappeared, never to be seen again, people who knew him were convinced Hoyt Chisholm had the worst luck with wives. Others weren't so sure.

There was at least one person—an insurance investigator—who suspected that Hoyt Chisholm had not only murdered all three wives, but would also do the same with his latest, Emma.

Dawson knew better. Hoyt was his father, the man who had adopted three motherless boys—Colton, Logan and Zane when the triplets' mother had died in child-birth, father unknown. He'd adopted Dawson, Tanner and Marshall when their mother had abandoned them, father also unknown.

Hoyt probably would have adopted even more children who needed homes if it hadn't been for the trouble with his wives.

Dawson, the oldest, was three when his father married his second wife, Tasha. They had been married only a short time before her death. He was five when Krystal came into their lives. She'd stayed an even shorter time. He doubted his brothers, who were all a few years younger, remembered any of them.

After that their father had raised them alone. All six of them now ranged from twenty-six to thirty-three. And then Hoyt Chisholm had met Emma.

A new wife had spurred all that old talk about Hoyt's other wives and brought former insurance investigator Aggie Wells back into their lives—until she'd gone missing. That was when their father's third wife's body had turned up. Aggie was still missing.

Dawson felt the temperature begin to drop up here in the mountains. He loved this ride from the sagebrush and prairie to the rocky mountain range, the towering pines and rush of snow-fed creeks. He'd been raised on a horse and felt as at home there as he did in the high country.

At heart he was a cattleman, he thought as he heard the comforting sound of cows lowing just over the ridge. There was nothing like that sound or seeing the herd scattered across a wide meadow.

He stopped a short way into the meadow and leaned on his saddle horn to admire the black cattle against the summer-green meadow. Chisholm Cattle Company raised the finest Black Angus beef there was—and lots of them.

At that moment he realized what a loner he was. Before Emma had left, he'd noticed that she'd seemed intent on seeing each of her stepsons settle down with the perfect woman. He shook his head at the thought. Was there a woman alive who could understand his need to ride up here and camp out for a few days with only cows as company?

He laughed at the thought, remembering some of the women he'd dated. Even hard-core country girls weren't all that up for roughin' it. He thought of the one woman he'd known who might have and quickly pushed the painful thought away.

A cold breeze stirred the deep shadows that had settled into the pine boughs. He glanced across the meadow to the spot where he usually camped and saw something move in the trees.

A hawk burst from a high branch. The cattle began to moo loudly and move restlessly in the bowl-like meadow. Something was spooking them. A mountain lion? A grizzly?

Dawson stared into the trees across the meadow and started to pull his rifle from the scabbard on his saddle, thinking it had to be a large predator for the cattle to get this nervous.

The first rider came out of the trees at a gallop. Dawson pulled his rifle as the rustler came into view and fired a shot into the air as warning before taking aim to fire another. The cattle began to scatter.

A second rustler appeared, then another and another broke from the pines; shots rang out across the grazing land as the rustlers tried to circle the now stampeding cattle.

Dawson realized the cattle were headed right for him—and so was one of the riders.

Chapter 2

With the stampeding cattle headed directly at him, Dawson realized there was nowhere to go to get away from them, and it was too late to try to outrun the herd. He was about to be caught in the middle of the stampede.

He reined his horse around in time to see one of the rustlers turn the herd at the last moment—and just enough that he was able to get out of the way. The cattle thundered past in a cloud of dust—the rustler with them.

Dawson sheathed his rifle, spurred his horse and took off after him. The rider was moving fast, bent over the horse and riding as if his life depended on it. It did, because Dawson was gaining on him. Just a few more yards…

Riding up behind him, Dawson dived off his horse, tackling the rustler. Both of them hit the ground at the edge of the thundering herd of cattle and rolled into the tall grass. Dust boiled up around them as they came to a stop at the base of a large pine tree, Dawson coming out on top.

As the dust settled, he got his first good look at the rustler. He blinked. A pair of big Montana-sky-blue eyes glared up at him from a face framed in blond curls.

A woman rustler?

"You have to let me go," she hollered as the roar of the stampeding cattle died off in the distance.

"So you can finish stealing my cattle? I don't think so."

"You don't understand."

"The hell I don't." He looked over his shoulder to see the last of the rustlers and cattle disappear through a gap in the trees. The rustlers had scattered the herd, but would still be able to cut out at least a hundred head.

He jerked the woman to her feet. "Where are they taking the cattle?"

She tested her left shoulder and grimaced, then she reached down to pick up her battered Western straw hat from the dirt.

"I think you'll survive," he said sarcastically.

She shot him a dirty look. "You could have killed me."

"It crossed my mind."

"Even after I saved you?" She narrowed those eyes at him.

"I beg your pardon?" He couldn't believe this woman.

"Do you think those cattle just happened to turn on their own?" She raised her chin as she said it, her gaze full of challenge. "I saved your life. Now you owe me. Let me go."

He laughed as he knocked the dust from his Stetson

and settled it back on his head. "The only place you're going is to jail."

"That would be a mistake," she said meeting his gaze. Her eyes were a heartbreaking blue in a face that could stop traffic with its surprising beauty. She looked too sweet and innocent to be a rustler.

"What the hell are you doing rustling my cattle?" he demanded, although he'd bet it had something to do with a man. It usually did.

"You wouldn't believe me if I told you," she said, and glanced toward where the cattle had disappeared through a wide spot in the trees.

"Try me."

Something came into her eyes, a subtle look that warned him. He mentally kicked himself for not thinking of it sooner. She reached for the gun strapped to her hip, hidden under her long barn jacket.

He grabbed the weapon before she could, his eyes narrowing as he assessed her. So much for sweet and innocent.

She wasn't just a woman whose boyfriend had talked her into some crazy stunt of rustling up a hundred head of cattle. The woman was armed and he'd already seen the way she could ride.

"How many others are there?" he demanded, grabbing a fistful of her jacket. "I think you'd better start talking before I tear into you."

She smiled. "I'm not sure you want to do that."

"Why is that?"

"You might not like the outcome."

He laughed again. He had a good ten inches on her and seventy pounds. She wasn't serious, was she?

Apparently she was, because before he could react, she punched him.

The blow caught him by surprise, breaking his hold on her and allowing her to take off running toward her horse, which had stopped a few dozen yards away.

Dawson went after her, bringing her down in the tall grass. She tried to fight him off, but he was onto her tricks this time and pinned her to the ground. He was suddenly aware of the soft curves.

"You have to listen to me." She ground out the words from between her gritted teeth. "You have to let me go. If you don't, they will come back for me and they will kill you. There are too many of them for you to fight off alone. You won't stand a chance and I don't want your blood on my hands."

"I'm touched by your concern for me. Especially after you just tried to pull a gun on me."

"I wasn't going to shoot you."

"You don't mind if I don't take your word on that, since you just punched me."

"You gave me no choice."

"Well, I'm giving you a choice now. Tell me how many of them there are."

She struggled under him for a few moments, then gave up and sighed. "Seven. How are those for odds?"

Not good. He'd heard about a large rustling ring that had been operating down in Wyoming and had only recently moved into southeastern Montana. He assumed it must be the same band of rustlers. Apparently they had now moved into north central Montana.

"When they realize I'm not with them, they will be back for me," she said.

Once the rustlers had the cattle settled wherever they

planned to keep them for the night, they would come looking for this woman, sure as hell—if they didn't notice her missing sooner.

He wondered how badly they would want to find her and how long they would look when they didn't. He figured only one or two of them would return. The others would stay with the cattle. That at least would even the odds.

Also it would be dark soon. It got dark fast up here in the mountains. He had to make sure the band of rustlers didn't find them until he decided what to do.

Eventually he'd have to deal with the possibly that all of them might come back for her, depending on her relationship to this gang. Holding off seven of them wouldn't be easy. Especially with this woman to worry about. What *was* he going to do with her?

"Look, we don't have much time before they realize I'm not with them."

She had a point. He hauled her to her feet and walked her the rest of the way to his horse. Reaching into his saddlebag, he pulled out a length of rope.

"You can't tie me up."

"What would you suggest I do with you?"

"You work for Chisholm, right?" She took his silence for yes. "You really want to die for a hundred head of his cattle?"

He pulled her hands behind her back and began to tie her wrists together.

"You're making a huge mistake," she said.

"It won't be my first."

She was watching the edge of the trees where the last of the cattle and rustlers had disappeared. He could feel the tension running through her. She knew they would be coming back for her. He thought about his first impression—that some man had talked her into this.

"So who is he?" Dawson asked as he finished binding her wrists and turned her around to face him. "This cowboy who talked you into becoming a rustler?"

Her expression changed and her gaze shifted away, making him pretty sure he'd pegged this one right. But, hell, given what he'd seen of her, she could be the leader of this group. Still, he thought it was more likely that some man was involved.

"What did he promise you?" he asked when she said nothing. "Adventure? Money? A chance to go to prison?"

"Rustlers seldom go to prison, because they are seldom caught," she snapped, sounding angry.

"Well, I caught *you*," he said, just as angry, since she was right. Convictions of cattle thieves were rare to nonexistent and with cattle going for a thousand dollars a head and times being tough, the rustlers had gotten smarter. With open range where there were no fences to worry about and back roads poorly patrolled, all a thief needed was a horse, maybe a good cattle dog and a semitrailer. There was always a crooked cattle buyer for a quick sale, and they could walk away with some good money after very little work on their part.

These rustlers, though, were going for the big reward, rustling a hundred head at least. From what Dawson had seen so far, they knew exactly what they were doing. Just like this woman.

She cocked her head at him. "You caught me, but how are you going to keep me when the others come back?"

"Don't worry, I'll think of something." He dragged

her over to her horse. "Let me help you up," he said and, before she could protest, hoisted her up into her saddle. Taking her reins, he headed for his horse. "You try anything and you'll be on the ground again in a heartbeat. I don't think you want that, do you?"

She glared at him before looking again toward the opening in the trees as if she expected the other rustlers to come riding in at any moment.

Dawson knew what would happen if the rustlers caught them out in the open. He had to get her to the other side of the large meadow, to a place he'd found when he was a boy, a place where he could hide her and make sure she didn't warn her partners in crime.

He swung up onto his horse and, leading hers, headed across the meadow. He needed to get them both out of sight until he could decide what to do with her—and how to get his cattle back.

"If you let me go, I can keep them from coming back," she said. "You have my word."

"Your word, huh? Like that is worth anything."

She let out an unladylike curse as he led her and her horse across the meadow. "I'm just trying to save your sorry neck."

He glanced back at her. "And I'm just going after my cattle."

"*Your* cattle? Don't you mean your *boss's* cattle?"

"I'm one of those Chisholms who you think can afford to lose a hundred and twenty-five head of cattle without even noticing it."

"You're a *Chisholm?*"

He could tell she liked it better when she thought he was just one of the hired hands. "Dawson Chisholm, and you are…?"

"Everyone calls me Jinx."

He chuckled. "I can see why."

Emma Chisholm woke with a terrible headache. She lay perfectly still and didn't dare open her eyes. There was a pounding at her temples and she felt sick to her stomach.

She inched her hand across the bed, hoping Hoyt was still lying next to her and hadn't gotten up early and gone to work already. Maybe if he got her something for her headache before she tried to get up—

The bed was empty. With a jolt she opened her eyes. Two thoughts hit her at once. She wasn't in her bed at the main house of Chisholm Cattle Company ranch and it wasn't morning.

Through the boards that had been nailed haphazardly over the only window in the room, she could see daylight, but from the angle of the shadows it appeared to be afternoon.

Emma struggled to sit up, taking in the unfamiliar small room with its paint-peeling faded walls, the mattress resting on the scarred wood floor, the tiny closet with two buckets, one full of water, and the tray near the door with a sandwich in plastic wrap, an apple and a thermos.

As her memory came back, she was suddenly aware of the cold air coming in through a broken pane at the window. She hugged herself for a moment before getting to her feet.

Her head swam and she had to drop back to her hands and knees. Crawling over to the tray, she opened the thermos. Coffee, and it was still hot. She poured herself some into the plastic cup it came with. Her fingers trembled as she took a sip and considered the situation she found herself in. It wasn't the first time she'd been drugged and locked in a room alone.

But it was the first time her captor had been a woman. Emma took another sip of the hot coffee to chase away the chill. She'd thought she'd been ready for Aggie Wells. She'd known the woman would come for her, but she'd underestimated Aggie.

When the former insurance investigator had disappeared a few weeks ago, Emma had been so certain Aggie was trying to make it appear that Hoyt had done something to her. But when Emma had recently come home from town and smelled the woman's perfume in the main house at the ranch, she'd known Aggie was alive.

She had wondered how Aggie had known that everyone was out of the house. That's when she'd found the listening devices Aggie had apparently installed in the house and she'd known that with Hoyt in jail and his six boys busy working on the ranch, it was only a matter of time before Aggie would come for her.

Emma remembered sitting in the kitchen after Hoyt was arrested, waiting to see what Aggie had planned next. She'd been sure that the woman's plan had been to frame Hoyt for the murder of his third wife—and then take advantage of Emma being alone at the ranch to what? Kill her?

Emma hadn't known, but she'd been armed and thought she was ready when Aggie suddenly appeared in the kitchen doorway.

Everything after that was still fuzzy. She drank more of the coffee, feeling a little better, unwrapped the sandwich—a ham and cheese—and took a bite before moving back over to the window and peering out a small hole the size of a fist between the boards.

Where was she? In some abandoned farmhouse near Whitehorse, Emma was fairly sure. The landscape looked familiar and she didn't think Aggie had driven far after she'd drugged her.

So what did Aggie have planned for her?

She thought about the first time she'd met the former insurance investigator at the bar at Sleeping Buffalo Resort north of town. She'd been surprised that Aggie was about her own age, early fifties, a tall, slim woman with an aura of intelligence and energy. Emma remembered thinking she was the kind of woman she could have been friends with—under other circumstances.

Aggie had told her that night about her suspicions that Hoyt Chisholm had killed his other three wives. Emma hadn't believed it. Still didn't, even though evidence had been found along with his third wife's remains that linked him to her murder.

She'd been all the more convinced of her husband's innocence when she'd realized that Aggie had faked her own disappearance to make Hoyt look guilty of yet another murder.

At a sound on the other side of the only door, Emma turned and braced herself. She didn't think Aggie planned to kill her—at least not yet. Otherwise, why bother to bring her here?

A dead bolt scraped in the lock, the knob turned and, as the door swung inward, Emma saw Aggie Wells framed in the doorway. She was holding a handgun in a way that made it clear she knew how to use it.

She laughed, because even if the woman had been

unarmed, Emma wasn't up to launching any kind of attack.

"You're in a good mood," Aggie said. "But then you are annoyingly cheerful most of the time, aren't you? It is one of the things I hate about you."

"You mean there are other things you hate about me?" Emma said, pretending to be crushed.

"I hate that you're married to Hoyt Chisholm."

Now they were getting somewhere, Emma thought as she watched the woman come into the room. For some time, she had suspected that the reason Aggie was so obsessed about Hoyt's case was that she'd fallen in love with the man. Emma could understand how that might have happened. Look how quickly Emma herself had fallen for him.

"You should eat," Aggie said, sliding the tray toward her.

Emma sat down, reached for the thermos and started to pour herself another cup of coffee but stopped, the cup and thermos held in midair.

Aggie chuckled. "Don't worry, it's not drugged."

She finished pouring the rest of the coffee into the plastic cup, thinking it was too late anyway if the coffee was drugged. She returned the stopper to the thermos and sat back against the wall as she took a drink. The coffee made her feel a little better and she needed to start thinking straight.

The only way she could get herself out of this was if she was very careful with this crazy woman, who she suspected was also a killer.

Aggie had caught her off guard at the main house at the ranch this morning. It had been just this morning, hadn't it? She thought so. She'd been expecting her. She'd even gotten a small pistol out of Hoyt's gun safe.

But then Aggie had appeared in the kitchen doorway and said, "I think it's time I told you the truth."

Emma had held the gun on her as Aggie had sat down across the table from her. "You framed my husband."

"I did much worse than that." Aggie had looked at Emma's coffee cup sitting on the table next to a small plate with cake crumbs on it. "I'll tell you everything, Emma. You deserve to know the truth. Is there any coffee?"

Emma thought she'd been watching Aggie the entire time she went to get another cup and the rest of the coffee in the pot. But that must have been when Aggie put the drug into her half-empty coffee cup.

Aggie had begun talking. Emma had listened, getting more drowsy by the moment and having a hard time making sense of what the woman was saying. It wasn't until she'd dropped her coffee cup that she realized she'd been drugged. She'd grabbed for the gun, but her movements had been too slow by then and Aggie had been much quicker.

She remembered Aggie walking her out to an old pickup and buckling her in. Emma couldn't be sure how far they had gone when Aggie got her out and up the stairs into the old farmhouse. That's the last she remembered until waking up thinking it was morning.

"What now?" Emma asked as she picked up the sandwich and took a bite.

"We wait," Aggie said.

"What for?"

Aggie merely smiled and turned to leave.

"You realize my family will be looking for me," Emma said.

"I wouldn't count on that. You left a note that said you couldn't deal with all of this."

"Hoyt won't believe it," she said with more confidence than she felt.

"Oh, I think he will. Along with the note, everything you brought into the marriage is gone from the house. If they bothered to check, which I don't think they will, they'd find that you bought a used pickup the day after Hoyt was arrested. The title is in the name of Emma Chisholm."

Zane had no idea how to find Emma. He started his search in Denver because that was where his father had met her. He flew into the mile-high city on the last flight out of Billings.

The cattleman's meeting had been held at one of the large hotels downtown. He had booked a room, feeling as if he was searching for a needle in a haystack. Armed with a photo of Emma taken at the ranch, he began with employees at the hotel.

"You a cop or a bill collector?" one of the clerks behind the main desk asked him.

"She's my stepmother," he said truthfully. "She's gone missing."

"And you think she's hiding out here at the hotel?"

"No, but I think she stayed here the beginning of May." Zane leaned closer and dropped his voice. "I didn't want to get into this, but...she met my father here, they eloped days later to Vegas and now she's disappeared and I haven't a clue how to find her."

"What about your father? He doesn't know how to find her either?"

"Seems they saw no reason to share their pasts or much else."

The clerk didn't look as if he believed a word of it.

"I just need to make sure she's all right," he said. "My father is worried about her." He laid a fifty-dollar bill on the counter, his hand covering all but the important parts of it. "Any help you can give me would be greatly appreciated."

"I didn't work here then, but I could take a look and see if she was registered back in May," the clerk said, smoothly cupping the fifty in his palm as Zane removed his hand. He tapped on the computer keyboard.

"It would have been under Emma McDougal."

The clerk skimmed the computer screen. "Nope. Sorry. No Emma McDougal registered as a guest here in the month of May. Or April, for that matter."

Now all Zane had to go on was what little had been on the marriage license he'd found in his father's safe. Apparently Emma had been born in Caliente Junction, California, fifty-three years ago. He'd looked on the internet. Caliente Junction was now nothing more than a wide spot in the road. Even if someone still lived there, which looked doubtful from what he'd seen, what were the chances anyone there would even remember her or her family?

Zane went to his room and called home to tell his brothers where he was headed in the morning.

"Where the hell is Caliente Junction?" Marshall asked.

"Apparently out in the desert near the Salton Sea. I don't think there is a town there—if there ever was—

from what I can tell. Just a few buildings on a two-lane road. What's going on there?"

"Just working. Dawson is still up in the mountains," his brother said. "You know him, he heads for high ground the moment there's trouble at the ranch. Nothing new there. Let us know what you find out about Emma. Dad keeps harping on us to find her."

Zane hung up and booked a flight into Palm Springs, California, for the next morning as he considered Caliente Junction on his laptop screen. He had a bad feeling his father wasn't going to like what he found out about his new bride.

Jinx Clarke rode along just feet from Dawson Chisholm, frantically trying to decide what to do. Her options were limited given that her hands were tied behind her and he was holding her horse's reins. One false move and, as he said, she'd be hitting the dirt again. Her left shoulder hurt as it was from her recent fall, thanks to him. She wasn't looking forward to being thrown to the ground again.

But she knew that at any moment Rafe could come riding out of the trees with all but a couple of his men with him. If he noticed she wasn't with them, he would hightail it back for her. More than likely, though, he wouldn't know they'd lost her until they got the cattle down to the first corral.

Which meant it would be some time before anyone would realize she was missing. But Rafe would come back. Even if he came alone, Dawson Chisholm was a dead man.

Jinx studied him as he led her across the wide meadow, trying to decide how much to tell him. The cattleman had coal-black hair and the darkest eyes she'd ever seen. She guessed he had some Native American in him. He was also handsome as sin—not that she would admit to noticing.

What worried her was why he'd shown up when he had. Either his timing was just his bad luck or it was no coincidence. It had been her idea to hit the Chisholm Cattle Company, because she'd thought it was big enough that they wouldn't be coming across anyone. But now she wondered if Rafe hadn't gone along with it too easily.

"So what's your real name?" Dawson asked, glancing back at her again. "I like to know who I'm dealing with."

"Jinx is all you get, Chisholm," she said.

He shook his head as if she was the most contrary woman he'd ever known. Clearly he hadn't known many women, if that was the case. "The sheriff will get your name out of you."

Jinx groaned. If he thought he could scare her with threats of the sheriff, he was sadly mistaken. She was far more worried about the killers she'd been riding with—and the dark-haired cattleman who had her tied and bound.

"I didn't check to see if you had some sort of identification on you," he was saying. "We might be able to settle this a whole lot quicker than waiting for the sheriff."

"Do you really think I'm stupid enough to carry identification on me?" she snapped.

"Do you really think I'm stupid enough to believe anything you say? At this point, you don't have a lot of credibility with me."

Neither did he with her. "How is it you just happened to show up when we were about to rustle your cattle, Chisholm?"

"Just luck, I guess," he said without turning to look at her.

She saw that they had reached the other side of the meadow and he was now leading her horse through the trees and up the mountainside to an outcropping of rocks. Did he think he could hold off seven men from there?

"These men I'm riding with are dangerous. When they come back for me—"

"What makes you so sure they'll be back for you?" he asked. "I'm surprised they even let a woman ride with them to begin with. A woman would be a liability. Especially one named Jinx."

Her temper flared from the insult. "I can ride with the best of men."

He chuckled. "I noticed. But I would imagine it took more than that to get into a group of men like this one."

She knew what he was insinuating and wished she could kick him where it would hurt the most. It hadn't been easy getting in with the rustling ring. She'd had to lie, cheat and steal. Fortunately that was as far as she'd had to go once she caught Rafe's attention at a bar down in Big Timber.

Rafe wasn't the ringleader. He got his orders from someone else. But he was the one the others listened to. He'd put up a fight for her. The other rustlers riding with him hadn't wanted a woman along, so she'd had to prove herself in their eyes. It wasn't enough that she could ride a horse and shoot. She had to have something they needed—information. She'd given them Chisholm Cattle Company.

Jinx grimaced at the realization that she was the one who was responsible if Dawson Chisholm got killed—and the way things were going there was nothing she could do to stop it.

Unless there was a chance Dawson was working with Rafe. That would explain why he was here. She wouldn't let herself worry about that right now. She had to keep her eye on her goal. Nothing could stop her. Not Rafe and all his men or this good-looking cattleman. When she got what she'd wanted, it would have all been worth it.

But as she stared at the determined set of Chisholm's broad shoulders, she wondered how high the price was going to get before this was over.

Chapter 3

Emma finished the sandwich. Her mind had been racing since Aggie left her alone in the small room of the abandoned old farmhouse. She'd listened, wondering if the woman was also staying here in this house. Where else could she be staying with every law enforcement officer in the state looking for her?

Glancing toward the window, Emma considered using the tray the next time Aggie left it to try to pry off the boards. It would be no easy task, since someone— probably Aggie—had nailed them on with large nails that would be hard to remove even with a claw hammer.

Not to mention what Emma would do after that. It was a two-story house. Was she going to throw out the mattress, then throw herself after it?

Thinking of ways to escape was better than considering why Aggie had left her alive. What was she waiting for?

Emma's first guess would have been Hoyt making bail. Once he was out, if Emma ended up dead, that would pretty much seal his fate. Somehow Aggie would plant evidence, as she had with Hoyt's third wife's body, to make him look guilty of her death, as well.

But Hoyt hadn't been able to make bail. Did Aggie have something planned to get him out?

And what was her motive for *any* of this? If Aggie had fallen in love with Hoyt, as Emma speculated, then why send him to prison for murder? It didn't make any sense unless… With a start, she realized why. What if they weren't dealing with a sane woman? Stalking Hoyt to the point where she'd lost her job certainly made Aggie look more than a little crazy.

From what Emma had been able to find out, Aggie had become obsessed with the insurance investigation into the death of Laura Chisholm, Hoyt's first wife. It had been ruled an accidental drowning, but since the body was never found…

When Hoyt's second wife had died, that must have been enough to make Aggie reopen the first wife's case.

So was that the problem? She was dealing with an insane woman bent on proving Hoyt was a killer—no matter the cost?

Her head still ached from the drugs and she was glad Aggie hadn't seen fit to drug her again. Which meant there were no other houses nearby, no chance of anyone just happening by, no one to hear her calling for help. So she would save her breath. Not that she was a screamer anyway.

Emma had learned early in life to accept things the way they were, good or bad. Wasn't that why she hadn't wanted to know Hoyt's past—because she hadn't wanted to tell him about her own?

The cave was on the side of the mountain, but few if any people knew about it. Dawson had found it on one of his trips up to the summer range when he was a boy. He'd been following a buck deer that had disappeared near the entrance. He'd almost missed seeing the opening for the overgrown brush. He'd put some of the brush back after he'd explored the cave, wanting to keep it a secret even from his brothers.

As he led the horses up into a stand of pines below the hidden cave entrance, he kept his eyes and ears alert for any sign of the rustlers. The sun had dipped behind the trees, forming deep shadows beneath them. The air had turned colder, as it did up here in the mountains.

"This is a mistake," Jinx said as he hauled her off the horse.

"You're the one who made the mistake when you decided to rustle my cattle."

She sighed deeply. "If you let me go, I will lead them away from you. I can tell them my horse stepped into a hole and I got thrown." She cocked her head at him. "I look like I got thrown to the ground, don't I?"

He glanced at her dusty clothing. There was a smudge of dirt on her cheek, her hat was crooked from where she'd hastily put it back on her head and her short curly blond hair had a twig in it. He removed the twig and tossed it over his shoulder.

"They'll come for me tonight. You can't hold off seven of them."

"Maybe. Maybe not."

"Isn't your life worth more than cattle?" she demanded.

"This isn't about money. Or even cattle. It's about defending what is yours."

She raised an eyebrow and glanced at his left hand. "Who was she?"

"I beg your pardon?"

"The woman you lost to someone else."

Dawson turned his back to her as he ground tied the horses.

"It must have been serious. High school sweetheart? Fiancée? Wife?" She let out a low laugh. "You didn't fight for her and you've regretted it ever since. So now you're damned sure going to fight for your cattle because of it. Is that it?"

He turned to face her. "You make a better rustler than a psychotherapist. Come on," he said, picking up his saddlebags. "I'm hungry and want to get something to eat before your friends come back. *If* they come back for you. Either way, I'm going after my cattle in the morning at first light."

Jinx stared at his backside as he started up the hill. Damn this cocky rancher. He acted as if he'd completely forgotten about her, but she wasn't fooled. This long, tall cowboy was aware of her every move, she thought as she started after him. She had no choice right now.

He could deny it all he wanted, but she was sure he'd lost some woman, a woman who'd hurt him badly. Because of it, he'd be happy to tackle her to the ground again. In fact, he'd take some pleasure in it.

She knew better than to try to make a run for it with

Rustled

her hands tied behind her and it getting dark. She'd be lucky if she didn't run into a tree and kill herself.

No, she had to wait, bide her time. Chisholm would make a mistake and she would get away. She had to. She'd come too far to let anyone stop her now. There had to be a way to get around this cocky cowboy—after all, he was a man.

And, oh, what a man, she thought as she studied him. Broad shoulders, slim hips, long denim-clad legs. Not to mention his face. Chiseled strong features, those dark, bottomless eyes and the way his lips quirked up on one side when he looked at her.

She wondered about the woman who'd broken his heart and made him the way he was. She must have been a beauty, probably some city girl who would have eventually left him anyway.

Jinx hated her stab of resentment at the thought of the kind of woman a man like Dawson Chisholm would have fallen for. She swore under her breath. How different she and that woman would have been.

She turned her thoughts to how to get away from him. She'd do whatever she had to because she couldn't let this man stop her. One way or another, she was going to get what she'd promised her father on the day she buried him.

Telling Chisholm the truth was out of the question. She couldn't chance it. It bothered her that he didn't seem worried about fighting off seven rustlers, and made her suspicious that he knew he wouldn't have to because he was in on this and was now waiting, like her, for Rafe to return.

The only thing that Jinx did believe about Chisholm was that he was angry about a woman riding with the rustlers. If he was in cahoots with Rafe, she had a feeling he planned to have it out with the rustler.

Either way, she was in trouble. Rafe liked to think of himself as the leader of the rustlers, but she knew better. And Chisholm must, too. If he demanded Rafe get rid of her, then Rafe would buckle like a bad saddle under the weight.

A sudden shiver of fear quaked through her as she had another thought. What if somehow they'd found out who she really was? She'd seen how surprised Dawson Chisholm had been when he'd tackled her. He hadn't expected her to be riding with the others. Or had he?

If he already knew, then that would explain why Chisholm had shown up when he had. He'd come up here to make sure she was stopped.

Unless she could stop Chisholm first.

Emma curled up on the mattress on the floor and pulled the blankets Aggie had thoughtfully provided over her. She could hear Aggie moving around somewhere in the house. She still felt woozy from the drug she'd been given.

At the sound of footfalls on the stairs, Emma sat up, holding the blankets to her chin as if they would protect her, and waited. The door opened. Aggie stood silhouetted in the doorway.

"You awake?"

"Yes," Emma said. "Not that the accommodations aren't delightful."

Aggie stepped into the room, closed the door and stood against it. Emma could barely see her in the dim light that came through the hole between the boards over the window.

"I like you," Aggie said. "I'm not going to hurt you."

"That's good." She figured she knew what was coming next.

"But I can't let you go back to the house and Hoyt."

"Why is that?" Emma asked.

Aggie let out an exasperated sigh. "I've told you. It's too dangerous."

"We both know that Hoyt is not a killer."

To her surprise Aggie said, "You could be right."

Was the woman merely trying to pacify her?

"Aggie, if you turn yourself in—"

She let out a laugh. "I haven't done anything."

Emma would beg to differ. "You abducted me, drugged me and are holding me prisoner."

"For your own good."

Now it was her turn to laugh. "And who are you protecting me from, Aggie?" When she didn't answer, Emma said, "Hoyt didn't kill anyone."

She heard Aggie slide down to sit on the floor and thought about trying to overpower her. But she knew that by the time she threw off the blankets and got up and launched herself at the woman, Aggie would be ready for her. Aggie was armed, probably with the same gun she'd been carrying earlier, and Emma wasn't in the mood for a suicide mission.

Also a part of her hoped that Aggie was finally going to tell her the truth.

"Do you know why I was such a good insurance investigator?" Aggie asked, seemingly out of the blue. She didn't wait for Emma to answer. "I studied everything about the people involved, and not just the surviving spouse. I wanted to know the deceased as intimately as if that person was alive."

"You're saying you got to know Hoyt's other wives?" Emma said. She had wondered what they had really been like. Nothing like herself, she would bet. They were probably tall, willowy and beautiful, not to mention young.

"I'm not sure Hoyt knew Laura as well as I have come to know her," Aggie said. "I could say the same for his two other wives, as well. But Laura..." She sighed. "She was like you, apparently totally enamored by Hoyt. At first. But I'm sure you've heard about how close the emotions are between love and hate."

"If you're telling me she grew to hate him, I don't believe you. I can't imagine anything Hoyt could have done that would have—"

"She believed he'd fathered his first three sons."

"I don't believe it. A simple DNA test would prove—"

"There wasn't DNA testing yet when Laura died."

"But there is now. And anyway, if he was the biological father to those boys, Hoyt would have admitted it."

"Why do you keep defending him?"

"Because I love him." She waited for Aggie to admit her own feelings for Hoyt. She heard the woman get to her feet again and quickly said, "I think you fell for him, as well." She didn't add that she thought Aggie had killed his other wives because she was jealous.

"I'll admit your husband is...charming. But historically, he is also dangerous to be around."

Not half as dangerous as you are, Emma thought. "So you're just trying to protect me," she said as she heard Aggie open the door to leave.

Aggie chuckled but didn't respond.

Emma lay back down on the mattress and pulled the

blankets over her, but she couldn't fight off the chill Aggie had left in the room.

Dawson heard Jinx behind him. She was as sure-footed as an expensive filly as she climbed up to the cave. He told himself that he could almost hear the wheels in her head turning. She would try to get away when the rustlers came back for her. Or at the very least, give away their location—if he let her. He was already outnumbered. He'd have to find a way to even the odds.

As he moved a piece of dried brush away from the entrance to the cave, he heard her come up beside him. He turned on his flashlight and shone it into the cavern. To his relief it wasn't occupied by any animals.

"Ladies first," he said with more gallantry than he felt.

She smirked at that as she bent to step through the small opening. Once inside, she stood to her full height of about five-seven.

Dawson stepped past her, going around a corner in the cave to the hidden cavern room. As he lit the kerosene lantern he'd left there on one of his trips to the high country, she followed him.

In the golden light he studied her, wondering what she'd try next. The one thing he knew for sure, there was plenty of fight left in this woman. He'd have to watch her closely or suffer the consequences.

"What now, Chisholm?" she asked as she glanced around. He could see that she'd been surprised by the size of the cave, surprised that he'd furnished it over the years with not only a lantern but with a cot, a collapsible table and stool, a few pots and pans and a Coleman stove.

"Sit down over here and take a load off," he said, opening the folding stool he used when he came up here.

"Take a load off, Chisholm?" she asked with amusement. She was slim, curved in all the right places, and she knew it.

"So to speak," he amended.

He didn't go far from the cave, not trusting her, but he had to take care of their horses. When he returned with some firewood, he found her sitting where he'd left her, which surprised him. But he didn't doubt she'd taken a look around for something to cut the rope binding her wrists behind her. Before he'd left he'd been smart enough to make sure there was nothing sharp she could use.

The way the cave was structured, the opening turned just inside, which meant that light from the stove or a fire couldn't be seen from the meadow. The cave was ventilated through a crack at the back that opened to fresh air on the cliff above them, so the smoke from a fire would draft upward high on the cliffs, on the same principle as a fireplace in a home.

If and when the rustlers returned for Jinx they might catch a whiff of smoke, but they would never be able to find the cave. He doubted they would even smell the smoke if they stayed down in the meadow.

He made a small fire at the back of the cave near the vent and close to Jinx. It would be getting cold once the sun went down. Then he started the Coleman stove and dug some food out of his saddlebag.

This cave had been a retreat for years, his own private sanctuary in the high country. A part of him resented that he'd had to bring her here, resented it even more when she asked, "So you come up here and play house by yourself a lot?"

He shot her a warning look before concentrating again on his cooking. He figured she was right about the other rustlers coming back to look for her—but not for a while, he thought. They'd have to secure the cattle. It would take a while for them to even realize they'd lost her after all that confusion earlier.

Dawson suspected that the main reason they would come back for her was that they wouldn't trust her. At least one of them, the boyfriend, would have another motive.

But given all that, he felt they were relatively safe in the cave, at least for the time being. He'd hidden the horses around the side of the mountain and covered the opening to the cave again with the dried brush. Even if they were found, the cave was high enough on the mountainside that he could hold them off for a long time. He hadn't brought an arsenal, but he always had extra ammunition.

"Dawson," she said, using his first name in a way that reminded him of melted honey and put him on guard. He'd been expecting her to make some kind of move and shouldn't have been surprised that she'd chosen this one.

"I don't want to see you get killed," she said, sweet enough to give him a toothache. "Maybe there is some way we can work this out so we both get what we want."

"I guess that depends on what you want," he said, not turning around. He heard her get up and come toward him and was glad he'd tied her hands behind her back. Otherwise he'd be worried about getting his head bashed in.

"All I need is for you to let me go."

"How would that get me back my cattle?" he asked, playing along.

"Well," she said softly right behind him. "If you just untie me..."

Jinx lowered herself to the cave floor next to him. He glanced over at her, eyes narrowing a little as she repeated his first name, her voice dripping with sugar. She saw the male spark in his eye as she moved closer. How sad that men were so much alike, she thought, a little disappointed in this one. She thought he was too smart to let himself be seduced by her.

She hated that she'd had to resort to such distasteful behavior, but too much was at stake. If she had to use her feminine wiles, she would.

"Yes?" He was close enough that she caught his very masculine scent.

She moved so her thigh brushed his. "Why don't we be honest with each other?"

"Why don't we?" He pressed his thigh against hers. His leg felt warm, even through his jeans. His dark eyes locked with hers. She felt a shiver that she quickly squelched. His eyes were golden like a big cat in the firelight. He really was magnificent.

It was the intellect in that gaze that gave her pause. She saw challenge in his eyes as well as a warning. This was a man you didn't want to fool with.

"Tell me what you're really doing up here," she said, not about to break eye contact first. He might be dangerous, but then again, he didn't realize the kind of woman he'd crossed paths with either.

"Checking my cattle, just like I told you."

He was either telling the truth or he was a damned good liar.

She reminded herself that he could just be playing along. If he knew who she was and what she was doing on his land… "Can't you please untie me?"

"No."

"You really think I'm going to get away?"

He smiled. "If I give you half a chance, yes." He turned back to his cooking.

"There wasn't another reason you just happened to come up here?" she asked quickly.

He turned off the stove and gave her his full attention. She found herself holding her breath. There was something about this man that scared her—especially the way he made her heart pound when he was this near, his gaze so intent on her that she feared he could see into her soul.

"As a matter of fact, there was another reason."

She expected him to finally tell her that he knew who she was. That she was the reason he was here.

"I wanted to spend a few days up in this country because I enjoy it. I thought I'd be alone. But since I'm not…" He was taunting her. Her feminine wiles were wasted on this man. "So, Jinx, what exactly are you offering?"

"If you think I'm going to sleep with you, you're going to be disappointed," she snapped and slid away from him.

He laughed. "Hell, I'm already disappointed. I thought we were being honest with each other."

"I should just let them kill you," Jinx grumbled, trying to get to her feet. With her hands tied behind her, it was a struggle.

Dawson rose abruptly, grabbed her waist and lifted her to her feet. His dark gaze bored into hers. "Now that we're being honest, no more games. Seduction might have worked on your rustler boyfriend, but quite frankly you aren't very good at it and anyway, you're not my type."

She swore as she tried to kick him in the groin. He'd obviously expected it, because he stepped to the side, grabbing her as she lost her balance and started to fall to the cave floor.

"Enough foreplay," he growled as he hauled her back over to the stool and pushed her down on it. Leaning over her, his gaze fired with anger as he said, "I'm getting my cattle back and you're going to jail, and if your boyfriend comes after you, he's going to get himself killed."

Chapter 4

Zane was too anxious to just sit around in his hotel room. He'd booked a flight to Palm Springs for the morning, but there was nothing more he could do today.

As he rode down in the elevator to the lobby, he noticed a woman going into the bar. She was probably in her forties, alone and wearing something provocative.

He was instantly reminded that his father had met Emma here in this hotel. What had she been doing here if she hadn't been a guest? As he stepped into the darkness of the bar, it took a moment for his eyes to adjust before he saw the woman who had gotten him thinking.

She had taken a stool at the bar and was now leaning toward the young male bartender, giving him a glimpse of her cleavage and asking him what he would suggest.

"I can make you a nice mango margarita," he said.

She smiled. "That sounds nice."

Zane took a stool down the bar from the woman.

"I'll be right with you," the bartender called to him.

Looking around, he saw that the bar was fairly empty, but then again by bar time standards, it was early. There was a couple at a table toward the back, two businessmen at another table and a lone fiftysomething man at the other end of the bar who had noticed the woman. She was hard to miss.

This was a scene Zane had seen played out many times before. Pretty soon the man would offer to buy the woman another mango margarita. She'd accept. He would move down the bar and strike up a conversation with her before taking the stool next to her.

Is this how his father had met Emma, Zane wondered with disgust. Had she been trolling the hotel bar?

He had a hard time believing that, given what little time he'd spent around Emma. But that was the problem. None of them actually *knew* Emma. That had become clear the moment he'd started looking for her. It could be that she was one of those women who kept reinventing themselves.

The bartender came down the bar, set a cocktail napkin in front of him and asked, "What can I get you?"

"A bottle of beer," Zane said. "Something local would be great."

"Dark or light?"

"Dark."

The bartender returned with a bottle of dark beer and set it down along with a frosted glass.

"Maybe you can help me," Zane said. He saw the bartender tense. "I'm looking for someone."

"Isn't everyone?"

"This woman," he explained as he pulled out the snapshot of Emma taken at the ranch.

The bartender glanced at the photo. Zane could tell he was ready to say he'd never seen the woman before, but something stopped him. He picked up the photo.

"What about her?" he asked.

"So she used to come in a lot?"

The bartender laughed and glanced down the bar, apparently catching Zane's drift. The lone drinker had skipped part of the script and had moved right in, pulling up a stool next to the woman.

"You're barking up the wrong tree," the bartender said. "Emma McDougal worked here at the hotel, at the front desk. As far as I know, she didn't drink." He tossed the photo back at Zane. "She's a nice woman. Everyone liked her. We were happy for her when we heard she'd fallen in love and gotten married. Is there any reason we shouldn't be happy for her?"

"I don't know. She's disappeared."

The bartender looked concerned. "And you're looking for her because...?"

"She's married to my father. He's worried about her, convinced she wouldn't just take off."

"No, she wouldn't. Unless she was forced to for some reason." The bartender glared at Zane. "Was there some reason?"

"My father adores her."

"Then you'd better find Emma, because I have a bad feeling she's in trouble," he said as the man down the bar ordered another mango margarita for his companion.

Jinx hid her embarrassment under her anger at herself for pulling such a stunt. She should have known better than to try to seduce the arrogant bastard, but she was desperate. She had to get away from him. As she watched him calmly go back to his cooking, she was all the more convinced he was toying with her. But was it because he knew who she was and why she was here?

Or because he thought her just another rustler and he was just another rancher about to lose his cattle and his life?

Well, if that was the case, then there was nothing she could do about it. She had tried to warn him. Now the smug cattleman was on his own.

She swore under her breath as she saw him tilt his head as if listening. Rafe *would* come looking for her, she was sure of that. The man he worked for wouldn't like there being any loose ends. The rustlers had already killed at least one rancher who got in their way on the orders of whoever was leading this gang. Even if she'd been thrown from her horse and broken her neck, Rafe would have to make sure she was dead so he could report back to his boss.

Chisholm moved around the corner of the cave to look out the entrance. She knew he was looking toward the trees where the cattle and rustlers had disappeared. Getting up, she stepped around the corner of the cave so she could see out.

A dusky gray light had fallen over the meadow, giving it an eerie feel. It was deceptive. She thought she saw ghostlike riders coming out of the mist only to have them evaporate before her eyes.

A darkness had settled in the pines even though it would still be light for several hours. She was surprised Rafe hadn't come back. Was it possible he hadn't realized yet that she was missing? Or was he too busy making sure the cattle were taken care of first?

Her being missing would spook all of them. Maybe they would decide to drive the cattle farther than planned.

She shifted her focus to Dawson Chisholm. What was he planning to do with her? She hated to think.

As he started to turn back in her direction, she quickly moved to her stool and sat down again, her mind racing. She had to find a way to hook back up with the rustlers before they became more suspicious of her.

Dawson went back to minding the meal he was making. She felt her stomach growl. She hadn't eaten since breakfast and the bacon he was frying smelled wonderful. Her stomach growled loudly and she saw him smile to himself as if he'd heard.

"Apparently it's a good thing you decided to ride up here when you did," she said as she watched him cook. He was making some kind of dough and now dropped it into the sizzling fat. Fry bread. She groaned inwardly as the smell filled the cave.

"Apparently it was. I'd heard about a band of rustlers operating near the Montana border down by Wyoming, but I didn't realize they'd worked their way this far north."

So he *had* heard. Had he also heard about the man who'd been killed down in Wyoming, his house burned to the ground by the rustlers?

"So how exactly did you pick my ranch?" he asked pointedly.

"What makes you think *I* had anything to do with the decision?"

He smiled. "I guess it's just my suspicious nature."

"Kind of like mine. Out of all the ranches around Whitehorse, you somehow knew yours would be hit next by rustlers? Maybe you knew before I did."

He laughed. "If you're insinuating that I'm somehow connected to the rustlers you're riding with—"

"That's exactly what I'm thinking. Chisholm Cattle Company is family owned. Six brothers, right? All adopted." She narrowed her eyes at him. "Wouldn't be unusual for one of the brothers to feel he was owed more than he was getting."

He chuckled. "You'll play any card, won't you? This tactic isn't going to work any better than the others you've tried." He turned the bread from the small pan onto the two strips of bacon he'd fried and folded the bread into a sandwich. He started to take a bite, but stopped as he glanced at her.

"Hungry?" he asked, even though he knew darned well that she was.

"No," she snapped, but her stomach growled loudly again, giving her away.

He laughed, pushed himself up and walked over to look down at her. He wiped the dust from a corner of the table and set down the sandwich. Then he untied her wrists, freeing one hand and tying the other to her leg.

"You really are the least trusting man I've ever met," she said as he put the sandwich into her free hand.

"Let's not forget that you and I only met because you were rustling my cattle."

She cocked her head at him. "You wouldn't have trusted me even if we'd met at church, and you know it."

His gaze met hers and held it for a long moment. "You might be right about that."

As he walked back to the Coleman, out of the corner

of his eye he watched Jinx take a bite of the sandwich. She moaned with pleasure and licked her fingers as some of the bacon grease tried to get away.

Dawson smiled, liking her more than he had, definitely more than he wanted to, as he started more fry bread for himself. The atmosphere in the cave seemed to have warmed considerably.

"Thank you," she said when she'd finished eating, licking her fingers before wiping her hand on her jeans.

"You're welcome." They sat around the cave in silence as he cooked and ate. He watched her, still afraid she would try to get away, but she seemed to have realized there was no way he was going to let that happen.

The crackling flames flickered, sending long shadows over the cave walls. The scent of the pine trees mixed with the smell of bacon and fried bread. The air had cooled outside the cave. Tonight would be cold. This high in the mountains was always cold at night even in the summer months.

He let the fire die down to hot embers as he considered the best way to get his cattle back. Making the long ride out to the ranch for help was out of the question. By then, the cattle and the rustlers would be gone.

He had no way to contact the ranch, since even if he carried a cell phone, it wouldn't have worked up here. Cells phones worked within only about ten miles of Whitehorse. After that, you were on your own.

Glancing over at Jinx, he knew she was his biggest problem. His every instinct told him not to trust her an inch. This was no small rustling operation, which meant there was a lot of money involved and whoever was behind it knew way too much about the ranchers—and cattle—they were going after. That worried him.

The rustlers he'd known hadn't been organized. They'd acted more on impulse, often after a few beers at the bar. But then, he'd never seen as large a gang as this one. Definitely not one with a woman riding along.

He remembered how much she'd known about the Chisholm ranch and his family. It galled him that anyone would hit Chisholm Cattle Company. He was more interested in getting his cattle back than trying to get justice, but just the fact that they'd hit his ranch made him dig his heels in. He wanted these bastards caught—including whoever was behind them.

He didn't doubt there was someone who was the brains of the band of rustlers who stayed behind the scenes, the man with the crooked cattle buyer contacts who financed the semitrucks and trailers needed for an operation this big.

But how was he going to get his cattle back, catch the rustlers and keep this woman from getting away?

He studied Jinx, wondering if she had realized yet that he planned to get his cattle back—even if it meant using her to do it.

It was dark by the time Dawson heard a sound outside the cave and moved quickly to Jinx's side.

"Jinx!" The word echoed faintly across the meadow. Just as she'd predicted, at least one of the rustlers had come back for her.

"Listen," she whispered as she glanced frantically toward the dark entrance of the cave. "We're on the same side. I can help you."

"On the same side?" Dawson chuckled as he quickly reached into his pocket for his bandanna. "Sorry, but I have to do this," he said as he used the bandanna for a gag, then tied her wrists and ankles with a length of the rope, securing it to his saddle. "If you try to get anyone's attention outside this cave, I will do a lot more than gag you. Understood?"

With her hands tied behind her and her ankles bound she might still be able to move, but she wouldn't get far dragging the saddle before he came back.

She glared at him, those blue eyes flaming with heat, as he picked up his rifle and headed for the mouth of the cave.

The night was clear and cold at this altitude. He slipped from the cave, looking back to make sure no light escaped. It appeared pitch-black inside the opening. The brush hid even that from the meadow. Assured that no one could find the cave without knowing where it was, he made his way down the mountainside, keeping to the blackness of the trees.

The rider had stopped in the middle of the meadow and now sat on his horse, shining his flashlight into the darkness at the edges of the trees. Could he smell the smoke in the air? Dawson didn't think so. At least, he was counting on that.

"Jinx!" the man called again, then seemed to sit listening.

Dawson had stopped behind a tree and now stood stone still, waiting for the rider to make a sound before he moved closer. He knew that if he shot the rustler, the sound alone might bring the others, depending on how far they'd driven the cattle. If this man didn't return tonight, Dawson didn't doubt that they would come looking for him.

As much as Dawson hated rustlers and put them right up there with horse thieves, he didn't like the idea of killing anyone. He'd just as soon let the law handle him. The problem was how to get his cattle back without getting rid of the rustler. Short of shooting someone, he wasn't sure how to do that.

He thought about what Jinx had said right before he gagged her. "We're on the same side." What did that mean? Or had it just been another ploy?

Shoving thoughts of Jinx to the back burner, he concentrated on the problem at hand. One of the rustlers had come back for her. The boyfriend? He thought about her earlier attempt at seduction and wondered just what she'd had to do to get into the rustling ring. That was another thought he didn't want to dwell on too closely—and definitely not right now.

The woman was nothing if not determined. He liked her spunk. The fact that she was cute as hell didn't hurt.

He reminded himself that she'd been trying to steal his cattle—and that if this was the same band of rustlers, which he suspected it had to be, then she and the others had already killed a ranch manager down in Wyoming who'd tried to stop them.

They'd burned down his house after trampling him in the stampeding cattle, which told Dawson that these rustlers were after more than cattle and the money they could get for them. They wanted to terrorize people they felt had more than they did and would take everything—including their lives.

With one rustler hog-tied in the cave and her boyfriend back for her, Dawson had to decide what to do. He didn't doubt for a moment that the man would kill him if he got the chance. But even if Dawson could capture him without it involving gunfire and bringing the other rustlers hightailing it back here, what would he do with him?

No way could he keep track of two prisoners and still go after his cattle. And while he might enjoy leaving them both tied up either in the cave or to a couple of trees, he couldn't be sure they would still be there by the time the sheriff was notified and could get up here to collect them. Not to mention that a grizzly bear or wolves would probably get them both before then.

He wondered if he would have felt this way if one of the rustlers hadn't been a woman and swore under his breath at the thought. The last thing he wanted to do was cut Jinx any slack, since she was one of them.

The contrast between the black trees and the starlit sky was enough that after a moment his eyes adjusted to the darkness. The meadow seemed bathed in a faint eerie light. As he hunkered in the trees, he could make out the cowboy on the horse moving slowly across the open space to the spot where the man had probably last seen Jinx. The rustler was searching the ground, but there was no way he could track her—or Dawson—not with the meadow all torn up from the stampeding cattle.

"Jinx!" the man called again. *"Jinx?"*

How long would this man look for her before he assumed she'd just taken off? Or gotten lost? Or was lying dead somewhere after being crushed by the cattle? Would he come back in the daylight to look for her? Or cut his losses and put all his efforts into getting the stolen cattle to a spot where they could be loaded onto a semitrailer and transported to wherever he planned to sell them?

The rustler kept looking, riding around the perimeter of the meadow. It made Dawson wonder again about the cowboy's relationship with the woman tied up in the cave. Jinx was a pretty young thing, the kind of woman who could definitely get her spurs into a man and take him for a wild ride.

But any man with a lick of sense could see that no man could get a lasso on a woman like her that would hold.

"Jinx!" the rustler called. "If you can hear me, try to be at the rendezvous spot in the morning." He finished riding in a wide circle around the meadow, his flashlight flickering in and out of the trees, then finally going out.

Dawson held his breath, listening, knowing the rustler was listening, as well. Then the rider began to move again through the meadow as if reluctant to leave, heading back the way he'd come. He stopped at the edge of the trees, called out one more time for her, then rode into the darkness of the forest and disappeared.

Hunkered down in the trees, Dawson stayed where he was for a few minutes to make sure the rustler was gone. Then he worked his way back toward the cave and the woman he hoped was still there waiting for him, because he wanted some answers.

Sheriff McCall Crawford kicked off her boots, plopped down next to her husband and put her feet up. It had been a long day and she was thankful to be home. As she settled in, she looked around the room. She loved the house her husband had built for them and this sitting room was her favorite.

A cool breeze scented with summer came in the open windows. She smiled over at Luke. He looked as if he'd had a rough day, as well.

"Any news?" he asked as he glanced over at her.

She shook her head. "Hoyt Chisholm wanted to see me earlier. Apparently Emma's left him. He swears Aggie Wells did something to her."

"Aggie Wells? The missing woman?"

McCall nodded. "I feel sorry for him, but I don't blame Emma for leaving him. If I'd been her, I would have hightailed it out of there the moment I heard about his third wife's body being found and his bolo tie being discovered at the scene."

"What happened to innocent until proven guilty?"

"You think he's innocent?" she asked her husband.

Luke sighed and leaned his head back against the couch cushion. "Admittedly, the evidence against him looks pretty bad."

"There's something about the missing Aggie Wells that is bothering you, isn't there?" she said, sitting up and turning to face him.

He smiled and reached out to caress her cheek. "Isn't it bothering you?"

"Yes! When Emma told me she'd smelled Aggie's perfume at the house, of course I didn't believe her. But this afternoon I got a letter from her. She had apparently mailed it before she left town. She claims Aggie bugged the main house at the ranch. She told me to check the fire alarms and even drew me a picture where I could find them."

"And?" Luke asked with interest.

"And I called the house. Emma is gone, just like Hoyt said. The sons are all staying there, but none of them were back at the house yet. I'm going out there tomorrow and see if there is anything to her story. But what if Emma is telling the truth?"

"You think Aggie kidnapped her?"

"I don't know what to think. Emma is convinced Aggie is behind her own disappearance. Hoyt believes Emma is in danger. If you'd seen his face…"

Her husband pulled her into his arms. "You can't do

anything about this until morning. What motive would Aggie have for kidnapping Emma?"

"Maybe she just wants to get rid of her so she can have Hoyt."

"Then why has she gone to so much trouble to make him appear guilty of his other wives' deaths?" her logical husband asked.

McCall groaned. "That's the part I can't figure. Maybe Aggie doesn't know herself what she wants out of this."

"That I find hard to believe. If she went to the trouble of staging her own disappearance and kidnapping Emma, then she has a plan, you can bet on that."

Jinx had no way of telling how long Chisholm had been gone. The fire had burned down to only glowing embers. When she looked toward the cave entrance all she saw was darkness. The quiet inside the cave was deafening. It fooled with her sense of time passing.

She'd known Rafe would come back for her. She hadn't been surprised when she'd heard him calling her name. He'd come, she knew, not because he had any real affection for her. He hadn't had a choice. The others didn't trust her. They'd been suspicious of her from the beginning and hadn't wanted her to ride with them.

But Rafe was their leader, though definitely not the brains behind the rustling operation. No, he was more the brawn, a tough ranch hand who'd done some time in the Wyoming pen. The others could push him only so far and she thought they knew it. Her disappearing would make them even more suspicious of her and question Rafe's judgment as well as his position.

Rafe would be worried that they were right. He

wouldn't trust her after this. Not unless she could convince him that she'd been captured and had gotten away.

She struggled to free her bonds, giving up when she realized Dawson had made sure she wasn't going anywhere. She froze, listening for a gunshot that would tell her which way the wind was going to blow, so to speak. There was still the chance that Dawson Chisholm was the ringleader and had gone down to meet Rafe and that they would both be coming back up here to decide what to do with her.

Why didn't she believe that scenario any longer? Because Chisholm had been nice to her? Because she'd shared his food? Because she was attracted to him and on a few scarce moments, liked him?

She cursed herself for telling him she was on his side. She'd taken a gamble based on nothing more than desperation. Normally she depended on her intuition, but with Chisholm she couldn't trust it.

Now he was out there with Rafe and she hadn't a clue what might be happening. Were the two of them at this moment discussing what to do with her? Or was Chisholm about to get himself killed? The thought sent an arrow of panic through her. Did he really think he stood a chance against a man like Rafe Tillman?

Another dire thought came on the heels of the first. She could die in this cave. If Chisholm didn't come back, Rafe would never find her and with her bound and gagged up here—

Jinx started at a sound at the entrance of the cave. She knew someone had entered, but it was too dark to see a thing in that direction. She sensed movement, heard the grate of boot soles on the cave floor approaching her and closed her eyes, bracing herself for the worst.

A moment later she felt a hand touch her arm and let out a startled cry, muted by the gag.

"I'm going to remove your gag," Chisholm whispered next to her. "Don't try to scream or call for help. Your boyfriend is gone."

She opened her eyes, blinked. He was little more than a shadow in the dying firelight. He snapped on a flashlight and laid it on the cave floor, then removed her gag.

She licked her dry lips. "He's not my boyfriend." She hated that her voice broke, that she sounded as frightened as she felt.

Chisholm smiled at that.

What had happened outside the cave? She hadn't heard a shot, but that didn't mean he hadn't killed Rafe. Or that the two weren't in cahoots. Her heart began to pound harder as she looked past him, expecting to see Rafe in the cave entrance. "Where is Rafe?" she finally managed to ask.

"Rafe, huh?" Chisholm said. "So that's your boyfriend's name."

"I told you, he isn't my boyfriend."

He started to untie her ankles, but stopped. She couldn't see his face, but she could feel his fingers brush her tender flesh. His touch was gentle, his fingertips cool and calloused.

She hadn't noticed how calloused his hands were before, and now it took her by surprise. Dawson wasn't one of those ranchers who drove around town in his new truck while someone else worked the place.

Jinx hated that this man had gotten to her. She didn't want to see him get killed, and yet how was she going to keep that from happening when he was determined to go after the rustlers and get his cattle back?

Chapter 5

"A few ground rules before I untie you," Dawson said quietly. "You try anything and I'll hog-tie you and leave you in this cave for the sheriff. And from here on out I don't want anything but the truth coming from those pretty lips of yours. Where are my cattle?"

She started to speak, but he stopped her with a hand on her arm.

"I'm warning you. Don't lie to me. And I want to know what you meant about us being on the same side."

Jinx met his gaze in the ambient glow of the flashlight. "There is something I need from you first, Chisholm."

He shook his head, looking amused. "Apparently you haven't noticed that you aren't in the best of bargaining positions right now."

Dawson saw the indecision in her expression. She didn't trust him any more than he trusted her.

She met his gaze. Tears shone in those big blue eyes

"I was only riding with the rustlers so I could get to the head of the rustling ring."

Dawson dropped to his haunches in front of her. "You expect me to believe that?"

"Under normal circumstances, I really wouldn't give a damn one way or the other," she snapped. Her eyes glittered with a sobering rage and, against his better judgment, he did believe her.

"Vengeance? Don't tell me this is because he stole *your* cattle."

"He killed my father."

Dawson frowned. "Your father?"

"The Wyoming ranch manager who was trampled in the stampede. Now do you understand why you have to let me go before it's too late?"

"I'm sorry about your father," he said, softening his words at the pain he saw in her pretty face. "But it's already too late."

She shook her head, clearly refusing to believe him. "Rafe came back for me. If I can catch up to him—"

"Jinx," he said, locking eyes with her. "Do you really think he could ever trust you? No matter what story you came up with, he's going to suspect you. Why didn't you tell me this from the get-go?"

"I would have, but I thought you might be involved. You definitely are coldhearted enough when it comes to your cattle."

He tried not to be insulted. "So you planned to single-handedly take down the rustling ring."

"I still do. Unless you want to help me."

He shook his head. "You're right. I'm coldhearted when it comes to what's mine. You want to get yourself killed, that's your business. I just want my cattle back."

"What about justice?" she demanded.

"Like you said, rustlers seldom get caught, and if they do, they hardly ever get any jail time."

"They *killed* my father."

Dawson nodded. "It's going to be hard to prove murder even if you can tie someone to the head of the rustling ring."

"I'm not worried about proving anything in a court of law." She lifted her chin, that defiant look back in her eyes. "All I need is a few minutes alone with the ringleader."

"Have you ever killed someone in cold blood?" he asked.

She looked away after a moment.

"That's what I thought." He shook his head as he got to his feet again. "But if you're determined to get yourself killed…"

As he started to walk away, she said, "I'll help you get your cattle back. I know where they took them."

The rendezvous point Rafe had mentioned? He stopped, lowered his head, struggling with his own good sense. He'd seen the passion in her eyes. He knew what it felt like to want to avenge a wrong, especially when it was against someone you loved. There was nothing he would have liked more than saving his own father.

He turned slowly.

"You just have to trust me."

"Trust you?" Dawson shook his head. "Let me get this straight. You rode with these rustlers, helping them hit other ranches?"

"This is my first."

"And you have no idea who is behind this rustling ring?"

"I had to gain their trust."

"Just as you're trying to gain mine now," he said with a smile. "Sorry, but I'm not going to let you jeopardize my life and my cattle so you can get yourself killed as part of some crazy revenge scheme."

"I told you. I'll help you get your cattle back, since that's all you care about," she said. "But don't try to stop me from going after what I want. It's a win-win situation."

He no longer had to ask himself how far this woman would go to get what she wanted.

"Chisholm—"

"I don't think you heard me. That cowboy who came after you tonight already suspects you, okay? You think they're going to believe any story you tell them? Hell, they might just shoot you outright the moment they see you."

"I'm willing to take that chance. Well?"

She was as stubborn as he was. He shook his head, angry that she would risk her life. "Let the law handle this. They'll catch these guys."

"Will they? I doubt it. And I know they won't get the person behind the rustlers."

"You don't think Rafe won't spill his guts when he gets arrested? Come on, Jinx, your father wouldn't want you doing this."

"You didn't know my father. You don't know me, for that matter."

He nodded, but he did know her. She reminded him of himself.

"At least I'm risking my life for something I believe in. You're risking yours for *cattle*, the dumbest animals on earth," she said. "So? Do you want your cattle back or not?"

He rubbed the back of his neck, studying her for a long moment. "It's your funeral."

"We have a deal then, Chisholm."

His gaze met hers and held it. Maybe she was a better poker player than he thought, because he was betting his life on the hand she was playing right now.

"Where are my cattle?" he asked as he began to untie her. "And where is the rendezvous point everyone is supposed to meet if something goes wrong?"

As it got late and things slowed down, Zane talked to a few more of the employees at the hotel. They all said the same thing about Emma McDougal.

"A delightful woman, always cheerful." That was the Emma he'd known at the ranch.

"We are so happy for her. You could tell that the two of them were in love." Zane had to agree from what he'd seen of his father and Emma together.

"Did she ever mention if she had family around here?" he asked each of them and got the same sad shake of the head.

"I think she might have had a family, maybe lost a husband or even a husband and a child. I sensed that about her," one woman from housecleaning told him. "I know she used to talk to her father on the phone. They seemed close."

"Any idea where he lived?" No. "A name?"

"I think I heard her call him Poppy."

As for employment records, Zane was told he would have to wait until the morning and talk to their supervisor. Initially, he was surprised that his father hadn't mentioned Emma had *worked* at the hotel. But then he realized his father wouldn't have found that little tidbit of information important. He probably also knew it might bias his sons if they'd known that from the beginning.

Zane was ashamed that was the case. He was realizing more and more that his father was a better man than he or his brothers were.

"Did she ever mention Caliente Junction, California?" he asked. No. "How about where she was from?" No.

"She never talked about the past."

But everyone had made up a past for Emma, a painful one filled with loss and regret.

He got the same answers from the bartender at closing. "Why does her past matter so much to you?" the young man asked as he wiped down the bar. The place was empty. The man and woman at the bar hadn't even made it until last call for alcohol. Both had been gone when Zane returned to talk to the bartender again.

"Her past is the only way I have of trying to find her," he said.

The bartender looked skeptical. "You're sure you aren't just trying to dig up some dirt on her?"

Zane couldn't deny he'd been worried when his father had rushed into marriage with a woman he clearly knew nothing about. "I like Emma," he said truthfully. "We all do. I just want to find her." That last part might not have been completely true.

If Emma had left his father of her own accord, then he was going to have to tell his father, and he doubted any dirt in Emma's past would be more heartbreaking than her deserting him.

* * *

Jinx told Dawson about the rustlers' plan to reach the first corral on the way out of the mountains and bed down the cattle for a night.

The cattle would be tired. If they didn't get them water, food and rest, the rustlers would lose them. Some would fall behind, and without support to pick up the stragglers, they would be left to die.

He swore under his breath at the thought. "So they are stopping at an old abandoned corral down the mountain for the rest of the night, then moving the cattle farther down tomorrow?"

She nodded. "They had planned to move the herd tomorrow on down to the next abandoned homestead. There's a large corral there for their horses."

"Then the next day, they push them on to the county road and the semitrucks waiting for them," Dawson said. "Where is this rendezvous spot?"

"If any of us got lost or anything happened, we'd meet at one of the corrals."

He nodded. But with her missing, he wondered if the rustlers wouldn't change their plans, try to move things up. They could move the cattle only so far each day without losing most of the herd.

"You realize that once I take my cattle back, your life will be in even more danger," Dawson said as they sat around the small fire he'd built. He'd made them coffee and they now sat next to each other, both staring into the flames. "There will be hell to pay and who do you think they are going to blame?"

"You just worry about getting your cattle back," she said without looking at him. "I can convince Rafe to let me tell his boss what happened," she said into the stony silence.

Dawson shook his head. "You and Rafe are that close?"

She let out an irritated sigh. "If you're asking if Rafe and I are lovers, the answer is no. I did what I had to do to get in with the rustlers, but there are lines I won't cross."

He glanced over at her, wondering if when she'd tried to seduce him earlier she would have crossed that line. He thought there was probably a better chance of finding himself with a gun barrel stuck in his ribs.

"This quest for justice, it won't bring your father back."

"Don't tell me you wouldn't do the same thing if it was your father," she said. "My father was a lot like you, determined not to let them take cattle that didn't even belong to him. It cost him his life."

Dawson rose and walked to the cave entrance. The fire had burned down to embers again, making the back of the cave glow warm with light and heat. But where he'd gone was dark. Starlight bathed the meadow in a shimmering silver.

He heard her come up behind him and tensed for a moment but didn't turn. In that instant, he knew she would have to overpower him. It was the only way he was going to let her go back to the rustlers.

She joined him in the cave opening, the two of them silhouetted against the night. He could make out a sliver of moon over the trees, the pines etched black against cobalt-blue. The air was crisp and fresh and he couldn't remember a time when he'd felt so aware of a woman.

The night seemed alive with an electric current that made everything about it more intense.

As he looked over at Jinx, he wondered what it would have been like to have met under other circumstances. She met his gaze. A shudder moved through him and it took all his strength not to pull her into his arms.

"You should try to get a couple hours of sleep," he said as he turned to go back into the cave.

Jinx let out the breath she'd been holding. Just moments before, she'd felt a connection to this man.... She shook her head, telling herself that she'd only imagined it. All Chisholm cared about were his damned cattle.

She followed him back into the cave. He seemed almost angry as he tossed her his bedroll. "We leave before daybreak, so you should get some rest. We are definitely going to need the element of surprise."

"I don't want to take your bedroll," she said and held it out to him. He didn't take it. Instead he asked, "So it was just you and your dad?"

Was he testing her? Was it possible he still didn't believe her story? She was too tired to care. She spread the bedroll out in front of the fire and sat down on it, leaning back against the cave wall. "My mother died when I was a baby."

Kindness filled his eyes. "I'm sorry." He sat down next to her. "You've had a lot of death to deal with." He leaned back and she saw exhaustion and something more in his eyes.

She'd heard about his father being arrested for murdering one of his wives. The story had made all the major papers because of who Hoyt Chisholm was. His arrest was one of the reasons she'd talked the rustlers into hitting Chisholm Cattle Company.

"I was fine with just my dad," she said. "I was raised on the ranch, started riding on my own as soon as I could sit a saddle. That life gets in your blood."

"Doesn't it, though," he agreed.

"What about you, Chisholm?"

He smiled. "You already know my story. You got it when you researched my family ranch to steal our cattle."

She didn't deny it, but she was sorry that he'd figured out the part she'd played in all this. Was this any better than him thinking she'd slept with Rafe to get her spot with the rustlers?

Jinx knew his story. With no father in the picture, he and his brothers had been adopted by Hoyt Chisholm. The triplets, Colton, Logan and Zane, had also gotten lucky—Hoyt later adopted them after their mother died in childbirth. All had been young and had needed a home where they wouldn't be separated. Hoyt Chisholm had provided it.

"At least you had your brothers. I was an only child. I did have a great-aunt who used to visit once in a while, though." She laughed softly at the memory. "If anyone influenced my life's decisions, it was Auntie Rose," she said, still smiling at the memories. "She was a rebel, a true outlaw, and she taught me everything I know about surviving in a man's world."

Chisholm shot her an amused look. "You obviously learned well."

Did she sense conflict in him? He'd said all he wanted were his cattle, but she wondered if he was having a hard time letting the rustlers get away—even when she assured him she wasn't going to let that happen.

"About the morning," she said.

"Don't try to talk me out of it."

She just didn't want to get him killed—and she feared she couldn't prevent it if he went after his cattle. "It's your funeral," she said, giving his own words back to him.

He said nothing, but when she looked over at him, she saw his dark eyes lit with amusement and his full sensual mouth turned up in a smile.

The kiss was so unexpected, Jinx gasped. One moment he was smiling at her and the next his lips were on hers. It couldn't have lasted more than an instant, but she felt herself melt into it, drawn to a desire that didn't take her completely by surprise. She'd felt the sparks between them at the front of the cave. Now she knew without a doubt that she hadn't imagined any of it.

He jerked back, looking as surprised as she felt. The next moment he was on his feet. But for that instant she'd seen the chink in his armor—she'd glimpsed the man behind the mule-headed, arrogant cowboy. Her heart beat a little faster because of it.

She said nothing as she watched him pick up his saddle and pour himself the last of the coffee before he headed back toward the cave entrance.

Did he expect Rafe to come back? Or was he just keeping his distance from her?

Chapter 6

Jinx came out of a deathlike sleep. She jerked awake and reached for her gun, only to find it gone. It took her a moment to remember where she was—and with whom.

She blinked, her eyes adjusting to the dim light, to find Chisholm standing over her. She felt such a wave of relief. For a moment she'd thought it was Rafe. Not that she would admit it to Chisholm, but Rafe scared her.

"What is it?"

"Time to go." He was looking at her strangely, giving her the impression that he'd been standing over her for some time watching her sleep. The thought made her heart beat faster.

"You haven't changed your mind, have you?" she asked as she threw off the sleeping bag and got to her feet.

"If you're asking if I trust you, the verdict is still

out," he said as he tied up the bedroll and turned to head out of the cave.

"I'm asking if you're going to let me go once we find the rustlers," she said to his retreating backside. There was something in the set of his shoulders that told her the verdict was still out on that, as well.

As she started after him, she noticed that their saddles were gone. She'd slept right through him packing up everything and apparently saddling their horses. Exiting the cave into the clear, cold darkness, she spotted their mounts in the starlight below them on the mountain. Without needing to check her watch, she knew it would be daylight in an hour or so. By then they would have reached the first corral.

Glancing over at Chisholm, she wished there was some way to talk him out of going with her. But she could see by his expression it would take nothing short of death.

Jinx gave only a moment's thought to taking off on her horse and trying to reach the corral before him. That was if she could outrun him. Her horse was fast, but she didn't like the odds, given what she'd seen of the rancher. After all, he'd caught her before and risked life and limb to stop her.

She didn't doubt he would do it again.

Warning Rafe and the rest of them would only get Chisholm killed. She was determined to keep that from happening. But he wasn't making it easy.

She would have to bide her time. All she could hope was that she got lucky and found a way to still get what she desperately needed—the leader of this rustling ring and the man she held responsible for her father's death. She would bring him down—then the others.

"I'm going to need my gun back," she said as they reached the horses.

Chisholm swung up into his saddle and she thought for a moment he hadn't heard her. "You'll get it back after I get my cattle."

"That's a mistake," she said as she mounted her horse. "You're going to need all the help you can get once we find the rustlers."

"Arming you could be an even bigger mistake. There is nothing like a woman bent on revenge." They were close enough she saw the gleam in his dark eyes. He thought she was dangerous. Determination had hardened the lines of his handsome face. But it was no longer just about his cattle. He was mad at himself for kissing her.

Emma woke to darkness. She wasn't sure at first what had startled her awake until she heard movement and rolled over to find Aggie standing over her.

"What is it?" she cried, hurriedly sitting up.

Aggie hadn't said a word. Nor had she moved. And yet Emma sensed something had happened and was filled with fear at the thought that she might never see Hoyt again. Under the fear was a deep ache that made it hard to breathe. Before Hoyt, she had never known this kind of love.

"What's happened?" she asked, sliding back to rest against the wall. It felt cold and yet solid, and right now she needed solid.

"Hoyt doesn't believe you left him," Aggie said. There was anger and frustration in her voice as she snapped on a flashlight, blinding Emma for a moment. "He seems to think something has happened to you."

Emma tried to hide the pleasure she felt. She'd prayed that Hoyt would know she would never leave him, that she believed in his innocence and would stand by him no matter what.

"Zane has gone to Colorado to try to find you."

She felt tears come to her eyes. Her wonderful stepsons—as tough as she'd been on them, now one of them was looking for her. Her heart swelled. Hoyt *did* know her. He wouldn't give up until he found her—even from jail.

Aggie looked disgusted in the ambient glow from the flashlight.

"This got you up before daylight?" Emma asked as a thought struck her. Had someone called Aggie to let her know about Zane's trip to Colorado? *No,* she thought with a curse. Aggie was probably still listening to everything that happened at the house. The sheriff either hadn't gotten her letter about the listening devices—or hadn't believed her.

"You're going to have to send Hoyt a letter," Aggie said as if the idea had just come to her. "You're going to have to convince him to call off his sons. For your safety—and theirs. Otherwise…"

Emma didn't want to think about the otherwise as Aggie left the room, locking the door behind her. Was she planning on mailing the letter from Denver to make it look as if Emma had gone there? Or somewhere even farther away from Whitehorse, Montana?

It had never crossed her mind that Aggie might have someone helping her. She'd thought the woman had been acting alone. But now she feared Aggie had resources no one knew about, including perhaps someone as fanatical as she was.

* * *

The huge Montana sky was getting lighter by the time they neared the abandoned corral. With it just over a rise, Dawson reined in his horse, aware of Jinx beside him. He glanced up at the last of the stars glittering overhead and said a silent prayer, knowing they might need it, since they had no idea what was awaiting them just over this hill.

Dawson could hear the cattle lowing in the predawn. The sound he had grown up with and loved now felt lonely.

He looked over at Jinx and wished to hell he'd left her tied up in the cave. But he knew that might have put her in even more danger if the rustlers went looking for her after he took back his cattle and before he could get help.

As Dawson studied her in the faint light of the new day, he wished he could change a lot of things. He was about to jeopardize both of their lives. The thought almost made him laugh. Even if he'd left Jinx in the cave, it wouldn't stop her from going after the rustlers and their leader. There was nothing like a woman set on revenge—or justice.

He turned his attention from Jinx to the best way to take the rustlers by surprise. The sky was lightening to the east. It wouldn't be long before dawn. He figured with Jinx missing, the rustlers would be up early—and expecting trouble.

They'd ridden through silvery darkness and now the old Mill Creek place was just over the rise.

"We strike fast," Dawson whispered now as he reached over and tied her hands with the hank of rope again—this time, putting her hands in front of her.

She looked up in surprise.

"I'm just trying to keep them from killing you," he said. "If they think I took you prisoner, they might believe you. I wouldn't bet on it, though." He pulled out his bandanna. His gaze met hers as she leaned toward him so he could tie the gag.

"Last chance to change your mind," he said.

She shook her head. He swore and gagged her.

He knew there was nothing else he could say, and daylight was burning its way up the mountain to the east. If they were going to do this, it had to be now.

"Good luck." He felt his heart pounding in his chest painfully. "I'd tell you to be careful, but…"

She nodded, a smile in her eyes. Then she spurred her horse and took off, as if like him, she feared what he might say. He was hot on her heels as they came up over the rise.

Sheriff McCall Crawford pulled up in front of the main house at Chisholm Cattle Company. It was early, the sun was just coming up off the prairie floor to the east, but she wanted to catch the Chisholms before they went off to do their chores.

As she stepped from her patrol SUV, Marshall Chisholm came out onto the porch. He looked wary. Like all the Chisholm men, he was handsome and exuded confidence. Three of the Chisholm brothers had the coal-black hair and eyes that reflected their Native American ancestry. The other three were blond with blue eyes.

"I'm here about Emma."

"You found her?" Marshall had the mocha coloring,

the dark hair and eyes and high cheekbones. There was a gentleness about him that belied his powerful size.

"No, I'm sorry. I take it you haven't heard from her?" McCall said.

He shook his head.

"She sent me a letter. Would you mind if I came inside?"

"You might as well," Marshall said. "My brothers are going to want to hear this."

Three of his brothers were sitting around the kitchen table when she walked in but they rose at the sight of her, all looking wary and worried. Colton and Logan were two of the fraternal triplets, both blond and blue-eyed and just as handsome as the others.

"Is this about Dad?" Colton asked. He'd recently become engaged to one of McCall's deputies, Halley Robinson.

"It's sheriff department business." McCall put a finger to her lips and stepped around the table to look up. The small smoke alarm was right where Emma had said it would be. "If you don't mind, I'd like to speak with all of you outside. I have something in my patrol car I need to show you."

They looked surprised but followed her out of the house. Once they were standing next to her SUV, McCall said, "Where's Zane and Dawson?" Zane was the third of the triplets.

"Dawson's up checking the cattle on summer range," Marshall said. Dawson was the older brother of Marshall and Tanner.

"Zane's gone to find Emma," Logan said. Unlike his brothers, he wore his blond hair long and was the rebel of the family, spending his off time not on horseback but on a motorcycle. "What's going on?"

"Emma left me a message at my office yesterday. She said that your house is bugged with listening devices."

"That's crazy," Marshall said.

"Maybe not," the sheriff said. "She told me what to look for. Did any of you put up that small smoke alarm hidden on the other side of your kitchen light?"

They all looked at one another. Logan spoke first. "I've never even noticed it before I saw you looking at it. Why would we put it there when Dad installed new smoke alarms last year all through the house in plain sight?"

"Emma believed that Aggie Wells isn't just alive, but that she's been in your house," McCall said. "That she's been eavesdropping on everything that is being said there."

"Are you telling us you agree with Dad, that Aggie Wells might have done something to Emma?" Colton asked as if seeing where this was going.

"I don't know what to believe at this point. But if Emma is right and Aggie Wells is alive and those smoke alarms in there are really listening devices... I know that's a lot of ifs, but that smoke alarm looks like one of the new high-tech listening devices any fool can buy off the internet."

"Well, we're about to find out," Marshall said, turning back toward the house.

McCall caught his arm to stop him. "Wait, if Aggie is listening in on your conversations, what has she heard? Did you mention that Zane had gone to look for Emma?"

Marshall swore.

"We've been staying here at the house, so I would

imagine she's heard everything that was said," Colton said. "Including that Zane has gone to Denver to try to find out anything he can about Emma."

The brothers looked as worried as McCall felt.

"These listening devices," Colton said. "Doesn't she have to be nearby with some sort of transmitter?"

McCall shook her head. "The new ones can be accessed through a cell phone or computer. Aggie doesn't even have to be in the area. But I do have an idea. There might be a way to make sure Emma was right about this. We need to disable the one in the kitchen, but we have to make it look like an accident."

"Are you suggesting a little roughhousing between brothers?" Marshall asked.

"Or a knock-down, drag-out fight," McCall said. "Think you can do that?"

They laughed at that. "Not that any of us ever fight. Then what?" Colton asked.

"If you all do most of your talking in the kitchen in the morning, if it is a listening device and if Aggie is alive and listening, then she's going to want to come and fix it. You'll just have to make sure she knows when all of you will be out of the house for a length of time. Emma said she found several other small smoke alarms in the house." She told them the locations.

"So she can still hear us if we're in the house," Colton said with a nod.

"Do you think she's hurt Emma?" Logan asked, sounding upset.

McCall hoped not. "If Aggie staged her own disappearance hoping to make Hoyt look guilty of her murder, then with Hoyt in jail, I believe she won't hurt Emma. Once he's out…"

"If she wants to frame him for Emma's murder, he has to be out of jail," Logan agreed.

"But Dad is trying to make bail. He's desperate to find Emma," Marshall said. "His new lawyer thinks he might be able to get him out by the weekend. He's pulling every string possible, including going to the governor."

"I doubt telling our father what's going on would make him slow down that process," Marshall said. "If anything, he will try to get out sooner."

"So we don't tell him," Logan said.

"If you're right, then Aggie is going to be curious about what you showed us in your patrol car," Colton said. "Is it anything we might want to argue about?"

The sheriff smiled. "More evidence against your father and a warning for you Chisholms not to interfere in my investigation. Is that sufficient?"

"Hell, we've never needed a reason to fight," Logan said. "You have to find Emma. If something happens to her…"

"Let's see if we can't draw out whoever installed these smoke alarms and start from there," McCall said. "That's *if* the smoke alarm is a high-tech listening device. I don't need to tell you that looking for Emma if Aggie has her in this part of Montana would be like looking for a needle in a haystack. My deputies are already looking for Aggie. Once you have the smoke alarm disabled, bring it to me. If it is a listening device, then we'll set the trap and see what falls into it."

Early-morning mist hung in the air as Dawson rode over the rise after Jinx. The minute he topped the hill, he saw the corral below bathed in the faint light of dawn and heard the bawling cattle and knew what the rustlers had done.

The rustlers had felt pressured and had been forced to leave some of the calves behind that couldn't go any farther.

Dawson had his rifle drawn, ready for the rustlers to show. But nothing but the calves in the corral moved in the abandoned ranch yard. No guard. The rustlers had been expecting trouble. Only the corrals still stood, the house nothing more than a decaying foundation of charred small stones and mortar after an apparent fire.

There was a chill in the air, a dampness from the morning dew that glistened on the grass. The calves bawled loudly as he and Jinx rode in. Dawson cursed the rustlers as he reined in.

Jinx had stopped a few yards from the corral and now sat looking despondent. Like him, she had to realize that her boyfriend Rafe was more than a little suspicious of her. The rustlers must have moved the cattle farther east, closer to where the semitrailers would be picking them up for quick sale to some crooked cattle buyer.

He swung down off his horse and walked over to untie her hands. As she took off the bandanna gag, even in the dim light, he saw her defeat.

"How far is it to the next corral they planned to use?" he asked. "I'll herd these cattle down to it today." It would be slower going, but he didn't want to leave them here.

As he started over to open the gate, she said, "They'll be expecting you to do that."

"I know," he said without turning around. "But I can't leave these calves here like this."

Dawson turned to look at her. She wanted to go after the rustlers, catch up with them. She didn't want to herd a bunch of calves down to the next corral.

"I can't stop you from leaving," he said, meeting her gaze. "It would probably be better that way. If they catch you riding with me…"

He could see from her expression that his offer had taken her by surprise. She actually looked at a loss for words. He wasn't just offering to let her go. He'd just told her he trusted her.

You're a damned fool.

Probably, he admitted. She could ride out, warn the rustlers and they would get away with as many cattle as they could herd to the truck. But if she had any chance of survival, given her determination to bring down this rustling ring, then she had to get as far away from him as possible.

He waited for her to overcome her initial surprise and take off like a shot.

But she surprised him.

"I'll ride with you as far as the next corral," Jinx said as she swung down from her horse and, taking off her straw hat, slipped through the corral fence to wave it in the air. The calves began to move toward the open gate.

She was going to help him move the calves down to their mothers? Didn't she realize how dangerous that was going to be if the rustlers were waiting in ambush?

He felt a hitch in his chest. As much as she wanted justice, she couldn't chance that Rafe would send a couple of his men back up this way to check out whatever story she came up with. She was worried about saving him.

The last thing Dawson wanted was that. The woman

was neck deep in a rustling ring. Whatever her good intentions, he suspected she'd been the one to target his ranch. Jinx was far from an innocent in all this and it aggravated him that he'd let her get to him.

"You sure about this?" he said as she turned away from him.

She let out a laugh as she swung up into her saddle and began to move the cattle east toward the rising sun. "I'm sure I'm a damned fool."

He knew the feeling. As he spurred his horse and they began to move the calves down the mountain in search of their mothers, he reminded himself that he hadn't changed Jinx's mind about going after the leader of the rustlers. He'd only postponed the inevitable.

He supposed he should be glad of that. Did he really think it possible to get her to come to her senses?

As they began to move the calves toward the next abandoned corral and hopefully their anxious mothers, he couldn't help watching Jinx. She was as good in the saddle rounding up cows as any cattleman he'd known.

He reminded himself that once they reached the next corral she'd be riding off into the sunset and not even looking back. She was a woman on a quest and a man didn't want to get in the way of a woman like that.

Keep your distance from this woman.

But the warning fell on deaf ears.

As they topped a rise, he looked out across the wild country. He knew the next corral wasn't far, from what Jinx had told him. Up here in this part of Montana there were a lot of abandoned old ranch places. It was big country, inhospitable a large part of the year with blizzards, howling wind that brought in dangerous storms and below-zero temperatures in the winter, and blazing heat, mosquitoes the size of bats and stunning sunsets all the other months.

The hardest part for some was the loneliness. Ranches were few and far between, the sky up here vast, the land seeming to go on forever without another living soul for miles. It took a special kind of person to appreciate it.

Dawson thought of Emma and his dad and felt a heart-wrenching ache. He'd actually thought his father had finally found the perfect wife for him.

As he looked over at Jinx, he saw that she had reined in and was looking out across the country with a kind of awe. She had removed her straw hat to catch some of the breeze that ruffled her blond hair. Her face was lightly tanned, her eyes the same blue as the big sky that spread out before them.

As hard as he tried not to, he lost a little piece of his heart.

Chapter 7

Aggie returned with paper and pen—and of course a gun. She dropped the paper and pen onto the mattress and leaned against the wall, the gun in her hand.

While Aggie had been gone, Emma had used the buckets in the closet. Just washing her face and cleaning up a little made her feel stronger.

"I'm going to need some fresh clothing," Emma said from where she'd been standing and peering out a space between the boarded-up window. "I assume you removed my clothing from the house and still have it."

She'd realized that if Aggie had gotten rid of her belongings, then she wasn't planning on letting Emma live.

Aggie studied her for a moment without answering, making Emma's heart pound. Was she upset that Emma had asked for a change of clothing? Or did she realize as

Emma did, that if she admitted to getting rid of Emma's things, then they would both know what her plans were?

Emma so far had been the perfect prisoner, not asking for anything, not trying to escape. She'd thought it better to bide her time.

But she needed fresh clothing and she was tired of pretending to be the perfect prisoner. However this ended, Emma wasn't about to go down in a cowardly fashion if she could help it.

"Write the letter and I'll get you some of your clothes," Aggie said.

Emma glanced toward the paper and pen on the mattress, relieved to hear that Aggie hadn't gotten rid of her things. That had to mean something.

Unless the woman was lying. That was always a possibility.

But Emma had little choice but to go along. "You left a note at the house." She shifted her gaze to Aggie. "I don't remember writing it."

"You didn't. I did."

She cocked a brow. "Aren't you afraid someone will check the handwriting and realize it isn't mine?"

Aggie laughed. "How long have you been in that house? Two months? I really doubt any of your stepsons would know your handwriting. Anyway, the note I left for you at the house was sloppy, hurried as if you were upset. I also made it short and sweet. Now, quit stalling."

Emma walked over to the mattress, sat down on the edge and picked up the paper and pen.

"Here, you can use the tray to write on," Aggie said, sliding it over to her with her foot. "Start by apologizing for running out on Hoyt." She smiled. "That is what

you would do, isn't it? Then tell them you are afraid
for your life."

At least that part Emma would write honestly.

"Now write, 'I'm having a friend drop this off at the
house.'" She lifted a brow. "You can't really say that
Aggie will be dropping it off when no one is home,
now, can you?"

So that was how she planned to get the letter to Chisholm Cattle Company quickly. Emma felt better already. Aggie didn't have an accomplice. She was all
alone in this. That definitely narrowed the odds—even
with Aggie holding the gun.

"Emma was delightful," the fiftysomething male supervisor at the hotel told Zane when they met that morning. "I hated to lose her. Everyone liked her."

"That's what I've heard. I need to find her." He filled
the man in on what he knew so far about Emma's disappearance, including the fact that she might be in danger,
something he thought very likely after his conversation with his brother Marshall first thing this morning.

He still couldn't believe that the house had apparently been bugged and that even the sheriff was beginning to consider that Aggie Wells wasn't just alive,
but that she might have faked her disappearance and
taken Emma.

"Did she ever mention family?" he asked the supervisor.

The man shook his head, visibly upset by the news
about Emma. "She had a father out in California. I believe they were close, but other than that…"

"Did she mention his name?"

"Sorry. Emma wasn't one to talk about herself."

"She didn't get any mail here?"

"Not that I know of."

"Do you know where she lived?" Zane asked.

"She had an apartment just down the street from here."

Zane glanced toward the front door and the street beyond it. "This is a pretty pricey neighborhood."

"I got the feeling she was careful with her money."

Was it possible she'd come from money? Or married it? Or was just careful with what she made?

She could have been divorced or widowed. Zane swore under his breath; there was no way of knowing. When he'd gone on the internet, he hadn't been able to find an Emma McDougal that matched her age.

"She was like family here at the hotel," the supervisor said.

And if she really had left on her own accord, she would have come back here, Zane thought. Clearly she could have gotten her old job back.

Letters. He thought of the note Emma had allegedly left. After talking to his brother Marshall this morning, he realized there was a chance she either hadn't left it or had been forced to write it.

"You wouldn't happen to still have anything that Emma had written?" he asked. "She left a note, but we suspect it wasn't her handwriting."

"As a matter of fact, I have her employment application. We keep those on file for five years." He went into the office and returned a moment later with a copy for Zane. "You don't see penmanship like this anymore. These kids and their texting—their handwriting is atrocious. I could show you applications that are barely legible."

Zane stared down at Emma's perfect script. There

was no way she'd written the note left at the house. Under former employment, the line was blank. The address line was also blank.

"There isn't much on this application," he noted.

The man shook his head. "She'd just gotten to town, didn't have an apartment yet, no past experience, but there was something about her, you know?"

Zane thought he did. He thanked the supervisor.

"When you find Emma, will you tell her that we all miss her?"

"I will," Zane said, aware that Hoyt Chisholm wasn't the only man who'd fallen for Emma at the Denver hotel.

The sun rose higher, taking the chill out of the mountain air, but Jinx felt little of the warmth. When she'd seen the calves in the corral, she'd known. Rafe wasn't taking any chances. He'd had his men leave the weaker calves that had been slowing them down. He was spooked, which meant he was suspicious of her.

She leaned back in the saddle to stretch her spine. Huge cumulus clouds floated in the sea of brilliant blue over the tops of the pines. The air up here felt so clean she swore it hurt to breathe. She was tired but Dawson, she noted as she glanced over at him, was exhausted. How much longer could he keep going without any sleep? She knew he hadn't gotten any last night.

As an old homestead cabin came into view, she saw Dawson rein in. Like her, he must have spotted the small creek nearby and the meadow of grass. They could push the calves only so hard. It had been slow going and they hadn't made much headway, but she also didn't think they'd left any strays for the wolves and grizzlies to eat.

"We have to stop," he said as she rode over to him. He looked as if he expected an argument from her. He knew how badly she wanted the leader of the rustling ring. So much she could taste it. But she couldn't leave him and the calves. She figured he was counting on that.

Rafe would be pushing the cattle down to the next corral, but he couldn't move up the delivery date because he would have no way to contact the truck drivers with no cell phone service for miles around.

There was time, she told herself as she swung down from her saddle. The calves had already found the creek. She headed for the old cabin. It looked as if it had been used by ranchers who brought their cattle up to summer range, maybe even the Chisholms, though not Dawson. He apparently liked the cave better.

"You can catch up to the herd if you leave now," Dawson said behind her. "I don't want you staying for the wrong reasons." She didn't turn, didn't answer. Rafe would be pushing the cattle toward the last corral, afraid something was amiss with her disappearance. She figured that meant he wouldn't be doubling back again to look for her—or anyone else.

Too bad that wasn't the real reason she was staying here.

"Jinx," Dawson said behind her. There was a softness to his voice as light as a caress. She turned around to face him, saw his expression and told herself she should have taken his advice and ridden out before she got in any deeper.

"Looks like things got rough," McCall said in her office. Marshall had brought her what was left of the listening device after the brothers had put on the fight at the kitchen table. "It's not a smoke alarm. It appears to be some sort of listening device, just as Emma suspected."

Marshall nodded. "She didn't bail on my father, did she?"

McCall studied the pieces he'd brought her. She was beginning to believe more and more that Emma had been right about a lot of things.

"Now what?" he asked.

"We have to assume whoever put this in the kitchen will have heard the fight up until the point where the device was destroyed," the sheriff said. "With luck, that person will wait until he or she is sure all of you are away from the house and then try to replace it."

He smiled, obviously noticing the way she was trying not to say Aggie's name. "Leaving yourself open just in case it isn't Aggie?"

"Just trying not to jump to conclusions."

He nodded. "I checked the house. There are at least two more of these things, one in the living room and another in my dad and Emma's bedroom, just as you said she told you in the letter."

McCall could see how angry he was. "We have to keep our cool," she warned. "If she gets any hint that we're onto her…"

"I know. We need her to lead us to Emma—if she has her."

"Have you heard anything from Zane?"

"He called this morning in the middle of the fight. I called him back from my cell phone away from the house and told him what was going on here," Marshall said. "He's flying to some place in California today, the last address he could find for Emma. I told him to keep looking for her—just in case we're wrong and Emma really did leave. I guess we're covering all our bets."

"Didn't you say your brother Dawson went to check on your cattle up on summer range?"

"Yeah." Marshall frowned. "I got the feeling he'd be gone for a couple of days at least. I don't think we need to worry about him showing up unexpectedly. My brothers and I were talking. We have some new fence we started putting in before Dad was arrested. It's up in the north forty far enough that we wouldn't be coming back to the ranch until late."

"That sounds good. We want her to know you'll be gone for a while. I'll take it from there," the sheriff said.

"You sure you won't need any help?" Marshall asked.

McCall smiled. "Thanks, but I think I can handle it." She knew that all the brothers would be there in a heartbeat if they thought they were needed. She liked the Chisholm men. They were all gallant, all loyal to family.

She thought of her newest deputy, Halley Robinson, and her fiancé, Colton Chisholm. They made a cute couple. Halley made a darn good deputy. McCall was happy for her and hoped Emma's situation had a happy ending, as well.

"Set it up for tomorrow," she said, afraid to put it off.

Marshall nodded. "Dad said Emma swore she smelled the woman's perfume in the house several times. The last time he didn't believe her. That's really weighing on him right now. He's convinced that not only is Aggie alive but that she might have already hurt Emma. He is doing everything possible to get out on bail. I know he has a call in to the governor."

"Hopefully this will all be over by tomorrow," the

sheriff said. If Aggie showed up, McCall was just praying she would lead her to Emma. If Emma was still alive.

The look in Dawson's dark eyes spurred Jinx's heartbeat into a gallop.

"Jinx," he said again, the soft timbre of his voice melting her resolve. She watched him yank his Stetson from his head and rake his fingers through his thick black hair. His expression was one of both desperation and desire.

She felt the same stir in her. "Chisholm…" She said his last name as if that could stop him.

It didn't.

In two long strides he closed the distance between them, wrapping his arms around her, dragging her to him, his mouth dropping to hers, stealing her breath, making her heart drum in her chest. She looped her arms around his neck, holding on tight as if in a fierce gale.

"What if Rafe comes back?" she said when he let her come up for breath.

"I don't give a damn about Rafe," he said as his mouth hovered over her lips. And then he was kissing her again, deepening the kiss.

Desire shot through her veins, hot and sweet. She told herself this was a mistake, but she no longer believed that as Dawson cupped her jean-clad bottom and lifted her against him. His mouth dropped from hers and trailed along her jaw to her throat to the tops of her breasts. She felt the heat of his breath, his mouth, as he ferreted one rock-hard nipple from her bra, then another.

With a cry, she arched against him and he lifted her higher, pressing her against the sun-warmed wood of the cabin as he peeled back her shirt, her bra, and found bare skin.

They never made it inside the cabin. As the sun rose high above the pines and clouds drifted past in the endless sea of blue overhead, they made love on their discarded clothing spread across the summer grass as the calves rested in the shade of the trees along the creek and the breeze stirred the leaves on the cottonwoods overhead.

Chapter 8

The plane banked, giving Zane a view of manicured golf courses, red tiled roofs and shimmering aquamarine swimming pools. After landing in Palm Springs, he rented a car and headed south toward the Salton Sea.

Caliente Junction was pretty much as he'd expected. A convenience store with lots of bars on the windows, a gas station, a boarded-up Mexican food place and several more empty buildings.

He could see what looked like a couple of houses behind the convenience store, small stucco houses sitting out in the middle of the desert. But he had little hope that the address Emma had used was anything more than one she'd pulled out of her hat.

Parking in front of the store, he got out and went inside. He was betting that Emma had some reason for wanting to hide her past and that was why she hadn't shared it with Hoyt.

A bell jangled over the door and he was hit with the rich wonderful scent of homemade tamales. His stomach growled.

An elderly Latino woman appeared behind the counter. "Can I help you?"

"I sure hope so." Zane pulled out the photograph he had of a smiling Emma McDougal Chisholm. "Do you recognize this woman?"

She barely glanced at the photo before asking, "What has she done?"

"She's missing and I'm trying to find her. Her last known address was Caliente Junction."

"Why do you want her? Are you a cop?"

He shook his head. "She's my stepmother. My father is worried something has happened to her. So am I."

The woman studied him for a moment. "You need to talk to Alonzo."

When she didn't say more, he asked, "Where do I find this Alonzo?"

She pointed toward the back of the building. "Last house at the end of the road. You can't miss his truck parked outside. It's blue."

The truck was a lot of blues, a monster vehicle with huge tires and a body that looked as if it had been pieced together by Frankenstein during his "blue" period. Zane parked and walked up to the door. It opened before he could knock.

"Yes?" the large elderly Latino man asked suspiciously. Alonzo was wearing baggy shorts and a huge faded Grateful Dead T-shirt. His feet were bare and it was impossible to tell his age. But if Zane had to guess, it would be late seventies.

He gave Zane the once-over. Zane had wisely left his

Stetson at home even though he felt half-naked without his hat. No way was he going anywhere without his boots and jeans, though, so he wore them and a Western shirt, which back home would have been standard ranchman's wear. He had fit right in back in Denver.

Now, though, he felt overdressed. "I just spoke with the woman at the store. She suggested I talk to you. I'm looking for Emma." He handed the man the photo. "I'm not a cop or a bill collector. Emma is my stepmother. I'm afraid she might be in some kind of trouble."

"Your *stepmother?*" The old man sounded disbelieving and for the first time, Zane thought he might be at the right place.

"My dad recently married her."

"Your *dad?*"

But he was getting tired of the echo. "Hoyt Chisholm of Chisholm Cattle Company out of Whitehorse, Montana."

The man laughed. "So Emma really did marry a cowboy? Come in," he said, pushing the door open wide and stepping back. As Zane entered, Alonzo said, "What's this about Emma being in trouble, though? If anyone can take care of herself, it's our Emma McDougal."

Dawson lay on his back staring up at the sky overhead. Not since his childhood could he remember watching clouds float by on a summer day and feeling so content. He breathed in the sweet scent of the crushed grass beneath him. It mingled with the scent of the woman next to him.

He never wanted to leave here, didn't even want to get up. Right now he would have let the rustlers take the cattle. All that mattered was being here with this woman on this summer day because he knew it couldn't last.

Jinx lay beside him, looking up at the expanse of blue sky dotted with big white clouds. There was a small smile on her lips, a softness to her expression that made him smile as well. The breeze ruffled her short blond curls and he felt an ache for her, a longing. There were some women you could never have, not in a way that promised they would always be there. Jinx was one of them.

"I can't let you go after the rustlers," he said, speaking the fear in his heart.

She turned her head slowly toward him. "Please don't, Dawson."

Dawson. Not Chisholm. He liked the sound of his name on her lips. Hell, he liked her lips on him.

He pushed himself up on one elbow and laid an arm over her warm stomach. Her soft skin spurred another jolt of desire that burned through him like an out-of-control wildfire. He knew that if he had a lifetime, he would never get enough of this woman, this capable, stubborn, determined woman who didn't think she needed anyone.

Well, getting the leader of the rustling ring was one thing he couldn't let her do alone. "Jinx—"

She slid out of his hold, picking up her jeans from the ground as she did. Her panties were still inside the jeans. She moved a few feet away and pulled on both before turning back to him.

He was sitting on the ground, his gaze on her. "You're still determined to go after him alone, aren't you?"

She reached for her Western shirt lying on the ground

next to him. He grabbed her wrist, met her gaze, and then slowly let go. "I have to finish what I started."

"Let me help you get him," he said.

"No." She shook her head, the look in her eye warning him not to bother arguing with her about this.

He nodded, chewing at his cheek as he tried to stem his anger. And his hurt. "What about this?" He motioned to the crushed grass, the scent of the two of them still lingering, the memory of the feel of her still fresh on his skin.

Jinx looked into his eyes and said the only thing she could. "It was a mistake." She wanted to take back the words the instant they left her lips. She saw the hurt in Dawson's eyes, but she knew that the one thing she couldn't risk was this man's life.

This was her crazy crusade for justice, a promise she'd made her father as she stood over his casket. She had to do this, but she wouldn't let Dawson get any more involved than he already was.

"I've come too far to stop now," she said, the words like gravel in her mouth as Dawson rose and began to dress, his movements hasty with anger. "It's something I have to do on my own."

"You go back to Rafe alone and you're a dead woman."

"Thanks for the vote of confidence," she snapped. "This is something I have to do. Alone, because that is the only way I can get near the man behind these rustlers. I thought you knew that."

"Knowing it is one thing. Accepting it…" He shook his head.

"I know how dangerous this is." Her voice broke. Dawson Chisholm was another danger, one she hadn't

planned on, one she couldn't regret either. But now she
had him to worry about and she was desperate to see
that nothing happened to him because of her.

"I should have ridden out this morning," she said,
pushing her straw hat down over her tangled blond hair.

"Why didn't you?" he asked, his gaze locking with
hers.

She could still smell him on her, still feel his phan-
tom touch on her flesh. "I'll ride with you as far as the
next corral. After that, you just concern yourself with
your cattle." She turned and headed for her horse.

It took all of his strength not to go after her and pull
her into his arms again. But Dawson knew if he did,
he wouldn't be able to let her go. Hell, he'd hog-tie her,
whatever he had to do to keep her safe, and she would
hate him for it until the day she died.

One look at her and he realized short of taking her
prisoner again, there would be no keeping this woman
from doing what she'd set out to do from the beginning.

Just as he'd felt about the first woman he'd loved.

The reminder sent an arrow of pain through him.
Jinx had nailed it when she'd said there'd been a woman
in his life who had been taken from him. Only, Jinx had
thought the woman had been taken by another man.
He'd lost her nonetheless and he still felt the pain of
that loss.

And now he'd met another headstrong woman who
was determined to get herself killed. He rose and
quickly dressed.

As he swung up in his saddle, she said, "I need you
to let me finish this, Dawson."

"Could I stop you?" He shook his head, furious with

himself for letting this woman get to him. And she had.
Maybe from the moment he'd tackled her thinking she
was one of the rustlers. Maybe in the firelight of the
cave. But she'd gotten to him. He thought now how apt
her name was.

"I've already tangled with one headstrong woman
who wouldn't listen to reason when it came to her wel-
fare," he said. "I'm not up to trying to corral another
one."

Anger flared in her eyes like a blue flame. "I'm not
one of your cattle, Chisholm. I don't need herding—or
corralling. I'm my own woman."

"You don't have to tell me that," he said. "I get it.
And you're right. This *was* a mistake." With that he
reined his horse around and rode down to the creek
to get his cattle. He didn't look back. He couldn't. He
wasn't letting another dangerous woman get her spurs
in him—at least not any deeper than Jinx already had.

McCall realized that telling her husband her plan
had been a mistake.

"I don't like this," Luke said. "If you're right and
Aggie Wells is alive and has Emma, then I shouldn't
have to tell you how dangerous she is."

"I'm the sheriff," she said with exasperation. "Forget
for a moment that I'm your wife."

"I never forget you're my wife. And I thank my lucky
stars." He took her shoulders in his big hands and drew
her closer. He had stopped by the sheriff's department
on his way to work and now the two of them stood in
the middle of her office, the door closed. "I just don't
like you being out there alone without backup."

"I'll have backup on the roads in and out of Chisholm

Cattle Company. I'll radio if I need help, but I think I can handle one woman."

"Are you sure that's all you're going to have to handle?" he asked. "You're that sure she's working alone?"

The question took her by surprise and it shouldn't have. If Aggie had abandoned her car out by the highway, had someone picked her up? Or had she already arranged for another vehicle that she simply got in and drove away?

"Uh-huh," Luke said. "You're convinced she has been working alone. What if you're wrong?"

"If it turns out she has a small army at her disposal, I will call for backup." She smiled at her husband. Touched that he was worried about her and a little concerned.

"How's your grandmother?" he asked out of the blue.

"Pepper?" McCall hadn't seen much of her lately. They'd both been busy. "Last time I talked to her, she and Hunt were settling in nicely. She loves having all her grandchildren on the ranch. They're building houses all over the place out there. Why are you asking about her?"

"Because she called me. She's worried about you. She thinks you work too hard. She wants us to come out for supper tomorrow. She also wonders when we're going to have a baby."

McCall quirked a brow. "*She* wonders?"

"She's also worried that you might not be around tomorrow for supper," he said, his gaze locked with hers.

McCall laughed and leaned in to kiss her husband. "Well, you can tell Grandmother or anyone else who's wondering that we'll be there tomorrow night."

He looked skeptical.

"And you can tell whoever else is interested that I think we should have a baby."

"Don't fool with me, McCall Winchester Crawford."

She chuckled. "Let's make a baby tonight."

He broke into a huge smile and pulled her to him, holding her as if he never wanted to let her go.

McCall was a little surprised at how worried he was. They were both in law enforcement, Luke a game warden trained just like she had been when it came to criminals. Often they ended up working together because of the shortage of law enforcement in this part of Montana.

He knew what her job entailed. It was strange that this case in particular had him so worried. Or did it have more to do with him wanting to have a baby?

Either way, it made her more anxious than she wanted to admit. If Aggie Wells was alive, then there was a good chance she had come unhinged. Those were the scariest criminals to confront and apprehend because you never knew what they would do.

McCall knew that was what had her husband worried. He didn't like the idea of her alone in an empty ranch house with a crazy woman. McCall wasn't that excited about it either.

"Ask my grandmother if there is anything I can bring for supper tomorrow night," she said later, trying to reassure them both as she gave him a conspiratorial wink. "By then with any luck, I'll already be pregnant."

Emma thought frantically about what she could say in the letter to let her stepsons know that she was being held captive by Aggie Wells.

But with Aggie watching over her shoulder with a

gun pointed at her, there was little chance of sending a message.

"Tell them to leave you alone, that marrying Hoyt was a mistake and that you don't intend to ever see them again," Aggie ordered.

Emma felt her eyes tear at the thought that she might not see her stepsons again, or Hoyt for that matter. Her heart broke at the thought. She couldn't bear to think that he might believe the words in the letter. Wouldn't he know it was a lie? Didn't he realize how much she loved him?

But she wouldn't be the first wife he believed had left him and, given his terrible luck with wives…or as one local called it, the Chisholm Curse, he might believe the words in the letter, and so might her stepsons.

It was actually the Aggie Wells curse, Emma thought as she wrote what the woman dictated. Aggie might deny that she was behind Hoyt's bad luck with wives since the first one had accidentally drowned, but Emma didn't believe it.

"There," she said as she finished.

"Sign it, Emma. Nothing more."

She did and handed the paper to Aggie.

"The pen, too."

Emma gave her an impatient look. "Did you think I was going to use the pen to break out of here? Or maybe carve it into a shank to use as a weapon?"

"I wouldn't be surprised," Aggie said as she took it. "You must be getting tired of sandwiches, but that's all we're going to have to eat for a while."

"Aggie, how long are we going to do this?"

The woman had stopped at the door. She had the

pen and paper in one gloved hand, the gun in the other. "Do what?"

"Stay here like this?"

"As long as it takes," Aggie said and stepped out, locking the door behind her.

It was a long slow ride to the next corral. The sun made a wide arc through the big Montana sky and had finally dropped over the horizon to the west, leaving streaks of color through the pines.

Farther to the north, though, a bank of dark clouds hunkered on the horizon in what could amount to a thunderstorm before the day was over.

Dawson hadn't said a word since they'd left the cabin. The only sound was the bawling of the calves and the occasional cry of a hawk in the sky over the towering pines as dusk settled in around them.

Jinx was sorry she'd told him that making love with him had been a mistake, but she figured he realized that now. It had been too intimate and she suspected it had left them both feeling vulnerable. They were vulnerable enough with a band of rustlers on the loose.

She wasn't sure Dawson realized how dangerous these men were, but she knew firsthand. The thought of her father lying in the dirt— She felt tears burn her eyes and quickly wiped them away. First she would take down the head of the rustling ring and the rustlers, then she would deal with her loss and let herself grieve.

Going after the rustlers and their leader had been the only way she could cope. She knew it wouldn't bring her father back, that it was dangerous, even stupid, but at least it was something she could do. Getting justice wouldn't fill the hole her father's death had left inside her. But it would maybe give her a little peace.

Ahead, she recognized a rocky bluff that sat high above a section of abandoned ranch. The calves had smelled water and were now bursting through the trees and into the open to get to it.

They both had reined in as they spotted the corral. It was empty.

For a moment neither of them moved as if taking this in and what it meant. Rafe and the others had moved the cattle out already. Or had never stopped here to start with.

"What the hell?" Dawson said, glancing over at her before he spurred his horse and rode down to the ranch. What was left of a small old cabin stood against a hillside. In front of it sat a cobbled rock wishing well. A frayed piece of rope hung from the well cover.

Jinx watched it move restlessly in the breeze as she tried to imagine the family who had lived here rather than think about Rafe. The ground was trampled from where the cows had been driven away. Rafe was more than suspicious of her. He was running scared.

Dawson had reined in his horse at the edge of the empty corral. Past him the land stretched out into the rolling prairie and the dark horizon. From here on out there would be no trees or mountains to hide in. Unless they traveled at night, they would be in open country—country where someone could see them coming for miles.

As she looked across it, Jinx thought she saw dust rising on the horizon. The cattle herd? They'd never be able to catch it unless they left the calves here and rode hard. Then what?

Suddenly it seemed too quiet even with the bawling calves. Jinx felt the hair rise on the back of her neck. "Dawson!"

But before she could warn him, the sound of a rifle shot filled the air.

Chapter 9

As Jinx raced down into the ranch yard, she saw Dawson flinch at the crack of the rifle. He reached for his own rifle but even as he did, she knew he was hit. A dark crimson splotch bloomed on his left shoulder.

"Get down!" he yelled as he dived from his horse.

Jinx felt as if everything was moving too fast. She bailed off her horse, diving behind the crumbling rock of the old well as another shot rang out. She couldn't see Dawson, could hardly hear with her heart in her throat and her pulse a war drum.

Another shot, then another. She and Dawson should have expected an ambush, been ready for it. But the ranch yard had seemed so deserted with the cattle gone.

She blamed herself. She knew Rafe had been leery of letting her ride with them from the first. When he hadn't been able to find her, he'd left someone to make sure she didn't turn up—just as Dawson had said.

She thought of her father. She'd been so hell-bent on vengeance, but Dawson was right. Her father wouldn't have wanted this.

"Let God settle the debt in his own time," her father used to say. "Don't think he isn't keeping track."

Tears welled in her eyes and her chest ached with regret and grief. If she'd gotten Dawson killed...

Suddenly she was aware of the eerie quiet again. Not a breath of air moved. She could see the calves down at the creek but they, too, had fallen silent. Somewhere in the distance she heard the song of a meadowlark, then everything fell silent again.

Jinx stayed down, afraid to move, afraid to breathe. If only Dawson had given her back her gun.

She heard the crunch of a boot sole on the dirt, then another. She looked around for anything she could use as a weapon. There was nothing.

A shadow fell over her. With dread, she looked up to see Rafe standing above her, his gun barrel pointed at her head.

Over homemade tamales, beans and rice, Alonzo told Zane about Emma.

"I was the one who found her," he said proudly.

"Found her?"

He nodded. "It was the middle of the night. I'd been down to the bar at the Salton Sea marina and was coming home. It is a miracle that I saw her." He crossed himself. "*La voluntad de Dios.* It was truly God's will," he translated. "I was driving along and boom! I blew a tire."

Zane was wondering when he was going to get to Emma. So far he couldn't imagine what about a night of drinking, then a flat tire, could be a miracle or had to do with Emma.

"I get out of my truck and realize my spare tire is flat," Alonzo said. "I was thinking what a terrible night it had been." He leaned toward Zane confidentially. "You see, I knew that when I got home Maria was going to be very upset with me. Maria was my wife of fifty-five wonderful years." He crossed himself again and said what Zane took to be a silent prayer.

"Emma," Zane reminded the man.

Alonzo laughed and passed him more tamales. Clearly this was a story he had told many times and with obvious relish.

"So I leave the truck and start to walk and all of a sudden—" his dark eyes lit up and a huge smile formed in his wrinkled face "—I heard what sounded like a kitten. The closer I got, though, I realized it was a baby cooing softly."

"Emma?" Zane said, with apparently enough surprise to please Alonzo.

The man clapped his hands. "Someone had left her beside the road wrapped in a dirty towel." He shook his head in disbelief even after all these years.

Zane was still in shock. "What did you do with her?"

"I brought her home, what else? I am no fool." He chuckled and gave his guest a wink. "I knew this little bundle of joy would keep Maria from being so upset with me."

"You raised her as your own?"

"We had always wanted children," he said with a shrug. "This one came from God. Try to explain that to Social Services. Much easier for us to let everyone think Maria had given birth at home. Maria named her

Emma after a character in a book she liked. The moment I saw her red hair I told Maria we'd have to give her a name that goes with that hair."

"So that's where the McDougal came from," Zane guessed.

"Emma McDougal Alvarez. Never was there a more cheerful child or a more mischievous one," he said with obvious affection. "She grew up here, making our lives blessed. We wanted her to go to college, but then Maria died." He shook his head. "Emma didn't want to leave me here alone, so she stayed for a while until I made her leave." A sadness came into his eyes.

"Something happened to her?" Zane asked, remembering what the people she'd worked with at the hotel in Denver had said. They had sensed some tragedy in her, perhaps the death of a husband or husband and child.

"She met a man. A bad man."

Rafe grabbed Jinx and dragged her to her feet. She told herself not to fight him, but as he pulled her up, she saw his men dragging Dawson's limp body behind the cabin.

"No," she cried and fought to get away. "You killed him?"

"Who is he?" Rafe demanded, shaking her into submission. "Who is your accomplice?"

When she didn't answer, he shook her harder.

"His name is Dawson Chisholm."

Rafe swore. "This is why you wanted to hit this ranch? You've been working with him all along?"

"Don't be stupid," she said and realized at once that was the wrong thing to say to a man like Rafe.

He backhanded her across the mouth.

She wiped her bleeding lip and glared at him. "He came up here to check his cattle and caught me. I've been his prisoner ever since."

Rafe gave her a scathing look. "You really do think I'm stupid, don't you? I saw the two of you ride in here together. You thought you could double-cross me?"

Jinx felt too sick to answer. She wanted to curl up and die. They'd killed Dawson. She started to slump back to the ground, but Rafe slammed her against the stone well, holding her up by a fistful of her jacket in his beefy hand. "How many others are there?"

She shook her head. "There aren't any others." She could tell he didn't believe her. "But when his five brothers find out what you've done…"

Rafe swore and shoved her toward her horse. "You try to make a run for it and I will personally shoot you," he said as his men came around the side of the house.

What had they done with Dawson's body? Her heart ached. She'd warned herself not to fall for him. But she had. And she'd gotten him killed. If the rustlers had hit any other ranch but Chisholm Cattle Company… Jinx knew that any rancher could have caught one of them and ended up like her father and Dawson, but still it wasn't any rancher who'd gotten killed. It was Dawson.

"Let's get these calves down to the rest of the herd," Rafe ordered.

Jinx realized that the dust she'd seen on the horizon hadn't been the rustlers at all. Dawson must have seen it and thought the same thing. No wonder they both hadn't been suspicious of an ambush.

But Rafe hadn't driven the cattle any farther than just over the hill into a lush meadow. She saw the dark

Angus cattle, heard the mothers begin to respond to the sounds of their bawling calves and move toward them.

Past the cattle, she saw the second abandoned ranch house set back against a hill with some outbuildings around it.

"She's going with us?" one of the rustlers demanded. They hadn't moved toward their horses.

Rafe laid his hand over the six-gun on his hip. "She's going with us as far as the trucks in case any more Chisholms show up. She is now our hostage."

The men looked as if they would have preferred Rafe kill her and leave her here with Chisholm, but they didn't put up an argument. Jinx knew that any one of them would gladly shoot her. They'd killed twice now. What was another body to get rid of out here in the middle of nowhere?

Jinx glanced toward the old cabin as Rafe led her horse and her toward the waiting cattle and the small ranch house. Now that he wasn't looking, she let the tears come.

I'm so sorry, Dawson. So sorry. Forgive me.

But she knew she would never forgive herself.

Aggie brought Emma dinner—another sandwich, an apple and more coffee.

Emma wasn't one to complain. She poured herself a cup of coffee and took a drink, needing the warmth. She couldn't help but think of Hoyt in jail, both of them prisoners.

"I'll bring you an extra sandwich in the morning," Aggie said.

"Why?" Emma asked, instantly suspicious.

"There is something I need to do, but don't worry, I'll be back later in the day."

She put down the coffee, having suddenly lost her appetite. "Don't hurt my family."

Aggie cocked a brow at her. "*Your* family?"

"I mean it. Do whatever you want with me, but leave the boys alone."

Aggie laughed. "The boys seem to be out of control over at the house. They got into a huge fight after the sheriff stopped by to talk to them this morning."

Emma felt sick. Her stepsons needed her more than ever with their father in jail. "You have to let me go to them. What is the point of keeping me here anyway?"

"Do you have any idea what evidence the sheriff might have wanted to show them?"

She shook her head. "Don't you? You hear everything that is going on at that house. Aggie, this is crazy, surely you realize that? What is it you hope to hear over there?"

"You wouldn't believe me if I told you."

"Try me," Emma said, although she suspected Aggie was right.

"I told you. Your life is in danger and someone is trying to frame your husband for murder. I'm just trying to prove it."

Emma shook her head and laughed. "*You're* the one who is trying to frame Hoyt for even *your* murder. You're the one who drugged me and now has me locked up here."

Aggie shook her head. "I knew you wouldn't believe me any more than the sheriff would if I took my story to her. There's more going on here than you know," she said mysteriously.

Emma groaned as Aggie moved to the door.

"You're just going to have to trust that I know what I'm doing."

Good luck with that, Emma thought but wisely didn't say as the woman left, locking the door behind her.

The thunderstorm that had been brewing on the horizon moved in so quickly, it seemed to take them all by surprise. They moved the calves down to the meadow, turning them out to find their mothers. The noise from the cows and their bawling calves at first hid the sound of thunder on the horizon.

Jinx noticed the wind first. It picked up, bending the tall tops of the pines and sending dust devils whirling across the patch of dirt in front of the old ranch house.

She squinted as dust filled the air. The clouds snuffed out the last of the light as they moved in. It felt as if someone had dropped a dark blanket over them.

Jinx felt nothing. A numbness had settled into her bones. She sat on her horse knowing that the rustlers were watching her, almost daring her to take advantage of the storm to make a run for it.

She knew if she made an abrupt move, one of them would shoot her and take their chances with Rafe. She saw him ride away for a moment to talk to his men, but she knew he was watching her out of the corner of his eye.

Any other time she might have taken her chances, spurred her horse and tried to make the top of the hill behind the old ranch house. She could see the deep eroded gullies around it and a part of her knew if she could reach one of them, she would get away.

But all the fight had gone out of her. Dawson was dead. She'd gotten him killed.

Lightning splintered the dark sky, followed only moments later by a burst of thunder that boomed as if right over their heads. The first drops of rain were hard and cold and made her stir as if she'd been in a daze.

Rafe grabbed her reins again and rode her over to the house. "Take care of the horses," he yelled to one of his men as he dragged her from her mount and shoved her toward the front door.

The huge drops of rain slanted down, stinging as they struck, the wall of rain obliterating everything around them. In a flash of lightning, Rafe threw open the front door and shoved her inside the dark cold house. Thunder rumbled around them.

She heard Rafe turn the skeleton key in the lock. Not that he probably needed to. She suspected he'd told his men not to come near the house no matter what they heard.

Jinx turned toward him, realizing what he had planned. She could barely see him in the darkness except when lightning flashed through the windows. She shivered, suddenly aware of the cold and her wet clothing that now stuck to her skin.

He let out a soft chuckle. "Now it's just you and me, Miss Brittany Bo 'Jinx' Clarke."

She felt the numbness leave her. He knew who she was. So he also knew why she was here. She thought she'd feel more fear knowing what this meant. Instead, her anger and need for justice rushed through her with a renewed fire.

"The boss really wants to see you."

"Oh yeah? I really want to see him," she said. She

knew now why he hadn't killed her. He was taking her to the boss. Isn't that what she'd always wanted?

She tried not to let herself think about the cost.

"By the way, who is the boss?"

He laughed and shook his head. "Not so fast, sweetheart."

Jinx stepped to Rafe, catching him off guard as she pressed her palms to his chest. "Why don't we go meet him right now? Or did you have something else in mind?"

In a burst of lightning, she saw him grin as he pressed his body to hers. "And here I thought I was going to have to force you."

She smiled up at him. "I've played enough poker to know when to throw in my hand."

Rafe chuckled. "I've been looking forward to this."

"Me, too." Jinx pulled his gun quickly, but Rafe surprised her with the speed with which he reacted. He grabbed for the pistol as she stepped back, his hand clamping down on her wrist.

She struggled to free herself as his other hand shot out to grab a handful of her hair.

"I was hoping you'd put up a fight," Rafe said, anger making his voice sound like sandpaper as he jerked her against him, both of them still struggling for the weapon. "You're going to regret this."

Jinx already regretted it. Her plan had been to walk him out of here at gunpoint. Force him to take her to his boss. End this once and for all.

Rafe was twisting her wrist and she could feel the weapon slipping from her fingers. Once he had the gun—

The gunshot boomed inside the empty old house like

the blast of a cannon. It echoed around her, the surprise of the sound making her freeze.

Rafe released his grip on her as he grabbed his chest. In a flash of lightning, he dropped to his knees in front of her. Thunder rumbled, rattling the windows.

"He'll kill you," Rafe said through gritted teeth.

"Tell me who you're working for," she said, dropping beside him.

He looked at her dumbly. She could see pain and shock in his eyes.

"Tell me," she pleaded.

He opened his mouth. A bubble of blood appeared at the corner of his lips. As another bolt of lightning splintered the sky outside, he fell face-first onto the dirty wooden floor.

Jinx stumbled back, her heart in her throat. "No!" For a moment she was too shocked and upset to think clearly.

At a sound beyond the broken window, she spun around, realizing the men might have heard the gun blast over the storm and would be busting down the door any moment. Thunder cracked overhead. Lightning illuminated the two of them in flickering flashes, followed by another crack of thunder that seemed to shake the floor under her as she stood, trembling, the gun dangling at her side.

What was she going to do now?

Chapter 10

Dawson came to slowly. At first all he felt was cold. Then came the pain, the confusion. He blinked for a moment, thinking he'd gone blind.

The darkness was total. He blinked again. Something sticky ran down into his eye and when he raised his hand to the spot over his eye, his fingers came away wet with blood from a gash in his forehead.

He wiped the blood away and tried to sit up, suddenly aware of his shoulder. It, too, was wet with blood. He lay there for a moment breathing in the damp, musty air. He could hear what sounded like gunfire outside and, between the volleys, could hear what sounded like rain. Under him he felt cold dirt and sensed he was underground.

With the memory of what had happened, he pushed himself up, fighting the pain; his only thought was of Jinx.

"Jinx?" he said as he felt around on the cold floor.

"Jinx?" He listened but heard nothing but the haunting echo of his own voice. Reaching out in front of him, he felt something cold and solid. A rock wall. He inched his fingers along it until he came to what felt like weathered wood. A door? He discovered a hinge and pulled himself to his feet, using the wall for balance until the dizziness subsided.

The doorknob was ice-cold to the touch. He turned it. The door swung open and the space filled with a dim, rain-streaked light. He stumbled out into a small covered space that ended in a row of stairs leading upward.

He could hear the thunder now, see flashes of lightning. Breathing in the sweet scent of rain, he stepped back out into the downpour. He still felt wobbly on his feet, but some of his strength was coming back.

Glancing back, he made sure that Jinx wasn't in a corner of what he saw was an old root cellar that had been dug back under the house. His attackers had shot him and thrown him down here, probably thinking no one would find his body.

But where was Jinx?

Dawson began to climb the steps, his memory coming back to him as he mounted each old stone step. The rustlers had waited in ambush and attacked. He told himself he should have known they would do that. Hadn't they already killed one man?

But he hadn't anticipated an attack. He'd believed that they were more interested in his cattle. Apparently they were more worried about Jinx than he'd thought they would be.

Still, something niggled at the back of his mind. First her father, and now they were after Jinx. Probably had inx. The thought sent his heart pounding. What would they do to her? He hated to think.

With dread, he went to find her.

The thunderstorm snuffed out most of the day's light. Low clouds hung over the ranch yard. Through the driving rain he saw the spot next to the wishing well where he'd last seen Jinx.

Their horses were gone. No big surprise there. As he moved through the downpour, he looked for any sign of her and saw nothing. The old cabin was small and empty. At the wishing well, he stopped and looked down. The well was too narrow to stuff a body down. He felt relieved, though only a little.

After a quick search, it was clear.

Jinx was gone.

So were the cattle and his horse. The rustlers had taken her. As he bandaged his shoulder as best he could and washed the blood from his face, he told himself that their taking her alive was a good sign. They had left him for dead and could have done the same thing with her. He had to assume they had a reason for keeping her alive—at least for the time being.

Though he wasn't fool enough to think she was safe. If anything, he was all the more worried about her. Where would they take her? In a flash of lightning he looked down the mountain toward the prairie. They wouldn't be crazy enough to try to move the cattle in a thunderstorm, would they?

For a moment he thought he heard the mooing of his cattle. He moved toward the sound, climbing up the small hill behind the cabin. At the top he waited for another crack of lightning. He didn't have to wait

long. The sky lit up, illuminating a ranch house in th
distance and a large herd of black cows.

Relief washed over him like the pouring rain. H
watched, trying to estimate how many of them ther
might be. He'd seen at least one rider and knew ther
would have to be several watching the herd. The cattl
would be spooked with the thunder and lightning. Jus
about anything could start another stampede and th
cattle could scatter for miles.

In the darkness that followed the lightning strike
Dawson saw what appeared to be a small fire glow
ing under an overhang on an outbuilding a little wa
from the house. There were no lights on in the house
no sign of Jinx. But there were horses in the corral, hi
and Jinx's included.

Dawson knew what he had to do. The bastards ha
tried to kill him. They'd left him for dead. Taken hi
horse. And his woman.

The thought of Jinx being his woman made hir
smile. She would never belong to any man. But a ma
would be damned lucky if he could talk her into shar
ing her life with him.

With each step, he thought about her and how t
get her away from the rustlers. He had no weapon an
he'd lost just enough blood that he was unsteady o
his feet. But he was alive, and with his last breath h
would find a way.

He smiled to himself as he realized that he wasn
going after the rustlers for justice. Or revenge. Or eve
his cattle. All he wanted was Jinx.

Zane watched the plane bank over the Billings rim
rocks and thought about what he'd learned in Californi

"I have been worrying about Emma," Alonzo had said. "She usually calls every few days to see how I am doing. I haven't heard from her yet this week."

"She doesn't come to visit?" Zane asked, surprised by that, since the two seemed close.

"She knows he has people watching the house."

"You're sure her former husband is still in prison?" he'd asked Alonzo. Apparently Emma had gotten involved with an abusive criminal who'd almost killed her. He'd ended up in prison for killing another man during a liquor-store holdup. Emma had turned him in. He'd sworn that when he got out he would find her and kill her.

"I check every week. He is still inside. But he comes up for parole next year. It's his friends I worry about," Alonzo said, looking even more worried.

"It might not be this ex-husband or his friends." Zane told him about Aggie Wells and how the sheriff in Whitehorse was planning to set a trap in the morning and his brothers were helping.

"It's good she has such wonderful stepsons," he'd said. "I don't want to believe that our Emma married another killer."

"She didn't. My father had nothing to do with the deaths of his other wives. The sheriff thinks this Aggie Wells might be behind it. Hopefully, we'll know tomorrow."

"I know Emma loves your father. All she talked about every time I spoke with her was Hoyt this and Hoyt that. I could hear the happiness in her voice. She would never have left him if she believed he was innocent."

"My father is convinced of that, as well."

Alonzo had crossed himself and said something i
Spanish he didn't understand. "You must find her."

Yes, Zane thought as the plane came into its final ap
proach. He was beginning to think his brothers wer
right about Emma having never left Montana—at lea
not of her own free will.

Zane had promised to let Alonzo know as soon a
he heard something and then he'd caught the last fligh
home. Now as the plane came in for the landing, h
couldn't wait to get back to the ranch. He still had
three-hour drive ahead of him, but he'd called Marsha
and filled him in on everything he'd found out.

His brothers were at the ranch waiting for him. I
the morning, the five of them would leave early to g
off to work on the new fence and leave the sheriff
spring her trap.

Zane hoped to hell it worked.

Jinx moved around the dark abandoned house cau
tiously. She didn't dare use the flashlight she'd foun
on Rafe. After she'd realized that the other rustlers mu
not have heard the gunshot over the noise of the storm
she'd searched Rafe, finding another gun, a knife an
the flashlight. She tucked the knife sheath into the to
of her boot, stuffed one of the pistols into her waistban
and held on to the one that had killed Rafe.

She avoided his body. She was shaking, from the col
and rain, from what had happened with Rafe.

She'd killed a man.

That realization, she knew, hadn't completely settle
in yet. Right now she just had to concentrate on gettin
away from the other rustlers. If they found out she'
killed Rafe, she had no doubt what they would do to he

Jinx checked the windows and saw where the other rustlers had gone. Through the pouring rain she could make out an old shed against the hillside with a lean-to on one side. They had built a fire and some of them were sitting around it. She was sure they were warmer than she was.

Counting the men around the fire, she figured three of them must be out with the cattle in the rain. She watched lightning zigzag across the open dark sky, listening as the thunder began to move off, and knew she couldn't wait much longer to make a run for it.

Even if the men were planning to spend the night here, eventually someone was going to come check on Rafe. His body lay in front of the locked door, blocking her exit. Fortunately there was a back door. In a flash of lightning she'd seen that it opened to a small gully that ran behind the house.

If she could stay down and keep moving, she might be able to get far enough from the house that the men wouldn't be able to find her.

In a burst of lightning that illuminated a corner of the house, she saw the saddlebags Rafe had brought in. She found hers and Dawson's and quickly went through them, stuffing anything she thought she might need into one and pulling on her slicker. She was still chilled and running scared.

But she knew she stood only one chance and that was to make a run for it.

Jinx moved to the door, waiting until the next lightning flash and the pitch blackness that followed it.

Dawson smelled the smoke and knew he had to be close. He'd been stumbling along in the darkness and pouring rain. He was soaked to the skin and chilled and

couldn't tell if his light-headedness was from his loss o
blood or from exhaustion and hypothermia.

He crouched down as he neared a rise and saw wha
was left of the old ranch buildings below him. He coulc
see the dark cattle through the steadily falling rain anc
the horses penned up in the corral.

As he moved closer, staying to the gully behind the
ranch house, he caught the sound of laughter, even a
snatch of drunken conversation. He inched closer, anx
ious to see Jinx, praying she was safe.

The smell of smoke grew stronger. As he came
around a bend in the gully he could see the light from
the campfire under the lean-to and several of the mer
sitting around the fire. He listened.

If Jinx was with them, she wasn't saying anything
He had to get closer. One of the men suddenly steppec
to the edge of the lean-to and looked toward the house
He said something over his shoulder to the other men

Dawson caught only the name Rafe and the words
that woman, followed by a raunchy laugh as the mar
rejoined the others.

Rafe was at the house with Jinx? Dawson felt his
stomach roil at the thought. Working his way back up
through the narrow gully he was almost to the back of
the house when the door opened.

He stepped back and waited, hoping it was Rafe.

Jinx darted out the door only to be grabbed, spun
around and slammed against the back wall of the house
Dawson pulled back his fist at the last moment. Rair
pounded. Lightning lit the sky.

"Dawson!" she cried and threw herself into his arms
as thunder rumbled around them. "I was so scared that

ou were dead." He grimaced in pain at her embrace
nd she quickly drew back. "How badly are you hurt?"
he asked, keeping her voice down as the thunder died.

"Never mind that. Where's Rafe?" Clearly he had
een expecting Rafe to come through that door—not
er.

"Dead. The others are either watching the cattle or
itting by the fire under a lean-to a ways from here."
he could see that he was still processing the news that
afe was dead.

"Anyone else in the house?"

She shook her head and he reached around her to
pen the door, leading her back inside. Jinx hadn't
anted to go back inside. It was dark and cold in the
ouse. Only the occasional lightning flash illuminated
he space. They stood just inside the back door out of
he rain.

When he glanced toward the front door and saw
afe's body in a flicker of lightning, she said, "It was
n accident. I…" She couldn't form the words to say
vhat Rafe had planned for her or how she'd gone for
is gun—another impulsive decision that had almost
ost her her life. "I didn't have a choice."

Dawson put his good arm around her and pulled her
lose. "Did he tell you who is behind the ring?"

She shook her head and nestled against his wet cloth-
ng, seeking the warmth beneath it. "I don't think the
thers will come around until morning."

"We can't take that chance," he said. "We need to get
o the horses. What do you have for weapons?"

She told him, handing him his gun and Rafe's pistol,
eeping her own and the knife.

"I'm going to sneak out and get us two horses," he said. "Can you get the saddles and tack?"

"Yes." She could feel his gaze on her.

"Be careful. We'll meet in the gully behind the house."

"Dawson—" She realized she'd almost blurted out that she loved him. "You be careful, too."

He disappeared out the back door, with her right behind him. The saddles and tack had been dumped on the porch of the house out of the rain. She rummaged through it quickly and as quietly as possible.

Dawson took two halters from Jinx and she watched him cross to the corral between flashes of lightning. It was far enough from the house and the lean-to that she doubted the rustlers would see him. But if the already spooked horses started acting up, one of the rustlers might brave coming out in the rain to check.

Jinx quickly gathered up what she could carry and took it around to the back of the house out of sight of the lean-to and the men under it to wait for Dawson.

He appeared a few minutes later leading two horses. They each saddled their horses quickly. The rain was letting up, but her fingers were still red and numb by the time she finished getting her horse ready to ride.

"I want you to ride up through that gully at the back of the house and meet me on the other side of the hill," he said.

She saw that he was still in a lot of pain and his shoulder had started bleeding again. He needed medical attention. Surely he wasn't still thinking of trying to get his cattle back. "What are you going to do?"

"I'm going to open the corral and run off the horses

then you and I are headed for Chisholm Cattle Company."

"What about the cattle?" she asked.

"All I care about is getting you away from here to some place safe. If you're still determined to go after the leader of this rustling ring—"

"I just want to get you to a doctor," she said.

He leaned into her, kissed her quickly and said, "Be ready to ride, then."

Just before daylight, Marshall picked McCall up and brought her to the Chisholm ranch. She was hidden in the king cab seat behind him as they drove in—as per the plan. She could see the mountains in the distance and the tops of the peaks encased in clouds.

Earlier she'd thought she'd smelled rain in the air, but the forecast for the prairie was warm and dry. The sky was lightening to the east, the sun peeking out from the horizon, promising a clear, sunny day.

The other Chisholm brothers had stayed at the main house last night and had made sure that anyone listening in would know they weren't leaving until morning.

Marshall parked where he could sneak her in the back way. She had her radio and deputies planted out of sight at strategic points on the roads so they could see anyone coming in or out of the ranch. They had been advised to simply report if they saw someone and not to apprehend.

McCall hoped they weren't all wasting their time.

As she slipped into the back of the house, the Chisholms went about their business, making themselves sack lunches as she took a look around. She looked for a comfortable place to wait, since she didn't know how long it might take.

There was a good chance that Aggie Wells wouldn't show, because she was dead and buried somewhere on the ranch. It wouldn't be the first time McCall had been wrong about a suspect. It took a kind of killer mentality to start from nothing and build an empire the way Hoyt Chisholm had. McCall reminded herself that she could be dead wrong about him and that would make Emma dead wrong, as well.

Finding a stool in the kitchen, she dragged it into the large walk-in pantry, leaving the door open a crack so she had a view of the kitchen table and the back door.

A few minutes later the brothers waved goodbye and made a show of leaving to go string barbed wire on the fence they were building too far from the house to return unexpectedly.

McCall listened as they drove away and a deathly quiet fell over the house. She thought about the way it must have sounded when all six sons and Hoyt and Emma and several hired help had been in this big old place. She also thought about the first time she'd met Emma and how much she'd liked her. It was clear just looking around the house that Emma had made it a home.

Now the place was empty. The brothers had been staying here to hold down the fort until their father was exonerated. If that happened. They were all old enough that they would soon want to go back to their own places, get on with their lives—no matter what happened with their father.

But she did wonder what would happen to Chisholm Cattle Company if Hoyt was found guilty. The brothers would try to keep the place going without him, but Hoyt had been the heart and soul of the ranch.

At the sound of a floorboard creaking, McCall started. She eased her weapon out of the holster, telling herself it was an old house. Old houses creaked and groaned. Another floorboard creaked and then another. The sound was coming from the living room. Whoever it was, was headed this way.

McCall stood and pressed her body against the pantry wall so she had a good view of the person who was about to appear in the kitchen doorway.

As Jinx rode up through the dark gully, the rain had slowed to a drizzle, but she barely felt it she was so worried about Dawson.

Her heart suddenly leaped to her throat as she heard shouts behind her, then the boom of gunfire. She looked back, but saw nothing through the rain and darkness. It took every ounce of common sense she had not to turn around and go back. Spurring her horse, she stopped at the edge of the hill. She could see the cattle were huddled in a shimmering sea of black bodies against the first signs of daybreak. No sign of any rustlers.

Reining in, she turned and stared back into the darkness of the hillside, telling herself Dawson would come riding over the rise at any moment. She saw movement, heard more shouts and gunfire. The cattle began to mill and bawl.

Jinx blinked as a rider emerged from the rain and darkness. She held her breath. As the figure drew closer, she felt her chest swell with relief. Dawson. Tears burned her eyes. Her heart felt as if it might burst.

She glanced behind him, expecting to see rustlers coming over the hill as he rode up to her. His face was etched in pain and she feared they would never make it to the ranch. He gave her a smile, even though she could tell it cost him. The rain had almost stopped. A fine mist hung in the air, making all of it seem surreal.

As they reined their horses around and rode into the new day, she looked back at the cattle. She could smell smoke from the rustlers' fire. Hear voices. Two rustlers on foot topped the hill as she and Dawson rode into the trees.

Rifle fire punctuated the wet morning air, but the men were too far away and their shots never reached the trees.

Jinx thought about the cattle they were leaving and wondered if Dawson would ever get any of them back. Or would the rustlers, after finding Rafe dead, only care about retrieving their horses and saving their own necks?

Dawson had come for her—not his cattle.

It filled her heart like helium and yet, as she rode, she couldn't help the feeling that she'd failed in so many ways. She'd almost gotten Dawson killed and herself as well and she still didn't know who was behind the rustling ring, who was ultimately responsible for her father's death.

She shivered in the cold as water dripped from the dark green branches of the pines and glanced over at Dawson. This wasn't over yet, she thought, realizing how weak he was. Nothing else mattered, she realized, but getting him to a doctor. She couldn't let him die. No, after everything they'd been through. She hadn't even gotten a chance to tell him that she loved him.

Chapter 11

Aggie Wells came into the kitchen as if she lived there. She carried a small box that she set on the table before she headed back into the living room.

McCall watched her from her hiding place in the pantry, but lost her when she left the kitchen. She could hear her in the living room and dining room. She seemed to just be wandering around the house.

McCall wondered if she was pretending she lived here. Her former supervisor had suggested that Aggie might have gotten too involved with Hoyt Chisholm and his case, that she had fallen in love with Hoyt.

The insurance company Aggie had worked for let her go after they found out she was still working the case on her own time—even after her investigation had been unable to prove anything other than Laura Chisholm's drowning had been an accident.

Aggie came back into the kitchen, shoved one of the chairs closer to the table and stood on it. Reaching into the box she'd brought, she took out what looked like a small smoke alarm and replaced the one the Chisholm brothers had destroyed.

She worked with a single-minded efficiency, making McCall wonder how many other houses she had bugged over the years.

McCall frowned as she realized she hadn't heard a vehicle. How had Aggie gotten here? Not by a road, or one of the deputies would have alerted McCall.

As Aggie finished reinstalling the listening device, she froze on the chair and looked around as if she suddenly sensed she wasn't alone. She lowered herself off the chair to the kitchen floor, clearly trying to be as quiet as possible, picked up her box and slipped out the back door.

McCall was ready to pitch the plan. Aggie had been spooked. What would she do? McCall couldn't bear to think that the woman might just take off and never be seen again. But what if she *had* taken Emma and was now going back to wherever she'd hidden her?

Arresting Aggie now might mean never finding Emma. McCall made herself stay where she was, counting to ten before she eased out of the pantry.

She caught a whiff of perfume as she edged to the back door and peered out. Aggie was a few hundred yards from the house, walking toward a four-wheeler.

McCall swore. That's why the deputies hadn't seen her. She hadn't taken a road, but had come across country.

Grabbing her radio, she barked out an order for the deputies to close in. Now! "She's on a four-wheeler."

She opened the back door, heard the four-wheeler crank over and saw Aggie take off through the pasture.

McCall realized the deputies couldn't possibly get there fast enough. Aggie was going to get away unless—

She raced through the house, slowing at the front door. It was standing wide open. She got another strong whiff of perfume. Why would Aggie leave the front door open?

McCall didn't have time to consider what it might mean as she sprinted to the corral. She'd never had a horse of her own, but she'd ridden any horse that would let her since she was a girl. Because of it, riding bareback was the only way she knew how to ride.

One of the horses came toward her. She grabbed a halter off the post by the gate and, slipping it on, led the mare out of the corral and swung up onto her back. Spurring the horse, she went after Aggie as the wind whipped the cottonwoods, sending dust swirling around her. In the distance she could see storm clouds over the mountains and smell rain in the air. The weatherman had been wrong.

As she rode the horse over the first rise, she caught sight of Aggie tearing through the open country on the four-wheeler. Dust churned up behind the rig, obscuring the rider. Even if Aggie looked back, she wouldn't be able to see McCall coming after her.

McCall leaned over the mare's neck and galloped across the pasture, keeping her focus on the four-wheeler and where it was headed.

Dawson topped the last rise and saw Chisholm Cattle Company sprawled below him. He reined in his horse.

He'd never seen anything more beautiful in his life. Except for the woman who rode up next to him.

She smiled over at him and he saw her concern. She must see how hard it was for him to even stay in the saddle he felt so weak.

"You going to make it?" she asked.

He smiled back at her. "I am now."

As they rode down toward the ranch, he saw dust boiling up along the road into the ranch. Two sheriff's deputy vehicles came racing up the road toward them.

Jinx rode out to flag down one of the deputies. "Dawson's been shot by some rustlers. He needs medical attention right away," she said.

As Dawson rode up, he recognized the deputy as his future sister-in-law Halley Robinson. She started to reach for her radio, no doubt to call an ambulance.

"There isn't time," Jinx said. "We need to take him in your patrol car."

Dawson felt the last of his strength seep out of him. He slumped over his saddle, only to feel someone pulling him down and into the patrol car. He lay back against the seat for a moment before Jinx drew him over, cradling his head in her lap. He felt her fingers brush back a lock of hair from his forehead, heard her say, "Please hurry."

The sound of the siren came on and he felt the patrol car turn around and head toward town. He closed his eyes.

"Listen to me, Chisholm," Jinx whispered next to his ear. "I didn't ride all the way off that mountain to have you die on me now." He heard the emotion in her voice and realized she was close to tears.

He opened his eyes, looked into her adorable face and tried to smile. That was the last thing he remembered.

McCall slowed the mare to a trot as she saw the four-wheeler turn onto an old dirt road. At the end of it sat an empty farmhouse. She eased the mare through the trees along the edge of a creek that ran the length of the property as she watched the four-wheeler come to a stop behind the farmhouse and Aggie climb off to disappear inside.

McCall kept to the trees, working her way to the back of the house, all the time keeping an eye on the dust-coated windows. Was Emma inside? She could only hope.

She thought about calling for backup as she slid from her horse, but a patrol car could be spotted for miles out here and McCall couldn't chance what Aggie might do to Emma. If Emma was even in there.

No, she thought as she drew her weapon and moved stealthily toward the back door. She couldn't risk Emma's life by tipping off Aggie they were onto her, and she had a strong feeling that Emma was inside.

The back door wasn't locked. It swung open with a creak that made McCall grimace. The old, bare kitchen was empty. She stepped inside. As she moved toward the front of the house, she heard voices upstairs.

Her heart soared. Aggie wasn't alone. Someone was with her. Emma?

Weapon in hand, McCall started up the stairs. Normally she would be thinking about what she was going to find at the top of the steps, but suddenly she had a flash of memory of lying in bed with her husband—

and the realization that she could already be pregnant, just as she'd joked with Luke last night.

The thought of having Luke's baby made her go soft inside. She hesitated on the stairs, surprised by this sudden well of emotion. McCall had never thought anything could keep her from doing her job.

And while she wouldn't let it now, she realized that having Luke's baby was going to change everything—especially the way she felt about risking her life.

She shook the thought away as she continued up the stairs, torn between her love for her job and her love for her husband and the thought of their child.

At the top of the stairs she stopped to listen, afraid the creaking stairs might have given her away. With relief she heard two women's voices coming from behind one of the closed doors. One of them was Emma's.

McCall inched toward the door, fearing it would be locked. Her hand closed over the knob. She took a breath, let it out and tried the knob. It turned in her hand.

On the count of three. One. Two. Three.

"I mean it, Dawson, don't you dare die on me, you hear me?" Jinx said as she cradled his head in her lap. He looked so pale and yet so handsome. Her heart broke at the sight. She checked his pulse again. He was still alive, but he'd lost so much blood....

She felt that if she kept talking to him, she wouldn't lose him. She whispered to him as the deputy drove, talking about anything she could think of, her childhood, her first boyfriend, her dreams, her hopes.

"I wish we'd met at a community dance, that you saw me from across the room and that you worked your way through the crowd, determined to dance with me," she whispered. "Our first dance would be a slow one and you would hold me close and—" her voice broke "—and you would never let me go."

She felt tears burn her eyes as the deputy said, "Once we get to the hospital, I'm going to have to get your statement about who shot him."

Jinx glanced up and nodded to the deputy looking at her in the rearview mirror, then started as she felt Dawson move in her lap, his voice a hoarse whisper.

"What's your real name?"

She looked down and saw that his eyes were open and he was staring up at her.

"Brittany Bo Clarke."

He smiled. "Easy to see why you go by Jinx." Then his eyes closed again.

She didn't know if he could hear her or if he had passed out again, but she kept talking to him. "I grew up on the Double TT Ranch. It was home even though we lived at the old homestead and my father was only the ranch manager all those years. My father worked for Hank Thompson. When he died his son, Lyndel, inherited the ranch."

Jinx couldn't help remembering her first run-in with Lyndel when they were both kids. Lyndel was only four years her senior, a son born to the older Hank and his young wife, who left him right after Lyndel was born.

Dawson groaned as if he sensed something unpleasant had happened with Lyndel and that was what had caused her to stop talking to him.

"My first boyfriend was a neighbor boy," she said quickly as she stroked Dawson's dark hair. "We used to swim together in the creek, ride horses, build forts, you

know the kind of puppy love best friends have as kids."
She wondered if there had been anyone like that in Dawson's life and realized how little they knew about each other. That seemed strange since they'd been through so much together and she was in love with him.

"I went off to college. My first boyfriend married a local girl. They have three children and raise horses. I always wanted to raise horses, live on a ranch, a ranch of my own...." Her voice broke again and she looked up to see that they had reached town.

Dawson groaned softly and she had to lean in to hear his words. "Why did they change their pattern at your ranch?"

She frowned, realizing he must be delirious and talking nonsense.

As the patrol car raced to the emergency room, sirens blaring, the staff came running out with a gurney. Jinx had to let go of Dawson as he was loaded onto it and wheeled into the emergency room.

She stood just inside the draped room, watching the doctor and nurses rushing around. "Is he going to be all right?" she asked, hating that she couldn't control the tears streaming down her face.

"He's lost a lot of blood, but it looks like a clean wound," the doctor said. "The bullet went right through the shoulder. This wound," he said, probing at the blood-dried injury on Dawson's forehead, "appears to be a graze, but you can never tell with a head wound. Are you next of kin?" She shook her head. "Family should be notified."

She watched them wheel Dawson down the hall, her heart in her throat. She realized the deputy was still waiting as well and wondered now why two sheriff's deputy patrol cars had been racing into the ranch this morning.

"What was going on at the ranch as we were riding in?" she asked the female deputy.

"I'm not at liberty to say. I am going to need your statement, though," Deputy Robinson said. She pulled out a notebook and pen.

"The doctor said I should notify his family."

"I already did. I'm engaged to Dawson's brother Colton."

Jinx nodded as she recalled that one of the brothers had gotten engaged to a sheriff's deputy.

"Why don't we start with your name?"

"Brittany Bo Clarke."

"Can you tell me what happened?"

"He was shot by rustlers," Jinx said. "Could you check with the doctor and ask how he is? *Please.* I'm so worried about him."

"You're the one who brought him out of the mountains?"

"Yes. I was afraid he wasn't going to make it. When I saw your patrol car…"

"How was it you were up there?"

Jinx had known that question was coming. She turned to look down the hallway. "Please. The doctor might tell you how he is. I have to know."

The deputy gave her a sympathetic nod, got up and, pocketing her notebook and pen, went to check on Dawson.

Jinx stood watching her go, thinking that she already had Rafe's blood on her hands. Not that she could do anything for Dawson now anyway. He was in God's hands—and the doctor's.

Suddenly Rafe's last words seemed to echo in her ears. *I see why he called you Jinx.*

Her heart began to pound harder. She saw the deputy talking to a nurse, then heard the nurse say Dawson had regained consciousness, his wounds didn't appear to be life-threatening and that they were getting fluids into him and he should be fine. Dawson's words came to her. *Why did they change their pattern at your ranch?* Yes, why had they?

She said a silent prayer for Dawson, then made sure no one was looking and slipped out the back of the hospital. Once outside, she took a deep breath and ran.

McCall turned the knob and eased open the door to the upstairs room in the old farmhouse. Aggie's back came into view, then the corner of an old mattress lying on the floor and finally Emma.

She appeared to be fine, though McCall couldn't tell if Aggie was holding a gun on her or not.

Easing the door open a little more— The hinges creaked and Aggie started to turn. McCall raised the gun as the former insurance investigator swung around in surprise.

"Don't move!" McCall ordered, relieved to see that Aggie was unarmed except for the pistol sticking out of her waistband. She quickly took the pistol and forced Aggie deeper into the room. "Emma? Are you all right?"

"Glad to see you," Emma said.

Aggie stood looking defeated. "Agatha Wells, you are under arrest," McCall said as she cuffed the woman and read her her rights.

"I only took Emma to protect her," Aggie said. "You don't understand. Her life is in danger."

McCall said nothing as she radioed for backup. "It's the old Harrington place. We'll be waiting outside for you." She helped Emma to her feet and led the two of them outside. She'd expected to see Deputy Robinson first, since she'd been the closest, and she was suddenly worried something had happened. She tried to radio Deputy Robinson and couldn't get through. Her concern grew.

What if Aggie hadn't been working alone?

"Where's Deputy Robinson?" McCall said when one of three deputies came racing up in a patrol SUV. She was anxious to get Emma back home and Aggie behind bars. A second patrol car roared up the road in a cloud of dust.

"Deputy Robinson was called away on an emergency," the deputy said so the others couldn't hear. "There's been a shooting. No details yet."

"Emma, you have to listen to me," Aggie was saying. "I know you all think I'm crazy, but the only reason I took you was to—"

McCall reminded Aggie that anything she said could be used against her as the deputy loaded Aggie into the back of the first patrol car. She asked the second deputy to please take Emma home and stay with her until one of her stepsons returned.

"Thank you," Emma said, giving the sheriff a hug before climbing into the patrol car.

"And if you wouldn't mind," McCall said, "return this horse to the Chisholm corral." She handed the deputy the reins once he was behind the wheel.

Climbing into the patrol car with Aggie Wells locked in the back, she told the deputy to take them to Whitehorse and the county jail.

"You're making a terrible mistake," Aggie said from behind the wire divider. "You're going to get Emma killed. If you'd given me just a little longer, I could have proved… Never mind. You wouldn't believe me." She fell silent, slumped in the backseat as the patrol car headed for Whitehorse.

"Where's Jinx?" They were the first words out of Dawson's mouth when he opened his eyes again.

"Jinx?" Deputy Robinson asked from the chair next to his bed. She appeared to have been waiting there for him to wake up.

"The woman I was with," he told his brother's fiancée, then registered her expression. "What did she do?"

"She asked me to check on you and when I turned around…"

He nodded. "She was gone. That's Jinx." He closed his eyes, hiding his disappointment. He'd hoped she would be sitting beside his bed. He should have known she would go after the leader of the ring on her own. She had before and nothing had really changed.

That wasn't true, he realized. At least not for him. He'd thought not for Jinx either.

"I need to ask you some questions," Halley said. "That is, if you're up to it. The sheriff should be here soon."

Dawson opened his eyes again. His shoulder was bandaged, and so was the spot on his forehead where a bullet had grazed him. There was an IV hooked to his arm.

The last thing he wanted to do was talk about what had happened up on the mountain. He was sure Jinx had felt the same way. He thought about her talking all the way from the ranch to the hospital. He'd been in and out of consciousness, but he could remember most of what she'd said.

"Dawson?" Halley asked.

"Sorry, I'm not sure what I can tell you." He touched the bandage on his forehead, stalling.

"The doctor said the bullet creased your forehead, but warned that there might be some memory loss."

He wished that were the case. He could remember everything—the way it had felt to lie naked with Jinx in the tall summer grass, the sound of her laugh, the feel of her touch. He closed his eyes again at the memory, reminding himself she was gone.

"Maybe it would be better later, Halley," he said without opening his eyes. The rustlers would be long gone by now, except for Rafe, even if the sheriff could get together a posse to ride up there.

He heard Halley rise from her chair.

"Do you have any idea where we can find Jinx?" she asked.

"No." He realized the moment he heard her leave his room that he was wrong. He did know where to find Jinx.

He remembered in the patrol car on the way to the hospital when she'd stopped talking. She'd been talking about the Double TT where she'd grown up, where her father had been ranch manger, where he'd died. She'd been talking about Lyndel Thompson, the new ranch owner.

"What are you doing?" the doctor demanded as he came into the room after the deputy had left, to find Dawson disconnecting the IV from his arm.

Dr. Brian "Buck" Carrey wore a cowboy hat over his

long gray ponytail. His face was tanned and weathered with deep lines around his bright blue eyes. "You're still too weak to be going anywhere, son."

"You patched me up fine, Doc." Dawson swung his legs off the gurney and stood. He felt a little light-headed, but not bad. "Where are my clothes?"

"Your family is on the way to the hospital," the doctor said, shoving back his cowboy hat. His look said he'd dealt with his share of stubborn cowboys in his day. "Anything you'd like me to tell them when they get here—other than the fact that you're a damned fool to be taking off right now?"

"Tell them our summer range cattle need to be rounded up. Oh, and have them give this to the sheriff." He scribbled a note on the pad by the bed and handed it to the doctor.

Buck sighed. "And as your personal secretary, what would you like me to say when they ask where the hell you've gone?"

"The Double TT Ranch in Wyoming. Just tell them I've gone after a woman. They'll understand."

Emma was waiting on the front porch when Marshall brought Hoyt home. She told herself she wasn't going to cry, but of course she did.

He stepped from the pickup and she ran to him, throwing herself into his arms. The sheriff had called earlier, saying Hoyt had made bail after the county attorney had heard about Aggie Wells's arrest. Hoyt's call to the governor hadn't hurt either.

"Emma," he said as he hugged her so tightly she couldn't breathe. Then he held her at arm's length and looked her over. "Are you all right?"

She nodded, unable to speak around the lump in her throat.

"God, I've missed you," he said and pulled her to him again. "I was so worried."

"But you knew I would never leave you."

He drew back to smile at her. "I knew no one could run you off, so something had to have happened."

"Aggie happened. She's crazy, Hoyt."

He nodded. "I guess when she couldn't prove I had something to do with Laura's death, she tried to frame me by killing Tasha and Krystal." He shook his head as if he couldn't believe it himself. "I'm just so glad she didn't hurt *you.*"

"She seemed to really believe that she was saving me from harm by abducting me. I feel sorry for her. That perfume she was wearing—"

He glanced away for a moment. "I should have told you right away. I recognized it. It was Laura's favorite."

Emma felt a cold chill snake up her spine. "Aggie said when she investigated a case, she tried to become the victim to understand what had happened to her. But wearing her perfume?" She shuddered as she realized just how sick Aggie really was and how lucky she was to be free from the woman.

"I'm sorry I didn't believe you when you said you smelled the perfume that day," Hoyt said.

Emma nodded, barely registering what he said. She was thinking about Aggie. "I wonder if she didn't want to become Laura? That is what must have happened. In her mind, she became Laura and couldn't bear to see you married to anyone else."

"Well, the sheriff told me they are planning to send her up to the state mental hospital in Warm Springs for a psychiatric evaluation. I'm not too sure she wil ever stand trial."

"What does your lawyer say?" Emma asked, stil worried.

"He thinks with Aggie's arrest I will be exonerated."

Emma let out a relieved sigh. "Oh, Hoyt, then it's finally over."

He smiled down at her, then swung her up into his arms and carried her into the house.

"Don't mind me," Marshall called after them, a laugh in his voice. "I'll just be going now," he said as the front door closed behind his father and stepmother.

Lyndel Thompson looked up as Jinx walked into the main ranch house at the Double TT without knocking He was standing behind the large breakfast bar in the kitchen about to pour himself a cup of coffee.

Surprise registered in his expression. He let out a soft chuckle as he finished pouring his coffee and pu the pot back. "Didn't expect to see you."

"Why is that, Lyndel?" She'd had a lot of time be tween retrieving her pickup where she'd left it on the edge of Whitehorse and the long drive to Wyoming to think. The pieces seemed to be falling into place and she wondered why it had taken her so long to figure it out

Dawson was the one who'd made her realize she hadn't been thinking clearly since her father's murder All the other rustling jobs had been about the cattle Her father's had been different for a reason.

Why had the rustlers changed their pattern?

"I thought you had moved on since the funeral," Lyn del said. "Didn't think you'd have any reason to come back here."

She smiled at that as she took in the ostentatious living room. Lyndel had built the house when he'd inherited the ranch. His father had cut off supporting him years ago but on his deathbed had relented and left the ranch to his only child—except it came with a small string attached.

He'd set up the inheritance where everything had to be run through Jinx's father, a man he trusted after all these years. The only way Lyndel would have full control was when he reached forty—or when her father died. Apparently Lyndel couldn't wait the eight years.

Her father had told her that Lyndel had been spending money as if there was no tomorrow—no doubt more money than the ranch had been taking in. And now he had the ranch up for sale. Her father had been fighting him—and losing. Under a clause in the inheritance, Lyndel could have lost the ranch if her father had taken legal action.

Her father had always been a fair and understanding man. He hadn't wanted to take legal action unless necessary, thinking Lyndel would come to his senses and settle down. If her father had, though, the ranch would have gone into state conservation land and Lyndel would lose everything.

"I didn't see any cattle on the way in to the ranch," she said as she ran a finger along the expensive marble countertop.

"After the rustlers hit us, I decided maybe it was time to just lease the land and get out of the cattle business."

"That right? Well, you never did have any interest in the day-to-day running of a ranch."

His smile never reached his eyes. "Jinx, I have a

feeling this isn't a social call. Why don't you just spit it out?"

"I've been doing some thinking."

He chuckled and leaned against the breakfast bar. "You sure that's a good idea, High Jinks?"

"High Jinks?"

"That's what my old man used to call you. Somewhere along the way it got shortened to Jinx."

She hadn't known where she'd gotten the nickname, just that everyone had called her Jinx as far back as she could remember. But, she reminded herself, Rafe had known where she'd gotten the name.

"What's on your mind?" Lyndel asked impatiently.

She studied him, remembering the mean, selfish boy he'd been and how he used to rub it in her face that she was just the ranch manager's kid while his daddy owned the ranch. He used to brag that someday it would be his and he could kick her and her daddy off it if he wanted to.

Well, now it was his and he was selling the ranch that had meant so much to his father—and to her own.

"I know how angry you were when you found out the ranch came with strings," she said.

"Is there a point to this?" Lyndel asked, putting down his coffee cup. He hadn't offered her a cup, but then that was no surprise.

"I met a friend of yours recently," she said. "Rafe Tillman."

He frowned and shook his head. "Doesn't ring a bell."

"Think harder. He knows *you*. That is, he *knew* you. He's dead."

Lyndel lifted a brow. "If I'd known him, maybe that would mean something to me. But—"

"That's funny, since he knew about my nickname."

"Maybe he knew my father." His voice had taken on an irritated clipped tone.

She slipped out of her jean jacket and casually hung it over the back of one of the breakfast bar's chairs. "He had something interesting to say before he died."

She had Lyndel's attention now. "You were with him?"

"Oh, didn't I mention? I hooked up with the rustlers."

"Why would you do—" The rest of his words seemed to catch in his throat. So he hadn't known that Rafe had let her join the gang. That shouldn't have surprised her. Rafe wasn't completely stupid. Lyndel wouldn't want him adding another rustler without his permission—let alone a woman. Any fool would know how much trouble that could cause among the gang of men.

But if Lyndel hadn't known, then that meant none of the other rustlers had told him. Because they hadn't known who was behind the rustling ring.

"They killed my father," she reminded him.

"So why would you have anything to do with them?"

"To get to the ringleader. I knew eventually Rafe would tell me who was behind it."

Lyndel had gone stone still.

"You killed my father."

"What are you talking about?" He picked up his coffee cup again and took a sip, avoiding her gaze. "Too bad this Rafe character is dead, because without him to verify your story…"

She shook her head. "I was so upset about what happened I wasn't thinking straight at first, but as someone pointed out to me, everything about the rustling on the Double TT didn't fit the rustlers' normal pattern."

"You're talking foolishness. If you had a shred of

proof you wouldn't be standing here, you'd be talking to the sheriff." He was back to his usual cocky self as he came around the end of the breakfast bar. "Now, get the hell out of my house."

"Why? Why did you have to kill him?"

He shook his head. "If you don't leave right now—"

"What are you going to do? Call the sheriff? Maybe you should. Maybe he would like to look at the ranch books. My father must have realized that you were up to something. Is that why you had to get rid of him?"

Lyndel smiled again, the old meanness coming back into his eyes as he advanced on her. "If the sheriff was to take a look at the ranch books he would find that your father had been stealing from the ranch for years."

"That's a bald-faced lie!"

He laughed. "Hard to prove otherwise, now, isn't it?"

"That's why you had him killed. He knew what you'd been doing. I remember him saying that your father wasn't fool enough to leave you the ranch without some kind of protection against you either running it into the ground or selling your legacy. The only way you could have the ranch to do as you pleased was to kill my father."

Lyndel swore under his breath. "If you want to blame someone, blame my old man. He gave me no choice."

"You would have gotten the ranch free and clear once you were forty."

"Forty?" He snorted. "It was *my* legacy, not your father's. I had every right to do whatever I wanted with this place. I was sick to death of hearing how I couldn't spend my own money. I should have killed him the moment I inherited the place, then I wouldn't have had to listen to his lectures."

Jinx let out a gasp. She'd known, and yet hearing Lyndel say it was like a stab through the heart.

"And you should have left things alone," he snapped.

As he took another step toward her, she pulled the gun.

He froze. His gaze went from the gun to her face. His smile returned. "You can't pull the trigger."

She ran her finger lightly over the trigger. "Try me."

He'd killed her father in cold blood and for what? Money, power, freedom from anyone telling him what to do? She had told herself that when she found the man behind the rustling ring, she would kill him. One shot through the heart—just like her father's death had felt to her.

But she could still hear the boom of the gunshot that had killed Rafe. She could still remember the feel of his warm blood on her hands and the way he had looked at her before he died.

She swung the gun to the right and touched off a shot. A large pottery vase exploded, sending shards spraying across the living room as the sound of the shot echoed through the house. She quickly swung the gun back to point at Lyndel's heart.

"Are you crazy?" he demanded. "I should have told them to wait to kill your father when you were home visiting him so you would be gone, too. My mistake."

Her finger skimmed over the trigger of the gun. Just a little pressure and—

Strong arms looped around her. The gun was wrenched painfully from her hand. She struggled, but it was useless in this bear of a man's arms.

"What kept you, Slim?" Lyndel demanded. "I buzzed the barn ten minutes ago."

Chapter 12

Dawson drove south down into the Missouri Breaks, across the dark green river, headed for Wyoming. The drive was long, especially with him worrying about Jinx the whole time. He'd tried calling the Double TT but the line had been disconnected and Lyndel Thompson had an unlisted number.

Why would the ranch line be disconnected? He tried not to panic, but in his gut he knew something was terribly wrong.

He'd had a lot of time to think about what had happened up in the mountains, a lot of time to think about Jinx.

Brittany Bo Clarke. He smiled, thinking how the tomboy he'd bet she'd been would have wanted to be rid of a name like that. No frilly dresses and pretty pink bows, not for that little girl.

He recalled that she'd told him her mother had died

when she was young and the aunt who had helped raise her had instilled the need for Jinx to be her own woman. The lessons she'd learned on the ranch with her father and her aunt had certainly done that.

Ahead he could see the outline of a huge house on the horizon. He slowed. There was a new Cadillac parked out front and an older model pickup. Both had Wyoming plates.

He wondered if the pickup belonged to Jinx. He hadn't asked her how she'd gotten to Montana and he wondered now how she'd made it back to Wyoming unless she'd had a vehicle.

As he parked and climbed out of the ranch truck he'd gotten Marshall to bring him at the hospital, he knew it wasn't like Jinx to leave her horse back in Montana. Whatever had sent her hightailing it down here must have been damned important. No way had she run to avoid the law. No, she had something else on her mind and he knew what it was.

The door was gigantic. He rang the bell and waited, feeling his anxiety growing with each passing moment. The ranch was for sale, so why had the main phone line been disconnected? Or was that the reason? Maybe it had already sold.

Dawson thought about Jinx's father. He'd been ranch manager. Had he known that Lyndel was selling the ranch? Or did Lyndel make that decision after his ranch manager was killed by the rustlers?

A large burly man opened the door. From the looks of him, he was one of the hired hands. Or Lyndel's muscle.

"I'm looking for Jinx."

"You have the wrong house," the man said in a gravelly voice. He started to close the door.

Dawson stuck his boot in it. "Then I'd like to see Lyndel Thompson."

The ranch hand scowled, a warning look in his gaze. Muscle, Dawson thought, but he was ready to go through this man if that was what it was going to take—even injured.

"Mr. Thompson isn't—"

"I know he's home, unless that's your Caddy out front, which I'm betting not," Dawson interrupted. "Tell him Dawson Chisholm is here to see him and I'm not leaving until I do."

The ranch hand started to make a threatening move when Lyndel Thompson stepped into view and said, "That's all right, Slim, I'll take care of this."

Dawson had met Hank Thompson on several occasions over the years when he'd attended cattleman meetings for the regional northwest. Lyndel was tall like his father, but that was about the only trait he seemed to have gotten from him. There was a softness to the younger Thompson, a weakness about the mouth and chin and definitely a lack of kindness in the eyes.

While Hank Thompson had been a working rancher, his son was a drugstore cowboy who Dawson would bet had never had manure on his boots. He was decked out in a fancy Western shirt, expensive jeans and boots and a brand-new Stetson as if he'd just come into some money.

"Mr. Chisholm," Lyndel said, sounding amused to find him standing at his door. Dawson was a little surprised that Lyndel knew who he was and it made him all the more convinced that Jinx was here and Lyndel had been expecting him. "What brings you all the way down from Montana? I heard there was trouble at your ranch. Seems you were in the middle of it," Lyndel said, motioning to the bandage on Dawson's forehead.

"I want to see Jinx."

He raised an eyebrow. "What makes you think she's here?" Slim was standing just a few feet away, his big arms crossed over his expansive chest, waiting as if expecting trouble.

Dawson thought about the Chisholm ranch. His father, while wealthy by most people's standards, had never had the need for a bodyguard. Why did Lyndel?

"I know Jinx came to see you," Dawson said as he pushed past the man into the opulent living room.

"Do you want me to throw him out?" Slim asked, hustling after him.

The main house at the Chisholm ranch was elegant but nothing like this. Lyndel had gone all out. Dawson said as much.

"Thank you," Lyndel said, not realizing it hadn't necessarily been a compliment. He motioned to Slim to back off. Slim pulled up his jeans and puffed out his chest to look as menacing as possible but stayed where he was. Until that moment, Dawson hadn't noticed the pistol the man had strapped to his leg.

"Don't you mean Brittany Bo Clarke?" Lyndel smiled. "I'm sorry, you just missed her."

Dawson returned his smile. "Mind telling me what she wanted with you?"

"As a matter of fact, I do. It's personal. You may not be aware of this, but Brittany Bo and I go way back from the time we were kids here on the ranch."

"Then you probably know how she got the nickname."

Lyndel chuckled. "My father gave it to her. It was actually High Jinks because of all the trouble she got into around the ranch. She really was quite the rascal, that girl." He smiled as if remembering her fondly.

"You also must know then how badly she wants the person behind the rustling ring who is responsible for her father's death."

"Yes, a horrible accident," Lyndel said.

"She seems to think it wasn't an accident. That someone wanted him dead and gave the rustlers the order to kill him."

Lyndel shook his head. "That sounds like our Jinx. She was always imaginative. Why would anyone want to kill my ranch manager?"

"I was hoping you might have some idea," Dawson said as he took a look around the living room. It opened into the kitchen. "I'm sure that's why Jinx came to see you." A wide, long hallway apparently led to the bedrooms, since the house was all on one sprawling level.

"She came to see me partly because of the good news, if you must know," Lyndel said. "The local sheriff called me earlier to tell me that the leader of the rustling ring was found dead up in Montana on your ranch. He was found shot to death after a botched attempt to rustle your cattle. I doubt I'm telling you anything you don't already know. I'm sorry, I didn't catch his name."

Had Jinx told him about riding with the rustlers and running into one of the Chisholms up in the high country? Or did Lyndel have other sources?

"You're mistaken. Rafe Tillman wasn't the leader. He had nothing to gain by killing Jinx's father," Dawson said as he stepped toward Lyndel. Slim moved in their direction, but Lyndel waved him off.

"Too bad we can't ask Rafe, isn't it?" Lyndel said as

he stepped away, moving to the bar to pour himself a drink. "I'd offer you a drink, but I have an important appointment I need to get to. You can probably catch Jinx if you hurry. I would imagine she's headed into town to one of the motels. Either that or headed out of town. I understand the local sheriff is anxious to talk to her."

"As close as you say the two of you are, I'm surprised you didn't ask her to stay here," Dawson said. "The place looks like it might be large enough for a guest or two."

Lyndel downed his drink and put down his glass a little too hard on the bar. "Now, it wouldn't be smart of me to harbor a fugitive, even one I consider a friend."

"You're so law-abiding," Dawson said sarcastically.

"I'm going to have to ask you to leave," Lyndel said, no longer pretending to be cordial.

Dawson saw that he wasn't going to get anywhere with Lyndel, and Slim was just itching to prove how tough he was. He moved toward the open front door, Slim shadowing him. "I see that your ranch is for sale."

"Not that it is any of your business, but it has already sold. I need a change of pace. I've picked up a little place in the Caribbean. Who needs the winters up here?"

Lyndel had managed to get rid of his ranch manager and his cattle to rustlers for both a profit and probably a good insurance settlement. Now he'd sold his ranch and was skipping the country. Things seem to be working out perfectly, he thought, and said as much.

"Good luck finding Jinx," Lyndel snapped from behind him.

Slim slammed the door behind him and, for a moment, Dawson stood on the front step trying to still his pounding heart.

He had spotted Jinx's battered straw hat hanging o
a hook in the hallway off the living room. He'd recog
nized the distinctive horsehair hatband. Next to the ha
had been a jean jacket that he would swear was Jinx's

He'd also seen scuff marks on the polished floo
where there had been a recent scuffle. Of course Jin:
would have put up a fight.

But where was she now?

Somewhere in the house, Dawson was betting a
he walked to his pickup, climbed in and drove just fa
enough away that Lyndel wouldn't send Slim after him

He found a place in a creek bottom to hide the truck
then, taking his shotgun, he headed to the house on foo
He just hoped Jinx didn't do anything crazier than sh
already had before he could get to her.

Jinx squirmed. She hated cramped, confined places
That was one reason she liked the wide open spaces o
Wyoming. She thought of Chisholm's Montana. Th
rolling prairie, the Little Rockies. She thought of th
man she'd fallen in love with.

He would think she'd abandoned him, taken off t
save her own neck. He would think she'd been impul
sive, going off half-cocked without a plan.

She squirmed again, trying to get her hands untied
Slim had done a bang-up job binding them behind he
Her wrists ached and she couldn't feel the tips of her fin
gers. He'd slapped a piece of duct tape over her mout
and shoved her into some broom closet at the back o
the house.

Did he really think she was going to start scream
ing? She knew how far the house was from anything
Who would hear her?

Unless someone had come to the house that he worried might hear her?

That was a comforting thought, but this far at the back of the house she really doubted anyone could hear her.

Only a little light bled through around the door. She'd tried throwing herself against it, but the lock had held. All she'd managed to do was hurt her shoulder. As she felt around to see if there was anything she could use to get out, she thought again of Dawson and wished she hadn't. It made her heart ache and took her mind off the problem at hand—getting out of here before Lyndel and his thug returned.

Jinx knew that Lyndel would feel he had to get rid of her. As far as he knew, she didn't have any proof he was behind the rustling ring. True, he'd admitted that he'd killed her father. But even though he could argue that it would be her word against his, she doubted he wanted to take the chance. He appeared set on selling out and getting out of Dodge.

Dawson had been right. There was a reason the rustlers had changed their pattern on the Double TT.

But his being right gave her little satisfaction. Lyndel was going to get away with murder and a lot more if she didn't get out of there.

She found some kind of cleaner on a shelf at the back, sprayed it on the rope she was bound with and tried sliding her hands out, without any luck. Feeling the clock ticking, she discovered a broom in the back corner of the closet. Using it like a lever, she pried it between the doorjamb and the knob. It took all her weight.

Just when she thought the broom handle was going

to break and the splinter would probably fly off and kill her, the knob snapped off and she tumbled to the floor.

For a moment she just lay there. She'd smacked her head when she fell and hit her elbow and she'd made one devil of a racket doing it. She listened, didn't hear anything and got to her feet.

A shaft of light spilled out of the hole where the doorknob had been. Turning her back to the door, she reached her fingers inside it and jiggled the piece of metal, at the same time pushing on the door. It swung open and she stumbled out into the hallway, wondering what she was going to do now, since her wrists were still bound.

Dawson slipped along the back edge of the house, keeping to the dark shadows. He'd checked the barn first and had been surprised to find a black pickup parked inside it. He'd thought the old pickup out front was Jinx's, but it must belong to one of the ranch hands. A quick check in the glove box verified it. It was Jinx's. The registration read Brittany Bo Clarke.

The keys were in the ignition and her purse was on the seat. He checked the bag, not surprised to find the gun missing that Jinx had had on her when they'd come out of the mountains.

He'd done a quick search of the barn, but no Jinx. He'd hoped that meant she was still somewhere in the house. He hadn't heard a sound coming from the house, but he'd managed to distract Slim for a while by opening a couple of the corral gates and shooing the horses toward the front of the house.

A few minutes ago he'd heard the big ranch hand swearing, then Slim and Lyndel arguing. As he neared the windows, he was glad to see one partially open. Hoping there wasn't a security alarm on the window, Dawson popped off the screen and shoved the window up enough to step inside. He didn't hear a sound, but that didn't mean that there wasn't a silent alarm.

Moving quickly through what appeared to be a guest bedroom, he opened the door to the hall and peered out. No sign of anyone. He knew Jinx was here somewhere, but he had no idea how to find her.

As he hurried as quietly as possible down the carpeted hall, he checked each room as he went. He had to assume that Slim or Lyndel had taken the gun from Jinx. He couldn't wait to see her and ask her what the hell she'd been thinking coming here alone—and, worse, armed.

He opened the last door at the end of the hallway, afraid now that he'd been wrong about Jinx being in the house. The room beyond the doorway was huge. So was the massive bed against one wall. He realized he'd found the master suite, Lyndel's lair.

Dawson was about to ease the door closed again when he heard a sound coming from what he guessed was the master bath. He listened for a moment. Was it possible Lyndel had hurried down here after his argument with Slim about the horses?

Doubtful. But possible.

He shifted the shotgun to his other hand and eased inside the room, closing the door behind him. The sound in the bathroom stopped. He didn't move a hair as he waited. The sound resumed and he tried for the life of him to figure out what it was. Cautiously he stepped toward the open doorway to the bathroom.

With shotgun ready, he peered in.

Jinx had a pair of scissors and was sawing at the ropes that bound her wrists behind her back. She spun around as if sensing someone behind her.

"Dawson?" She dropped the scissors and threw herself at him.

"I know what you're thinking, Chisholm," Jinx said as Dawson put down the shotgun and, taking the scissors, cut the rope binding her.

"You don't know what I'm thinking."

"Sure I do," she said as she tried to work some feeling back into her hands. "You're thinking, 'Jinx must have been out of her mind to come here by herself.' It isn't like I came here unarmed."

She'd noticed the relieved expression on his face when he'd seen her. He'd been unable to hold back the smile she'd caught in the bathroom mirror as he'd cut her wrists free. He hadn't been surprised that she'd gotten away—at least partially. And he'd come all the way to Wyoming for her. That had to mean something, even if he did think she was a fool.

He still didn't say anything as he put the scissors aside and picked up his shotgun again.

"Aren't you going to say anything?" she asked.

"Now that you mention it, I was going to say I think we should get out of here."

She shook her head. "Not yet. There's something I need."

He gave her a look that said he didn't believe this.

"My jean jacket. It wasn't with me in the broom closet where they left me. I need it."

"I'll buy you another jean jacket. Hell, I'll buy you two."

"Like I said, I know you think I was a fool for coming here like I did, but there's a reason I need my jean jacket. The digital recorder I bought is in it. It will have Lyndel's confession on it. He had my father killed." Her voice broke. "He admitted it."

"I'm sorry, Jinx."

She nodded. "I wanted to shoot him. I really did."

"I'm glad you didn't. As a matter of fact, I'd like to get out of here without anymore bloodshed."

"That might not be so easy."

"Lyndel said he had an appointment he was anxious to get to."

She smiled at that. "I should mention Lyndel Thompson isn't just a killer. He's a liar."

Dawson shook his head as if she amused him, the hint of a smile on his lips, and then he kissed her. She melted against him—until she heard a sound from the hallway.

Chapter 13

"I told you Aggie had been in our house," Emma said to Sheriff McCall Crawford when she stopped by the ranch that evening. "Isn't that right, Hoyt?"

The three of them were sitting at the kitchen table over a cup of coffee and some warm banana bread.

"Yes, you did," McCall said. "I should have listened to you. I'm just glad you sent me that letter about the listening devices."

Hoyt smiled over at his wife. "Emma is something, isn't she?"

The sheriff smiled. "Yes, she is."

"That first time in the house, Aggie took Hoyt's bolo tie clasp and put it in Krystal's grave to frame him, just as she left her car nearby so you'd find Krystal's remains and think Hoyt had done something to her, as well," Emma said in one breath.

"That is the theory," McCall admitted.

"Surely the county attorney hasn't changed his mind about taking Hoyt to trial," Emma said, suddenly worried.

"No. The charges have been dropped."

"Unless new evidence turns up," Hoyt said, sounding skeptical that this could be over.

Emma shook her head. "Stop thinking like that, Hoyt Chisholm. It's over." She turned to the sheriff. "How is Aggie?"

"I'm surprised you'd ask, given what she's put you through," McCall said.

"I can't help it—I liked her. She was misguided, I'll admit."

"I'm afraid she might be more than that," the sheriff said. "Based on some of the statements she's made, the county attorney has decided that a psychiatric evaluation is needed. We are going to be sending her to the state mental hospital soon for testing."

Emma nodded. "I suppose she told you that she tried to become Laura Chisholm to get inside her head to find out what had happened to her, including acting like her, wearing the kind of clothes she wore and even wearing the same perfume."

McCall nodded. "She swears that she was only in your house twice. That the other time it was..." the sheriff glanced toward Hoyt before saying "...your first wife, Laura. She swears that Laura didn't drown and that she is responsible for the deaths of your second wife and third wife and that she will be coming for Emma."

Hoyt had gone white as a sheet.

Emma felt her heart jump at his reaction. He seemed too frightened by the ramblings of a deranged woman. "You don't really believe—"

But it was the sheriff who answered. "No, I don't, but Aggie seems to. She said that was what she was trying to prove when she put the listening devices in your house."

"How does she explain knowing where Krystal's body was buried?" Emma asked.

"According to Aggie, she got a message from you to meet at that spot on the river where her car was found. It was dark when she arrived. She said she was sitting in the rental car waiting when someone attacked her and tried to kill her. She didn't see her attacker. At first she said she thought it was Hoyt. She managed to escape."

"Escape? But her car—"

"She left it because she doubted she would be believed. She said she thought that once her car was found, I would start looking into the case again. Her injuries were minor, a nosebleed, which explains the blood on the car seat. She swears she didn't know anything about Krystal's body being buried beside the river near there and only realized who her attacker had been after you, Emma, had said something about smelling her perfume three times when Aggie swears she was only in your house twice."

"That all sounds…unbelievable," Emma said. "First she blames Hoyt, then a woman who drowned more than thirty years ago?"

McCall nodded.

Hoyt still looked as if he'd seen a ghost. Emma felt her stomach knot.

"That is apparently when she put in the listening devices, hoping to catch Laura in your house," the sheriff finished. "She'd wanted ones that also supplied video, but couldn't find any that small."

"Hoyt took them all down," Emma said, getting to her feet. "We kept them as you requested in case you ever need them for evidence. But I can tell you now, I won't press charges against Aggie."

That seemed to bring Hoyt out of his shocked state. "Emma—"

"No, I liked her. Clearly she's sick. But prison isn't the place for her. She needs help."

McCall nodded and got to her feet. "Thank you for the coffee and banana bread, but I need to get going. By the way, did you get your cattle all rounded up?"

"Most of them," Hoyt said. "My sons brought the majority down earlier. They're going back up tomorrow for the ones they missed. Here, let me carry that box for you. I'll walk you out."

Emma knew her husband wanted to talk to the sheriff alone. That's why she waited, then snuck around the house to a dark corner so she could listen.

"Aggie's story about Laura, it's crazy," Hoyt said.

"Yes," the sheriff agreed as she took the box of listening devices and set them in the back of the patrol SUV. "So why are you still worried about Emma?" she asked as she closed the car door.

"You're sure Aggie worked alone?"

"From what we can tell. There isn't any chance Laura is alive, is there?"

Hoyt rubbed a large hand over his neck as he always did when he was worried. "I can't imagine how, and yet…"

"And yet?"

"Her body was never found."

McCall nodded. "It's not that unusual in a lake that

size, plus during a storm and that time of year. Unless you know something I don't?"

"No, it's just that..." He rubbed his neck again. "I never told anyone, but Laura was insanely jealous."

"Insanely?" the sheriff asked.

"It was what we were fighting about the day she drowned," Hoyt said, his voice full of pain. "She attacked me. I was trying to hold her off...." He let out a sound like a sob.

Emma closed her eyes and leaned into the side of the house. The wood felt cool to the touch. She wanted to run to her husband, throw her arms around him, comfort him. She knew what was coming, feared it bone deep.

"I swear to you, McCall, I didn't push her overboard," Hoyt was saying. "She pulled away from me. I thought she'd lost her balance. But the truth is... I think she might have purposely fallen overboard."

Dawson grabbed Jinx's hand and pulled her back into the bathroom as the bedroom door slammed open. As heavy footfalls thudded across the floor, he raised the shotgun, motioning for her to be quiet.

As if that was necessary. From Jinx's expression, he figured she was thinking the same thing he was. Lyndel had discovered that Jinx wasn't in the broom closet and now they were turning the house upside down looking for her.

Dawson listened to someone rummaging around in the bedroom. Lyndel? Slim? Or had someone else arrived? And what were they searching for in the master bedroom?

He heard a drawer close, then the familiar snick of a bullet being jacked into the chamber of a gun before

he person left, slamming the door behind them. Who-
ver had come into the room was now armed as well
s dangerous.

Dawson let out the breath he'd been holding. Getting
ut of there without any bloodshed was seeming less
nd less likely. They would be looking for Jinx inside
he house and out. For all he knew, Lyndel had called
n more ranch hands to help. Or possibly even the rest
f the rustlers back from Montana.

He eased the bathroom door open and peered out.
inx did the same next to him. The bedroom was empty.

The way he saw it, they had two options. Trying to
scape through the back way without the digital re-
order. Or going out the front door with it.

Dawson walked over to the phone beside the bed
nd picked up the receiver, remembering belatedly that
yndel had had it disconnected. He wasn't in the habit
f carrying a cell phone. They were pretty worthless
nless you lived in Whitehorse. A few miles out, you
ouldn't get any service, so what was the point when
ou lived on a ranch miles from town?

But he wished to hell he had one right now. He
oked over at Jinx.

She shook her head. "Mine's in the other pocket of
ny jean jacket."

Great. "Come on," Dawson said. "We're getting out
f here. We'll call the sheriff as soon as we reach town
nd have him get your jacket and the digital recorder
vith the evidence on it." He'd expected her to put up an
rgument and was surprised when she didn't.

For once Jinx wasn't taking chances? It gave him
ope.

He moved to the door, grabbed the knob and slowly

turned it. As he pulled the door open a crack, he peere
out. The hallway was empty. "Stay behind me."

Jinx nodded and they slipped out of the master sui
into the hallway.

Dawson could hear raised voices coming from th
front part of the house and knew any moment the
would be searching the house. He hoped they'd alreac
done a preliminary search of all of the rooms excep
the master suite. It was far enough off the grid that the
might not have bothered with it the first time around

He headed for the first exit they came to, stopping
the door to look back at Jinx. He figured if there was
security system installed, it would be on now.

"The moment I open this door we hightail it for th
grove of trees east of the house. You lead. I'll be rigl
behind you with the shotgun."

She nodded, looking as anxious as he was.

He shoved open the door and they sprinted acros
the moonlit ranch yard toward the dark grove of trees i
the distance. Dawson could hear voices in the distance
the yelp of a dog. Glancing back, he saw no movemer
from the house.

Ahead he saw several of the horses he had release
standing broadside against the dark horizon. He hear
a vehicle engine rev in front of the house and mor
shouting.

Jinx had reached the trees. Her dark shadow blende
with the deep shadows of the trees and for a mome
he lost sight of her. Then something glinted in a sli
of moonlight that cut down through the tree limbs ar
leaves.

And he saw Jinx. Lyndel had one arm locked aroun

her throat. In the other he held a gun, the barrel catching the moonlight as he pointed it at her temple.

"Drop the shotgun, Dawson, or I'll kill her right now."

"What is this about Dawson getting caught in the middle of a rustling ring?" Hoyt asked his wife later as they lay in their large bed. A light breeze played at the curtains at the window. Moonlight spilled in along with summer-scented air.

Emma filled him in on what she knew, which wasn't much. "Apparently he met a woman up on the mountain. McCall thinks she was riding with the rustlers."

"Are you trying to tell me that Dawson has fallen in love with a rustler?" her husband demanded.

She hated to tell him that might be the least of it. "McCall has had to put an APB out on her for questioning. One of the rustlers' bodies was found in an old abandoned ranch house up on the mountain."

"So we don't know who killed him," Hoyt said. "Could have been one of the other rustlers. Or this woman. Or Dawson." He raked a hand through his thick blond hair. It was beginning to gray and had seemed to gray even more since Emma had come into his life, she thought with regret.

"We need to talk about the past sometime," she said. "I need to tell you about my former husband."

He took her hand and met her gaze. "I never doubted that you had a past, Emma. If you want to tell me about it, fine. But I'm not asking. I don't need to know. I know you."

She smiled. "Yours might not be the only past that comes back to haunt us, but it can wait for now."

He nodded. "Tell me what you know about this woman rustler, then."

"Apparently she had gone undercover to bring down the rustling ring."

Hoyt raised a brow. "And almost got my son killed."

Emma couldn't argue that. "I've always known it would take a special woman for each of your 'boys,'" she said, smiling over at her husband. Like her husband, though, she feared that this woman Dawson had gone after might get them both killed before this was over. "You know your son."

He swore under his breath. "Yes," he said and started to get out of bed.

"Where do you think you're going?" she demanded.

"I have cattle to help round up, a son to find—"

She caught his hand. "Hoyt, they aren't boys anymore. They've been running this ranch just fine without you. They can run it a few more hours without your help. Anyway, it's too late to do anything tonight and you know it."

He smiled down at her, then came back to bed, taking her in his arms. She thought about what she'd overheard him telling the sheriff and pushed the thought away. No one other than Aggie was involved in what had happened.

Laura might have been *insanely* jealous, but Aggie was apparently just plain insane. At least she was locked up where she couldn't hurt anyone else, Emma thought as she snuggled into her husband's strong, warm body.

"Put down the shotgun, Dawson," Lyndel said again.

"Don't listen to him," Jinx said. "He can't kill me and get away with it."

Lyndel laughed. "That's only if her body is ever found."

Jinx saw movement at the edge of the trees. "Dawson, look out!"

But the warning didn't come quickly enough. Two men sprang from the trees behind him, wrenched the shotgun away and threw him to the ground.

"Don't hurt him," she cried. "He doesn't have anything to do with this."

"Bring him along," Lyndel ordered. "He sealed his fate when he threw in with you." He grabbed her arm roughly and shoved her back toward the house. "I knew he wouldn't just go away and leave well enough alone. Apparently he got himself *jinxed* by the likes of you and now it is going to cost him his life."

To her surprise, Lyndel didn't take them to the house but to his Cadillac running out front. He shoved her into the front seat at gunpoint and climbed in after her. Dawson was thrown into the backseat with one of Lyndel's men, also at gunpoint, as Slim slipped behind the wheel.

Out of habit, Jinx reached for her seat belt.

"You won't be needing that," Lyndel said with a chuckle.

She snapped it on anyway, making him shake his head.

"Take us to the quarry," he ordered.

Jinx swallowed as she realized what he had planned. He wasn't joking about their bodies never being found. The rock quarry on the ranch had filled in with water years ago. As a girl she'd been warned not to go there because the water was so cold and deep. She knew Lyndel hadn't heeded warnings about it and had almost drowned there one summer. The girl who'd been with him had drowned and Hank Thompson had fenced the quarry, adding several strings of barbed wire along the top and locking the gate in.

The headlights cut a swath of golden light on the narrow ranch road. There was no other ranch within miles, no one around out here in the middle of nowhere. Jinx thought of Dawson in the backseat. He'd come after her and now it was going to cost him his life. She couldn't let that happen. No matter what she had to do.

Slim slowed and turned down an even narrower dirt road. In the moonlight she could see the tall cottonwoods around the quarry. The light glinted off the steel fence Lyndel's father had built around the deep, water-filled hole.

Large rocks rose up from the edges of the quarry. Slim pulled up to the gate and got out to unlock it.

Jinx's mind raced. She had to do something desperate. This time her situation actually demanded it. Lyndel was going to kill them either way, so she didn't see that she had anything to lose. She glanced in the rearview mirror, saw Dawson. Their gazes met and she tried to send a silent message.

Slim returned, slid behind the seat and shifted the car into gear as he pulled through the open gate. Lyndel must have been selling the quarry stone again, because this end of the quarry sloped down to the water and she could see where workers had been blasting.

"Drive down to the edge," Lyndel ordered.

Moonlight shone on the dark surface of the cold, deep water as Slim drove closer to the edge and what appeared to be no more than a fifteen-foot drop to the water at this end.

As Slim started to slow, Jinx shot Dawson a glance, then slipped her foot over and tromped on the gas. She heard Dawson snap on his seat belt. Jinx had hoped she could catch Slim by surprise. But she couldn't take the chance that he would go for the brake. Or even throw the car into Reverse.

Fortunately Slim wasn't quick, not mentally or physically, and she had managed to catch him by surprise. She'd also shoved against him, slamming him into his door as she tromped on his big foot on the gas pedal, throwing him off balance enough that he didn't recover before it was too late.

Beside her, Lyndel let out a curse and grabbed for her, latching on to her arm to pull her back toward him, then quickly letting go as the car soared over the edge and began a nosedive for the water below. Jinx braced herself and prayed that she hadn't just killed them all.

Dawson couldn't believe it. When he'd looked into Jinx's eyes, he'd known she was going to do something desperate. He'd been trying to come up with something himself, since it was clear what Lyndel had planned for them when he realized what she was going to do.

He braced himself as the engine revved and he felt the vehicle go airborne. It seemed to hang in the air, then did a slow nosedive, rolling forward. The ranch hand who'd been beside him flew forward along the headliner as they struck the water with a force that shook Dawson's teeth.

The car plunged, then bobbed up as it flipped over on its top. Everything went quiet except for the slosh of waves against the sides of the car and the sound of the water rushing in.

Dawson found himself alone, suspended upside down by his seat belt in the backseat. "Jinx?" he cried, seeing her hanging, as well. The others seemed to be piled on the windshield upfront, none of them moving. At least not yet.

He quickly unsnapped his seat belt and dropped to the interior roof of the car. Hurriedly he crawled to the front. Water was rushing into the car at every crack and crevice. His movements made the car pitch as if it was a boat. A sinking boat.

Jinx was fumbling with her seat belt.

"Are you all right?"

She nodded. He saw that there was a cut over her eye and it was bleeding. He helped her unsnap the belt and lowered her to the headliner, which was now already soaked with water.

One of the ranch hands or Lyndel moaned. They'd all been thrown into the windshield. The water around them was turning red with their blood.

Dawson looked around for something to break out one of the windows, as the water seemed to be coming in faster, leaving less air space. It wouldn't be long before the weight of the water would sink the car.

He spotted his shotgun and remembered Slim picking it up and carrying it toward the car. "I'm going to bust out the back window, but when I do the water is going to rush in. We won't be able to swim out until it fills the car."

Jinx nodded.

"Hang on to the seat. Hold your breath, then take my hand, okay?" He met her gaze. "We're going to get out of this."

Another groan from the front of the car. Hurriedly Dawson took a swing at the back window with the butt of the shotgun, his back to what was happening behind him.

*   *   *

Dawson didn't see Lyndel push himself away from Slim and the other man, both of them unmoving. But the movement caught Jinx's eye. She watched in horror as Lyndel's hand snaked out and latched on to a gun that had been lying at the edge of the bodies.

"You really are a jinx," he said, his words slurred, his eyes wild.

"Dawson!" she cried as Lyndel lifted the gun and aimed it at her head.

Dawson was already in midswing with the butt of the shotgun. He started to turn when the glass shuddered. The water came rushing in like a tidal wave. Jinx saw Lyndel's eyes widen as Dawson was washed back toward them. Lyndel might have gotten off a shot. Jinx didn't know. If he did, the shot went wild. The wave surrounded her, slamming her back against the seat she'd been holding on to as the car quickly filled with water and began to sink.

The water was colder than anything Jinx had ever felt in her life. It stole the breath she'd been holding and she was sure she would drown. But then she felt Dawson take her hand and he was swimming her out through the gaping hole where the back window had been.

She could see moonlight above them. Her lungs felt as if they would burst. They weren't going to make it. The surface was farther than they'd thought. She felt his hand tighten on hers and a moment later they burst to the surface.

Jinx gasped for breath, choking and crying.

"You're all right," Dawson said as he pulled her to him.

She couldn't catch her breath and the cold had seeped

into her bones, leaving her numb. He drew her over to the edge of the rock quarry and pulled them both up the rock ledge and into the warmth of the summer night and his strong arms.

"It's over, Brittany Bo. You're safe and I'm never letting you out of my arms ever again."

Epilogue

"I'd like to make a toast." Everyone turned their attention to Hoyt Chisholm at the head of the table. "We've had one interesting year so far and it isn't even half over." He raised his glass. "Here's hoping the next six months aren't half as eventful."

Everyone said, "Hear, hear," and raised their glasses.

Emma smiled across the table at her soon-to-be daughter-in-law, Halley. The deputy had eyes only for her fiancé, Colton, though. She was smiling up at him as they touched glasses.

Next to them Dawson and Jinx were also smiling at each other. Dawson hadn't let her out of his sight after everything that had happened to them. Emma shivered at even the thought of the two of them underwater with killers in the quarry in Wyoming. She gave a silent thanks to God that they had survived, and that the men who had been trying to kill them had perished—only

because she didn't want Jinx and Dawson to have to go
through a lengthy trial.

Emma liked Jinx. She was a good strong woman, ca
pable and smart. She'd had the good sense to get Lyn
del Thompson's confession on a digital recorder, which
she and Dawson had given to the sheriff in Wyoming
The rustlers had been rounded up and were facing seri
ous charges in connection with Jinx's father's murder

Across the table, Tanner and Billie Rae were shar
ing a private toast of their own. Emma loved the way
Billie Rae seemed to radiate with happiness when she
was with Tanner. He'd said he'd fallen in love with her
at first sight. Emma loved nothing better than a happy
ending.

"It's been a good year so far, too," Emma added after
everyone had taken a drink of their champagne. She'd
thought that the night had called for prime rib from one
of their beef and champagne and all the trimmings
"We have a lot of celebrate, including those who have
joined us tonight."

She lifted her glass to Colton and Halley, then Jinx
and Dawson, then Tanner and Billie Rae, turning to
smile down the long table at Sheriff McCall Crawford
and her husband, Luke. The sheriff was glowing and
Emma wondered if it was possible...

She turned back to her own husband. As she touched
his glass, her eyes locked with his. A silent look of love
and relief passed between them.

"To even happier times," she said, followed by ap
plause.

"Now can we please eat?" Marshall joked.

Emma loved the sound of laughter around the table
as her gaze took in her other stepsons. Zane had gone

clear to California looking for her. Her father had said how lucky she was to have such wonderful stepsons. Didn't she know it.

Next to him, Logan seemed lost in thought. Of the six, he puzzled her. She knew he loved the ranch, but as they said, he definitely heard a different drummer, with his long hair and his love of his motorcycle over horses. Emma knew he was also a puzzle to his father, but she had great hopes for him.

She'd seen a change in Marshall after everything that had happened and wondered what had caused it. He was now in the process of remodeling the farmhouse where he lived. It was part of the Chisholm Cattle Company, the most isolated of the places.

When she'd first married into the family only months ago, she'd been determined to bring the family together and she'd had this crazy idea of finding each of her stepsons the perfect mate.

She chuckled at her naïveté. Three of them had found mates in the least likely places. Emma had tried to help things along with Colton and even a little with Tanner, but she'd had nothing to do with getting Dawson and Jinx together.

Not that she had given up matchmaking. *No,* she thought as she looked at the three stepsons who were still single. She was making no promises. Now that her own life had settled down, the cattle all rounded up, Hoyt cleared of any criminal charges and Aggie soon to be headed for the state mental hospital, Emma thought she might see what she could do to help Cupid along for Marshall, Zane and Logan. Look how happy the other three were! she thought.

* * *

"She shouldn't give you any trouble," the deputy said as Aggie Wells was loaded into the back of the state mental hospital van. "Doc gave her something to calm her down."

The driver glanced back at the woman in his rear-view mirror, but made a point of not making eye contact.

"You must be new," the deputy said.

"Just started yesterday," the driver said. "Needed a job and this was all I could find."

"I guess there are worse jobs," the deputy agreed. "At least it's not the middle of winter where you have to fight icy roads and blowing and drifting snow a lot of the times. Good luck," he said as he started to close the van door.

"Thanks. I hope I don't need it." As he pulled away, he saw the deputy go back inside the sheriff's department.

He didn't look at the woman again until they were out of Whitehorse and headed across the open prairie. It was twilight, the sun somewhere behind the Little Rockies and the Bear Paw Mountains.

The driver checked his side mirror first. No cars behind him and none ahead as far as he could see. This really was an isolated part of the state—even during tourist season in the summer.

He finally glanced back at his passenger. "How are you doing, Aggie?"

She looked up, her gaze meeting his. "Okay, now that you're here."

He hadn't had a choice when he'd gotten her message. He owed her and had told her a long time ago that if she ever needed him... Years ago she'd proved that his wife had been systematically selling off the jewelry he gave her and replacing it with fakes, which she then paid her boyfriend to steal so she could collect on the insurance money.

He'd gotten rid of the boyfriend, kept the wife and gone into business with her. They had a nice life and he didn't have any more trouble with his wife after she'd seen what he'd done to her boyfriend.

Aggie Wells? Well, he was indebted to her in a big way.

"Did you have trouble getting the van?" she asked.

"Nothing I couldn't handle."

* * * * *

Nicole Helm grew up with her nose in a book and the dream of one day becoming a writer. Luckily, after a few failed career choices, she gets to follow that dream—writing down-to-earth contemporary romance and romantic suspense. From farmers to cowboys, Midwest to *the* West, Nicole writes stories about people finding themselves and finding love in the process. She lives in Missouri with her husband and two sons and dreams of someday owning a barn.

Books by Nicole Helm

Harlequin Intrigue

A Badlands Cops Novel

South Dakota Showdown
Covert Complication
Backcountry Escape
Isolated Threat
Badlands Beware
Close Range Christmas

Carsons & Delaneys

Wyoming Cowboy Justice
Wyoming Cowboy Protection
Wyoming Christmas Ransom

Stone Cold Texas Ranger
Stone Cold Undercover Agent
Stone Cold Christmas Ranger

Visit the Author Profile page at Harlequin.com for more titles.

STONE COLD
UNDERCOVER AGENT

Nicole Helm

The first romance novel I ever read was a romantic suspense, and I never thought I'd be able to write one. Thank you, Helen and Denise, for helping me prove past me wrong.

Chapter 1

Gabby Torres had stopped counting the days of her captivity once it entered its sixth year. She didn't know why that was the year that did it. The first six had been painful and isolating and horrifying. She had lost everything. Her family. Her future. Her *freedom*.

The only thing she currently had was…life itself, which, in her case, wasn't much of a life when it came right down to it.

For the first four years of her abduction, she'd fought like a maniac. Anyone and anything that came near her—she'd attacked. Every time her captor got up close and told her some horrible thing, she'd fought in a way she had never known she could.

Maybe if the man hadn't so gleefully told her that her father was dead two years into her captivity, she might have eventually gotten tired of fighting. She might have accepted her fate as being some madman's kidnapping victim. But every time he appeared, she remembered how happily he had told her that her father had suffered a heart attack and died. It renewed her fight every single time.

But the oddest part of the eight years of captivity was that, though she'd been beaten on occasion in the midst of fighting back, mostly The Stallion and his men hadn't ever forced themselves on her or the other girls.

For years she'd wondered why and tried to figure out their reasoning…what their *point* was. Why she was there. Aside from the random jobs The Stallion forced her and the other girls to do, like sewing bags of drugs into car cushions or what have you.

But she was in year eight and tired of trying to figure out why she was there or what the point of it was. She was even tired of thinking about escape.

She'd been the first girl brought to the compound and, over the years, The Stallion had collected three more women. All currently existing in this boarded-up house in who knew where. Gabby had become something like the den mother as the new girls tried to figure out why they were there, or what they had done wrong, or what The Stallion wanted from them, but Gabby herself was done with wondering.

She had moved on. After she'd stopped counting every single day at year six, the past two years had been all about making this a reality. She kept track of Sundays for the girls and noted when a month or two had passed, but she had accepted this tiny, hidden-away compound as her life. The women were as much of a family as she was ever going to have, and the work The Stallion had them doing to hide drugs or falsify papers was her career.

Accepting at this point was all she could do. If sometimes her brain betrayed her as she tried to fall asleep, or one of the girls muttered something about escape, she pushed it down and out as far as it would go.

Hope was a cancer here. All she had was acceptance.

So when just another uncounted day rolled around and The Stallion, for the first time in all of those days, brought a man with him into her room, Gabby felt an icy pierce of dread hit her right in the chest.

Though she'd accepted her fate, she hadn't accepted *him*. Perhaps because no matter how eight years had passed, or how he might disappear for months at a time, or the fact he never touched her, he seemed intent on making her *break*.

Quite honestly, some days that's what kept her going. Making sure he never knew he'd broken her of hope.

So, though she had accepted her lot—or so she told herself—she still dreamed of living longer than him and airing all his dirty laundry. Outliving him and making sure he knew he had never, *ever* broken her. She very nearly smiled at the thought of him dead and gone. "So, who are you?"

The man who stood next to The Stallion was tall, broad and covered in ominous black. Black hair—both shaggy on his head and bearded on his face—black sunglasses, black shirt and jeans. Even the weapons, mostly guns, he had strapped all over him were black. Only his skin tone wasn't black, though it was a dark olive hue.

"I told you she was a feisty one. Quite the fiery little spitball. She'll be perfect for you," The Stallion said, his smile wide and pleased with himself.

The icy-cold dread in Gabby's chest delved deeper, especially as this new man stared at her from somewhere behind his sunglasses. Why was he wearing sunglasses in this dark room? It wasn't like she had any outside light peering through the boarded window.

He murmured something in Spanish. But Gabby had never been fluent in her grandparents' native language and she could barely pick out any of the words since he'd spoken them so quickly and quietly.

The Stallion's cold grin widened even further. "Yes. Have lots of fun with her. She's all yours. Just remember the next time I ask you for a favor that I gave you exactly what you specified. Enjoy."

The Stallion slid out of the room, and the ominous click of the door's lock nearly made Gabby jump when no sounds and nothing in her life had made her jump for nearly two years.

While The Stallion's grin was very nearly...psychotic, as though he'd had some break with reality, the man still in her room was far scarier. He didn't smile in a way that made her think he was off in some other dimension. His smile was... Lethal. Ruthless. *Alive.*

It frightened her and she had given up fear a very long time ago.

"You don't speak Spanish?" he asked with what sounded almost like an exaggerated accent. It didn't sound like any of the elderly people in her family who'd grown up in Mexico, but then, maybe his background wasn't Mexican.

"No, not really. But apparently you speak English, so we don't have a problem."

"I guess that depends on your definition of problem," he said, his voice low and laced with threat.

What Gabby wanted to do was to scoot back on the bed as far into the corner as she possibly could, but she had learned not to show her initial reactions. She had watched The Stallion get far too much joy out of her flight responses in the beginning, and she'd learned to school them away. So even though she thought about it, even though she pictured it in her head complete with covering her face with her hands and cowering, she didn't do it. She stayed exactly where she was and stared the man down.

He perused the bedroom that had been her life for so long. Oh, she could go anywhere in the small, boarded-up house, but she'd learned to appreciate her solitude even in captivity.

The man opened the dresser drawers and pawed through them. He inspected the baseboards and slid his large, scarred hands up and down the walls. He even pulled at the boards over the windows.

"Measuring for drapes?" she asked as sarcastically as she could manage.

The man looked at her, still wearing his sunglasses, which she didn't understand at all. His lips curved into an amused smile. It made Gabby even more jumpy because, usually, the guards The Stallion had watching them weren't the brightest. Or maybe they'd had such rough lives they didn't care for humor of any kind. Either way, very few people, including the women she lived with, found her humor funny.

He was back to his perusal and there was a confident grace about him that made no sense to her. He wasn't like any of the other men she'd come into contact with during her captivity. He was handsome, for starters. She couldn't think of one guard who could probably transfer from a life of crime into a life of being a model, but this man definitely could.

It made all of her nerves hum. It gave her that little tingle that mysteries always did—the idea that if she paid enough attention, filed enough details away, she could solve it. Figure out why he was different before he did her any harm.

She'd begun to wonder if she hadn't gone a little crazy when she noticed these things no one else seemed to. She was pretty sure Tabitha thought she was out of her mind for having theories about The Stallion's drug and human trafficking operations. For coming up with a theory that he spent three months there and split the other seasons at three other houses that would ostensibly be just like this one.

She'd been here for eight years and she knew his patterns. She was sure of it. Things puzzled together in her head until it all made sense. But the girls all looked at her like she was crazy for coming up with such ideas so she'd started keeping them to herself. She'd started trying to stop her brain from acting.

But it always did and maybe she had gone completely and utterly insane. Eight years ago her life had been ripped away from her, but she didn't even get to be dead. She had to be here living in this weird purgatory.

Wouldn't that drive anyone to the brink of insanity? Maybe her patterns and theories were gibberish.

Finally the man had looked through everything in the room except her bed where she was currently sitting. He advanced on her with easy, relaxed strides that did nothing to calm the tenseness in her muscles or the heavy beating of her heart. She couldn't remember the last time in her captivity she'd felt so afraid.

He didn't say anything and she couldn't see his eye

underneath the sunglasses, so whatever he was thinking or feeling was a blank-expressioned mystery.

Finally, after a few humming seconds, he lifted a long finger up to the ceiling. She frowned at him and he made the gesture again until she realized he wanted her to get off the bed.

Since most of the guards' preferred way of getting her to do something was to grab her and throw her around, she supposed she should feel more calm with this man who hadn't yet touched her.

But she wasn't calm. She didn't trust him at all.

She did get up off the bed and, instead of scurrying away, tried to measure her steps and very carefully move to the farthest corner from him.

The man lifted every single blanket on her bed and then, in an easy display of muscles, the heavy mattress and box spring, as well. He got down on all fours and looked under the bed and, finally, she realized he was searching for something in particular.

She just had no idea what on earth he could be looking for.

"No bugs?"

She stared at him. What, did he have some weird fear of ladybugs or ants or something? Then she realized the intensity with which he was staring at her and recalled how carefully he had looked through every inch of this little room. Yeah, he wasn't looking for insects.

"I've been here for eight years. As far as I know, he's never bugged or videotaped individual rooms."

The man raised his eyebrows. "But he films other rooms?"

Gabby trusted this man almost less than she trusted The Stallion, which was not at all. She offered a careless shrug. The last thing she was going to do was to share all of her ideas and information with this stranger.

"Tell me about your time here."

There was a gentleness to his tone that didn't fool her at all. "Tell me who you are."

He smiled again, an oddly attractive smile that was so out of place in this dire situation. "The Stallion told me you'd be exactly what I was looking for. I don't think he knew just how perfect you'd be."

"Perfect for what?" she demanded, trying to keep the high-pitched fear out of her voice.

"Well, he thinks you'd be the perfect payment. A high-spirited fighter—the kind of woman who would appeal to my baser instincts."

This time Gabby couldn't stop herself from pushing back into the corner or cowering. For the first year she'd been held captive, she'd been sure she'd be sexually assaulted. She'd never heard about an abduction that hadn't included that, not that she'd had any deep knowledge of abductions before.

But no one had ever touched her that way and she'd finally gotten to a point where she didn't think it would happen. That was her own stupid fault for thinking this could be her normal.

The man finally took off his sunglasses. His eyes were almost as dark as his hair, a brown that was very nearly black. Everything about his demeanor changed, the swagger, the suave charm, gone.

"I'm not going to hurt you," he said in a low voice.

Maybe if she hadn't been a captive for eight years, she might have believed him. But she didn't, not for a second.

"You're just going to need to play along," he continued in that maddeningly gentle voice.

"Play along with what?" she asked, pushing as far into the corner as she could.

"You'll see."

Gabby wanted to cry, which had been an impulse she'd beaten out of herself years ago, but it was bubbling up inside her along with the new fear. It wasn't fair. She was so tired of her life not being fair.

When the man reached out for her, she went with those instincts from the very first time she'd been brought there.

She fought him with everything she had.

Jaime Alessandro hadn't worked his way up "The Stallion's" operation by being a particularly *nice* guy. Undercover work, especially this long and this deep, had required him to bend a lot of the moral codes he'd started police work with.

But thus far, he'd never had to beat up or restrain a woman. This woman was surprisingly agile and strong, and she was coming at him with everything she had.

He was very concerned he was going to have to hurt her just to get her to stop. He could stand a few scratches, but he doubted The Stallion was going to trust him with the next big job if he let this woman give him a black eye—no matter how strong and "feisty" she was.

God, how he hated that word.

"Ma'am." He tried for his forceful FBI agent voice as he managed to hold one of her arms still. He didn't want to hurt the poor woman who'd been here eight years—a fact he only knew because she'd just told him.

He shouldn't have been surprised at this point. He'd

learned very quickly in his undercover work that what the FBI had on Victor Callihan, a.k.a. The Stallion, was only the tip of the iceberg.

If he thought about it too much, the things The Stallion had done, the things Jaime had done to get here... Well, he didn't, because he'd had to learn how to turn that voice of right and wrong off and focus only on the task at hand.

Bringing down The Stallion.

That meant if she didn't stop flailing at him and landing some decent blows, he was going to have to restrain her any way he could, even if it caused her some pain.

Though he had her arm clamped in a tight grip, she still thrashed and kicked at him, very nearly landing a blow that would have brought him to his knees. He swore and, though he very much didn't want to, gave her a little jerk that gave him the leverage he needed to grab her from behind with both arms.

She still bucked and kicked, but with his height advantage and a full grip on her upper body, he could maneuver her this way and that to keep her from landing any nasty hits.

"I'm not going to hurt you. I'm going to help you, I promise."

She spat, probably aiming for him but missing completely since he had her from behind. It was only then he realized he'd spoken in Spanish instead of English.

He'd grown up speaking both, but his work for The Stallion and the identity he'd assumed required mostly speaking Spanish and pretending he struggled with English.

It was slipups like that—not realizing what language

he was speaking, not quite remembering who he was—that always sent a cold bolt of fear through him.

He needed this to be over. He needed to get out. Before he lost himself completely. He could only hope that Gabriella Torres would be the last piece of the puzzle in getting to the heart of The Stallion's operation.

"I'm not going to hurt you," Jaime said in a low, authoritative tone. Certain, self-assured, even though he didn't feel much of either at this particular moment.

"Then let go of me," she returned, still bucking, throwing her head back and narrowly missing head-butting him pretty effectively.

He tried not to think about what might have happened to her in the course of being hidden way too long from the world. It was a constant fight between the human side of him and the role he had to play. He wouldn't lose his humanity, though. He refused. He might have to bend his moral code from time to time, but he wouldn't lose the part of him that would feel sympathy. If he lost that, he'd never be able to go back.

Jaime noted that though Gabriella still fought his tight hold, she was tiring.

"Be still and I'll let you go," he said quietly, hoping that maybe his outer calm would rub off on her.

She tried to land a heel to his shin but when that failed she slumped in his arms. "Fine."

Carefully and slowly, paying attention to the way she held herself and the pliancy of her body, Jaime released her from his grip. Since she didn't renew her fight, he took a few steps away so she could see he had no intention of hurting her.

When she turned and looked at him warily, he held his hands up. Her breathing was labored and there were droplets of sweat gathered at her temples. She had a pretty face despite the pallor beneath her tan complexion. She had a mass of dark curls pulled back and away from her face, and he had to wonder how old she was.

She looked both too young and too world-weary all at the same time, but he couldn't let that twist his insides. He'd seen way worse at this point, hadn't he? "I'm not going to harm you, Gabriella. In fact, I want to help you."

She laughed, something bitter and scathing that scraped against what little conscience he had left.

"Sure you do, buddy. And this is the Taj Mahal."

Yeah, she'd be perfect for what he needed. Now he just had to figure out how to use her without blowing everything he'd worked for.

Chapter 2

Gabby was wrung out. Physically. Emotionally. It had been a long time since she'd had something to react so violently against. Her breathing was uneven and her insides felt scraped raw.

She wanted to cry and it had been so long since she'd allowed herself that emotional release.

She couldn't allow it now. Not with the way this man studied her, intently and far too interested. She had become certain of her power in this odd world she'd been thrust into against her will, but she didn't believe in that power in the face of this man.

She closed her eyes against the wave of despair and the *need* to give up on this whole *surviving* thing.

"Gabriella. I know you have no reason to trust me, but I'm going to say it even if you don't believe it. I will not hurt you."

The worst part was that she was so exhausted she

wanted to believe him. No one had promised her safety in the past eight years, but just because no one had didn't mean she could believe this one.

"I guess it's my lucky day," she returned, trying to roll her eyes but exhaustion limited the movement.

"I know. I know. I do. Don't trust me. Don't believe. I just need you to go along with some things."

"What kind of things? And, more important, *why*?" She shook her head. Questions were pointless. The man was going to lie to her anyway. "Never mind. It doesn't matter. Do whatever you're going to do."

"You fought me."

"So?"

He stepped forward and she stumbled away. He shook his head, holding his hands up again, as if surrendering. "I'm sorry. I won't. I'm not going to touch you." He kept his hands raised as he spoke. Low, with a note to his voice she couldn't recognize.

Panic? No, he wasn't panicked in the least. But there was something in that tone that made her feel like time was running out. For what, she had no idea. But there was a *drive* to this man, a determination.

He had a goal of some kind and it wasn't like The Stallion's goals. The Stallion had a kind of meticulous nature, and he never seemed rushed or driven. Just a cold, careful, step-by-step map in his head to whatever endgame he had. Or maybe no endgame at all. Just… living his weird life.

But *this* man in her room had a vitality to him, an energy. He was trying to *do* something and Gabby hated the way she responded to that. Oh, she missed having a goal, having some *fight* in her. The weary acceptance of the past two years had given her less and less to live for. Helping the other girls was the only thing that kept her getting up every morning.

"What do you want from me?"

"Just some cooperation. Some information. To go along with whatever I say, especially if The Stallion is around."

"Are you trying to usurp him or something?"

He released a breath that was almost a laugh. "N—" He seemed to think better of saying no. "Who knows? Right now, I need information."

"Why should I give you anything?"

He seemed to think about the question but in the end ignored it and asked one of his own. "Is it true…?" He trailed off, giving her a brief once-over. "They haven't touched you while you've been here?"

She stared hard at the man. "One time a guard tried to touch my chest and I knocked his tooth out."

The man's full mouth curved a little at that, something so close to humor in his expression it hurt. Humor. She missed…laughing. For no reason. Smiling, just because it was a nice day with a blue sky.

But she couldn't think about all the things she missed or her heart would stop beating.

"What happened to the guard?"

Gabby shrugged, hugging herself against all this *feeling*. Thoughts about laughter, about the sky, about using her mind to put the pieces of the puzzle together again.

You gave that up. You've accepted your fate.

But had she, really, when the fight came so easily and quickly?

"I don't know. I never saw him again."

"Was it only the one time?"

Gabby considered how much information she wanted to give a stranger who might be just as evil as the man who held her captive. She could help him boot The Stallion out…and then get nothing for her trouble. She wasn't sure if she preferred to take the risk. The devil you knew and all that.

But there was something about this man… He didn't fit. Nothing about his demeanor or mannerisms or his questions fit the past eight years of her experience. What exactly would be the harm in telling him what she knew? What would The Stallion do? He'd been the one to leave her with this man.

"As far as I know, they can knock us around as long as they don't break anything or touch our faces. If they go overboard, or get sexual, they disappear."

The man raised an eyebrow. "How many have disappeared?"

Gabby shrugged, still holding herself. "It was more in the beginning. Five the first year. Three the second. Only one in the third. Then five again the fourth. Two the fifth, then none since."

Both his eyebrows raised at this point, his eyes widening in surprise. "You remember it that specifically?"

Part of her wanted to brag about all the things she remembered. All the specifics she had locked away in her brain. All the patterns she'd put together. None of the girls had ever appreciated them. She had a feeling this man would.

But it would be showing her hand a little too easily for comfort. "Not a lot to think about in this place. I remember some things."

"Tell me," he said, taking another one of those steps toward her that made her want to cower or run away to whatever corner she could find. But she stood her ground and she shook her head.

If she told him, it would be in her own time, when she thought telling might work in her favor in some way.

He stood there, opposite her, studying her face as though he could figure out how to get her to talk if he simply looked hard enough.

So she looked right back, trying to determine something about *him*.

He had a sharp nose and angular cheekbones, a strong jaw covered liberally with short, black whiskers. His eyes looked much less black close up, a variety of browns melding to the black pupil at the center.

He had broad shoulders and narrow hips and even the array of weapons strapped to him didn't detract from the sexy way he was built. Sexy. Such an odd thing. She hadn't thought about sex or attractiveness or much of anything in that vein for eight long years.

She didn't know if she was glad she could still see it and recognize it or if it just made everything more complicated. Far more lonely.

The eerie click of a lock interrupted the moment and he looked back at the door, then at her. His expression was grave.

"I'm not going to hurt you," he whispered. "But this may scare you a little bit. That's okay. Fight back."

"Fight ba—"

He reached out and grabbed her by the shirt with both large hands. She screeched, but he had her shirt ripped in two before she landed the first punch.

Jaime pretended to laugh as Gabby pounded at him. He glanced at The Stallion, doing his best to stand between the man and his view of Gabby. He'd tried not to look himself, but he needed the illusion of a fight. A sexual one.

He couldn't let his disgust at that show. *"Senor?"* The Stallion always got some bizarre thrill when Jaime called him that, so he'd done it with increasing regularity. Being the egomaniac that he was, The Stallion never got tired of it. "An hour, no?"

"I'm sorry to interrupt, but I need you immediately. Your hour will have to wait."

Jaime scowled. He didn't have to fake it, either. He wanted more information from Gabriella. If the woman had remembered how many guards were dismissed every year...who knew what other kind of information she might have.

Jaime inclined his head as if he agreed, though he didn't at all. He wanted to get information out of Gabriella as soon as possible. The more he got and the sooner he got it, the less he'd have to do for The Stallion.

He gave her a fleeting glance. Those big, dark eyes were edged with fury, and she crossed her arms over her chest. The bra she wore was ill-fitting and he couldn't help but notice the way her breasts spilled over the fabric even under her crossed arms.

He quickly looked back at The Stallion. He handed Gabriella the remains of her shirt. *"Perdón,"* he offered, making sure he didn't sound sorry in the least.

The Stallion chuckled as Jaime walked to meet him at the door. "You could be so much better at your job if you weren't so easily distracted," the man said, clapping him on the shoulder in an almost fatherly manner as he pulled the door closed, leaving Gabby alone in the room.

He didn't lock the door this time and Jaime was surprised at how much freedom he allowed the women he kept there. Of course, the front and back doors were chained and locked even when The Stallion was inside, and all the windows were boarded up in a permanent, meticulous manner.

There were no phones in the house, no computers. Absolutely no technology of any kind aside from kitchen appliances. But even that was relegated to a microwave and a refrigerator. No stove and no knives beyond dull butter ones.

He wondered if the women inside knew that only a couple of yards away, in a decent-size shed, The Stallion kept all the things he denied the women. Computers and phones and an array of weapons, which was where The Stallion was leading Jaime now.

"We have a situation I want you briefed on. Then you may go back to our Gabriella and finish your…" He trailed off and shook his head as he locked and chained the back door they'd exited into an overgrown backyard. "Sex is such a *base* instinct, Rodriguez. Women are a worthless expense of energy. I'm fifty-three, for over half my life I have searched for the perfect woman and failed time and time again. Though, I will admit the women I've kept are of exceptional quality. Just not quite there…"

The man got a far-off look on his face as they walked through the long grass toward his shed. It was the kind of far-off look that kept Jaime up at night. Void of reason or sense, completely and utterly…incomprehensible.

The Stallion patted his shoulder again, tsking. "I know this is all going over your head. You really ought to work on your English."

Jaime shrugged. It suited his purpose to be seen as

not understanding everything that went on because of a language barrier, and at times it had been hard to remember he was supposed to barely understand.

But when The Stallion started going on and on about women, Jaime never had any problems keeping his mouth shut and his expression confused. It was broken and warped and utter nonsense.

The Stallion unlocked the shed and stepped inside. Two men were sitting on chairs around The Stallion's desk, which was covered in notes and technology. The man strode right to it and sat on his little throne.

"Herman's gone missing," he said without preamble, mentioning The Stallion's most used runner in Austin. "He didn't deliver his message today, and so far no one has figured out where he disappeared to. Wallace, I'm giving you the rest of today to find him. He can't have gone too far."

The fair-haired man in the corner nodded soundlessly.

"If he *somehow* gives us the slip that long…" The Stallion continued. "Layne, you'll take him out."

Layne cracked his knuckles one by one, like he'd seen too many mobster movies. "Be my pleasure. What happens to him if Wallace finds him, though? I wouldn't mind getting some information out of him."

The Stallion's mouth curved into a cold, menacing line that, even after two years, made Jaime's blood run cold. "Rodriguez will be in charge if we find him. I'd like to see what he can do with a…shall we say, recalcitrant employee. *¿Comprende?*"

"*Sí, senor.*"

"Wallace, you're dismissed. Report every hour," The

Stallion said with the flick of his wrist. "Layne, have the interrogation room readied for us, please."

Both men agreed and left the shed. Jaime stood as far from The Stallion as he could without drawing attention to the purposeful space between them. The man steepled his hands together, looking off at some unknown entity Jaime was pretty sure only he could see.

Jaime stood perfectly still, trying to appear detached and uninterested. "Did you need me, *senor*?"

The Stallion stroked his forehead with the back of his thumb, still looking somewhere else. "Once we figure out what's going on with Herman, I'll be moving on to a different location." His cold, blue gaze finally settled on Jaime. "You'll stay here and hold down the fort, and Ms. Gabriella will be yours to do whatever you please with her."

Jaime smiled. "Excellent." He didn't have to fake his excitement about that, because Jaime was almost certain Gabriella had exactly the information he'd need to pull the sting to end this whole nightmare of a job.

And then Jaime could go back to being himself and figuring out…who that was again.

Chapter 3

Gabby considered taking a nap in lieu of lunch. Her little *visit*, which she couldn't begin to understand, however, had eradicated any appetite she'd had.

That man had acted like two different people. Even the way he talked when The Stallion was present and when he wasn't was different. His voice, when he'd spoken with her, had only the faintest touches of Mexico, reminding her of her parents' accents—a sharp, hard pang of memory.

But when he spoke to The Stallion, it was all rolled R's and melodic vowels. Even his demeanor had changed. That goal or determination or whatever she thought she'd seen in him just…disappeared in the shadow of The Stallion. He was someone else. Something more feral and menacing.

But, despite the very disconcerting shirt-ripping, and

the way his gaze had most definitely lingered on her chest, he had been honest with her thus far.

He hadn't hurt her, but he'd let her hurt him. Blow after blow. Considering she'd gotten into the habit of exercising to keep her overactive mind from driving her crazy, she wasn't weak. She had punched him with everything she had, and though he hadn't made too much of an outward reaction, it had to have hurt.

She shook away the thoughts, already tired of the merry-go-round in her head. If she couldn't nap or eat, she'd do the next best thing. Exercise until she was too exhausted to think or to move or to do anything but sleep.

She rolled to the ground, then pushed up, holding the plank position as she counted slowly. It had become a game, to see how long she could hold herself up like this. The counting kept her brain from circling and the physical exertion helped her sleep better.

A knock sounded at the door, which was odd. No one here knocked. Except the girls, but that was rare and only in case of emergency.

Before she could stand or say anything, the door squeaked open and in stepped the man from earlier.

She scowled at him. "I only have so many clothes, so if you're going to keep ripping them, at least get me some duct tape or something."

He pulled the door closed as he stepped inside. "I won't rip your clothes again...unless I have to." He studied her arms, eyebrows pulling together. "You're awfully strong."

"Remember that."

"It could definitely work in our favor," he muttered. "Now, where were we?"

She pushed into a standing position. "You don't want to go back to where we were. I'll hit you where it *really* hurts this time." Why he smiled at that was completely beyond her.

"You might literally be perfect."

"And you might literally be as whacked as Mr. Stallion out there."

He shook his head in some kind of odd rebuttal. "Now—"

"You act like two very different people."

He froze, every part of his body tensing as his eyes widened. "What?"

"You act like two completely different people. In here alone. With him. Two separate identities."

He was so still she wasn't even sure he breathed.

"Two separate identities, huh?"

"Your accent is different when he's not here. The way you hold yourself? It's more…relaxed when he's with you. Rigid with me. No…almost…" She cocked her head, trying to place it. "Military."

She knew she was getting somewhere at the way he still didn't move, though he'd carefully changed his wide-eyed gaze into something blank.

Yeah, she was right. "You were military."

"No."

"Police then?"

"You're an odd woman, Gabriella." He said her name with the exaggerated accent, and it reminded her of her long-dead grandfather. He hadn't been a particularly nice man or a particularly mean man. He'd been hard. Very formal. And while everyone else in her family had called her Gabby, he'd been the lone holdout.

He'd never appreciated the "Americanization" of his family, even though he'd immigrated as a young man.

"I'm right. You're…" Her eyes widened as she put it all together. Him not hurting her. Him gathering information. Being someone else with The Stallion.

He gave a sharp head shake so she didn't say anything, but she did step closer. "But you are, aren't you?"

"No," he returned easily, nodding his head as he said it.

Her heart raced, her breathing came too shallow. He was an undercover police officer. She had to blink back tears. "Tell me what it means, that you're here. Please."

He let out a long breath and stepped toward her. This time she didn't scurry away. She needed to know more than she was afraid of him. He'd checked the room for bugs before, and she knew they were safe to talk in there, but she also understood how a man like him would have to be inordinately careful. *Undercover.* What did it mean? For her? For the girls?

He inclined his mouth toward her ear, so close she could feel his breath against her neck. "I can't promise you anything. I can only tell you that I am trying to end this, so whatever information you can give me, whatever you can tell me, it'll bring me closer to finishing out my job here."

He pulled back, looking at her, his gaze serious and that determination back in his dark eyes.

She tried to repeat those first five words. *I can't promise you anything.* It was important to remember, to not get her hopes up. Just because he was an undercover police officer…just because he wanted to take The Stallion down…it didn't mean he *would.* Or that he'd get her out in the process.

"How did you put it all together?" he asked. "I'm not..."

"You're very good. Very convincing. I'm probably the only person you let your guard down for, right?"

He nodded, still clearly perplexed and downright worried she'd figured it out.

"I don't know, ever since I got here... I remember things, and I can see...patterns that no one else seems to see. I thought I was going crazy. But... I don't know. I was always good at that. Observing, remembering, figuring out puzzles and mysteries. It just works in my head."

"Clearly," he muttered. "Hopefully you're the only one around here with that particular talent or I'm screwed."

"How long?" she asked. Was he just starting out? He was so close to The Stallion, surely...

"Two years."

She let out a breath. "That's a long time."

"Yes," he said, a bleak note in his voice that softened her another degree toward him. He'd voluntarily held his own identity hostage, separated himself from his life. He'd probably had no idea the things he'd end up missing or wanting.

God help her, she hadn't had a clue in that first day, week, month, even year. She'd had no idea the things that would grow to hurt her.

She felt a wave of sympathy for the man and, even if it was stupid or ill-advised, she had to follow it. She had to follow this first possibility in *ages* that there might be an end to this. "How can I help?"

"So, you trust me?"

"I don't trust anyone anymore," she returned, feeling

a little bleak herself. "But I'll try to help you. Because I believe you are what I think you are."

"That'll work. That'll work. But there's something you have to understand. Being a different person means being a *different* person. The ripping-your-shirt thing…"

"It was for him to think that you were…having your way with me." She shuddered a little at the thought, at how close they might have to come to…proving that.

"Yes. There may be times I have to push that a little bit. Because he is…" He cleared his throat. "What do you understand about your position here? Is there a reason you were kidnapped? Is there a reason he's kept you girls…untouched?"

"I'm not really sure. I have no idea why I was taken. I was waiting at my dad's work for him to get off his shift and all of a sudden there were all these people and men talking and I was grabbed and thrown into a van with some other people. They took us somewhere that I don't know anything about. It was all dark and sometimes we were blindfolded or there were hoods put on our heads."

Gabby felt ill. She didn't relive the kidnapping anymore. She'd mostly gotten beyond *that* horror and lived in the horror of her continual imprisonment. Going back and thinking about coming here brought up all sorts of horrible memories.

How awful she'd been to her mother that night when she'd had to cancel her date to pick up Dad. All that fear she hadn't known what to do with or how to survive with when she'd been taken, moved, inspected. But she had. She had survived and lived, and she needed to remind herself of that.

"Eventually, after I don't know how long… Actually that's not true." She didn't have to lie to this man about her memory or pretend she didn't know exactly what she knew like she did with so many people. "It was two days. It was two days from the time they took me and put me in the van to the time they took me to this other place, kind of like a warehouse. They took me—and all the people from that first moment—there and then we were sorted. Men and women went to different areas. And then The Stallion came."

"Keep going," he urged, and it was only then she realized she'd stopped because she could see it. Relive every terrifying detail of not knowing what would happen to her, or why.

"I didn't know that's who he was at the time, but he walked through and he asked everyone if we knew who he was. One woman in my group said yes and she was immediately taken away."

"Did he say his name or offer any hints about who he was beyond The Stallion?"

"No. I've gone over it a million times in my head. He must've…he must be someone, you know? He had to be someone with some kind of profile?"

"Yes, he is."

"He is?" She stepped toward the man who could mean freedom, a scary thought in and of itself. "Who? What's his name? Why is he doing this?" she demanded, losing her cool and her calm in an instant.

"I can't answer those questions."

She grabbed his shirtfront, desperate for an answer, a reason, desperate for those things she'd finally given up on ever getting. "Tell right this second, you miserable—"

"I'm sorry," he said so gently, so *emotionally*, she could only swallow a sob.

"He kidnapped me. He brought me here. He separated me from my family for eight years, and you can't tell me who he is?" she demanded, her voice low and scratchy but measured. She was keeping it together. She would keep it together.

"Not now. There are a lot of things I can't tell you, because everything you know jeopardizes what I'm doing here. You deserve the answers, you do, but I can't give you what you deserve right now. But if you help me, you'll have the answers, and you'll have your *life* back."

Odd *that* prompted a cold shudder to go through her body. "You can't promise me that."

"No, I can't, but I promise to put my life on the line to make it so."

She didn't know what to do with that or him, or any of this, so she turned away from him, hugging herself, trying to calm her breathing.

There were no promises. There were no guarantees. But she had a *chance*. She had to believe in it. She had to *fight* for it. With everything she had. If not for herself, for the three girls she shared this hell with. For their family's, and hers, even if they probably thought he was dead.

She owed it to a lot of people to do what this man said he would do: put her life on the line to make it so.

Gabriella was clearly brilliant. The way she described remembering things and figuring out patterns no one else did, to the point she thought she was crazy... it sounded like a lot of the analysts he knew. Because when you saw things no one else saw, it was very easy to convince yourself you were wrong.

But she wasn't wrong, and she had *so* much information in that pretty head of hers… Jaime was nearly excited even though she now had the power to end his life completely.

He didn't care because he was so close now. So damn close to the end of this.

She might be brilliant, but he was a trained FBI agent, after all. He wasn't going to let her figuring him out be the end. No way in hell.

"Tell me about what happened after the woman who knew who he was disappeared."

Gabriella nodded. "She was taken away from the room. She had no chance to say anything at all. After that, the rest of us women were separated into groups, and I tried to find a rhyme or reason for these groups, but I really couldn't. Except that all of the women in my group were young and reasonably fit. Dark hair, though none of the same shade—it ranged from black to light brown."

Jaime thought back to The Stallion's odd statement about searching half his life for the perfect woman. He couldn't make sense of it, but that had to be connected to this.

"At that point, it was just six of us. The Stallion lined us up and, one by one, he inspected us."

"Inspected you how?"

Gabriella visibly shuddered, and Jaime hated that she had to relive this, but she did. If they were going to put The Stallion away, she'd probably have to relive it quite frequently.

"He touched our hair and…smelled it." She audi-

ly swallowed, hugging herself so tightly he wished he
ould offer some comfort, some support.

But he was nothing to her.

"He had one of his cronies measure us."

"Measure you?"

"You know, like if you've ever been measured for
lothes?" She turned to face him again, though her dark
yes were averted. But she gestured to her body as she
poke. "Shoulders, arms, chest, hips, legs, inseam, and
he guy yelled out each number and The Stallion wrote
all down on this little notepad."

She was quiet for a few seconds and instead of pushing this time, he let her gain her composure, let her take
he time she needed.

Time wasn't on his side, but he couldn't…lose the
umanity. That was his talisman. *Don't lose your humanity.*

"He dismissed everyone except me."

Jaime didn't know how to absorb that. He could pic-
ure it too easily after everything he'd done with and for
The Stallion. The fear she must have felt having been
aken for no reason, having been chosen for no reason
hat she understood.

It was dangerous to fill her in on the things he knew.
ut he had already entered dangerous territory when
e had allowed himself to behave differently enough
rith her for her to figure out who he was. *What* he was.

"He's a sick man," Jaime offered.

"A sick man who is very, very smart or very, very
ucky since he hasn't gotten caught in eight years. Prob-
bly more than that."

"Yes. Listen, there are a lot of things The Stallion
oes. But this thing you're involved in… He told me

something just now about how he spent over half his life looking for the perfect woman. That women are basically stupid and you shouldn't dirty yourself with them unless you find this perfect specimen."

"Oh, how lovely. I'd love to show him how *stupid* I can be. With my fists."

He smiled at the irritation in her tone because it was *life*. A spark. It wasn't that shaky fear that had taken over as she had relived her kidnapping experience.

"Let him have his delusions. They might get us out of this mess." He wanted to reach out and take her shoulders or…something. Something to cement this partnership, but he was still a strange man in her room who'd ripped her shirt. He had to be careful. Human. "Between what you said and he said, I think that's what he's been doing with this arm of things. Searching for the perfect woman."

"So that's what the measuring was, then. He has a perfect size, I just bet." Gabriella rolled her eyes. "Disgusting pig. And then when we got here he, like, tested me. He would ask these questions, and I never answered. I only fought. For weeks, every time he opened his mouth, I'd just attack. I thought maybe that's why…"

She took in a shaky breath, still hugging herself. Jaime hadn't been lying when he'd said she might be perfect. She was smart, she was strong—not just physically. Strong at her core.

"I thought for sure I would be raped, but I never have been, and I've never understood why."

"He thinks women are dirty. At least, in this context of looking for the perfect woman. I can't rationalize a madman, but the point is that you were brought here

ecause he thought you *could* be the perfect woman.
he fighting, I guess, proved to him that you weren't."

"I thought that for the longest time, but that isn't it.
smine—she was brought here my second year—she
idn't fight him at all. She told him she'd do whatever
e wanted as long as he would let her go. I was the only
ne who fought, but he hasn't touched any of us. No
atter what our reactions were, he found us lacking in
ome way, I guess."

Gabriella shook her head. "So, he brought us here
ecause we were a possibility, then he tests us and de-
ides we're not perfect, but then why does he keep us?"
he looked up at him for answers.

Jaime hated that he couldn't give them to her—and
at hate kept him going. Because at least he still had
conscience. He'd started to worry. "That's where I
ome in. I've been working my way up to get close to
guring out who he was. When I did that, it was de-
ided I'd stay and get enough information on him that
e can arrest and prosecute."

"And you don't have that yet?"

"Not to the extent my superiors would like. Which
why we came up with a plan."

"Let me guess. You can't tell me about the plan."

"Actually, this one I can. A little. You're a gift to me."

She physically recoiled and he could hardly blame
er.

"Excuse me?"

"I've slowly become his right-hand man and as I
arned about the girls he keeps locked up... I wanted
 get close to one of you to figure out how I could get
ou out. How we could all work together to get you out.

So I convinced him that a woman would be better payment than drugs or money. I mean, I get paid, too, bu—"

"Of course you do. I'm sure you get money and a horse and forty acres of land. The payment of a woman is simply pocket change, right?"

"Gabriella."

She began to pace the tiny room, her irritation and anxiety so *recognizable* to him he started to feel the same build in his chest.

"This is insane," she muttered. "This is so impossible. These things don't happen! They don't happen to people in my family. They don't happen to people! This is movie craziness."

"No. It's your life," Jaime returned firmly. He needed her to focus, to get past the panic. "There's one of his compounds that has the most evidence on his whole operation, and it's the only one that I don't know where it's located. So, as I work with him right now, that's what I'm trying to figure out. If you've been watching, paying attention, listening…you might have the answer. But we have to pretend like…"

"Like I'm the gift to you. And you can do whatever you want with me," she said flatly.

"Yes. But the key here is that it's pretend. I'm not going to hurt you. I've done a lot of things that will stick with me for a very long time." He stopped talking for a few seconds so he could regain his composure. He didn't like to think back at some of the chances he'd had to take or some of the people he'd had to hurt. Though he hadn't actively killed anyone, he had no doubt some of the things he'd been involved in had led to the death of someone else.

There were a lot of terrible things you could do to a person without killing them.

He had to get hold of himself, so he did. He forced himself to look at Gabriella. She was studying him carefully, as though she could see the turmoil on his face.

To survive, he had to believe this was a very special woman who could see things no one else could. Because if she could see these things and other people could, as well, they would probably both end up dead.

"I know it sounds crazy," she said carefully, "but I know what it's like. I've helped hide drugs that I'm sure have killed people. I've had to dig holes that I think were…so he could bury people. I've had to do terrible things, and sometimes I'm not even sure that I had to. Just that I did."

"No." He took a step toward her and though he knew he had to be careful so he didn't startle her, he very slowly and gently reached out and took her hand in his. He gave it a slight squeeze.

"We've done what we had to do to survive. In my case, to bring this man to justice. We have to believe that. Above everything else."

She looked down at their joined hands. He had no idea what she saw or what she felt. It had been so long since he'd been able to touch someone in a kind way, in a gentle way, it affected him a bit harder than he'd expected.

Her hand was warm and it felt capable. She squeezed his back as though she could give him some comfort. This woman who'd been abducted from her family for eight years.

When she raised her gaze to his, he felt an odd little

jitter deep in his stomach. Something like fear but not exactly. Almost like recognizing something or someone, but that didn't make sense, so he shook it away.

Chapter 4

Gabby looked at her hand, encompassed by a much larger one. She wondered if the small scars across his knuckles were from his undercover work or if he'd got them before.

What would he have been like before his assumed identity?

And what on earth did *that* matter?

She forced her gaze back to him, his dark brown eyes somehow sure and comforting, when nothing in eight years had been *comforting*. It shouldn't be potent. It was probably part of his training—looking in charge and compassionate.

She'd never been too fond of cops, though that may have been Ricky's influence. Her first serious boyfriend. A poster child for trouble. Gabby had been convinced she could change him, that everyone saw him all wrong. Her parents had been adamant that she could *not* change what was wrong with that boy.

They'd barred him from their house. Insisted Gabby live at home through her coursework at the community college, and had been making noise about her not transferring to get her bachelors.

It had all seemed like the most unjust, unfair fate. They didn't have enough money, they didn't have any trust. The world had seemed cruel, and Ricky had been nice...to her.

She was twenty-eight now and that was the only relationship she'd ever had. A boy, really, and she'd only been a girl.

This man holding her hand was no *boy*, but she wasn't sure what she was. Except a little off her rocker for having this line of thought.

She cleared her throat and pulled her hand away. "So. What is it you need from me?"

He was quiet for a moment, studying his hand, which he hadn't dropped—it still hovered there in the air between them.

"My main goal is to find the last compound," he finally said, bringing his hand down to his side. "It's the one he's the most secretive about. So much so, I'm not sure he takes any of his employees there."

"I don't know if I can help with that. I did have this theory..." She trailed off. "I wish I had something to write on," she muttered. She searched her room for something...something to illustrate the picture in her head.

She opened one of her drawers and retrieved her brush, pins and ponytail holders, some of the few "extras" The Stallion afforded her. A giddy excitement jumbled through her and maybe she should calm it down.

But this was something. God, *something* to do. Something real. Something that wasn't just pointless fighting but actually working toward a *goal*.

Freedom.

She settled herself at that word. It had come to mean something different in eight years. Or maybe it had come to mean nothing at all.

She shook those oddly uncomfortable thoughts away and looked around for a place to create her makeshift map. "I can't explain it without props," she said, setting a brush on the center of the floor.

"Let's do it on the bed instead of the floor, so if anyone comes in we can…" He rubbed a hand over his unkempt if short beard. "Well, cover it up."

Right. Because to The Stallion she was a *gift*. No, that was too generous. She was a thing to be traded for services. She shuddered at the thought but…the man kneeled at the bed. The man who hadn't used her as payment but was using her as an informant.

The man whose name she didn't know.

"What should I call you?" she asked suddenly. Because she was working with this man to free—no, not to free anything, but to bring down The Stallion—and she hadn't a clue as to what to call him.

He glanced at her and she must be dreaming the panic she saw in his expression because it disappeared in only a second.

"They call me Rodriguez," he said carefully. "But my name is Jaime A— I…" He shook his head as he focused, as he seemed to push away whatever was plaguing him. "Call me Rodriguez. It's safest."

She knelt next to him, biting back the urge to repeat *Jaime*. Just to feel what his name would sound like in her mouth.

Silly. "All right, Rodriguez." She placed the brush at the center of the bed. "This is Austin. The bed is Texas. I don't have a clue..." She trailed off, realizing this man would know where they were. He hadn't been blindfolded or hooded. He actually *knew* if they were still in Texas, if they were close to home.

She breathed through the emotion swamping her. "Where are we?" she whispered.

"An hour east of El Paso. Middle of nowhere, basically. Only a few small towns around."

She blinked. El Paso. She'd had theories about where they could be, and El Paso had factored into them, but theories and truths were...

"Take your time," Jaime said gently.

"But we don't have much time, do we?" she returned, staring into compassionate eyes for the first time in eight years. Because as much as all the girls felt sorry for each other, they felt sorry for themselves first and foremost.

Jaime nodded toward the bed. "Technically, I don't know how much time we have. I only know the quicker we figure it out, the less chance he has of hurting people. More people."

She took a deep breath and returned her focus to the bed. "The brush is Austin. I get the feeling that's something like...the center. I don't know if it's a headquarters or..."

"Technically, he lives in Austin. His public persona, anyway."

His public persona. Though it fit everything she

knew or had theorized, it was hard to believe The Stallion went about a normal life in Austin and people didn't see something was wrong with the man. Warped and broken beyond comprehension.

"So, we've got his personal center at Austin," Jaime continued for her, taking one of the rubber bands she'd piled next to her. He reached past her, his long, muscular arm brushing against her shoulder. "And this is the compound close to El Paso."

"Right. Right." She picked up another rubber band. "He seems to work by seasons, sort of. I started wondering if he had a place in each direction. If this is west, he has a compound in the north, the south and the east. Unless Austin is his east." She placed rubber bands in general spots that represented each direction, creating a diamond with Austin at the somewhat center.

"He has a compound in the Panhandle. Though I haven't been there, he's talked of it. I've been to the one on the Louisiana border. I didn't think he had women there, but... Now that I've seen this setup, maybe he did and I just didn't know about it."

The idea that there'd been women to help and he hadn't helped them clearly bothered him, but he kept talking. "But south... He's never mentioned any kind of holdings in the south of Texas." He tapped the lower portion of her bed. "It has to be south."

"It would make sense. The access to drugs, people."

"It would make all the sense in the world, and you, Gabriella, are something of a miracle." He grinned over at her.

"It's... Gabby. Everyone, except *him*, calls me Gabby."

His grin didn't fade so much as morph into something else, something considering or...

The door swung open and the next thing Gabby knew, she was being thrust onto the bed and under a very large man.

Jaime hadn't had a woman underneath him in over two years, and that should not at all be the thought in his head right now. But she was soft underneath him, no matter how strong she was…soft breasts, soft hair.

And a kidnapping victim, jackass.

"Rodriguez. Boss wants you." Layne's cruel mouth was twisted into a smirk, clearly having no compunction about interrupting…well, what this looked like, not so much what it was.

Damn these men and their interruptions. He was getting somewhere, and he didn't mean on top of Gabriella.

Gabby.

He couldn't call her that. Couldn't think of her like that. She was a tool, and a victim. Any slipups and they could both end up dead. He glanced down at her, completely still underneath him, and it was enough of a distraction that he was having trouble deciding how to play things in front of Layne.

She blinked up at him, eyes wide, and though she wasn't fighting him, he'd scared her. No matter that she understood him, his role here, he didn't think she'd be trusting him any time soon. How could he blame her for that?

Wordlessly he got off Gabby and the bed and straightened his clothes in an effort to make Layne think he was more rumpled than he really was.

"We'll finish this later," he said offhandedly to Gabby, hoping it sounded to Layne like a hideous threat.

Jaime sauntered over to the door, not looking back

at Gabby to see what she was doing, though that's desperately what he wanted to do. He grabbed his sunglasses from his pocket and slipped them on his face as he stepped out into the hallway with Layne.

"Awfully clothed, aren't you?" Layne asked.

Jaime closed the door behind him before he answered. "Still trying to knock the fight out of her. Wouldn't want to intimidate her with what's coming." Jaime smirked as if pleased with himself instead of disgusted.

"It's a hell of a lot better when there's still a little fight in them," Layne said, glancing back at Gabby's door as they walked down the hall.

Jaime's body went cold, but he reined in his temper, curling his fingers into fists, his only—and most necessary—reaction.

"Do you think *senor* would be pleased with that world view?" he asked as blandly as he could manage.

Layne's gaze snapped to Jaime and his threat. The man sneered. "Not every idiot believes your Pepe Le Pew act, buddy."

Jaime flashed his most intimidating grin, one devoid of any of the *humanity* he was desperate to believe he still had. "Pepe Le Pew is French, *culo*."

"Whatever," the man said with a disinterested wave. "You know what I mean."

"I know a lot of things about you, *amigo*," Jaime said, enjoying the way the man rolled his eyes at every Spanish word he threw into the conversation.

Layne didn't take the hint. "Maybe you want to pass her around a bit. Boss man's been pretty strict about us getting anything out of these girls but you—"

Jaime stopped and shoved Layne into the wall. What

he really wanted to do was punch the man, but he knew that would put his credibility in jeopardy, no matter how much dirt he had on Layne. He wrestled with the impulse, with the beating violence inside him.

No matter what this man might deserve, he was not Jaime's end goal. The end goal was to make this all moot.

So, he held Layne there, against the wall, one fist bunched in the man's T-shirt to keep him exactly where he wanted him. He stared down at the man with all the menace he felt. "You will not touch what is mine," Jaime threatened, making his intent clear.

"You've already stepped all over what's mine," Layne returned, but Jaime noted he didn't fight back against Jaime's hold—intelligence or strategy, Jaime wasn't sure.

"I ran this show before he brought you in," Layne growled.

"Well, now you answer to me. So, I'd watch your step, *amigo*. I know things about you I don't think The Stallion would particularly care to hear about. A hooker in El Paso, for starters."

Layne blustered, but underneath it the man had paled. This was why Jaime preferred everyone think of him as muscle who could barely understand English. They underestimated him. But Jaime hadn't walked in here blindly. He knew The Stallion's previous head honchos wouldn't take the power share easily. So he'd collected leverage.

Thank God.

"Now, are you ready to keep your disgusting tongue and hands to yourself?" Jaime asked with an almost pleasant smile. "Or do I have to make your life difficult?"

Layne ground his teeth together, a sneer marring his features, but he gave a sharp nod.

"Muy bueno," Jaime said, pretending it was great news as he released the piece of garbage. "Let's proceed, then." He gestured grandly down the hall to the back door.

Layne grumbled something, but Jaime was relieved to see concern and fear on the man's face. He could only hope it would keep the man in line.

They exited the house and Jaime waited while Layne chained everything up. The late summer sun shimmered in the green of the trees, and if Jaime didn't know what lurked in the shed across the grass, he might have relaxed.

As it was, relaxing wasn't happening any time soon.

Jaime let Layne lead the way to the shed. He preferred to touch as little as possible in that little house of horrors.

Both men stepped in to find The Stallion pacing, hands clutched behind his back, and Wallace looking wary in the far corner.

The Stallion looked up distractedly. "Good. Good. We've gotten news of Herman before Wallace even got anywhere." The man's hands shook as he brought them in front of him in fists, fury stamped across his face. The usual calm calculation in his eyes something darker and more frenzied. "With the Texas Rangers and a hypnotist." The Stallion slammed a fist to the desk that made the creepy-ass dolls on the shelf above shake, their dead lifeless eyes fluttering at the vibration.

Jaime forced himself to look away and stare flatly at his boss. *Fake boss*, he amended.

"Luckily, Mr. Herman doesn't know enough to give them much of a lead, but he certainly represents a loose end." The Stallion took a deep breath, plucking one of the brunette dolls from the shelf. He cradled it like a child.

It took every ounce of Jaime's control and training to keep the horror off his face. Grown men capable of murder cradling a doll was not…comforting in the least.

"I've sent a team to get rid of Herman. Scare the hypnotist. I don't think I want to extinguish her yet. She might be valuable. But I want her *scared*." He squeezed the doll so tight it was a wonder one of its plastic limbs didn't break off.

"There we are, pretty girl," The Stallion cooed, re-settling the doll on the shelf and brushing a hand over its fake hair.

Jaime shuddered and looked away.

"Until this mess is taken care of, you are all on lock-down. No one is leaving the premises until Herman is taken care of."

"Then, boss?" Layne asked a little too hopefully.

The Stallion smiled pleasantly. "And then we'll decide what to do about the hypnotist."

Lockdown and death threats. Jaime tried to breathe through the urgency, the failure, the impossibility of saving this man's life.

He'd try. Somehow, he'd try. But he had the sinking suspicion Herman was already gone.

Chapter 5

Gabby couldn't sleep. It wasn't an uncommon affliction. Even in the past two years, exercising herself to exhaustion, giving up on things ever being different, avoiding figuring out the pieces of The Stallion puzzle, insomnia still plagued her.

Because no matter how she tried to accept her lot in life, she'd always known this wasn't *home*.

But what *would* be home? Her father was dead. Her sister would be an adult woman with a life of her own. Would Mom and Grandma still live in the little house on East Avenue or would they have moved?

Did they assume she was dead? Would they have kept all her things or gotten rid of them? The blue teddy bear Daddy had given her on her sixth birthday. The bulletin board of pictures of friends and Ricky and her and Nattie.

Her heart absolutely ached at the thought of her sister. Two years apart, they hadn't always gotten along, but they had been friends. Sisters. They'd shared things, laughed together, cried together, fought together.

Tears pricked Gabby's eyes. She hadn't had this kind of sad nostalgia swamp her in years, because it led nowhere good. She couldn't change her circumstances. She was stuck in this prison and there was no way out.

Except maybe Jaime.

That was not an acceptable thought. She could work with him to take down The Stallion, and she would, but actually thinking she could get out of there was… It was another thing altogether.

She froze completely at the telltale if faint sound of her door opening. And then closing. She closed her hands into fists, ready to fight. She couldn't drown that reaction out of herself, no matter how often she wondered if giving in was simply easier.

"Gabby."

A hushed whisper, but even if she didn't remember people's voices so easily, she would have known it was Jaime—*Rodriguez*—from a man calling her Gabby.

Gabby. She swallowed against all of the fuzzy feelings inside her. Home and Gabby and what did either even mean anymore. She didn't have a home. The Gabby she'd been was dead.

It didn't matter. Taking The Stallion down was the only thing that mattered. She sat up in the dark, watched Jaime's shadow get closer.

The initial fear hadn't totally subsided. She wasn't *afraid* of him per se or, maybe more accurately, she wasn't afraid he would harm her. But that didn't mean there weren't other things to be afraid of.

She had sat up on the bed, but he still loomed over

her from his standing position. She banked the edgy nerves fluttering inside her chest.

He kneeled, much like he had earlier today when they'd been putting together her map. Except she was on the bed instead of her makeshift markers.

"Do you have any more ideas about the locations? Aside from directions?" he asked, everything about him sounding grave and...tired.

"I have a few theories. Do we...do we need to go over all that tonight?"

"I'm sorry. You were sleeping."

"Well, no." She had the oddest urge to offer her hand to him. He'd taken her hand earlier today and there had been something... "Is something wrong?"

He laughed, caustic and bitter, and she didn't know this man. He could be lying to her. He could be anyone. Then there was her, cut off from normal human contact for *eight* years. The only place she had to practice any kind of compassion or reading of people was with the other girls, and she'd been keeping her distance lately.

So she was probably way off base to think something was wrong, to feel like he was off somehow.

But he stood, pacing away from the bed, a dark, agitated shadow. "It doesn't get any easier to know someone's going to die. I tried..." He shook his head grimly. "We should focus on what we can do."

"You tried what?" Gabby asked, undeterred.

"I tried to get a message to the Rangers, but..." He kneeled again and she couldn't see him in the dark, found it odd she wanted to.

"But?"

"I think it was too late."

Gabby inhaled sharply. Whether she knew him or

not, whether she'd lost all ability to gauge people's emotions, she could all but *feel* his guilt and regret as though it were her own.

She didn't know what the answer to that was…what he might have endured in pretending to be the kind of man who worked for The Stallion. Gabby couldn't begin to imagine… Though she'd ostensibly worked for the man, she'd never had to pretend she liked it.

"If we're an hour west of El Paso, I would imagine each spot would be likely the same distance from the city in its sector," she said, because the only answer she knew was bringing The Stallion down.

It couldn't bring dead people back, including herself, but it could stop the spread. They had to stop the spread.

She kept going when he said nothing. "He's very methodical. Things are the same. He stays here the same weeks every year. He eats the same things, does the same things. I would imagine whatever other places he has are like this one. Possibly identical."

In the dark she couldn't see what Jaime's face might be reflecting and he was completely and utterly still.

"Jaime…"

"Rodriguez. We have to…we can't be too complacent. There's too much at stake. I am Rodriguez."

"Okay," she returned, and she supposed he was right, no matter how much she preferred to call him something—anything—other than what The Stallion called him.

"But you're right. The eastern compound was around an hour west of Houston. I wonder… He is methodical, you're right about that. I wonder if the mileage would be exactly the same."

"It wouldn't shock me."

"Have you seen the dolls?"

Gabby could only blink in Jaime's shadow's direction. "Dolls?"

"He has a shelf of dolls in his office. They sit in a row. I'd always thought they were creepy, but today…" Jaime laughed again, this one wasn't quite as bitter as the one before, but it certainly wasn't true humor. "You should get some rest. I didn't mean to interrupt you. We can talk in the morning." He got to his feet.

She didn't analyze why she bolted off the bed to follow him. Even if she gave herself the brain time to do it, she wouldn't have come up with an answer.

He was a lifeline. To what, she didn't know. She didn't have a life—not one here, not one to go back to.

"I wasn't sleeping." She scurried between him and the room's only exit. "What about the dolls?"

He was standing awfully close in his attempt to leave, but he neither reached around her for the door nor pushed her out of the way. He simply stood there, an oppressive, looming shadow.

Gabby didn't know what possessed her, why she thought in a million years it was appropriate to reach out and touch a man she'd only met today. But what did it *matter*? She'd been here eight years and worrying about normal or appropriate had left the building a long time ago.

So she placed her palm on his chest, hard and hot even through the cotton of his T-shirt. Such a strange sensation to touch someone in neither fight nor comfort. Just gentle and…a connection.

"Tell me about the dolls," she said in the same tone she used with the girls when she wanted them to listen and stop whining. "Get it off your chest."

* * *

His chest. Where Gabby's hand was currently touching him between the vee of straps that kept his weapons at hand. Gently, very nearly *comfortingly*, her hand rested in the center of all that violent potential.

Jaime was not in a world where that had happened for years. His mother had hugged him hard and long that last meal before he'd gone undercover, and that had been it. Two years, three months and twenty-one days ago.

He had known what he was getting himself into and yet he hadn't. There had been no way to anticipate the toll it would take, the length of time and how far he'd gotten.

That meant bringing The Stallion to justice was really the only thing that could matter, not a woman's hand on his chest.

And yet he allowed himself the briefest moment of putting his hand over hers. He allowed himself a second of absorbing the warmth, the proof of beating life and humanity, before he peeled her hand off his chest.

"He cradled the doll like a baby. Talked to it. Damn creepiest thing I've ever seen—and I've seen some things." He said it all flippantly, trying to imbue some humor into the statement, but it felt good to get it out.

The image haunted him. A grown man. A doll. The threat on a man who would most certainly be dead even if Jaime's secret message to his FBI superiors made it through.

Dead. Herman, a man he'd never met and knew next to nothing about, was dead. Because he hadn't been able to stop it.

"Dolls." Gabby seemed to ponder this, and though

her hand was no longer on his chest, she still stood between him and the door, far too close for anyone's good.

"If there are identical dolls in every compound, I'll never be able to sleep again after this is all over."

Even in the dark he could see her head cock, could *feel* her gaze on him. "Do you think of after?"

"Sometimes," he offered truthfully, though the truth was the last thing they should be discussing. "Sometimes I have to or I'm afraid I'll forget it isn't real."

"I stopped believing 'after' could be real," she whispered, heavy and weighted in the dark room of a deranged man's hideout.

He wanted to touch her again. Cradle her small but competent hand in his larger one against his chest. He wanted to make her a million promises he couldn't keep about *after*.

"I... I can't think about after, but I can think about ending him. If we're an hour west of El Paso, give or take, and the western compound is an hour west of Houston, then what would the southern compound be? San Antonio?"

"If we're going from the supposition it's the closest guarded one because it's closest to the border, I think it'd be farther south."

"Yes." She made some movement, though he couldn't make it out in the dark. Likely they could turn on the lights and no one would think anything of it, she had been a gift to him, after all, but he found as long as she didn't turn on the lights, he didn't want to, either.

There was something comforting about the dark. About this woman he didn't know. About the ability to say that a man's life wasn't saved probably because of him. Because who else could he express that remorse to? No one here. No one in his undercover life.

He finally realized she had moved around him. She wasn't exactly pacing, but neither was she still in the pitch-black room.

He couldn't begin to imagine how she'd done it. This darkness. This uncertainty. For eight years she had been at someone else's mercy. As much as he sometimes felt like he was at someone else's mercy, it was voluntary. It was for a higher purpose. If he really wanted to, if he didn't care about bringing The Stallion down, he could walk away from all this.

But she was here and said she couldn't even think about after. Instead she lived and fought and puzzled things together in her head. Remembered things no one would expect her to.

She was the key to this investigation. Because she'd been that strong.

"Loredo, maybe?" she offered.

"It's possible," Jaime returned, reminding himself to focus on the task at hand rather than this woman. "Doesn't quite match the pattern of being close to bigger cities like Houston and El Paso."

"True, and he does like his patterns." She was quiet for a minute. "But what about the northern compound? There isn't anything up there that matches Houston or El Paso, either. Maybe whatever town in the south it's near matches whatever town is north."

"I haven't been to the northern one, so I don't know for sure, but one would assume Amarillo. Based on what I know."

"Laredo and Amarillo would be similar. Was the place west of Houston similar to this?"

It was something Jaime hadn't given much thought to, but now that she mentioned it… "I never went in the house, but there was one. It didn't look the same from the outside, but it's very possible that the layout inside was exactly the same."

"If you didn't go in the house, where did you go there?"

It confirmed Jaime's suspicion that the girls didn't know anything about the outside world around them. "He has a shed for an office outside."

"It must be in the back. He had us dig holes in the front."

It shouldn't shock him The Stallion used the women he kidnapped for manual labor, and yet the thought of Gabby digging shallow graves for that man settled all wrong in his gut. "Did you ever see…?"

"We just dug the holes and were ushered back inside," she replied, her tone flat. Though she had brought it up yesterday when they'd first met, so clearly it bugged her. "It's the only time I've been out…" She shook her head. "The office shed. Is the one here the same as the one in the west?"

He wanted to tell her she'd make a good cop—focusing on the facts and details over emotions—but that spoke of an after she couldn't bring herself to consider. So he answered her question instead.

"The one he has here is a little bit more involved than the one he had there. And no dolls."

"The doll thing really bothers you, huh?"

"Hey, you watch a grown man cradle and coo at a doll the way a normal person would an infant and tell me you wouldn't be haunted for life."

Though it was dark and Jaime had no idea if his instincts were accurate without seeing her expression, he thought maybe she was teasing him. An attempt at lightening things a little. He appreciated that, even if it was a figment of his imagination.

"As long as I'm on lockdown, I can't share any of this information with my superiors. It would be too dangerous and too risky, and I've already risked enough by trying to warn them about…" He trailed off, that inevitable, heavy guilt choking out the words.

"If the man ends up dead, it has nothing to do with you," Gabby said firmly.

"It's hardly nothing. I knew. And I didn't stop it."

"Because you're here to bring down The Stallion. Doing that is going to save more men than saving one man. Maybe I wouldn't have thought about it that way years ago, but… You begin to learn that you can't save everyone, and that some things happen whether it's *fair* or not. I hate the word *fair*. Nothing is fair."

That was not something he could even begin to argue with a woman who'd been kidnapped eight years ago.

"Do you know who this man was?" she demanded in the inky dark.

"He delivered messages for The Stallion."

"Then I don't feel sorry for him at all."

"You don't?" he asked, surprised at her vehemence for a man she didn't know.

"No. He worked for that man, and I don't care who you are or how convincing he is in his real life, if you work for that man, you deserve whatever you get."

She said it flatly, with certainty, and there was a part of him that wanted to argue with her. Because he knew things like this could make you hard. Rightfully so, even. She deserved her anger and hatred and her uncompromising views.

But he could not adopt them as his own. He was afraid if he did that he would never find his way out of this. That he would become Rodriguez for life and forget who Jaime Alessandro was. It was his biggest fear.

He felt sorry for Gabby, but it made him all the more determined to make sure she got out. He would make sure she had a chance to find her compassion again.

"Until I can get more intel to my superiors, the next step is to keep gathering as much information as we can. The more I can give them when the time comes, the better chance we have of ending this once and for all."

"End." She laughed, an odd sound, neither bitter nor humorous. Just kind of a noise. "I'm not sure I know what that word means anymore."

"I'll teach you." That was a foolish thing to say, and yet he would. He would find a way to show her what endings meant. And what new beginnings could be about.

Because if he could show her, then he could believe he could show himself.

Chapter 6

Gabby was tired and bleary-eyed the next day. Jaime had stayed in her room for most of the night and they had talked about The Stallion, sure, but as the night had worn on, they'd started to veer toward things they remembered about their former lives.

She'd kept telling herself to stop, not to tell yet another story about Natalie or not to listen to another about the birthday dinners his mother used to make him. And yet remembering her family and the woman she'd been years ago—which had never been tempting to her in all these years—had been more than just tempting in a dark room with Jaime.

She should think of him as nothing but Rodriguez. She shouldn't be forming some odd friendship with a man whose only job was to bring down The Stallion. Knowing those things seemed to disappear when she was actually in a room with him.

He was fascinating and kind. She missed kindness. In a way she hadn't been able to articulate in the past eight years. The other kidnapped girls were mostly nice. Alyssa was a little hard, but Gabby had spent many a night holding Jasmine or Tabitha as they cried. She had reassured them they wouldn't be hurt and hoped she wasn't lying. She had given them all kindness and compassion, but there was something about being the first—the older member, so to speak—that meant none of the girls offered the same to her.

Gabby was the mother figure. The martyr to them. Everyone thought she was strong and fine and somehow surviving this. But she wasn't. She was broken.

Jaime saw the victim in her, though. It should be awful, demoralizing, and yet it was the most comforted she'd felt in eight years.

But it would weaken her. It *was* weakening her. There was this war in her brain and her heart whether that weakening mattered.

Maybe she should be weak. Maybe she should lean completely on this strange angel of a man and let him take care of everything. If it all worked out in the end and The Stallion was brought down, and she was free—

She wasn't going to go that far. She'd save thinking about freedom for after.

So she sat at the kitchen table with Jasmine, Tabitha and Alyssa eating breakfast and wondering what Jaime would be up to this morning. Would he be as exhausted as she was? Would he be thinking of her?

Foolish girl. But it nearly made her smile—to feel foolish and stupid. It was somehow a comfort to know she could be something normal. Stupid felt deliciously normal.

At Jasmine's sharply inhaled gasp, Gabby glanced up from her microwaved oatmeal. All the girls were looking wide-eyed at the entrance to the hallway.

Jaime stood there in his dedicated black, weapons strapped against his chest. Those sunglasses on his face. Gabby wondered if there was a purpose to always wearing them. So no one could see the kindness in his eyes. Because even in the dark she had to think that kindness would radiate off a man like him.

Since the girls seemed scared into silence, she nodded toward him. "Rodriguez."

"You know him?" Jasmine squeaked under her breath.

"He's The Stallion's new right-hand man." She looked back at Jaime and tried to work on the sarcastic sneer she sent most of the guards. "Right?"

Jaime's lips quirked and she could almost believe it was in pride, but she saw the disgust lingering underneath it.

Was she the only one who saw that? Based on the way Jasmine scooted closer to her, as though Gabby could protect her from the man, Gabby wondered.

"Senorita."

It took everything in her not to roll her eyes at him and smile at that exaggerated accent.

"You're wanted privately, Gabriella," he said with enough menace she should have been scared. She didn't think the little fissure of nerves that went through her was *fear.*

"But, please, finish your *desayuno.* I am nothing if not gracious with my time."

Gabby began to push her chair back, the crappy

packet oatmeal completely forgotten. But Jasmine's fingers curled around her arm and held on tight.

"Don't go, Gabby. Fight."

Gabby looked down at Jasmine, surprised that none of the women seemed to see the lack of threat underneath Jaime's act. But then, they didn't know what she knew. Maybe that made all the difference.

"It's all right. When have I ever not been able to handle myself?" She smiled reassuringly at… Sometimes she thought of the girls as her friends. Sometimes as her charges. And sometimes simply people she didn't really know. She didn't know what she felt today. But she patted Jasmine's arm before peeling the woman's fingers off her wrist. "I'll be back for lunch."

"Don't make promises you can't keep, *senorita*."

She shot Jaime a glare she didn't have to fake. He didn't have to make these women more scared. They already did that themselves.

She walked over to where Jaime stood in the entrance to the hallway. He made a grand gesture with his arm. "After you, Gabriella."

Again she had to fight to mask her face from amusement. He should go into acting once this was all over. The stage where his over-the-top antics might be appreciated.

As she began to walk down the corridor to her room, Jaime's hand clamped on her shoulder. Hot and hard and tight. She didn't have to feign the shiver or the wild worry that shot through her.

It wasn't comfortable that he could turn himself on and off so easily. It wasn't comfortable that, though she was intrigued by the man and convinced of his kindness, she didn't know him at all. Anything he'd told her so far could be lies.

When he acted like this other man, she could remember she shouldn't trust him. She couldn't believe everything he said. He could be as big a liar as The Stallion, and just as dangerous.

But they walked to her room with his hand clamped on her shoulder and somehow in the short walk it became something of a comfort. A calming presence of strength. She missed someone else having strength. True courage. Not the strength The Stallion or his guards exerted. Not that physical, brute force.

No, Jaime was full of certainty. Confidence. He was full of righteous goodness and she wanted to follow that anywhere it would lead.

She wanted to believe in righteous goodness again. That it was possible. That it could save her.

And what will happen after you're saved?

Jaime closed the door behind them, taking off his sunglasses and sliding them into his pocket. Immediately his entire demeanor changed. How did he do it? She opened her mouth to ask him but he seemed suddenly rushed.

"We don't have much time. There's a meeting in ten minutes and Layne will be sent to fetch me. I need… when he comes…"

She cocked her head because he didn't finish his sentence. He studied her and then he swallowed, almost nervously. "I'll have to, uh, do what I did the other day."

"The other day?"

"I'll try not to rip your shirt, but I'm going to need to…er, well, grab you."

"Oh." She let out a shaky breath, the white-hot fear of

that moment revisiting her briefly. "Right. Well, okay. But, uh, you know, not ripping my clothes would be preferred, if only because I don't have many."

His lips almost curved, but mostly something heavily weighted his mouth and him. She supposed he could play the part of Rodriguez easily enough in front of whoever walked through, but demonstrating the physical force expected of him? No. She couldn't imagine Jaime ever getting comfortable with that.

Maybe she was wrong. Maybe she was making everything up. Maybe he enjoyed scaring women and she was stupidly coping by turning him into a hero.

If a hero hadn't saved her in the past eight years, why would she think one would now?

"What do you know about his schedule? You said something about him staying certain times in certain places. Is he usually here, at this location, at this time?"

Gabby filtered through her memories. The ways she used to count days. Her many theories about The Stallion's yearly travel.

"Yes. He'd usually be here, but getting ready to leave." She tried to work out the days that would be left, but she'd stopped paying such close attention to the days and—

The thought hit her abruptly—a sharp blow to the chest as she met his intense brown gaze. "You know what day it is." She'd meant that to be a question, not the shaky accusation it had turned into.

He blinked down at her. Something in his face softened and then shuttered blank. "August 23, 2017."

She did the math in her head, trying to get through the shaky feeling of knowing what day it was. What actual day. For so long she'd known, but in the past two years she'd let it slide to seasons at most.

It was 2017. She'd been here for the entirety of the 2010s.

"Gabby." He touched her shoulder again, not the hard clamp of a guiding hand but a gentle laying of his palm to the slope of her arm. It was weird not to flinch. Weird not to want to. She wanted to lean into the strong presence. To the way he seemed to have everything under control…even when he didn't.

"August twenty-third. I would say usually he leaves for the southern compound on the twenty-sixth. I think. Around there. Never quite at the end of the month, but close."

Jaime smiled down at her, clearly pleased with the information.

When was the last time she'd seen a smile that wasn't sarcastic? When had anyone tried to smile at her reassuringly in eight long years? It hadn't happened.

She quashed the emotional upheaval inside her. Or, at least, she tried. It must've showed on her face, though, because he moved his hand up to her cheek, a rough, calloused warmth against her skin.

She knew he wanted to fix this for her. To promise her safety. But she didn't want to hear it. Promises… No, she wanted nothing to do with those.

Jaime was losing track of time and it wouldn't do. But she looked so sad. So completely overwhelmed by the weight of her existence here. He wanted to do something, anything, to comfort her. To take the tears in her eyes away, to take the despair on her face and stamp it out. He wanted to promise her safety and hope and a new life.

But he could promise none of those things. This was dangerous business, and they could easily end up dead. Both of them.

No matter that he would do everything in his power to not let that happen, it didn't mean it wasn't possible. It would be worse to promise something he couldn't deliver than to fail his mission.

"That means we'll have to wait about three more days. If he has me stay here while he goes to the southern compound, it gives me the opportunity to get this new information to my superiors. If he wants me to go with him, then I'll know where it is. Either way, we win."

"We may win the battle but not the war," she stated simply, resolutely. He wondered if she was just a little too afraid of getting hopes up herself.

He brushed his thumb down her cheek, even though it was the last thing he should've done. But though she was probably more gaunt than she would have been had she been living her actual life, though she was pale when the rich olive of her complexion should be sun-kissed, she was soft. And something special.

Her eyebrows drew together, but she wasn't looking at him. She was looking at the door and she mouthed something to him, but he couldn't catch what it was. She didn't hesitate. She grabbed him by the shoulders and pulled him close, her big brown eyes wide but determined. She mouthed the words again and this time he thought he caught them.

The door. Someone was at the door. Behind the door. That meant there was only one thing he could do. He choked back his complicated emotions and dropped his mouth to her ear.

"I'm going to kiss you. It won't be nice. The minute the door opens, shove me away with everything you've got. Understand?"

Her eyes were still wide, her hands on his shoulders. As if she trusted him.

She gave a nod and all he could do was say a little prayer that this would not be…complicated. But if someone was listening at the door, he had to prove he was Rodriguez and nothing more. That meant not being nice. That meant taking what he wanted whether it was what she wanted. And then, somehow, not getting lost in that. Humanity. His calling card. To keep his humanity.

But first… First he had to be Rodriguez. That meant he could not gently lower his mouth to hers. He had to take. He had to plunder.

And he had to stop talking to himself about it and do it.

He slid his arm around her waist and pulled her to him roughly. It was both regret and something far darker he didn't want to analyze that twined through him. He crushed his mouth to hers if only to stop his brain from moving in this hideous circle.

He focused on the fact that it wasn't supposed to be nice or easy. It was supposed to scare and intimidate. If she trembled, he was only doing his job. He was proving to everyone that he was Rodriguez—awful and mean, a broken excuse for a human being.

He thrust his tongue into her mouth and tried not to commit her taste to memory. But when was the last time he'd tasted a woman? Sweet and hot. Uncertain, and yet, brave with it. She let his tongue explore her mouth and she did not fight him.

He scraped his teeth along her plump bottom lip and

fought to remember who he really was. Not this man, but a man with a badge. A protector. A believer in law and order.

Gabby's fingers tensed on his shoulders and then relaxed. She did something that felt like a sigh against his mouth, and then he was being pushed violently back and away from sweet perfection.

He allowed himself two steps from the shove before stopping. He did everything to ignore the way his body trembled. Ignored the desperate erection pressing against his jeans. Ignored the inappropriate desire running through his blood. It was wrong and it was cruel but surely his body's natural reaction to that sort of thing after such a long absence.

Or so he told himself.

He didn't look at Gabby because it would surely unman him completely. Instead he turned to face the interruption with a sneer on his mouth.

Layne didn't need to know the hatred in his expression was for himself, not the interruption.

"You have the worst timing, *amigo*," he said, trying to eradicate the affectedness from his voice. "I grow weary of it."

Layne snorted. "You knew I was coming to fetch you at one. And here you are, yet again, clothed and being pushed around by a woman. Starting to question your strength, Rodriguez."

"Question all you want. Then test me. I'd love you to."

Layne merely crossed his hands over his chest. "Boss wants us now."

"*Sí.*" Jaime strode to the door, making sure never to look back at Gabby. The only reason Jaime paused in the hallway instead of going straight to The Stallion was to ensure Layne left Gabby's room without saying a damn thing. Because if that man said something to her...

Jaime balled his hands into fists. He had to get his temper under control. He wasn't pissed off at Layne. The man had done exactly what he was supposed to.

Jaime was pissed at himself.

Much like the afternoon before, Jaime let Layne lead him down the hall and outside. When they entered the shed this time, The Stallion's demeanor was calm rather than the unhinged anger of yesterday. He was sitting at his desk all but smiling.

"You're late. I suggest you get that kind of impulse under control. I demand timeliness in all things, gentlemen."

"Sí, senor."

"Now that that's been taken care of, we have our next target."

"The hypnotist?" Wallace asked from the corner.

"Yes, but not just her. A Texas Ranger has taken it upon himself to protect this young woman. I sent two men to follow them and to bring her to me." The Stallion reclined in his chair, his smile widening.

"What about the Ranger?" Jaime asked.

"He's of no use to us. I want her," The Stallion said with a sneer. "I hate when law enforcement try to get in my way. Bunch of useless pigs. We'll get rid of him and take the girl. The girl is *very* important." The Stallion's empty blue eyes zeroed in on Jaime. "There is a message I want you to deliver to our Gabriella, Rodriguez."

Jaime tried to maintain a blank expression, but it was hard with the addition of Gabby into the conversation.

That should be a warning in it of itself that he was letting himself get too wrapped up in this whole thing.

"The hypnotist has quite the interesting connection to our oldest guest."

"Connection?" Jaime repeated, hoping he covered the demand with enough confusion in his tone to make The Stallion think it was a language barrier issue.

"Natalie Torres is our hypnotist. Whatever Herman told her and this Ranger, I want to know it. But more, I want the girl." The Stallion turned his computer screen to face Layne and Jaime. "The resemblance. Do you see it?"

Jaime schooled himself into complete indifference. *"Sí."* The woman in the picture was more slight of build than Gabby and she had a softer chin and a sharper nose. But she had the same mass of curly black hair. The same big brown eyes.

"Tell our Gabriella her sister will be joining us soon. Make sure you mention how close she was to being the perfect woman. Perhaps her sister will fit the role she could not." The Stallion leaned back in his chair, smiling a self-satisfied smirk.

Jaime tried to match it, afraid it only looked like a scowl. But if he failed, The Stallion was too happy with himself to notice.

Chapter 7

Gabby knew it was beyond foolish to wait in the dark and hope Jaime would come to her again. She'd answered the questions he'd needed answered and he probably had henchman things to do.

Besides, she didn't really want to see him. Not after that kiss, which was hardly fair to call a kiss since it wasn't real. Like her life. It was a shallow approximation of something else. No matter how his mouth on hers had rioted through her like some sort of miracle.

She was clearly delirious or crazy. Maybe it was some sort of rescue-fantasy type thing that all kidnap victims succumbed to. She didn't know, and it wouldn't matter. Because it had all been fake. It had been a show.

Layne was… Gabby didn't know if "suspicious" was the right word, but he clearly didn't like Jaime and that was going to be dangerous. Because he would be watching him and making sure that whatever moves he made matched up with the man he was supposed to be. Making enemies as an undercover agent had to be incredibly dangerous and Layne was clearly Jaime's enemy.

Maybe she should think up something that could help Jaime in that regard. Surely there had to be something she'd witnessed or put together that would make all of this moot. Something he could tell his superiors that would make sure they felt like they had enough to prosecute.

Maybe if she told him the exact location of the holes she'd had to dig two summers ago, Jaime could find out what was buried there. Maybe that would be enough. Surely a dead body or two would be something.

If they could get through the next two days, and The Stallion left, surely Jaime could do a little figurative and literal digging.

She could make a map, like the one they'd made when trying to figure out the locations of the other compounds. But it would be difficult without paper. It would be difficult without being outside and working through landmarks. Maybe Jaime could sneak her out once The Stallion was gone.

She very nearly laughed at herself. Yes, after eight years she was going to sneak outside and bring The Stallion down with an undercover FBI agent. That was about as plausible as getting kidnapped, she supposed. But then what? She'd go back to her life? Eight years missing and she'd just waltz back into her old life? Twenty-eight with eight years of absolutely no education or work experience. Eight years without a *life*.

Maybe she could add digging shallow graves to her

résumé. *Excellent seamstress. Know just where to hide the drugs.*

This was such stupidity. Why was she even going down this road? The future had never held any appeal, and it still didn't. Jaime was here to do a job, and she'd do whatever he needed, but she certainly wasn't going to allow fantasies about escaping. About helping him or saving him from his gruesome undercover work.

The door opened and Gabby's heart jumped to her throat. Not as it had the night before. That night, she'd been scared. This night she was anything but.

She scrambled into a sitting position. But instead of staying in the dark, or saying her name, Jaime turned on the light. She blinked against the sudden brightness.

"I apologize," he said, his tone strangely bland, maybe a little tense. "I should've warned you."

"It's all right," she replied carefully, trying to read the blank expression on his face. He was tense and not like she'd ever seen him before. Because this wasn't his Rodriguez acting, and it wasn't exactly the honest and competent Jaime, either.

"Is everything all right?" she asked after he stood there in silence for ticking seconds.

"I want you to know that it will be. But there is some uncomfortable information I have to share with you."

Her heart sank, hard and sharp. She realized who this Jaime was. FBI Agent Jaime. A little aloof, delivering bad news. Probably how he delivered the news to a family that someone was dead.

"Uncomfortable?" she repeated, because surely if another one of her family members was dead it would be more than *uncomfortable.*

"If I could spare you this, I would," he said, taking a

step toward her, some of his natural-born compassion leaking through. "But I have to do what The Stallion asks right now."

A shiver of fear took hold of her, with deep awful claws, and she pressed herself into the corner of where her bed met the wall.

But this was Jaime, and he wasn't going to hurt her just because The Stallion told him to. She wanted to believe that. But for a moment she wondered if something in her would have to be sacrificed to take The Stallion down.

"It's just a message, Gabby," he said softly. "I won't hurt you. I promise. No matter what."

Part of her wanted to cry. Over the fact he could see through her so easily. The fact she could feel guilty over making him think that she thought he was going to hurt her. She wanted to cry at the unfairness of it all, and that was just…so seven years ago.

She straightened with a deep breath and fixed him with her most competent I-can-handle-anything expression. "Just tell me. Say it outright."

"The Stallion is after your sister."

Gabby thought she couldn't be surprised at what horrors The Stallion could do. After all, he'd gleefully informed her of her father's heart attack. Made it very clear she had been the cause. She knew The Stallion killed, and extorted, and hurt people.

He was after her sister. Her Nattie. There was no way to be calm in the face of it. She jumped off the bed and reached for Jaime.

"He doesn't have her," he said calmly. So damn calm. "And she's with a Texas Ranger who will do everything in his power to protect her—that, I know for sure."

"But he's after her. He's after *her*. Purposefully. Why? Why?"

Jaime took her by the shoulders, looking her directly in the eye. She could see all of that compassion and all of the right he wanted to do. No matter how she told herself not to believe in it. No matter how she told herself it was a figment of her imagination and that he couldn't really be good, she felt it. She *believed* it and knew it. No amount of reason seemed to change the fact that she trusted him.

"She has something to do with the dead messenger. I don't know the whole story yet, but I think she knows something. She's a hypnotist working with the Rangers, and if she's with the police… This could be… It could be a positive development. I know it doesn't feel like that, but this could be a positive."

"Is she…is she looking for me?" Gabby asked, ashamed that her voice wavered. But Nattie, a hypnotist, working with the Rangers? It didn't make sense. And Gabby was afraid of whatever the answer would be. If Natalie was looking for her, Nat had wasted eight years of her life. If she wasn't and this was some cosmic coincidence…

Jaime's strong hands squeezed her shoulders. Comforting. Strong. "I don't know. I don't know why your sister was in that interrogation room with The Stallion's messenger. I don't know why…" He shook his head, regret and frustration in the movement. "I wish I knew more, but I don't. But The Stallion wants you to know he's after your sister because he wants to break you."

Maybe if it had been her and The Stallion alone delivering his message, it would have succeeded in breaking her. But something about having Jaime there,

omething about feeling his strength and his certainty
hat this could work out…

"He won't break me," Gabby said firmly.

Jaime's mouth curved, one of those kind smiles that
ried to comfort her. It made her feel as though…as
hough there was hope. That was dangerous. Hope was
uch a dangerous thing here.

"You're an incredibly brave woman," Jaime said,
;iving her shoulders yet another squeeze.

The compliment warmed her far too much. Much
nore so than when the girls gave it to her. Then it felt
ike a weight, a responsibility, but when Jaime said it,
t sounded like an *asset*.

"It's not exactly brave to survive a kidnapping. You
lon't get much of a choice." No, choice was not some-
hing she had any of.

"There is always a choice. And the ones you've made
lave made this possible, Gabby. The things you remem-
)er, the theories you've come up with… You're mak-
ng this all the more possible. I know you don't believe
n endings, or maybe you can't see the possibility of
hem, but I am going to end this. One way or another,
ve will end him."

We. It was that final straw, a thing she couldn't fight.
[o be a "we" after so long of feeling like an I. Like the
)nly one who could do something or be something or
ight something.

"I believe you," she whispered. *Too much.* She
houldn't feel it, and she shouldn't say it. She should
eel none of the things washing through her at the way
ris face changed over her saying she believed him.

She shouldn't want to kiss this man she'd known for
wo days. She shouldn't want to feel what it would be

like for him to kiss her for real. Without weapons and
fake identities between them.

But there was something kind of beautiful about
being a kidnap victim in this case. That she had no life
to ruin, no self to endanger. Nothing to lose, really.
There was only her.

What choices did she have? Jaime thought she had
a choice, but he was wrong. She was nothing here. A
ghost at best. What she did or didn't do didn't truly
matter.

Even now, with The Stallion after Natalie, there was
nothing she could do except hope and pray the Texas
Ranger with her was a smart man, and a good man
and would protect Natalie the way Jaime was protecting Gabby right now.

Because no matter that he shouldn't, she knew that
was the decision he'd made. He would protect her above
himself.

Tentatively she touched her fingertips to the vee of
his chest between the straps of guns. She could feel underneath her fingertips the heavy beating of his heart.
A little fast, as though he had the same kinds of swirling emotions inside him that she had inside her. She
glanced up at him through her lashes, trying to read
the expression on his face. A face she'd memorized.
A face she thought she would always remember now.

There was enough of a height difference that she
would have to pull him down to meet her mouth.

It was such an absurd thought, the idea of wrapping
her arms around his neck and pulling his lush mouth
to hers. She smiled a little at the insanity of her brain.
And he smiled back.

"Thank you for that," he said.

She had lost the thread of the conversation and had no idea what he was thanking her for. All she could think about was the fact he was stepping away from her. Letting her shoulders go and making enough distance that her fingers fell from his chest.

"I should let you sleep," he said, backing slowly away and toward the door.

Gabby should leave it at that. She should let him go and she should sleep. But instead she shook her head.

"Please don't go. Stay."

It was wrong. It would be wrong to stay. It would be wrong to let her touch him. It would be wrong to let her belief in him change anything. It didn't matter. All that mattered was doing his duty. His duty included protecting her, not...

"There are things I could tell you," Gabby offered, for the first time in all their minutes together seeming nervous without fear behind it. "More things to help with making sure we can end this."

It didn't escape him the way she halted over the word "end." Like she still didn't quite believe a life outside these walls could exist, but she was trying to believe in me. For him? For herself? He had no idea.

He only knew that everything he should do was tangled up in things he shouldn't. Right and wrong didn't always make sense anymore, and it would take nothing at all for him to lose sight of the fact that anything more than a business partnership with her was a gross dereliction of duty. It was taking advantage of a woman who had already been taken so much advantage of.

But she wanted him to stay. She wanted him to stay. Not the other way around.

"I was just thinking before you got here that if I could tell you where the holes were that we dug two years ago, you might be able to connect it all together. If The Stallion does go in a few days, you'd be able to dig it up or something, and... Maybe that would be... Surely finding a body would be enough. Your superiors would want to press charges at that point, wouldn't they?"

The way she cavalierly talked about digging holes for bodies scraped him raw. It had always been hard to accept that there were people in the world who could hurt other people in such cruel and unusual ways. He'd always had a hard time reconciling the world as he wanted it—with law and order and good people—to the world that was with people who broke those laws and that order and had no good intentions whatsoever.

He didn't know what to do with the kinds of feelings that twisted inside him when he knew that nothing should have ever happened to her. She had been a normal girl, picking her father up from work, and she'd been kidnapped, measured and emotionally tortured into this bizarre world of being hidden away. Not touched, but put to work digging graves and hiding drugs.

"Don't you think?" she repeated, stepping closer to him.

She reached out to touch him and he sidestepped. He was too afraid if she touched him again, all of the certainty inside him would simply disappear and he would do something he would come to deeply regret. Something that would go against everything he'd been taught and everything he believed.

He was there to protect her, and that meant any deeper connection—physical or otherwise—was no ethical. It was screwing with a victim, and he wouldn't allow himself to fall that low. He had to keep a dispassionate consideration for her own good, not develop a passionate one.

"It's possible that evidence would be sufficient," he finally managed to say, his voice sounding raw. "But even if The Stallion goes to another compound, Layne and Wallace will still be here. Me doing any kind of digging is going to be hard to explain."

"Not if you told them that The Stallion ordered you to do it. He stays away for three months. So you'd have time before they'd tell him, wouldn't you?"

"I don't know how they communicate with him when The Stallion isn't here. I'm sure there'd be a way for them to keep tabs on me, and we both know that's exactly what Layne will be doing whether he's supposed to be or not."

"What about Wallace?" Gabby demanded.

Jaime scratched a hand through his hair. "I don't think Wallace is the brightest, but he's the most loyal. Layne is out to get me. Wallace will do whatever it takes to protect The Stallion. Either way, I don't think I have much hope of getting anything past them. At least, not anything tangible like digging."

Noticing her shoulders slump, he hurried on.

"But that doesn't mean it's not useful information. Maybe we can't use it right this second to shut this whole thing down, but every last shred of evidence we have when we finally get to that point is another nail in The Stallion's coffin. Men like him—powerful, wealthy men with connections… They're not easy to take down. We need it all. So it's still important."

"Right. Well. What else could I tell you that would help?" she asked hopefully.

A million things, probably, but he thought distance might do them both a bit of good. Too close, too alone, too much…bed taking up a portion of the room. "Don't you want to sleep?" Because he wanted to convince himself sleep was why he was thinking about beds.

She looked at him curiously. "I haven't had much to do in eight years except sleep. Day in and day out."

"Right, but…" He struggled to find a rebuttal and failed.

The curious look on her face didn't disappear and he couldn't exactly analyze why he suddenly felt bizarrely nervous. He'd been prepared for a lot of things as an undercover FBI agent, but not what to do with nerves over a woman.

A woman he'd known for all of two days. Who knew his secret now, and was thus her own dangerous weapon, but even in his most suspicious mode, he couldn't believe she'd turn him in. They were each other's best hope.

"Is it hard to switch back and forth?" she asked earnestly.

"Switch back and forth?" He'd been so lost in his own thoughts he was having a hard time following hers.

"Between the real you and this character you have to play?"

"Are you sure they're so different?" He'd tried to say it somewhat sarcastically, or maybe even challengingly, but the minute it came out of his mouth, he knew what he really wanted to hear was that she could tell the difference. That she absolutely knew he was two separate people. Because if she could see it, if this stranger could

ee it, then maybe it was true. Maybe he really hadn't
urned into someone else altogether.

"I've been nothing but Rodriguez for two years.
You're the only one who knows any different. I don't
now if it's easy. I only know that… This is the first
ime I've had to do it."

She stepped toward him again and he should side-
tep again. He knew he should. Everything about Gabby
alled to him on a deep cellular level, though, and he
idn't know how to keep fighting that call. There was
nly so much fighting a man could do.

She brushed her fingertips across his chest again.
Do you always wear these?"

Jaime looked down at the weapons strapped to his
hest. "I try to. Not a lot of trustworthy men around."

Her fingertips traced the leather strap, which was
trangely intimate considering the fact he never let any-
ne touch his weapons. It was a part of the persona he'd
reated. Slightly paranoid, always armed and always
angerous. No one touched his weapons.

Yet, he was letting her do just that. Touching them in
ays she couldn't begin to understand he was touched.

"You could take them off in here." She looked up at
im through the long spikes of her eyelashes.

It was tempting enough to lose his breath for a mo-
nent. "Wouldn't be smart," he rasped, surprised how
isceral the reaction was to the thought of not being
trapped to the hilt with guns and ammo. What would
hat feel like? He'd forgotten.

"Right. Of course not." She offered him a smile,
omething he supposed was an attempt at comfort, and
nat, too, was out of the ordinary. Something he didn't
emember.

"I have to go."

"Why?"

He should lie. Tell her he had important henchman duties to see to, but the truth came out instead. "I can't stay in my own skin too long. It's too hard to go back otherwise."

Then she did the most incomprehensible thing of all. She rolled up on her tiptoes and brushed her lips across his cheek. His cheek. Soft and sweet. A soothing gesture. She came back down to be flat-footed and gave him a perilous smile.

"Then you should go. Good night, Jaime."

That, he knew, to be a challenge. He should correct her. Tell her that she absolutely had to call him Rodriguez. Lecture her until she wished he'd never come into her room.

Instead he returned her smile and said, "Good night, Gabby," before he left.

Chapter 8

Gabby didn't know the last time she'd felt quite so light. Probably never here. It was probably warped.

Maybe if Jaime had showed up in her first year, it wouldn't be quite so easy to fall into comfort or friendship or even pseudo-flirting. Maybe there would have been enough of the real world and non-ghost Gabby to keep her distance or to keep her head straight.

But she had been here eight years, and all of those things before ceased to exist. All she had was these past eight years, and they had been dark and dreary and horrible. It was nice to have something to feel *light* about.

It didn't mean she wasn't worried about Natalie. It didn't mean she was happy to be kidnapped. It didn't mean a lot of things, but it did give her the opportunity to feel somewhat relaxed. To breathe. To smile as she thought of Jaime's bristled cheek under her mouth.

She made breakfast for the girls, which she did every

Sunday. Even after she'd stopped counting the days, she made sure to know what days were Sundays so she could do this for them. Give them something, if not to look forward to, something that felt like this was home and not just prison.

She didn't know if any of them still believed in home. She didn't. This was a prison no matter what, but sometimes it was nice to feel like it wasn't.

"We've been talking," Alyssa announced with no preamble, which was her usual way of broaching a subject. She had only been here for two years and one of the illuminating things about being imprisoned with other people was the realization that victims could be good and bad people themselves.

Alyssa was a bit of a jerk. Had been from the first moment, continued to be these two years later. She was too blunt and always abrasive, never kind to the softer girls. In real life, Gabby thought she might have ended up punching the woman in the nose.

But this wasn't real life.

"What about?" Gabby asked pleasantly, as if she cared.

"Rodriguez and his interest in you."

That certainly caught her off guard, but she feigned interest in her breakfast. "Interest?"

"He's traipsing in and out of your room at all hours."

Gabby slowly turned to face the trio of women in the exact same situation as her. They should be friends and yet all she felt like was an irritable babysitter. "Are you watching me, Alyssa?" Gabby asked, not bothering to soften the threat in her voice.

She wouldn't let anyone figure out what was going on, mostly because she didn't think the girls could hack it, but also because she didn't trust any of them. Perhaps same circumstances should have made them something like sisters, but when you were struck by senseless tragedy it was damn hard to remember to be empathetic toward anyone else.

"I've been watching *him*," Alyssa said with a sniff. "Are you sleeping with him?"

Gabby blinked. She couldn't tell if it was jealousy or fear or *what* that sparked Alyssa's interest. She only knew she was tired. Tired of navigating a world that didn't make any sense, and yet she barely remembered one that did.

She sighed. "The Stallion has *gifted* me to Rodriguez. I'm supposed to do whatever he wants." She almost smiled thinking about how surprised The Stallion would be to discover what Jaime really wanted.

Alyssa's eyes narrowed at the information but Jasmine gasped in horror and Tabitha looked frightened.

"Why you?" Alyssa demanded.

"I'm sorry, did you want to be offered up as payment for a job well done to any bad guy who walks through?" Gabby snapped.

Alyssa fidgeted, her expression losing a degree of its hostility. "Will it get you out?"

Gabby didn't know what to say. What little pieces of her heart that were left cracked hard for Alyssa thinking there was any possible way of getting out. And then there was the very fact that if anyone was ever going to get them out, it would be Jaime.

But not like Alyssa meant. "No," Gabby replied flatly. "Nothing we do for them gets us anything. We're things to them, at best. Certainly not people."

"What do we do then?" Jasmine asked, her voice wobbly and close to tears.

"We wait for him to die," Tabitha said morosely, lowering herself to a seat.

Jasmine sniffled and sat next to Tabitha, but Alyssa still stood, staring at the girls and then at Gabby. "Maybe we hurry that along."

Gabby's eyebrows winged up. It wasn't that she'd never wondered what it might take to kill The Stallion and escape on her own. It was just… She never thought the other women would have the same thoughts.

But Alyssa's face was grim and impassive, and the other girls were contemplatively silent.

"There's four of them, though," Tabitha offered in a whisper, as though they were plotting and not merely… thinking aloud.

"And four of us," Gabby murmured. A few days ago she would have shut this conversation down. She would have reminded them all that there was no hope and they might as well make the best of their fates.

She would have been wrong. Wrong to squash their hope, and their fight, like she'd been wrong to squash her own.

Jaime had brought it back, had reminded her that life did in fact exist outside these walls. Natalie, on the run. Blue skies. Freedom.

A dangerous kind of hope built in her chest. An aching, desperate need for that freedom she'd tried to forget existed. Even as Jaime had talked of ends and bringing him down, she had tried to fight this feeling away.

But it was all his fault she'd lost the reserves, because he'd appeared out of nowhere and trusted her in his mission. He'd somehow crashed into her world and opened her up *to* life again, not just existence.

"How would we do it?" Tabitha asked, her eyes darting around the kitchen nervously.

Alyssa eyed Gabby still. "Rodriguez wears a lot of guns, and if you are a gift, it means he gets awfully close to you."

"I couldn't steal his gun without him noticing."

Alyssa shrugged easily. "That doesn't mean you couldn't get it and shoot before he had a chance to notice."

The three women looked at her expectantly and she wondered if they hadn't all gone a little crazy. "Or, he stops me and shoots me first."

Alyssa raised a delicate shoulder. "Maybe it'd be worth the risk."

"Then you risk it," Jasmine said, surprising Gabby by doing a little standing up for her. "It was your idea, after all."

This time Alyssa smirked. "But Gabby is the one with access to his *guns*."

Gabby couldn't think of what to say to that. She had access to a lot of things, but she couldn't and didn't trust Alyssa with the information, and she wasn't sure she could trust Jasmine or Tabitha, either. All it would take was one woman to slip up or break and Jaime could end up dead.

It wasn't safe to let them into this, and it wasn't fair to refuse these women some hope, some power.

Leave it to Alyssa to make an already complicated, somewhat dangerous, situation even more twisted.

Gabby took a deep breath and tried to smile in some appropriate way. Scheming or interested or whatever, not irritated and nervous. Not…guilty. "I'll see what I can do, okay?"

"Don't put yourself in harm's way, Gabby," Jasmine said softly. "What would we do without you?"

Alyssa snorted derisively, but Gabby pretended she didn't notice and smiled reassuringly at Jasmine. "I'll be careful," she promised.

A whole lot of careful.

Jaime stood in the corner of The Stallion's well-lit shed while the man paced and raged at the news Wallace had just delivered.

"How did they get away? How did my men get arrested? I demand answers." He pounded on his desk, the dolls shaking perilously, like little train wrecks Jaime couldn't stop staring at.

"I don't know," Wallace said, shrinking back. "I guess the Ranger tangled 'em up with the local cops."

The Stallion whirled on Wallace. "Who is this Ranger?"

"Er, his name's V-Vaughn Cooper. With the unsolved c-crimes unit. Uh—"

Jaime lost track of whatever The Stallion's sharp demand was at the name. Vaughn Cooper. He *knew* Vaughn Cooper. Ranger Cooper had taught a class Jaime had taken in the police academy.

Christ.

"Rodriguez." It took Jaime a few full seconds to engage, to remember who and where he was. Not a kid in the police academy. Not an FBI agent. Rodriguez.

"¿Senor?" he offered, damning himself for his voice coming out rusty.

"No. Not you. Not yet." The Stallion muttered, wild

eyes bouncing from Jaime to the other men. "Wallace. Layne. You find them. You track them down. The girl, you bring to me. The Ranger, I don't give a damn about. Do what you will."

Layne grinned a little maniacally at that and Jaime knew he had to do something. He couldn't let Cooper get caught in some sort of ambush. He couldn't let a man who'd reminded them all to, above all else, maintain their humanity, get killed. Especially with Gabby's sister.

"*Senor*, perhaps you could allow me to take care of this problem." He smiled blandly at Layne. "I might be better suited to such a task."

The Stallion gave him a considering once-over. "Perhaps." He paced, looking up at his collection of dolls then running a long finger down the line of one's foot.

Jaime barely fought the grimace.

"No, I want you here, Rodriguez. We have things to discuss."

That wasn't exactly a comfort, though he did remind himself that as long as he was here, Gabby was safe. He wasn't so sure Layne would leave her be if Jaime wasn't around, even with The Stallion's distaste over hurting women.

Jaime assured himself Ranger Cooper knew what he was doing, prayed he knew what he was up against. If the man had outwitted the first two of The Stallion's men, surely he could outwit Wallace and Layne.

"You have three days to bring her to me. The consequences if you fail will be dire. I would get started immediately."

The other two men rushed to do their boss's bidding, hurrying out of the shed, heads bent together as they strategized.

Jaime remained still, trying to hide any nerves, any concern, with cool disinterest.

The Stallion turned to him, studying him in the eerie silence for far too long.

"I hope you're being careful with our Gabriella," The Stallion said at last.

"Careful?" Jaime forced himself to smile slyly. He spread his arms wide, palms up to the ceiling. "Care was not part of our bargain, *senor.*"

The Stallion waved that away. "No, I'm not talking about being gentle. I'm talking about being *careful.* Condoms and whatnot."

Jaime stared blankly at the man. Was he…giving him sort of a sex-ed talk?

"Women carry diseases, you know." The Stallion continued as though this was a normal topic of conversation. "And she's not a virgin, according to her."

"I…" Jaime couldn't get the rest of the words out of his strangled throat. The "according to her" should be some kind of comfort, but why had the man been quizzing her on the state of her virginity? Why did he think Jaime—er, Rodriguez, would care?

"Perfect in every way, save for that," The Stallion said, shaking his head sadly. "Oh, well, then there were her toes."

"Her…toes?"

"The middle one is longer than the big toe. Unnatural." The Stallion shuddered before running his fingers over his dolls' feet again.

Jaime knew he didn't hide his bewilderment very well, but it was nearly impossible to school away. What on earth went through this man's head? He ran corporations. Jaime doubted very much anyone in Austin knew Victor Callihan was really a madman. Perhaps eccentric, somewhat scarce when it came to social situations, but he was still *known*. Somehow he could hide all this…whatever it was, warped in his head.

"Regardless, if you are to be my right-hand man, and insist upon indulging in these baser instincts inferior men have, I expect you to keep yourself clean."

"I… *Si*." What the hell else was there to say?

"Good. Now, I held you back because I have some concerns I didn't want to broach in front of Layne and Wallace. I think we've been infiltrated."

There was a cold burst of fear deep within Jaime's gut, but on the outside he merely lifted an eyebrow. "Where?"

"Here," The Stallion said grimly, tapping his desk. "I don't believe that Ranger was smart enough to outwit my men unless he was tipped off. This is why I sent Layne and kept you with me."

"I do not follow."

The Stallion sighed exhaustedly. "You're lucky you're such a good shot, but I suppose I wouldn't want anyone too smart under me. How could I trust them to follow my lead?" He shook his head. "Anyway, if Layne and Wallace fail, I will be assured it's one of them, and they'll be taken care of. If they succeed, then I know my suspicions are wrong and we can carry on."

Jaime inclined his head and breathed a very quiet sigh of relief.

"If they fail, you will be in charge of punishing them suitably." The Stallion frowned down at his desk. "I don't like to alter my schedule…"

"If there's somewhere you need to be, I can be in charge here. I can mete out whatever punishments necessary, gladly."

The Stallion made a noise in the back of his throat. "This situation is priority number one. I need to do some investigating into this Ranger, and I want to be here for the arrival of Gabriella's sister to do my initial testing. For now, you're free to fill your time with our Gabriella. Get it out of your system before her sister gets here, if you would, please."

Jaime bowed faintly as if in agreement.

"You did give her my message, didn't you?" The Stallion asked, his gaze sharp and assessing.

"Sí."

"And how did she react? Were there tears?"

The Stallion sounded downright ecstatic, so Jaime lied. *"Sí."*

He sighed happily. "I should have done it myself, though I do like you telling her and then doing whatever it is you must do with her. Yes, that's a nice punishment for the little slut."

Jaime bit down on his tongue, hard, a sharp reminder that defending anyone wasn't necessary, no matter how much it felt it was.

"May I go, *senor*?" he asked through clenched teeth.

The Stallion inclined his head. "Do what you can to make her cry again. Yes, I like the idea of proud Gabriella crying every night. And when her sister comes… well, I'll bear witness to that."

All Jaime could think as he left the shed was *like hell he would.*

Chapter 9

Gabby didn't see Jaime all day. She'd expected him—
to pop into her room, to come into the kitchen at dinner,
something. But she'd eaten with the girls nearly an hour
ago and she'd been in her room ever since...waiting.

She shouldn't be edgy, yet she couldn't help herself.
The more time she had alone—or worse, with the other
girls—the more her mind turned over the possibility of
actually killing a man.

Actually escaping.

But she had Jaime for that, didn't she? Alyssa's cold
certainty haunted Gabby, though. Should she have
thought of this before? Not just as angry outbursts, but
as a true, honest-to-God possibility?

Of course, this was the first time in eight years
Gabby'd had access to anything that might act as a vi-
able weapon. If she could count Jaime and his guns as
accessible.

Where was he? And what was he doing? Had The Stallion sent him on some errand? Was he gone for good?

Her heart stuttered at that thought. Somehow it had never occurred to her that something might happen to him or that he might get sent elsewhere, but Layne and Wallace, and the other three men who sometimes guarded them were forever leaving for intervals of time. Some never to return.

Oh, God, what if he never came back and she'd missed all her chances? What if she was stuck here forever? What if all that hope had been a worthless waste of—

Her door inched open and Jaime stepped inside, sunglasses covering his eyes, weapons strapped to his chest. Strong and capable and *there*.

She very nearly ran to him, to touch him and assure herself he was real and not a figment of her imagination.

The only thing that stopped her was the fact that in three short days she'd come to rely on this man, expect this man, and in just a few minutes she'd reminded herself why she couldn't let that happen.

He could be shipped out. He could be executed. Anything—*anything* could happen to him and if she didn't make a move to protect herself and Jasmine, Alyssa and Tabitha…they'd all be out in the cold.

She tamped down the fear that made her nauseous. Jaime seemed to remind her of the best and worst things. Hope. Freedom. An end to this hell. Then how it could all be taken away.

"I have a bit of good news for you," he said, slipping his glasses off and into his pocket.

Some of the fear coiled inside her released of its own

accord. It was so hard to fear when she could see his dark brown eyes search her face as if she held some answer for him. Some comfort.

"Okay," she said carefully, because she wasn't sure she had any for him.

"Your sister and the Texas Ranger she's with escaped The Stallion's first round of men."

"First…round."

"And I know the Texas Ranger she's with. He's a good man. A good police officer."

"But he's sending another round of men," Gabby said dully, because though she'd not spent a lot of time with The Stallion, she knew his habits. She knew what he did and what he saw. When he saw a challenge, he didn't back down.

"Layne and Wallace," Jaime confirmed, crossing to where she sat on her bed. He crouched in front of her and, after a moment, took her hands in his. "I tried to get him to send me, but he thinks Layne is leaking things to the cops."

Gabby jerked her gaze up from where it had been on their joined hands. "He thinks there's a leak," she gasped. That meant Jaime was in danger. That meant once The Stallion figured out it wasn't Layne, he'd figure out it was Jaime and then—

Jaime squeezed her hands. "I don't actually think he thinks that because of anything I've done. He thinks it too convenient that Ranger Cooper and your sister outwitted those men, but he's underestimating the Ranger."

"Maybe he's underestimating my sister."

Jaime smiled, and not even one of those comforting ones. No, this seemed closer to genuine. A real feeling, not one born of this place. It smoothed through her like a warm drink on a cold day, which she barely remembered as a thing, but his smile made her remember.

"Maybe that is it. He certainly underestimates you."

"But you don't." She touched his cheek, brushed her fingertips across his bristled jaw. Five seconds in his company and she'd forgotten all the admonitions she'd just made to herself. But in his presence—calm and strong and comforting—she forgot everything.

Her gaze dropped to the weapons strapped to his chest and she sighed. Well, not everything. Alyssa's words were still there, scrambling around in her brain.

She dropped her fingers from his face to his holster of weapons. She traced her hand over a gun. She didn't know anything about guns. He'd have to somehow teach her to fire one, and it wasn't as if she'd be able to practice anywhere.

But maybe one of the other girls knew how to shoot. If she got one to them…?

She sighed, overwhelmed. This was why she'd given up making a plan. Too many variables. She could analyze a problem, remember a million facts and figures, puzzle together disparate pieces, but when it came to all the unknown fallout of her possible actions…

It made her want to curl up in her bed and cry.

"What's wrong?"

She had to put it all away. Emotion had never gotten her anything in this place. Unless it was anger. Unless it was fight.

"Would they notice?" she forced herself to say strongly and evenly. "If you gave one of these to me, would anyone notice it missing?"

His expression changed into something she didn't recognize. Into something almost like suspicion. "You want one of my guns?" he asked, moving out of his crouch and into a standing position. He folded his arms across his chest and looked down at her, and it was a wonder anyone who really paid attention didn't see the way his demeanor screamed *law enforcement*.

"What do you want to do with it?" he asked carefully, the same way she thought he might interrogate a criminal.

She wasn't sure what she'd expected, but she didn't like *that*. Trust was a two-way street, wasn't it? Didn't he have to trust her for her to trust him?

"What's going on, Gabby?"

She looked away from his dark brown gaze, from the arms-crossed, FBI-agent posture. She looked away from the man she didn't know. Hard and very nearly uncompromising.

She shouldn't tell him about the girls' plan. It felt like a violation of privacy, and yet, if she kept it from him he could just as easily be hurt, or accidentally hurt one of the girls.

It was a no-win situation, which should feel familiar. She'd been living "no win" for eight years.

Then his finger traced her cheek, so feather-light, before he paused under her chin, tilting her head up so she would look at him.

She was tired of hard things and no-win situations and *this*. But Jaime… It was as though he looked at her as neither just another kidnapping victim nor as the strong leader, not as anything but herself.

"What do you know about me, Jaime?" she asked, not even sure where the question came from but knowing she needed an answer. She needed something.

He cocked his head, but he didn't ask her to explain

herself. Instead he pulled her up into a standing position, gripping her shoulders and staring down into her eyes. Everything about him intense and strong and just...*him*.

"I know you're brilliant. That you're beyond strong. I know you love your family, and it eats at you that you can't protect Natalie from this. I know you've been hurt, and you're tired. But I also know you'll endure, because there is something inside of you that cannot be killed. No matter what that man does. You're a fighter."

It was a torrent of words. Positive attributes she'd thought about herself, questioned about herself. All said in that brook-no-argument, no-nonsense tone, his gaze never leaving hers. She knew he had to be a good liar to have survived undercover for two years, and yet she couldn't believe this was anything but the truth.

Jaime saw who she was—not what she'd done or how long she'd been here. He saw her. In all the different ways she was.

"The girls want to—" Gabby swallowed. She had to trust him. She did, because he was her only hope, and because he saw her like no one else had in eight years. "They want me to try to get a gun from you, and then go after The Stallion."

Jaime's forehead scrunched. "They can't do that."

"Why not?" she demanded, something like panic pumping through her. She wanted to be out of there. She wanted a *life*. Even if it wasn't her old life, she wanted...

Him. She wanted him in the real world, and she wanted her.

"I'm here to take him down, Gabby. I'm here to make sure he goes to jail, not just for justice, but so we can put an end to all the evil this man is doing. We can't shoot him in a blaze of glory. That just leaves a power vacuum someone else can take."

"I don't care," she whispered, feeling too close to tears for even her own comfort. But she didn't care in the least. The Stallion was going after her sister and she just wanted him *dead*.

"I understand that. I do. But—"

"My freedom isn't your fight." She sat back down on the bed, slipping through his strong grasp. He could see her. Maybe he even felt some of the things she felt, but her fight was not his fight.

He crouched again, not letting her pull into herself. He took her hands and he waited, silent and patient, until she raised her wary gaze to his.

"It's part of my fight," he said, not just earnestly but vehemently, fervently. "It's a part I don't intend to fail on. I will get you out of here. I will. But I need to do my job, too. It is why I'm here."

A tear slipped out, and then another, and she felt so stupid for crying in front of him, but everything ached in a way she hadn't let it for a very long time.

He brushed one tear off with his thumb then he leaned forward, his mouth so close she inhaled sharply, drowning a little in his dark eyes, wanting to get lost in the warm strength of his body.

"Don't cry," he said on a whisper before he brushed his mouth against another tear, wiping it from her jaw with his mouth.

He pulled his face away from hers, shaking his head. "I shouldn't—"

But she didn't want his shouldn'ts and she didn't want him to pull away, so she tugged him closer and covered his mouth with hers.

* * *

He'd dreamed of this. Gabby's mouth under his again. Not because he was trying to be someone else. Not because he was trying to convince *anyone* he was taking what he wanted.

No, he'd dreamed of her mouth touching his because they'd both wanted it, not from anything born of this place. On the outside. Free. Themselves. He'd imagined it, unable to help himself.

Even having dreamed of it, even in the midst of allowing it to happen in the here and now, he knew it was wrong. Not just against everything he'd ever been taught in his law-enforcement training, but against things he believed.

She was a victim. No matter how strong she was. No matter how much he felt for her. She was still a victim of this place. Kissing her, drowning in it, was like taking advantage of her. It was wrong. It flew in the face of who he was as an FBI agent, as a law-enforcement agent.

But he didn't stop. Couldn't. Because while it went against all those things he was, it didn't go against who he was. Deep down, this was all he wanted.

Her tongue traced his mouth and she sighed against him. Melting, leaning. Crawling under all the defenses he wound around himself. False identities. Badges and pledges. Weapons and uniforms and lies.

He should pull away. He should stop this madness.

He curled his fingers into her soft hair. He angled her head so that he could taste her better. He ignored every last voice in his head telling him to stop. Because she was touching him. Tracing the line of his shoulders. Pressing her hand to his heart. She scooted closer, brushing her chest against his.

She whispered his name against his mouth. His real name. And he wanted to be able to be that. He wanted to be able to be the man who could give her everything she wanted and everything she deserved.

But he wasn't that man. Not here. Not now. He couldn't even let her have fantasies of ending The Stallion's life.

He mustered all of his strength and all of his righteous rightness. Somehow...*somehow* he did the thing he least wanted to do and pulled away from her.

Her breath was coming in heavy pants, as was his. Her dark eyes were unfathomably warm, her lips wet from his mouth. He wanted to sink himself there again and again until they thought of nothing but each other.

"Jaime," she said on a whisper.

"We can't do this. I can't..." He tried to pull away but her arms were strong around him.

"Do you know how long it's been since someone's kissed me? Since I *wanted* someone to kiss me?"

"Gabby," he returned, pained. Desperate—for her and a way this could be right.

"I know it isn't the time or the place. I know it isn't prudent or whatever, but I have lived here for eight years without anything I wanted. I survived here without anyone touching me kindly, comfortingly or wanting to. Without anyone seeing me as anything other than a *thing*. If I'm going to believe in an *end*, I have to believe I can go back to being something real, not just this...ghost of a person."

"Getting involved with the victim is not an acceptable—"

She pulled away from him quickly and with absolutely no hesitation. She turned her head away, shaking it. He'd stepped in it, badly.

"I know you don't want to see yourself as a victim," he began, trying to resist the impulse to reach for her. "But in my line of work—"

"I understand."

But she didn't understand. She was angry and she didn't understand at all. "I do know how you feel," he offered softly.

She rolled her eyes.

"It hasn't been eight years, but two years is a long time to go without anyone seeing you for who you are. There aren't a lot of hugs and nice words for the bad guy, Gabby. Even the *other* bad guys don't like me because I've been slowly taking them down so that I could be the one next to The Stallion. It isn't all fun and games over here."

"Are you asking me to feel sorry for you?" she asked incredulously.

"Of course not." He raked a hand through his hair, trying to figure out what he *was* trying to ask of her. "I'm saying that I understand. I'm saying that I would love to give you what you want. I would…"

"I'm just a victim. And you can't get involved with the victim. I get it."

"You don't, because if you thought it was that simple… I have never in my entire career even considered kissing someone who was involved with a case I was part of. I have never once been unable to stop thinking about a woman who had anything to do with *work*. I have never been remotely—*remotely*—tempted to go against everything I believe. Until you."

That seemed to dilute at least some of her anger. She still didn't look at him, which was maybe for the best. He wasn't sure if she looked at him that he'd be able to stay noble.

Because her soft lips tempted him. And the defiant look in her eyes... Everything about her was very near impossible to resist.

He hadn't been lying that he'd never wanted someone the way he wanted her. Even if he took the police part out of it. No woman, no matter how short or long a period of time they had been in his life, had made him feel the way Gabby made him feel.

He wondered if that wasn't why she was upset. Not that he'd stopped the kiss, but that she thought he didn't see her the way he did.

She'd asked what he knew about her, and he'd been completely honest and open about all the things he *knew* she was. Maybe he shouldn't have been, but she was everything he'd said, and he knew being attracted to her, caring about her, wasn't as simple as whatever label a therapist would likely put on it.

It was Gabby, not the situation, that called to him. But the situation was what made everything far too complicated.

"I can't give you a weapon," he offered into her stubborn silence.

"All right," she said, and she didn't sound angry. She sounded tired. Very close to giving up. But then she straightened her shoulders and inhaled and exhaled slowly. Then she met his gaze, fierce and strong.

"I have to have a story for the girls... I have to... They want out, Jaime." Something in her face changed, a kind of empathetic pain. "I used to be able to tell them it wasn't any use to think about getting out, but we can't keep doing this. Alyssa is right. Staying here isn't worth being alive for."

"So what kept you alive for so long?" he asked because he couldn't imagine. He couldn't *fathom*.

"My family, I guess. Daddy died because of his guilt over me. The least I could do was still be alive. The least I could do was get back somehow." She looked down at her hands, clenched in her lap. "I thought I'd given up that hope, but I don't know. Maybe I just convinced myself I had."

He covered her clenched fists with his own. "I'm going to get you back to your family." God, he'd do it. Come hell or high water. If he had to *die* first, he would do it.

"Not so long ago you said you couldn't promise me that."

"Not so long ago I was doing everything by the book." He believed in the book, but he also…he also believed in this woman. "You're right. Things can't stand. It's been too long. We can't keep waiting around. We have to make something happen."

She finally looked at him, eyebrows raised. "Really?"

"As soon as we get word that your sister has escaped Layne and Wallace, we'll…" It was against everything he'd been taught, everything he was supposed to do, but he couldn't keep telling Gabby to wait when he could be getting her out.

"Once we know your sister is safe, we'll figure out an escape plan. You can't tell the others who I am but… Maybe you can tell them I'm sympathetic, if you trust them to keep that to themselves. Tell them that if you work on me for a few days, you might actually be able to get a weapon from me. If anything slips up to The Stallion or anyone else, I'll tell him it's part of my plan. If you get the girls to stand down a few days. I don't want to risk getting out and something happening to your sister."

"Why?" she asked, still studying him, her forehead creased.

"Because you love her."

Something in her face changed and he couldn't read it. But she moved. Closer to him. No matter that he should absolutely avoid it, he let her kiss him again.

Slow and leisurely, as if they had all the time in the world. As if it was just the two of them. Gabby and Jaime. As if that were possible.

And because the thought was so tempting, so comforting in this world of dark, horrible things, he let it linger far too long.

Chapter 10

Gabby had kissed four men in her life. Ricky, of course. Corey Gentry on a dare in eighth grade. A guy at a frat party—she didn't know his name—and now Jaime.

In the past eight years she would've considered this part of her dead. The part that could care about kissing and touching. The part of her brain that could go from that to sex.

It was a miracle and a joy to still have the same kind of desire she'd had before. It was a miracle and a joy to be kissing Jaime, his lips so soft, his touch nearly reverent. As though she were something of a miracle to him.

Ricky had never kissed her like this and she'd been convinced she loved him. But he'd been a boy and she'd been a girl. They'd been selfish and Jaime... Jaime was anything but selfish. A good man. A strong and honorable man.

That somehow made the kiss more exciting, knowing he thought it was wrong but couldn't quite help himself. Knowing he felt the same simmering feelings and that he didn't think it was because of their situation. It was because of who they were.

Gabby. Jaime.

She thought she hadn't known who she was anymore, but she was learning. Jaime was showing her pieces of herself she'd forgotten. He was bending his strict moral code for her and that, above all else, spoke to a feeling most people wouldn't believe could happen in three days. She herself wasn't sure she'd believed something like this could grow in three days.

But here she was feeling things for a man that she'd never felt before. She wanted to be able to make sacrifices for him, and she wanted him safe, and she wanted him *hers*.

He pulled away slightly and it was another wondrous thing that every time he pulled away she could *feel* how hard it was for him to do so.

"I have a meeting with The Stallion," he said, his voice very nearly hoarse. "I can't be late again or things could get ugly." He tried to smile, probably to make it sound less intimidating, but it didn't work.

She clutched him harder. "Come back," she blurted. She said it spontaneously, but she still meant it. She wanted him to come back. She wanted more than a kiss.

"So we can…" He cleared his throat. "Plan, right?"

She smiled at him because it was cute he would even think that. "We can plan, too." She watched him swallow as though he were nervous. She didn't mind that the least little bit.

"Gabby."

"Come back tonight. Spend the night with me."

It was a wonderful thing to know he wanted to. That though he was resisting, something deep inside him wanted to or he wouldn't question it at all. It was so against his inner sense of right and wrong, but he wouldn't fight with that if he didn't truly want her.

"It wouldn't be right. To… It would be taking advantage," he said, as though trying to convince himself.

"You're worried about me taking advantage of you?" she asked as innocently as she could manage.

He laughed, low and rumbly. It struck her that this was the first time she'd heard it, possibly one of the very few times she'd heard nice laughter in *years*.

"Gabby, you've been through hell for eight years."

As if she needed the reminder. "I guess that's all the more reason to know exactly what I want," she said resolutely. She knew what she wanted and if she could have it… If she could have him… She'd do it now. She wouldn't waste time. "I want you, Jaime."

He inhaled sharply, but he didn't say anything. "I have to go," he said, getting to his feet.

She gave him a nod, but she thought he'd be back. She really thought he'd return to her. Because he felt it, too. He had to feel it, too. No matter how warped she sometimes felt, this was the most real she'd felt in eight years. The most honest and the most true. The most certain she could survive getting out of this hell. That she wanted to.

That settled inside her like some weird evangelical itch. She wanted to be able to give that same feeling to the other girls. They deserved something, too. Something to believe in. They hadn't spent as much time as her, no, but they had spent enough. They had all spent enough.

Jaime was willing to break the rules and get them there, as soon as Natalie was safe. Not because that helped him any, but because she loved her sister and he knew that meant something to her.

Gabby left her room. She didn't know where exactly Jaime had gone, but she wasn't after him quite now. First, she wanted to find Alyssa. She wanted everyone to know that she was on board, maybe not in the way they thought, but regardless. They were going to find a way out of this.

She walked into the common room, which was basically their workroom opposite the kitchen and dining area.

Tabitha and Jasmine were sitting on the dilapidated couch working on a project The Stallion had assigned them a few days ago. Gabby realized she'd forgotten all about the project and what her role in it was supposed to have been. But ever since Jaime had arrived, it hadn't even occurred to her. Then again, she supposed to The Stallion her job now was to be payment to Jaime. Though she was surprised the girls hadn't asked her for help.

Jasmine looked at her first, eyes wide. She looked from Alyssa, who was riffling through drawers frantically in the kitchen, back to Gabby.

"Did you…?" she whispered then trailed off.

Gabby nodded. "I didn't get a gun or anything, but I think I can. If you give me some time." There was hope. She needed to give them hope.

Alyssa slammed a cabinet door closed and stormed over to them. "What does that mean?" she demanded.

"It means I couldn't quite sneak a weapon off of him, but he seemed a little…sympathetic almost. Like if I keep feeding him our sob story he might…"

"What you really need to do is willingly sleep with him, not fight him off," Alyssa said flatly, giving her a once-over. "When he thinks you're not fighting him, it'll give you time to grab his gun and shoot him."

Gabby couldn't hide a shudder. Maybe if they'd been talking about any of the other men, she wouldn't have felt an icy horror over Alyssa's words. But this was Jaime. Still, she couldn't let even the other girls think he'd gotten to her.

She forced herself to look at Alyssa evenly. "And then what?"

"What do you mean and then what?" Alyssa demanded.

"There are at least three other men here almost at all times. What do you suggest I do after I shoot him? I'm pretty sure gunshots can be heard somewhere else in this little compound, then one of them is going to come running to shoot me. They've got a little more experience with guns and killing people than I do."

Alyssa pressed her lips together, neither mollified nor understanding.

"You just have to give me some time," Gabby said, trying for calm and in charge. "If not to convince him to give me a weapon, then at least time to find a way to sneak one off him without him noticing right away. We do this without a plan, without thinking everything through, then we're all dead. You can't just…"

Alyssa's face was even more mutinous, turning red almost. Gabby tried for conciliatory, though it grated at her a bit. "I know we all want out." She looked at

Tabitha and Jasmine, who were watching everything play out from where they sewed on the couch. "And I know once you start thinking about all of the things you could do once you got out of here that it builds inside you and everything feels… Too much. You start to panic. But if we are going to survive getting out of here, we have to be smart. Okay?"

"Does it matter if we survive?" Alyssa asked, all but snarling at Gabby.

Jasmine gasped and Tabitha straightened.

"Of course it matters," Tabitha shouted from the couch. She took in a deep, tremulous breath, calming herself as Jasmine patted her arm. "I'd rather be alive and here for the next *ten* years than die and never get a chance to see my family again." Her voice wavered but she kept going. "We have to have patience, and we have to do this smart. This is the first time any of us has access to a weapon, and we can't waste the chance. It won't happen again. At least, not for a very long time."

Alyssa scoffed, but she didn't pose any more arguments. "I'm going crazy in this place," she muttered, hugging herself.

"Why don't you help us work?" Jasmine offered. "I know it isn't any fun, but it'll at least keep your mind busy."

"You two can be his slave. I have no interest."

Tabitha and Jasmine exchanged an eye-roll and Alyssa stomped back to the kitchen. She riffled through the drawers again, inspecting butter knives and forks.

Gabby hoped Natalie and her Ranger escaped The Stallion's men once and for all, and quickly. Not just for her own sake, and for Jaime's, but because she wasn't certain Alyssa would last much longer.

If she didn't last, if she kept being something of a loose cannon, then they were all in danger. Including Jaime.

Jaime didn't go to Gabby that night. He knew it was cowardly to avoid her. He also knew it was for the best. For both of them. He wouldn't be able to resist what she offered, and it wasn't fair to take it. So he kept himself away, falling into a fitful sleep that was never quite restful.

The next day he busied himself outside. He fed The Stallion a story about wanting to come up with some new security tactics, but what he was really trying to do was to see if he could find any evidence of a shallow grave.

The Stallion was so obsessed with Layne and Wallace's progress in finding Ranger Cooper and Gabby's sister, Jaime felt pretty confident he could get away with a lot of things today.

Including going to see Gabby for only personal reasons.

He shook the thought away as he toed some dirt in the front yard. Unfortunately the entire area, especially in the front, was nothing but hardscrabble existence. Scrub brush and tall, thick weeds. It was impossible to tell if things had been dug, if things had grown over, if empty patches of land were a sign of a grave or just bad soil.

Being irritated with himself over his inability to find a lead didn't stop him from continuing to do it.

Until he heard the scream. A howling, broken sound. Keening almost. Coming from inside. From a woman.

"Gabby," he said aloud.

He forgot what he'd been doing and ran full-speed to the front door. He struggled with the chains on the doors and cursed them. It took him precious minutes to realize the door wasn't just locked and chained, it had been sealed shut with something. There was no possible way of getting to her through this door. He swore even louder and rushed around to the back.

Was The Stallion inside or in his shed? Was he hurting them? Jaime grabbed one of the guns from his chest. If he was hurting Gabby—if he was hurting any of them—this was over. Jaime wasn't going to let that happen. Not for anything. Not for any damn evidence to be used in a useless trial.

He'd just kill him and be done with it.

Nearly sweating, Jaime finally got all the locks and chains undone. He hadn't heard another scream and didn't know if that was a good or bad sign. He ran down the hall, looking in every open door. Gabby wasn't in her room and it prompted him to run faster.

He reached the main room and skidded to a halt at the sight before him. Gabby was standing there in the center of the room looking furious, blood dripping down her nose.

"What the hell happened?" he demanded, searching the room and only seeing the other women.

Gabby's gaze snapped to his and she widened her eyes briefly, as if to remind him he had an identity to maintain. It wasn't Demanding FBI Agent. *Or concerned...whatever you are.*

Either way, he'd forgotten. He'd let fear make him reckless. He'd let worry slip his mask. He very well could have ruined everything if not for that little flick of a gaze from Gabby.

He took a breath, calming the erratic beating of his heart. He moved his gaze from Gabby's bloody face, fighting every urge to grab her and pat her down himself to make sure she wasn't hurt anywhere else.

"Well, *senoritas*?" he demanded, rolling his R's in as exaggerated a manner as he could manage in his current state. He glared at the other three women. The two blondes were holding the brunette down on the couch.

The brunette was breathing heavily, her nostrils flaring as she glared at Gabby. Slowly, she took her gaze off Gabby and let it rest on him.

She sneered and then spat. Right on one of the girls holding her. The slighter blonde shrieked and jumped back, which gave the brunette time to throw off the other woman and jump to her feet.

It wasn't wasted on him that Gabby immediately went into a fighter stance.

"First shot was free, but you hit me again, I will beat you," she said, angry and menacing as the brunette stepped toward her.

Jaime stepped between them. "I will say this only once more. What is going on?" He realized he was still holding his gun and gestured it at the angry brunette threateningly.

The girl who'd been spit on squeaked and cowered while the girl who'd been flung off the brunette turned an even paler shade of white.

"Let's have story time, Alyssa. Tell our captor here what you're after," Gabby goaded.

"I'm going to get out of here," Alyssa yelled, whirling from Jaime to the blondes. "I don't care if I kill all of you." She pointed around him at Gabby. "I am going to get the hell out of here."

Jaime didn't want to feel sorry for the girl considering she was clearly at fault for Gabby's bloody nose, but he looked at Gabby and watched her shoulders slump and the fury in her eyes dim.

Damn it. He couldn't blame the woman for losing her mind here. Not in the least. But it was the last thing they needed if they were actually going to put something in motion that might get them out.

"You would be dead before you killed anyone, *senorita*. Calm yourself."

She bared her teeth at him. "I can't do this anymore. I can't do this anymore. Shoot me." She lunged toward him. "God, put me out of my misery."

"Hush," he ordered flatly, tamping down every possible empathetic feeling rising up inside him. "I'm not going to kill you. And you are not going to kill anyone. You're going to calm yourself."

"Or what? What happens if I don't?" She got close enough to shove him, even reached out to do it, but Gabby was stepping between them.

Jaime was certain the woman would throw another punch at Gabby and he would have to intervene, but Gabby did the most incomprehensible thing. She pulled the woman into a hug.

And the woman began to sob.

The others started, too. All four of them crying, Gabby with her nose still bleeding.

Jaime had to clench his free hand into a fist and pray for some kind of composure. It was too much, these poor women, taken from their lives and expected to somehow endure it.

"What is all this?" The Stallion demanded and Jaime was such a fool he actually jumped. Where had all his instincts gone? All his self-preservation? He'd lost it, all because Gabby had gotten under his skin.

Jaime steeled himself and turned to face The Stallion.

"Your charges were getting out of hand. I had to do some knocking around," Jaime offered, nodding at Gabby's nose. If any of the girls wanted to refute his story, it would possibly end his life.

But none of them did.

"She is mine, no?" Jaime continued, hoping the fact Gabby was a gift meant he'd forgive him for the supposed violence that had shed blood.

The Stallion was staring oddly at Gabby, and it took everything in Jaime's power not to step between them. In an obvious way. Instead he simply angled his body and hoped like hell it wasn't obvious how much he wanted to protect her.

"Crying," The Stallion said in a kind of wondering tone. "Well, I am impressed, Rodriguez. No one has ever gotten her to cry."

Gabby flipped him the finger and Jaime nearly broke. Nearly ended it all right there.

"I trust our friend has told you that your sister will be joining us soon," The Stallion said, watching her far too carefully no matter how Jaime tried to angle himself into the picture.

"And yet she isn't here yet. Why is that?" Gabby returned in an equally conversational tone.

Jaime might have fallen in love with her right there.

The Stallion, however, snarled. "You're lucky I don't want to touch your disease-ridden body. But I have found someone who will. Take her away from me, Rodriguez. I don't want to see that face until her sister is here. Make sure to lock her room once you're done with her. She's done with outside privileges."

"And these?" Jaime managed to ask.

The Stallion snapped his fingers. "To your rooms. Don't make me turn you into gifts, as well."

The girls, even the instigator, scattered quickly.

The Stallion squinted at Gabby and maybe it was her unwillingness to cower or to jump that made her a target.

If Gabby cared about that, she didn't show it. So Jaime took Gabby by the arms, as gently as he could while still appearing to be rough to The Stallion. "I will take good care of her, *senor*," he said, donning his best evil smile.

"I'm glad you're willing to soil yourself with this," The Stallion said. "I should have had someone do this long ago. I don't care what you have to do to make her cry. Just do it."

Jaime gave a nod since he didn't trust his voice. He nudged Gabby toward the hallway and she fought him on it, still staring at The Stallion.

"You're a disgusting excuse for a human being. You aren't a human being. You're a monster." And then, apparently taking a page out of Alyssa's book, she spit at him.

The Stallion scrambled away and then furiously scowled at Jaime.

"Are you going to let her get away with that?" he demanded, fury all but pumping out of him.

Oh, damn, Gabby and her mouth. How the hell was he going to get out of this one?

Chapter 11

Gabby had gone too far. She realized it a few seconds too late. She'd wanted to make sure The Stallion didn't think she was happy to go with Jaime. She wanted The Stallion to think she hated Jaime as much as she hated him, and she didn't know how to show it considering she didn't hate Jaime even a little bit.

But she'd put Jaime in an impossible position. The Stallion expected Jaime to hurt her now. In front of him.

And how could he not?

Jaime's jaw tightened and Gabby knew it wasn't because he was getting ready to hurt her. It was because he didn't want to and he was having a hard time figuring out how to avoid it. But he didn't need to protect her.

She lifted her chin, hoping he would understand. "Hit me with your best shot, buddy," she offered.

Much like when he'd come into the room, guns blazing, not using his accent at all, she gave him a little open-eyed glance that she hoped would clue him in.

He had to hit her. There was no choice. She understood that. She wouldn't hold that against him. Besides, he'd pull the punch. It'd be fine.

He raised his hand and she had to close her eyes. She didn't want the image in her head even if she knew he had to do it. She braced herself for the blow, but it never came.

Instead his fingers curled in her hair, a tight fist. Not comfortable, but still not painful, either.

"It appears you need to be taught some respect, *senorita*. Let's go to your room where I can give you a thorough lesson. I teach best one-on-one."

Gabby opened her eyes, ignoring the shaking in her body. She didn't dare look at The Stallion—she didn't want to know if he'd bought that ridiculous tactic or not. She couldn't look at Jaime, because she didn't want anything to give him or her away.

So she sucked in a breath as though Jaime's fingers in her hair hurt and stared at the floor as if he was forcing her. She stumbled a little as he nudged her forward, trying to make it appear as if he'd pushed her. She put everything into the performance of making it look like he was being rough with her when he was being anything but.

"I will come to give you a full report when I'm done, *senor*."

"Excellent." The Stallion sounded pleased with himself. Satisfied.

Jaime continued to nudge her all the way to her room, and she let out a little squeak of faked pain. When Jaime finally gave her a light push into her room, she could only sag with relief.

Jaime closed the door and flicked the lock. Before she had a moment to breathe, to say a thing, she was being bundled into his arms and gently cradled against his hard chest and the weapons there.

She relaxed into him, letting him hold her up. She was shaking more now, oddly, but it was such an amazing thing to be cradled and comforted after everything that had just happened, she couldn't even wonder over it.

"We need to get you cleaned up," Jaime said, his voice low and sounding pained.

She waved him away, wanting to stay right there, cradled against him. "Leave it. Maybe it'll convince him you were suitably rough with me if we let it bleed more."

"He's not going to see you again," Jaime said fiercely, his arms tightening around her briefly. "You're under lock and key now, and if he tries to come in here, I will kill him myself."

She looked up at him curiously. He was… He'd avoided her for days, and Gabby couldn't blame him because she knew he was trying to do something noble. Still, she didn't quite understand his anger.

Frustration or fear, maybe even annoyance, she might have understood, but the beating fury in his eyes, completely opposite to the gentle way he held her, was something she couldn't unwind.

"What was the other woman's problem?" he asked, studying her nose.

"She hit the two-year mark," Gabby stated with a tired sigh.

"What does that mean?"

Gabby sighed. "Oh, I don't know. It just seems that

around two years in here you start to realize how stuck you are. How no one's going to come and save you. I think we all have a little bit of a meltdown at two years."

"Did your two-year meltdown include punching another woman in the face?"

"No. I was alone. I did try to use a butter knife to stab a guard," she offered almost cheerfully.

His mouth almost…almost quirked at that.

"I was desperate," she continued. "With that desperation comes a kind of insanity. Alyssa's hitting that same wall. Losing it. Wondering what it's worth being stuck in this horrible place. Of course, she has the worst possible timing, but what can we do? We just have to try and end it as soon as we can."

"You hugged her." Jaime's voice was soft, awe-filled.

Gabby turned away from him and his comforting, strong arms, uncomfortable with the way he said it as though she'd done something special. But she hadn't. Not really.

"You forget sometimes, when you're in here, that a simple hug can be reassuring. She needed someone to be kind. You…you reminded me of that. Humanity. Compassion. So, I did what you've done to me."

"You did it after she punched you in the nose," he pointed out.

"I let her punch me. I thought it would help her get some of the rage out of her system. I'm hoping getting some of it out will stop her from just…losing it completely."

"You are a marvel," he said, like she was some kind of genius superhero. It shouldn't have warmed her. She should tell him she wasn't.

But she wanted to believe there was something marvelous about her.

"I'm washing you up," he said, taking her arm and pulling her into the little nook that acted as a bathroom. There was a toilet and a sink, but no door, no privacy. Still, Jaime grabbed a washcloth from the little pile she kept neatly stacked in the corner.

He flicked on the tap and soaked the cloth in warm water. He squeezed it out before holding it up to her face gently. Ever so gently, he wiped away the blood that had started dribbling out of her nose after Alyssa had hit her.

"You're lucky she didn't break it," he muttered.

Gabby rolled her eyes. "I *let* her hit me, and I pulled back a bit. I'm a lot stronger than all that bluster."

He cupped her face with his hands, long fingers brushing at her hairline. "That you are," he said with a kind of fervency that had a lump burning in her throat.

"You've been avoiding me," she rasped.

"Yeah," he said. "I'm trying to do the right thing."

"What about instead of doing the right thing, you do what I want? How about you give me something I want?"

He sighed and shook his head. "I don't know how I ever thought I'd resist you." Then his mouth was on hers.

Potent and hot. Not quite so gentle. Gabby reveled in the fact that he could be both. That he could give her everything and anything she wanted.

"Tell me if I hurt your nose," he murmured against her mouth, never breaking contact. His hands trailing through her hair, his body pressed hard and tight against hers.

She could barely feel the ache in her nose. Not with

Jaime's tongue sliding against hers. Not with the smell of him and leather and what might be outside if she even remembered what outside smelled like.

She realized whatever this was, it was frantic and needy. It was also something that could be temporary all too easily. The chances she'd have to touch him, to be with him…

She needed to grasp and enjoy and lose herself in this moment, in the having of it. She molded her hands against his strong shoulders, slid them down his biceps and his forearms. Everything about him was honed muscle, so strong. He could've been brutal with someone else's heart, but Jaime was anything but that.

His hands smoothed down her neck and, for the first time, he dared to touch more than just her face or her shoulders. The fingers of one hand traced across her collarbone over her T-shirt. His other hand slid down her back, strong as he held her against him.

She could feel him, hot and hard against her stomach. It had been a long time since she'd done this, and it was possibly the most inappropriate moment, but there wasn't time to think.

She didn't want to think. She wanted to sink into good feelings and let *those* take over for once.

She arched against him and the fingertips tracing her collarbone stilled. Then lowered. He palmed one of her breasts and she moaned against his mouth.

"We can stop whenever," he said, so serious and noble and *wrong*.

"I don't ever want to stop." She wanted to live in a moment where she had some power. Where she had some hope. "Take off your guns, Jaime."

He stilled briefly and then reached up to the shoulder

of the harness and unbuckled it. He pulled the strand of weapons off his body, his eyes never leaving hers. He hesitated only a moment before he laid the weapons down next to her bed.

He took a gun from his waistband she hadn't known was there and placed it on the little table next to her bed. Something almost resembling a smile graced his mouth as he reached to his boots and pulled a knife out of each.

There was something not just weighty about watching him disarm, but something intimate. She watched him strip himself of all the things he used to protect himself. All the things he used to portray another man. To do his job, his duty.

"I think that's all of them," he said in a husky voice.

She didn't have any weapons to surrender, so she grabbed the hem of her shirt and pulled it off. She moved her hands to unbutton her pants, but Jaime made a sound.

"Stop," he ordered.

She raised a questioning eyebrow at him.

He crossed back to her, a hand splaying against her stomach, the other sliding down her arm. "Let me."

She swallowed the nerves fluttering to the surface. No, nerves wasn't the right word. It was something more fundamental than that. Would he like what he saw? Would he still be as enamored with her when they were naked? When it was over?

She wanted to laugh at her momentary worry about such things. But, like so many other thoughts, it was a comforting reaction—a real-life response. That she could still be a woman. That she could still care about such things.

His hands were rough against her skin. Tanned

against how pale she was with no access to sunlight. She watched as he traced the strangest parts of her, as if fascinated by her belly button or the curve of her waist. But he was still fully clothed, though he'd surrendered all his weapons.

She gave the hem of his shirt a little tug. "Take this off," she ordered, because it was nice to order. More than nice to have someone obey. Power. Equality, really. He could order her and she could order him, and they could each get what they wanted.

He pulled his shirt off from the back, lifting it over his head and letting it hit the floor. He really was perfection. Tall and lithe and beautiful. He had scars and smooth patches of skin. Dark hair that drew a line from his chest to the waistband of his jeans.

She moved forward and traced the longest scar on his side. A white line against his golden skin.

"How did you get this?" she asked.

"Knife fight."

She raised her gaze to his eyes, but his expression was serious, not silly. "You were in a *knife* fight?"

He shrugged. "When I first started out as Rodriguez, I was doing some drug running for one of his lower-level operations. Unfortunately a lot of those guys try to double-cross each other. I was caught in the cross... well, cross-stabbing as it were."

He said it so cavalierly, as if that was just part of his job. Getting stabbed. Horribly enough to leave a long, white scar.

"Did you go to the hospital?"

Again he smiled, almost indulgently now. "There was a man who did the stitching back at our home base."

"A man? Not a doctor?" she demanded.

"Doctors were saved from more…life-threatening injuries. Even then, only if you were important. At that point, I wasn't very important."

Gabby tried to make sense of it as Jaime shook his head.

"It's a nonsensical world. None of it makes sense if you have a conscience, if you've known love or joy. Because it's not about anything but greed and power and desperation."

She traced the jagged line and then bent to press a kiss to it. He sucked in a breath.

"I bet there was no one to kiss it better," she said, trying to sound lighthearted even though tears were threatening.

"Ah, no."

"Then let me." She raised to her tiptoes to kiss him. To press her chest to his. She still wore a bra, but the rest of her upper body was exposed and she tried to press every bare spot of her to every bare spot of him.

She tasted his mouth, his tongue, and she wanted the kiss to go deep enough and mean enough to ease some of those old hurts, some of that old loneliness.

For both of them.

There were things Jaime should do. Things he should stop from happening. But Gabby's kiss, Gabby's heart, was a balm to all the cruelties he'd suffered and administered in the past two years. She was sweetness and she was light. She was warmth and she was hope.

At this point he could no longer keep it from himself, let alone her. She wanted this. Perhaps she needed it as much as he did. Regardless, there was no going back. There was only going forward.

Her skin was velvet, her mouth honey. Her heart beating against his heart, the cadence of a million wonderful things he'd forgotten existed.

Her fingertips were curious and gentle as they explored him, bold as though it never occurred to her she shouldn't.

All of it was solace wrapped in pleasure and passion. That someone would want to touch him with reverence or care. That he wasn't the hideous monster he'd pretended to be for two years. He was still a man made of flesh and bone, justice and right.

And despite her time here as a victim, she was still a woman. Made of flesh and bone. Made of heart and soul.

He smoothed his hands up and down her back, absorbing the strength of her. Carefully leashed, carefully honed.

He reached behind her and unsnapped her bra, slowly pulling it off her and down her arms. It meant he had to put space between them. It meant he had to wrestle his mouth from hers. But if anything was worth that separation, it was the sight before him. Gabby's curly hair tumbled around her face. Her lips swollen, her cheeks flushed.

The soft swell of her breasts, dark nipples sharp points because she was as excited as he was. As needy as he was. He palmed both breasts with his too-rough hands and was rewarded by her soft moan.

Of course this amazingly strong and brave woman before him was not content to simply let him look or touch. She reached out and touched him, as well, her hands trailing down his chest all the way to his waistband. She flipped the button and unzipped the piece of clothing with no preamble at all.

He continued to explore her breasts with his hands. Memorizing the weight and the shape and the warmth, the amazing softness her body offered to him. And it was more than just that. So much more than just the body. A heart. A soul. Neither of them would be at this point if it wasn't so much more than *physical*. It was an underlying tie, a cord of inexplicable connection.

She tugged his jeans down, his boxers with them. And then those slim, strong hands were grasping him. Stroking his erection and nearly bringing him to his knees.

He needed to find some sort of center. Not necessarily of control but of reason. Sense and responsibility. This was neither sensible nor responsible, but that didn't mean he couldn't take care of her. That didn't mean he wouldn't.

Gently he pulled her hand off him. "I need to go get something. I'll be right back."

She blinked up at him, eyebrows furrowed. Beautiful and naked from the waist up.

He pressed his mouth to hers as he pulled his jeans up, drowning in it a minute, forgetting what he'd been about to do. It was only when she touched him again that he remembered.

"Stay put. I will be right back." When she opened her mouth, he shook his head. "I promise," he repeated, his gaze steady on hers. He needed her to understand, and he needed her to believe him.

She pouted a little bit, beautiful and sulky, but she nodded.

"Right back," he repeated and then he was rushing to

his room, caring far too little about the things he should care about. If The Stallion was around… If the other girls were okay… But it hardly mattered with Gabby's soul entwined with his.

He went to his closet of a room and grabbed the box that had been given to him. The box was still wrapped and he had no doubt about the safety of its contents.

And he would keep Gabby safe. No matter what.

With a very quick glance toward the back door, Jaime very nearly *scurried* back to Gabby. That back door was clearly shut and locked. Surely The Stallion had disappeared into his lair to obsess over Layne and Wallace's progress.

Jaime entered Gabby's room once again, closing and locking the door behind him quickly. She wasn't standing anymore. She was sitting on the edge of her bed and she was still shirtless.

He walked over and placed the box of condoms on the nightstand next to his smaller gun. He watched her face carefully, something flickering there he didn't recognize as she glanced at the box.

"We still don't have to," he offered, wondering if it was reticence or something close to it.

Her glance flicked from the box to him. "Why do you have these?"

"If you haven't noticed The Stallion is a little convinced women have—"

"Cooties?" Gabby supplied for him.

Jaime laughed. "I was going to say diseases. But, yes, essentially, cooties."

"So he gave those to you?"

"When I convinced him that only female payment would do, he insisted I take the necessary precautions."

She frowned, puzzling over the box. He didn't know what to say to make her okay. But eventually she grabbed the box and ran her nail around the edge. Pulling the wrapping off, she ripped open the box and took out a packet.

She studied him from beneath her lashes and then smirked. "I think this is where you drop your pants."

He laughed again. Laughing. It was amazing considering he couldn't think of the last time he'd laughed. With Gabby he felt like he wasn't just a machine. He wasn't simply a tool to bring The Stallion down or a tool to help The Stallion out. He'd been nothing but a weapon for so long it was hard to remember that he was also real. Capable of laughing. Capable of humor. Capable of feeling.

Capable of caring. Perhaps even loving.

He'd never been a romantic man who believed in flights of fancy and yet this woman had changed his life. She'd changed his heart and he didn't have to know how she'd done it to know that it had happened.

He pushed his jeans the remainder of the way down, watching her the entire time. Her gaze remained bold and appraising on his erection.

She scooted forward on the bed, tearing the condom packet open before rolling it on him. Finally she looked up at him. Her gaze never left his as she lay back on the bed and undid the fastenings of her pants. She shimmied out of her remaining clothes and then lay there, naked and beautiful before him.

He took a minute to drink her in. Because who knew how much time they would have after the next couple of days. He would save her—he would do anything to save her—and he did not know what lay ahead. He did know he had to absorb all of this, commit it to memory, connect it to his heart.

He stepped out of his jeans and then crawled onto the bed and over her. She slid her arms around his neck and pulled his mouth to hers. The kiss was soft and sweet. An invitation, an enchanting spell.

He traced the curve of her cheek with one hand, positioning himself with the other. Slowly, torturing himself and possibly her, as well, he found her entrance. Nudged against it. Taking his sweet time to slowly enter her.

Joined. Together. As if they were a perfect match. A pair that belonged exactly here. How could he belong anywhere else when this was perfect? When she was perfect?

She arched against him as if hurrying him along, her fingers tightening in his too long hair.

"We have time, Gabby. We have time." He kissed her, soft and sweet, indulging himself in a moment where he was simply seeped inside of her.

A moment when he was all hers and she was all his. And she relaxed, melting. His. All his.

Chapter 12

Gabby had known sex with Jaime would be different for a lot of reasons. First and foremost, she wasn't a young girl sneaking around, finding awkward stolen moments in the back of a car. Second, he wasn't a little boy playing at being a hard-ass bad man.

He was a strong, good, *amazing* man, doing things her ex-boyfriend would have wilted in front of.

But mostly, sex with Jaime was different because it was them. Because it was here. Because it mattered in a way her teenage heart would never have been able to understand. Perhaps she never would have been able to understand if she hadn't been in this position. The position that asked her to be more than she'd ever thought she'd be able to be. Because the truth of the matter was, eight years ago she had been a young woman like any other. Selfish and foolish and not strong in the least.

She would never be grateful for this eight years of

hell. She would never be happy for the lessons she'd learned here, but that didn't mean she couldn't appreciate them. Because whether she was happy about it or not, it had happened. It was reality. There was only so much bitterness a person could stand.

With Jaime moving inside her, touching her, caring about her, bitterness had no place. Only pleasure. Only hope. Only a deep, abiding care she had never felt before.

He kissed her, soft and gentle, wild and passionate, a million different kinds of kisses and cares. His body moved against hers; rough, strong, such a contrast. Such a perfect fit.

Passion built inside her, deep and abiding. Bigger than anything she'd imagined she'd be able to feel ever again. But Jaime's hands stroked her body. He moved inside her like he could unlock every piece of her. She *wanted* him to.

The blinding spiral of pleasure took her off guard. She hadn't expected it so quickly or so hard. She gasped his name, surprised at the sound in the quiet room. Surprised at all he could draw it out of her.

He still moved with her. Growing a little frantic, a little wild. She reveled in it, her hands sliding down his back. Her heart beating against his.

She wanted *his* release. Wanted to feel him lose himself inside her.

Instead of galloping after it, though, he paused, as if wanting to make this moment last forever. Satisfied and sated, how could she argue with that? She would stay here, locked with him, body to body forever.

He kissed her neck, her jaw. His teeth scraped against her lips and she moved her hips to meet with his. But he was unerringly slow and methodical. As though they'd been making love for years and he knew exactly how to drive her crazy. How to make her fall over that edge again and again. Because she was perilously close.

Aside from the tension in his arms, she would have no idea he was exerting any energy whatsoever. That spurred something in her. Something she hadn't thought she'd ever feel again. A challenge. And need.

She tightened her hold on his shoulders, slicked though they were. She sank her teeth into his bottom lip, pushing hard against him with her hips. He groaned into her mouth. She slid her hands down his back, gripping his hips, urging him on. One hand tightened on her hip, a heavy, hot brand.

She looked into his eyes and smiled at him. "More," she insisted.

He swore, sounding a little broken. That control he'd been holding on to, that calm assault to bring her to the brink, snapped. He moved against her with a wildness she craved, that she reveled in.

She'd brought him to this point, wild and a little broken. *She* could be the woman that did this to him, and that was something no one could ever take away. *She* was the woman who had made him hers. Maybe she wouldn't always have Jaime, but she'd always have this.

He groaned his release, pushing hard against her, and it was the knowledge she'd brought him there that sent her over the edge again herself. Pulsing and crashing. Her heart beating heavy, having grown a million sizes. Having accepted his as her own.

He lay against her, and she stroked her hand up and down his back, listening to his heart beat slowly, slowly, come back to its regular rhythm. He made a move to get off her, but she held him there, wanting his weight on her for as long as it could be.

"Aren't I crushing you?" he asked in her ear, his voice a low rumble.

"I like it," she murmured in return.

He nuzzled into her neck, relaxing into her. As though because she'd said she liked it he would give her this closeness for as long as he could. She believed that about him. That he would always give her whatever he could. Once they knew Natalie was safe, he'd agreed to get her out under any means possible, and she believed.

For the first time in eight years she believed in someone aside from herself. For the first time in eight years she had hope and care and pleasure.

She might've told him she loved him in any other situation, but this was no regular life. Love was… Who knew what love really was? If they got away, back into the real world, maybe…maybe she could learn.

Jaime slept in Gabby's bed. It was a calculated risk to spend the night with her. He didn't know how close an eye The Stallion was keeping on him with everything going on. In the end, perhaps a little addled by her and sex, he'd figured, if pressed, he'd explain all his time as making sure Gabby paid for her supposed lack of respect.

It bothered him to have to think of things like that. Bothered him in a way nothing in the past two years had. That he had to make The Stallion think he was hurting Gabby. It grated against every inch of him every time he thought about it.

So he tried not to think about it. He spent the night

in her bed and the next day mostly holed up with her in her room. They made love. They talked. They *laughed*.

It felt as though they were anywhere but in this prison. A vacation of sorts. Just one where you didn't leave the room you were locked into. He wouldn't regret this time. It was something to have her here, to have her close.

They didn't talk about the future or about what they might do when they got out. Jaime would have some compulsory therapy to go through. A whole detox situation with the FBI, along with preparations for the future trial. Any further investigating that needed to be done would at least fall somewhat within his responsibility.

But he was done with undercover work. He'd known that before he'd met Gabby. These past two years had taken too much of a toll and he couldn't be a good law-enforcement officer in this position anymore. He didn't plan to leave the FBI, but undercover work was over.

Once he got Gabby out, he would make sure that "something different" included her. She would need therapy, as well, and time to heal. It would take time to find ways back to their old selves.

He could wait. He could do anything if it meant having a chance with her.

But their time here in this other world was running out. The Stallion would be expecting a full report from Rodriguez, and Jaime had put it off long enough.

He would do all the things he had to do to protect her. To free her.

"You have to go meet with him," she said, her tone void of any emotion.

He turned to face her on the bed. It was too narrow and they barely fit together, and yet he was grateful for the lack of space, for the excuse to always be this close. "How'd you figure that out?"

"You got all tense," she replied, rubbing at his shoulders as though this was something they could be. A couple. Who talked to each other, offered comfort to each other.

He couldn't think of anything he'd ever wanted more, including his position with the FBI.

"He's expecting a report from me."

Gabby frowned and didn't look at him when she asked her question. "Are you going to tell him I cried?"

He'd been planning on it. He knew it poked her pride, but it would be best if The Stallion thought her broken. It would be best if Jaime made himself look like a master torturer.

"Do you not want me to?"

"You would tell him you failed?"

He shrugged, trying to act as though it wasn't a big deal, though it was. "If you want me to. I don't think it would put me in any danger to make it look like I'd failed one thing considering everything else that's currently going down."

"You don't *think*?"

"He's not exactly the most predictable man in the world, no matter how scheduled and regimented he is."

"That's very true," she mused, looking somewhere beyond him.

"Gabby."

Her dark gaze met his, that warrior battle light in them. "Tell him I cried. Tell him I sobbed and begged. What does it matter? I didn't actually."

"If it matters something to you—"

"All that matters to me is you." She blinked as if surprised by the force of her words. "And getting out of here," she added somewhat after the fact.

He pressed a kiss to her mouth. Whatever tension he'd had was gone. Or perhaps not *gone*, but different somehow.

Screw The Stallion. Screw responsibility. She was all that mattered. He wanted to believe that as he fell into the kiss, wanted to hold on to that possibility, that new tenet of his life. Gabby and only Gabby.

But life was never quite that easy. Because Gabby, being the most important thing, the central thing for him, meant he had to keep her safe. It meant that responsibility *did* have a place here. It was his responsibility to get her out. His responsibility to get her *free*.

He started to pull away but she spoke before he could.

"Go have a meeting. Find out if there's any news about Nattie, and make sure you remember every last detail. And then, when you can…" She smoothed her hand over his chest and offered him a smile that was weak at best, but she was trying. For him, he knew.

"When you're done, when you can, come back to me," she said softly.

He brought her hand to his mouth and pressed a kiss to her palm. "Always," he said, holding her gaze. Hoping she understood and believed how much he meant that.

He slid out of bed, because the sooner he got this meeting with The Stallion over with, the sooner he could find a way to make sure that this was over. For Gabby and for him.

Jaime collected his weapons. He could feel Gabby's eyes on him though he couldn't read her expression.

She had perfected the art of giving nothing away and as much as it sometimes frustrated him as a man, he was certainly glad she had built such effective protective layers for herself.

He put the knives back in his boots and then strapped on his cross-chest holster with all of his guns. He buckled it, still watching her expressionless face.

She slid off the bed and crossed to him. She flashed a smile Jaime didn't think had much happiness behind it, but she brushed her lips against his.

"Good luck," she said as though she were scared. For him.

"I have to lock the door," he said, regretting the words as they came out of his mouth. Regretting the way her expression shuttered.

"Yeah, I know." She gave a careless shrug.

Her knowing didn't make him feel any better about doing it, but he had to. There were certain things he still had to do. Things that would keep her safe in the end, and that was all that could matter.

He kissed her once more, knowing he was only delaying the inevitable. He steeled all that certainty and finally managed to back himself out of the room. Away from her smile, away from her sweet mouth.

Away from his heart and soul.

He closed the door and locked it from the outside. He regretted having to add the chain, but any regrets were a small price to pay to get her out. He would keep telling himself that over and over again until he believed it. This was all a small price to pay for getting her out.

He walked briskly down the hall, noting the house was eerily quiet. It wasn't unusual, but often in the afternoon there was a little bit of chatter from the common rooms as the girls worked on their projects or fixed dinner.

Jaime cursed and retraced his steps to check on them. The two calm ones from yesterday were sitting on the couch working on something The Stallion had undoubtedly given them to do. Alyssa was pacing the kitchen.

None of them looked at him, so he could only assume he'd been quiet enough. Satisfied that things seemed to be mostly normal, he backed out of the room. Alyssa's frenzied pacing bothered him a bit. Gabby was right, the girl was a loose cannon, and it was the last thing they needed. But what could he do about it?

There wasn't anything. Not now.

He walked back along the hallway, going through the hassle of unlocking and unchaining the door, stepping out, then redoing all the work. His thoughts were jumbled and he had to sort them out before he actually saw The Stallion.

He paused in the backyard, taking a deep breath, trying to focus his thoughts. He forced himself to hone in on all the strategies he'd been taught in his years as a police officer and FBI agent.

He had to put on the cloak of Rodriguez, get the information he was after, lie to The Stallion about Gabby, then go back to her. Once this was over, he could go back to her.

With a nod to himself, he stepped forward, but it was then he heard the noise. Something strange and faint. Almost a moan. He paused and studied the yard around him.

The next sound wasn't so much a moaning but almost like someone rasping "Rodriguez" and failing.

Jaime started moving toward the noise, listening hard

as he walked around the backyard. He held his small handgun in one hand, leaving his other hand free should he need to fight off any attacker.

He rounded the front of the house, still listening to the sound and following the source. When he did, he nearly gasped.

Wallace and Layne were sprawled out in the yard. Layne was a little closer to the house than Wallace, but they were both caked with blood and dirt.

"Rodriguez. Rodriguez." Layne moved his arm wildly and stumbled to his feet. "I've been dragging this piece of shit for who knows how long. Go get The Stallion. And water. By God, I need water."

"Where is your vehicle?" Jaime asked, his tone dispassionate and unhurried.

"Only go so far..." Layne gasped for air, stumbling to the ground again. "Asshole shot our tires. Got as far as I could."

Jaime looked at both men in various states of bloodied harm. "You don't have her."

Layne's dirty, bloody face curled into a scowl, but he gave brief shake of the head.

"I don't know if you want me to get The Stallion if you don't have her."

"He shot us," Layne said disgustedly. "That prick shot us. Wallace might die. We need The Stallion. We need *help*."

"You may wish you had died," Jaime said, affecting as much detached disinterest as he could.

On the inside he was reeling. Gabby's sister had escaped these men with Ranger Cooper, which meant that it was time. It was time to move forward. It was time to get the hell out. Her sister was safe and now it was her turn.

"Go get The Stallion," Layne yelled, lunging at him. He had a bloody wound on his shoulder and he was pale. Still, he seemed to be in slightly better shape than Wallace who was lying on the ground moaning, a bullet wound apparently in his thigh.

After a long study that had Layne growling at him as he tried to walk farther, Jaime inclined his head and then began striding purposefully back to The Stallion's shed. He knocked and only entered once The Stallion unlocked the door and bid him entrance.

"What took you so long?" The Stallion demanded and Jaime was more than a little happy that he had a decent enough excuse to explain his long absence in a way that didn't have anything to do with Gabby.

"*Senor*, Wallace and Layne are in the yard. Injured."

The Stallion had just sat in his desk chair, but immediately leaped to his feet. "They don't have her?" he bellowed.

"No."

"Imbeciles. Useless, worthless trash. Kill them. Kill them both immediately," he ordered with the flick of a wrist.

Jaime had to curb his initial reaction, which was to refuse. He might find Wallace and Layne disgusting excuses for human beings, he might even believe they deserved to die, but he was not comfortable with it being at his hand.

"*Senor*, if this is your wish, I will absolutely mete out your justice. But perhaps…"

"Perhaps what?" he snapped.

"You will want to go after the girl yourself, *si*?"

The Stallion frowned as he walked over and stood by his dolls, grabbing one hand as though he was holding the hand of a little girl.

Jaime had to ignore that and press his advantage. "Clearly the Ranger is smarter than your men. But certainly not smarter than you. If you go after him, you can do whatever you want with both of them. Surely you, of all people, could outsmart them."

The Stallion had begun to nod the more Jaime complimented him. "You're right. You're right."

He dropped the doll's hand and Jaime nearly sagged with relief.

"You'll have to go with me, Rodriguez."

Jaime stilled. That was not part of his plan. "Tell Layne and Wallace they're in charge of the girls. We'll leave immediately."

"Their injuries are severe. Shot. Both of them. Surely incapable of watching after anything. You must have other men you can take with you, and I'll stay—"

"No." The Stallion shook his head. "No, you're coming with me. Wallace and Layne, no matter how injured, can keep a door locked. I'll send for another man, and he can kill them and take over here. Yes, yes, that's the plan. I need you. I need you, Rodriguez." The Stallion took one of the dolls off the shelf. He petted the doll's dark hair as though it were a puppy. "If you prove your worth to me on this, there is nothing that I wouldn't give you, Rodriguez." He held out the doll between them.

Jaime was afraid he looked as horrified as he felt, but he kept his hands grasped lightly behind his back. He forced himself to smile languidly at the unseeing doll. "Then I am at your service, *senor.*"

"Go tell them the plan," The Stallion said, gesturing

with the doll, thank God not making him take it. "Not the killing part, of course, just the watching-after-the-girls part. Pack all your weapons and all your ammunition. Pack up all the water in my supplies and put it in the Jeep. We'll leave as soon as you've gotten everything together. Do you understand?"

Jaime nodded, trying to steady the panic rising inside him. *"Sí, senor."*

It wasn't such a terrible thing. He'd be there to stop The Stallion from getting any kind of hold on Gabby's sister and Ranger Cooper. But it left Gabby here. Exposed.

And he only had limited time to figure out how to fix that.

Chapter 13

Gabby tried to ignore how locked in she felt. She'd been a victim for eight years. A prisoner of this place. Being locked in her room and unable to leave was certainly no greater trial to bear.

But she hadn't been locked in her room for any stretch of time since the very beginning. Mostly she'd been able to go to the common room or the kitchen whenever she wanted.

She'd gotten used to that freedom, and it was clawing at her to have lost some of it. That made it a very effective punishment all in all.

She wondered what the girls were doing. Had Alyssa calmed down? Was she ranting? Was she bringing reality to her threat to kill everyone in an effort to get out of there?

Gabby buried her face in her pillow and tried to block

it all out, but when she inhaled she could smell Jaime and something in her chest turned over.

Oh, Jaime. That was part of why this locked-up thing was harder to bear, too. She'd felt almost real for nearly twenty-four hours. She and Jaime had spent the night and most of today, having sex and talking and enjoying each other's company. As though they lived in an outside world where they were themselves and not undercover agent and kidnapping victim.

It made it so much harder to be fully forced into what she really was. Victim. Captive. Not any closer to having any power than she'd been twenty-four hours ago.

Except she'd stolen a moment of it, and wasn't that something worth celebrating?

She heard someone unlocking her door from the outside and sat bolt upright in bed. Jaime hadn't been gone very long. If he was back already, it had to be bad news.

If it wasn't Jaime on the other side, so much the worse.

But it was the man she'd taken as a lover who stepped into her room, shutting the door behind him with more force than necessary. His face reminded her of that first day. Rodriguez. The mask, not the man.

"Do you have anything in here you'd want to take with you?" he demanded.

"What?" She couldn't follow him as he walked the perimeter of her room as if searching for something valuable.

"I don't have time to explain. I don't have time to do anything but get you out now."

"What happened?" she asked, jumping off the bed.

His hand curled around her forearm, tight and with-ut any of its usual kindness. "Is there anything you need to take?" he repeated, glaring at her.

"What's happened?" she pleaded with him. Her heart beat a heavy cadence against her chest and she couldn't think past the panic gripping her. "Is it Nattie? Is—"

He began pulling her to the door. "Your sister and the Ranger escaped."

"Escaped? Escaped!" Hope burst in her chest, bright and wonderful. "So we're...we're just running?"

He looked up and down the hallway. "You are. I'll get the other girls after."

That stopped Gabby in her tracks, no matter how he pulled on her arm. "What?" she demanded.

"Layne and Wallace are hurt. I can get one of you out now without raising any questions because you're supposed to be locked up, but I can't get you all out. Not right this second. I have to go with The Stallion to track down your sister. Which is good," he said before she could argue with him or ask him what the hell he was talking about. "Because I will obviously make sure that doesn't happen. I have—" he glanced at his watch "—maybe five seconds to contact my superiors to let them know to raid this place, and then to try to find one just like it in the south." He shoved her into the hallway, but she fought him.

"You can't take me and not them."

His gaze locked on hers. "Of course I can. And that's what we're doing."

"No. You can't. They'll fall apart without me."

"They won't. And they'll be saved in a day or two. Three tops."

"You really expect me to leave Tabitha and Jasmine here with Alyssa? Alyssa will instigate something. You know she will. They'll all be dead before…" She didn't want to say it out loud, no matter how much he wasn't being careful himself.

He grabbed her by the shoulders and gave her a little shake, his eyes fierce and stubborn. "But you won't be."

It was her turn to look up and down the hallway. She didn't know where the girls were, where Wallace and Layne or The Stallion were milling about. Jaime was losing his mind and it was her… Well, it was her responsibility to make him find it.

"You have to get it together," she snapped in a low, quiet voice. "You have to be sensible about this, and you have to calm down."

He thrust his fingers into his hair, looking more than a little wild. "Gabby, I do not have time. You have to do what I say, and you have to do it now."

"Take Alyssa," she said, though it pained her to offer that. A stabbing pain of fear, but it was the only option.

"Wh-what?" he spluttered.

"Take Alyssa. I can handle more days here. Tabitha and Jasmine… We can hack it, but Alyssa cannot take another day. You know that. Take her. Get her out, we'll cover it up, and when the raid comes, you will come and get me."

"Have you lost your mind?"

"No! You've lost yours." Part of her wanted to push him, or reverse their positions and shake him, but the bigger part of her wanted to reach something in him. She curled her fingers into his shirt. "You know it isn't safe to take me out. Why are you risking everything?"

"Because I love you," he blurted, clearly antagonized into the admission.

She only stared up at him. It wasn't… She…

Love.

"I do not have time to argue," he said, low and fierce.

That, she was sure, was absolutely true. He didn't have time to argue. He didn't have time to think. But she knew the girls better than he did. She knew...

She reached her hands up and cupped his face. She drew strength from that. From him. From love. "If you love me," she said, low and in her own kind of fierce, "then understand that I know what they can handle. What they can't. I couldn't live with myself if I got out and they didn't. Not like this."

She wasn't sure what changed in him. There was still an inhuman tenseness to his muscles and yet some of that fierceness in him had dimmed.

"What am I supposed to do if something happens to you?" he asked, his voice pained and gravelly.

"I can take care of myself." She knew it wasn't totally true. A million things could go wrong, but she had to trust him to leave and save Nattie, and he needed to trust her to stay and keep the girls alive.

That she'd have a much easier time of doing if he took Alyssa. No matter that it made her want to cry. No matter that she wanted to be selfish and take the spot. But she couldn't imagine living the rest of her life if their deaths were on her head.

If there was a chance to get them *all* out, alive and safe, she had to take it. Not the one that only saved her. "You know I'm right."

He looked away from her, though his tight grip on her shoulders never loosened. "You understand that I have to go. I don't have a choice."

"I want you to go. To save my sister."

His gaze returned to hers, flat and hard. "I'm not taking Alyssa."

"What? You have to." She gripped his shirt harder in an attempt to shake him. "If you can get one of us—"

"Gabby, I could get you out. Because you're supposed to be locked up, but more because I know you could do it. I could trust you to handle anything that came our way. I can't trust Alyssa. I can't trust her to keep her mouth shut when it counts. I can't trust her to get home. Like you said, she can't hack it. If I can't leave her here, then I can't take her, either."

"Then take one of the other girls!"

"You said it yourself. Alyssa would blab someone was missing. She'd… You can't trust her not to get you all killed. Don't you understand? It's you or no one."

"Why are you doing this?" she demanded, tears flooding her eyes. It wasn't fair. It wasn't right. He should take someone. Someone had to survive this.

"I'm not doing anything. I saw a chance for you— you, Gabby, to escape. If you won't take it, there's no substitute here. There is only you or nothing."

"Why are you trying to manipulate me into this? If you love me—"

"Why are you trying to manipulate my love? I know what the hell I'm doing, too. I have been trained for this. I have—"

"Gabby?"

Gabby and Jaime both jerked, looking down the hallway to Jasmine standing wide-eyed at the end of it. "What's going on?"

Jaime shook his head. "I can't do this. I don't have time to do this." Completely ignoring Jasmine, he got all up in Gabby's face, pulling her even closer, his dark eyes blazing into her. "I can save you *now*, but you have to come with me now. This is your last chance."

"It's your last chance to think reasonably," she retorted.

He looked to the ceiling and inhaled before crushing his mouth to hers, as though Jasmine wasn't standing right there. He seemed to pour all his frustration and all his fear into the kiss, and all Gabby could do was accept it.

"Goodbye, Gabby," he said on a ragged whisper, releasing her. "I love you, and I will get you safe."

She started to say his name as he walked away, but stopped herself as she looked at Jasmine. She couldn't say his real name. Even if she trusted Jasmine, she couldn't… This was all too dangerous now.

She wanted to tell him to save her sister. She wanted to tell him she loved him. She wanted to tell him he was being unfair and wrong, and yet none of those words poured out as he started to walk away. She wanted to tell him to be safe. That it would kill her if he was hurt.

But Jasmine was watching and she had to let him walk away. To save her sister. To save them all.

"What's happening?" Jasmine asked in a shaky voice. "I don't understand anything that I just saw."

Gabby slumped against the wall. "I don't know. I don't…"

"Yes, you do," Jasmine snapped, her voice sharp and uncompromising.

Gabby felt the tears spill unbidden down her cheeks. What was happening? She didn't understand any of it. But she knew she had to be strong. If they were going to be saved, she had to be strong.

She reached out for Jasmine, gratified when the girl offered support.

"We need to make a plan," Gabby said, sounding a lot stronger than she felt.

Jaime wasn't sure he could hide his dark mood if he tried. He was furious. Furious with Gabby for not coming with him. Furious at The Stallion for being the kind of fool who needed him to be there to do all the dirty work. Furious at the world for giving him something beautiful and then taking it all away.

Or are you just terrified?

He ground his teeth together and slid a look at The Stallion. The man sat in the passenger seat of the Jeep, typing on his laptop, swearing every time his Wi-Fi hotspot lost any kind of signal. He had a tricked-out assault rifle sitting precariously on his lap.

Jaime drove fueled on fear and anger. He'd had to leave the compound before he'd been able to be certain his message to his superiors had gone through. For all he knew, he could be out there alone with no backup. Gabby could be alone with no backup.

He wanted to rage. Instead he drove.

They were in the Guadalupe Mountains now, having driven through the night. Apparently, Gabby's sister and Ranger Cooper had run this way. Jaime was skeptical, considering how isolated it was. How would they be surviving?

But it didn't really matter. If they were on the wrong track, all the better.

What would actually be all the better would be reaching down to his side piece and ending this once and for all. It would put an end to two years of suffering.

Eight for Gabby. Who knew how much suffering for everyone else.

But no matter how much anger and fury pumped through his veins, he knew he couldn't do it. Those same people who had been victims deserved answers and they deserved justice. In an operation like The Stallion's, so big, so vast, taking the big man out would produce perhaps a confused few days, but someone would quickly and easily usurp that power. Taking over as if The Stallion had never existed. It would create even more victims than already existed.

He couldn't overlook that. His duty was his duty. Intractable no matter how unfair it seemed. No matter what Gabby would think of it.

Gabby had implored him to trust her and, in the moment, he hadn't. He'd been too blinded by his fear and his anger that she wouldn't go with him.

In the quiet of driving through these deserted mountains, Jaime could only relive that moment. Over and over again. Regret slicing through him. He'd ended things so badly, and there was such a chance—

No. He wouldn't let himself think that way. There was no chance he wouldn't see Gabby again. No good chance they didn't escape this. He would find a way and so would she.

"Drive up there." The Stallion pointing at, what seemed to Jaime, a random mountain.

"There is no road."

The Stallion gave him a doleful look. "Drive to the top of that mountain," he repeated.

Jaime inclined his head. *"Sí, senor."* He drove, adrenaline pumping too hard as the Jeep skidded and halted up the rocky incline. He gripped the wheel, tapping the brakes, doing everything he could to remain in control of the vehicle.

Finally, The Stallion instructed him to stop. The man pulled out a pair of high-tech binoculars and began to search the horizon.

Jaime watched the man. He looked like any man, hunting or perhaps watching birds. He appeared completely sane and normal, and yet Jaime had seen him fondle dolls like they were real people.

"*Senor*, may I ask you a question?" It was a dangerous road to take. If The Stallion read anything suspicious into his questioning, Jaime could end up dead in the middle of this mountainous desert.

But The Stallion nodded regally as if granting an audience with the peasants.

"If you believe women are diseased, so you say, why do you keep so many of them?"

The Stallion seemed to ponder the line of questioning. Eventually he shrugged. "Waste not, want not."

Jaime didn't have to feign a language barrier for that to not make sense at all. "I… Come again?"

"Waste not, want not," The Stallion repeated. "I find them hideous creatures myself, as the perfect woman remains elusive. But some men, like yourself, require certain payments. Why should I waste the work they can do for the possible insurance they can offer me? It only makes sense to keep them. To use them. In fact, it's what women were really meant for. To be used. Perhaps the perfect woman is just a myth. And my mother was a dirty liar." The Stallion's fingers tightened on his gun, though he still held the binoculars with his other hand.

Jaime said nothing more. It was best if he stopped asking for motives and started focusing on what he was going to do if they found Natalie and Ranger Cooper. Focus on thwarting The Stallion's plans without tipping him off to it.

Or you could just kill him.

It was so tempting, Jaime found his hand drifting down to the piece on his left side without really thinking about it.

"There!" The Stallion shouted, pointing.

Jaime blinked down at the bright desert and mountain before them.

"I saw something down there. Get out of the Jeep. Remember, I don't care what happens to the Ranger, but I want the girl alive."

The Stallion jumped out of the Jeep, scrambling over the loose rock, his gun cocked, laptop and binoculars forgotten in the passenger seat.

Though Jaime wanted nothing to do with this, he also jumped out of the car. He had to make sure The Stallion did nothing to Ranger Cooper or Gabby's sister.

Jaime grabbed a gun for each hand. It was easy to catch up with The Stallion given Jaime's legs were longer. Since The Stallion had his gun raised to his shoulder, Jaime pretended to accidentally skid into him as he fired his weapon.

"Damn it, Rodriguez. I had a shot!" The Stallion bellowed.

Jaime surveyed the ground below. He could see two figures standing like sitting ducks in the middle of the desert. They were too far away to make a shot a sure thing, but why weren't they moving after that first shot?

Jaime raised his gun. "Allow me, *senor.*"

Jaime was surprised that his arm very nearly shook as he took aim. He'd used his guns plenty in the past two years, though usually to disarm someone or to scare them, not to kill them.

This was no different. He aimed as close as he could without risking any harm and fired.

"You idiot!"

"They are too far away. We have to be closer."

"Like hell." The Stallion raised his gun again and since Jaime couldn't run into him again, he did the only other thing he could think of. He sneezed, loudly.

Again, The Stallion's shot went wide. He snapped his furious gaze on Jaime, and as his head and body turned toward him, so did the gun.

Jaime held himself unnaturally still, doing everything he could to show no fear or reaction to that gun pointed in his direction. He couldn't clear his throat to speak, and he could barely hear his own thoughts over the beating of his heart.

"*Perdón, senor*, but we need to be closer," Jaime said as if a gun that could blow him to pieces wasn't very nearly trained on him at close range. "If you want to ensure the Ranger is dead and the girl is yours, we need to be closer." Jaime pointed out over the desert below, where the couple was now running.

With no warning, The Stallion jerked the gun their way and shot. The woman scrambled behind the outcropping, but Jaime watched as Ranger Cooper jerked. Jaime winced, but Cooper didn't fall. He kept running. Until he was behind the rock outcropping with Gabby's sister.

"Get in the Jeep," The Stallion ordered with calm and ruthless efficiency, making Jaime wonder if he was really crazy at all.

Jaime nodded, knowing he was on incredibly thin ice. The Stallion could shoot him at any time.

You could shoot him first.

He could. God, he could all but feel himself doing it, but Gabby was back in that compound, defenseless. And if the message hadn't gotten through to his superiors... Even if he shot The Stallion his cover would be blown. He'd have to take Ranger Cooper back, and the FBI would intercept all that. Then they'd make him follow their rules and regulations to get Gabby out.

As long as he remained Rodriguez, there was a chance to get Gabby, and the rest of the girls, out by any means necessary.

So he drove the Jeep like a madman down to where the couple had been hiding.

"They are gone by now," Jaime said, perhaps a little too hopefully.

"Keep driving. Find them." The Stallion clenched and unclenched his hand on the rifle.

Jaime did as he was told, driving around mountains until The Stallion told him to stop.

"Stay in the Jeep," The Stallion ordered. "Turn off the ignition. When I call for you, you run. Do you *comprende*?"

Jaime nodded and The Stallion got out of the Jeep, striding away. Jaime thought about staying put for all of five seconds and then he set out to follow his enemy.

Chapter 14

Gabby sat in the common room with Jasmine, Tabitha and Alyssa. They were huddled on the couch, pretending to work on a project The Stallion had given them a few days ago. Layne and Wallace were groaning and limping around the house. Both clearly very injured and yet not seeking any medical attention.

"They're vulnerable. We have to press our advantage now. We have to hit them where it hurts," Alyssa whispered fiercely, staring daggers at the men who were currently groaning about in the kitchen.

Jasmine looked down at her lap, pale and clearly not wanting any part of this powwow, but...

"Unfortunately she's right," Gabby said. "It's our only chance. They've had time to call for backup. The longer we wait...the more chance someone else comes."

She felt guilty for not telling them about the possibility of an FBI raid. They deserved to know the full truth, and they deserved to know what possibilities lay ahead, but Gabby knew they had to get Alyssa out of there before she got killed or got them all killed. They couldn't wait for the FBI to come. They couldn't wait for Jaime to magically fix everything.

No, they had to act.

"We have to time it exactly and precisely. Two of us against one, the other two against the other. Same time. Same attack. Same plan."

Gabby took stock of the two men grousing in the kitchen then of the three women huddled around her. Alyssa practically jumped out of her seat, completely ready to go, Tabitha looked grim and certain, but Jasmine looked pale and scared.

Gabby didn't want to draw attention to that. Not with Alyssa as...well, whatever Alyssa was. Without looking at her, Gabby reached over and gave Jasmine's hand a squeeze.

"I'm just not strong like you, Gabby," she whispered. "What if I mess up?"

Alyssa started to say something harsh but Gabby stopped her with a look. "That's why we're doing it in pairs. We're a team. Me and Jasmine. Alyssa and Tabitha. Right?"

Alyssa mostly just swore and Gabby watched her carefully. Jaime's words about trusting her rang through her head. Because how could she trust a woman who'd clearly lost her mind? Who'd just as soon kill them all as anything else?

But Jaime had been too cautious. Too afraid for her safety. Gabby didn't have anyone's safety to be afraid for right now. She and the girls were getting to the now-or-never point. Alyssa was already there, and though

Tabitha and Jasmine had been somewhat more resilient, they had to feel as she did. They had to be losing that perilous grip on who they were.

Jaime had given herself back to her. Hope, a possible future, but those women hadn't had that. So she had to get them free.

"We'll take Layne," Gabby said, nudging Jasmine with her shoulder. "You two will have Wallace."

"But he's the bigger one," Jasmine whispered.

"It'll be fine. He has a gunshot wound to the shoulder. Wallace has one to the leg. We're four healthy, capable women."

"B-but what do we do, exactly? After we attack them, what do we do? Run?" Tabitha asked, clearly forcing herself to be strong.

"Kill them. We want to kill them. They did this to us. They deserve to die," Alyssa all but chanted, a wild gleam to her eyes.

Gabby wasn't sure why she hesitated at that. She had indeed been stripped from her life by men like these two, and they surely deserved death. But she found she didn't want to be the one to give it to them.

"We're going to use their injuries to our advantage, hurt them, and then tie them up so we can get away without fear of being followed."

Alyssa scoffed. "I'm going to kill him."

Gabby reached over and grabbed Alyssa's hands, trying to catch her frenzied gaze. "Please. Understand. I don't want to be haunted by this for the rest of my life. I want to leave here and leave it *behind*. No killing unless we absolutely have to. If we have a hope of getting out of here as unharmed as we are in *this* moment, we don't kill them. We incapacitate them."

"And then what? We're just going to run? Run where?"

"I have a vague notion of where we are, and that will help get us out. We've survived this, we can survive walking until we find a town."

Alyssa shook her head in disgust, but Gabby squeezed her hands tighter.

"I need you with me on this. We need to all be together and on the same page. Don't you want to be able to go home and go back to your old life and not have that on your conscience?"

"Who said I have a conscience?" Alyssa retorted, and for a very quick second Gabby believed her, believed that coldness. She'd seen nothing but cold for eight years.

Until Jaime.

That made Gabby fight so much harder. "The four of us are in this together. The four of us. They can't take that away from us. We have survived together, and when we get out, we will still be indelibly linked by that. We're like sisters. They can't make us turn on each other. You can't let them. As long as we work together, as long as we're linked, they can't hurt us."

Gabby wasn't certain that was true. They had guns and weapons, after all. But they were hurt. She had to believe it gave her and the girls an advantage.

Alyssa was looking at her strangely. "Sisters," she whispered. "I don't... No one's ever fought with me before."

"We will," Tabitha said, adding her hand to Gabby's on top of Alyssa's. Then Jasmine added her hand.

"We don't get out of this without each other," Gabby

said, glancing back at Wallace and Layne. Wallace was still moaning, but Layne was glancing their way.

"We'll slowly make excuses to go to our rooms, but you'll all come to mine," she whispered as she pulled her hand from the girls.

Jasmine brought her sewing back to her lap and Tabitha pretended to examine the next package they were supposed to hide in the stuffing of a toy dog.

Gabby got to her feet, but Layne was there and, with his good arm, he shoved her back down.

Well, crap. This wasn't going to go well.

"Problem?" she asked sweetly, looking up at his suspicious gaze. She probably should avert her gaze and show some sort of deference to the man with a gun in his waistband and a nasty expression on his face.

"Aren't you supposed to be locked up?"

"I was just going back to my room when you shoved me back to the couch so rudely."

"I'd watch how you talk to me, little girl," Layne seethed, getting his face into hers.

Gabby bit her tongue because what she really wanted to do was tell *him* to be careful how he talked to her, and then punch him in his bloody bandage as hard and painfully as she could.

Instead she slowly got to her feet, unfolding to her full height. Though he was still much taller than she was, she affected her most condescending stare, never breaking eye contact with him as she stood there, shoulders back.

She was more than a little gratified by the way he seemed to wilt just a teeny tiny bit. As if he knew he couldn't break her.

"I'll just be going to my room now. Feel free to lock my door behind me."

"You little—" He lifted his meaty hand, she supposed to backhand her, and she probably should have let him hit her. She probably should let this all go, but whatever instincts to defend herself she'd tried to eradicate surged to life. She grabbed his hand before it could land across her face, and then put all her force behind shoving him, trying to make contact with his injury.

He stumbled back, though he didn't fall. He let out a hideous moan as, with his bad arm, he pulled the gun from his waistband and trained it on Gabby.

She was certain she was dead. She stood there, waiting for the firearm to go off. Waiting for the piercing pain of a bullet. Or maybe she wouldn't feel it at all. Maybe she would simply die.

But before another breath could be taken, Alyssa was in front of her, and then Tabitha and Jasmine at her sides.

"You'll have to get through us to shoot her, and if you shoot all of us?" Alyssa pretended to ponder that. "I doubt The Stallion would be too pleased with you."

"I'll kill all of you without breaking a sweat, you miserable—"

"Isn't it cute?" Alyssa said, looking back at Gabby. "He thinks *he's* in charge, not his exacting, demanding boss. Well, I guess it takes some balls to be that stupid."

Gabby closed her eyes, she didn't think goading him was really the road to take here, but he hadn't fired.

Yet.

There was a quiet standoff and Gabby tried to rein in the heavy overbeating of her heart. Jasmine's hand slid into hers and Tabitha's arm wound around her shoulders. Alyssa faced off with Layne as if she had no fear whatsoever.

Together, they couldn't be hurt. God, she very nearly believed it.

"If you aren't in your rooms in five seconds, I will shoot all of you," Layne said menacingly.

Gabby didn't believe him, but she didn't want to risk it, either. The girls in front of her hurried down the hall first, and Gabby tried to follow, but Layne grabbed her arm as she passed, digging his heavy fingers into her skin hard enough to leave bruises.

"Tonight you'll be screaming my name," he hissed.

Gabby smiled. It was either that or throw up. "Maybe you'll be screaming mine." She yanked her arm out of his grasp.

She was pretty sure the only thing that kept Layne from shooting her at this point was Wallace's sharp stand-down order.

When Gabby got to her room, she locked the door behind her. It wouldn't keep her safe from Layne since he undoubtedly had a key, but it at least gave her the illusion of safety.

When she turned back to face her room, the girls were all there, Tabitha and Jasmine on her bed, Alyssa pacing the room.

"And now we plan," Alyssa said, that dark glint in her eyes comforting for the first time.

Jaime stalked The Stallion. It wasn't easy to carefully follow a man who was carefully following another man, especially through a weirdly arid desert landscape dotted by mountains and rock outcroppings. But then, when had any of this been *easy*?

The Stallion stopped as though he'd seen something, and Jaime waited a beat. He realized The Stallion was peering around a swell of earth, and when The Stallion didn't move forward in the swiftly calculating pace he'd been employing, Jaime sucked in a breath.

On a hunch and a prayer, Jaime snuck around the other side of it. He kept his footsteps slow and quiet.

And then a shot rang out.

Jaime took off in a run, skidding to a halt when he saw The Stallion and Ranger Cooper standing off.

Jaime couldn't hear their conversation, but both men were unharmed and The Stallion didn't fire. Jaime dropped the small handguns he'd been carrying for ease of movement and unholstered his largest and most accurate weapon.

He trained it on The Stallion, only occasionally letting his gaze dart around to try to catch sight of the woman who remained hidden somewhere. The Stallion and Ranger Cooper spoke, back and forth, guns pointed at each other, lawman and madman in the strangest showdown Jaime had ever witnessed.

That gave Jaime the presence of mind to *breathe*. To watch and bide his time. Without knowing where Natalie Torres was, he couldn't act rashly. He—

Something in The Stallion's posture changed and Jaime sighted his gun, ready to shoot, ready to stop The Stallion before anything happened to Ranger Cooper. But before he could line up his shot and pull the trigger without accidentally hitting Cooper, Cooper fired.

The gun flew from The Stallion's hand and he howled with rage. Why the hell hadn't Cooper shot the bastard in the heart? Jaime was about to do just that, but the woman appeared from a crevice in one of the rocks, holding her own weapon up and trained on The Stallion.

She reminded him so much of Gabby it physically hurt. There wasn't an identical resemblance, but it was that determined glint in Natalie's dark eyes that had him thinking about Gabby. If she was safe. If any of them would make it through this in one piece.

He shook that thought away. They would. They all damn well would.

And then Natalie pulled the trigger. She missed, but before Jaime could step out from the outcropping, she'd fired again. Even from Jaime's distance he could see the red bloom on The Stallion's stomach.

"Rodriguez!" he screamed, followed by The Stallion's sad attempt at Spanish. Jaime sighed. He could only hope Cooper recognized him, or that they wouldn't shoot on sight. He could stay there, of course, but it would be worse if he waited for Ranger Cooper to find him.

He stepped out from behind the land swell and walked slowly and calmly toward his writhing fake boss.

Ranger Cooper watched him with the dawning realization of recognition, but Natalie clearly didn't have a clue as she kept her gun trained on him.

Jaime thought maybe, maybe, there was a chance he could maintain his identity and get back to Gabby, so he nodded to Cooper. "Tell your woman to put down the gun," he said in Spanish.

Cooper looked over at the woman. "Put it down, Nat," he murmured, an interesting softness in the command. One Jaime thought he recognized.

Wasn't that odd?

"I won't let anyone kill us. Not now. Not when that man has my sister," Natalie said, her hands shaking, her dark eyes shiny with tears. The Torres women were truly a marvel.

The Stallion made a grab for Jaime's leg piece, but Jaime easily kicked him away. No, he wasn't Rodriguez anymore. He had to be the man he'd always been, and he had to do his duty.

He wasn't Rodriguez, a monster with a shady past. He was Jaime Alessandro, FBI agent, and regardless of *who* he was, he'd find a way to get Gabby to safety as soon as he got out of there.

"Ma'am, I need you to put your weapon down," Jaime said, steady and sure, making eye contact with Natalie. "I'm with the FBI. I've been working undercover for Callihan." Jaime ignored The Stallion's outraged cry, because he saw the way the information tumbled together in Natalie's head.

She didn't even have to ask about Gabby for him to know that's what she needed to hear. "I know where your sister is. She's…safe."

Natalie didn't just lower her gun, she dropped it. She sank to the rocky ground and Jaime had to raise an eyebrow at Ranger Cooper sinking with her.

He couldn't hear what they said to each other, but it didn't matter. He turned to The Stallion. Victor Callihan. The man who'd made his life a living hell for two years.

He was still writhing on the ground, bloody and pale, shaking possibly with shock or with the loss of blood. He might make it. He might not. Jaime supposed it would depend on how quickly they worked.

Jaime slid into a crouch. "How does it feel, *senor*,"

Jaime mused aloud, "to be so completely outwitted by everyone around you?"

"You think this is over?" The Stallion rasped. "It'll never be over. As long as I *breathe,* you're mine, and it will never, *ever,* be over."

Jaime had been through too much for those words to have any impact. The Stallion thought he could intimidate him? Make him fear? Not in this lifetime or the next.

"There's already an FBI raid at all four of your compounds." He was gratified when the man's eyes bulged. "Oh, did you think I didn't put it together? The southern compound? You know who helped me figure out its location? Ah, no, I don't want to ruin the surprise. I'll let you worry about that. You'll have plenty of time to ruminate in a cell."

The Stallion lunged, but he was weakened and all Jaime had to do was rock back on his heels to avoid the man's grasp.

"Everyone should be out by the time I get back, and you know what my first order of business will be? Burning every last doll in that place," he whispered in the man's ear, before standing.

Jaime turned to Cooper who'd gotten Natalie to her feet. He ignored The Stallion's sputtering and nodded in the direction of the Jeep. "I have rope in my vehicle. We'll tie him up and take him to the closest ranger station."

And then he'd find a way to get to Gabby.

Chapter 15

Gabby stood at the door to her room, Jasmine slightly in front of her. Alyssa and Tabitha had already gone back into the common room, plan in place.

Gabby felt sick, but she pushed it away. The girls were counting on her and so was… Well, she herself. She was the architect of this plan, the leader, and if she wanted them all to survive, she had to be calm and strong.

Jaime was out protecting her sister, and no matter how mad he might be at her for not leaving, she knew he'd do everything to keep Natalie safe.

And she hadn't even told him…

She forced it all away as Alyssa's cue blasted through the house. Gabby exchanged a look with Jasmine. Alyssa was supposed to yell at Tabitha, not scream obscenities at her.

As Gabby and Jasmine slid into the room, Alyssa attacked, stabbing one of her butter knives into Wallace's leg with a brutal force Gabby had to look away from.

Jasmine threw the cords they'd gathered at Tabitha. Wallace screamed in a kind of agony that made Gabby's blood run cold, but she couldn't think about that now. Layne was her target.

His eyes gleamed with an unholy bloodlust and his gun was in his grasp far too fast. But somehow everything seemed to move in slow motion. Before Gabby could even flinch, Jasmine was throwing her body at Layne's legs.

The impact surprised Layne enough that he fell forward, on top of Jasmine, who cried out, mixing with Wallace's screams.

Gabby scrambled forward, pushing Layne off Jasmine so he hit the hard floor on his injured shoulder. He howled in pain, but he didn't let go of the gun as Gabby grabbed it.

She jerked and pulled, but Layne didn't let go. He screamed, but she couldn't wrestle the weapon from his grasp.

Until Jasmine got to her feet and started stomping on his bad shoulder, a wholly different girl than the woman who'd, pale-faced and wide-eyed, told Gabby she wasn't strong enough. Gabby finally wrested the gun free of his hand, trying to think past the high-pitched keening from both men.

"Rope," she gasped then yelled louder. She glanced at Alyssa and Tabitha. Wallace thrashed, groaning in pain as he swung his hands out, but Tabitha had tied his legs tightly to the chair and Alyssa had already wrestled the gun out of his hands.

Alyssa kicked one of the cords Gabby's way and Gabby grabbed it as Layne tried to scuttle away from Jasmine, cursing and, Gabby thought, maybe even sobbing.

Jasmine stomped another time on his wound, which had now bled completely through his bandage and shirt. His face went white and his eyes rolled back in his head, and it was only then that Gabby realized Jasmine was crying and that Wallace had gone completely silent.

Feeling a sob rise in her throat, Gabby knelt next to Layne and jerked his arms behind his back, doing her best to tie the cord around his thick forearms and wrists. She pulled it as tightly as she possibly could and tied as many knots as the length of cord would allow.

She breathed through her mouth, because something about the smell of Layne—him or his wound—nearly made her woozy.

"I've got his legs," Tabitha said, moving to the end of Layne's lifeless body. Gabby could see the rise and fall of his chest, so he wasn't dead.

She almost wished he was, which was enough to get her to her feet. She glanced back at Alyssa who had ripped off half her shirt and tied it around Wallace's face like a gag. The man still wiggled, but the cords and knots were holding and if he tried to escape too much longer, he'd likely knock the whole chair over.

Alyssa held the gun far too close to Wallace's head.

Gabby crossed to her, holding her hand out for the gun. "Tabitha is going to guard them."

Alyssa didn't spare Gabby a glance. "My suggestion of just killing them stands," she said, her hands tight on the gun, sweat dripping down her temple.

"I need your help to gather evidence."

"They can," Alyssa said, jerking her chin toward Jasmine, who stood with Layne's gun trained on his unmoving form and Tabitha finishing up the knots at his ankles. She never looked at them, just gestured toward them.

"No, I need you," Gabby said firmly.

Alyssa's gaze finally flickered to Gabby. "You need me?"

"Yes. You're the strongest next to me. We'll be able to break down the doors easiest and carry the most stuff. I need you."

Gabby didn't really know if Alyssa was stronger, but it was certainly the most plausible. Clearly it also got through to her since she'd looked away from Wallace.

Maybe it would be easier to kill the men, but Gabby... She didn't want to have to relive that for the rest of her life, and she didn't want the other girls to have to, either.

Alyssa waved the gun a bit. "We might need this to bust the lock off."

Gabby remained steadfast in holding her hand out, palm upward. "Give me the gun, Alyssa. We need to do this as a team."

The woman's mouth turned into a sneer and Gabby thought for sure she'd lost the battle. Any second now Alyssa would pull the trigger and—

She slapped the gun into Gabby's palm. "Let's go get those doors open," she muttered.

Gabby nodded, looking at Tabitha and Jasmine. Jasmine had Layne's gun and Tabitha had what looked to be a dagger of some kind that she must have taken off one of the men.

"Scream if you need anything," Gabby said sternly. "Once we have whatever evidence we can carry, we'll come get you and lock this place back up, and then we'll start out."

Jasmine and Tabitha nodded, and though they'd handled themselves like old pros, everyone seemed a little shaky now. Far too jumpy. She and Alyssa needed to hurry.

They raced down the hall to the door. "Give me one of those knives."

Alyssa pulled one out of her bra and if Gabby had time she might have marveled at it, but instead she used it to start picking the lock. Turned out Ricky and his ne'er-do-well friends *had* taught her something.

She got the locks free and pushed on the door. It creaked open only a fraction. Alyssa inspected the crack. "It's chained on the outside," she said flatly. "Give me the gun."

Gabby hesitated. "What if it ricochets?"

Alyssa raised an eyebrow. "It won't."

What choice did Gabby have? A butter knife wasn't cutting through chain any more than anything else, and Alyssa might be losing it, but she was sure. They had to be a team.

Gabby handed over the gun. Alyssa shoved the muzzle through the crack, barely managing to fit it, and then a loud shot rang out.

The chain clanked and then after another quick and overly loud shot, Alyssa was pushing the door open.

Both women stumbled into the bright light of day. It very nearly burned, the bright sunshine, the intense blue overhead. Gabby tried to step forward, but only tripped and fell to her knees in the grass.

"Oh, God. Oh, God," Alyssa whispered.

Gabby couldn't see her. Her eyes couldn't seem to adjust to the bright light, and her heart just imploded.

She could smell the grass. She could feel it under her knees and hands. Hot from the midday sun. Rocky soil underneath. It was real. Real and true. The actual earth. Fresh air. The sun. God, the sun.

The one time they'd been let out it had been a cloudy day, and The Stallion hadn't allowed for any reaction. Just digging. But today…today the sun beat down on her face as if it hadn't been missing from her life for eight years.

Gabby tried to hold back the sobs, she had a job to do, after all. A mission, and leaving Tabitha and Jasmine alone with dangerous men no matter how injured or tied up wasn't fair. She had to act.

But all she could seem to do was suck in air and cry.

Then Alyssa's arms were pulling her to her feet. "We have to keep moving, Gabby. We've got time to cry later. Now, we have to move."

Gabby finally managed to blink her eyes open. Alyssa's jaw was set determinedly and she pointed to a fancy shed in the corner of the yard.

Gabby took a deep breath of air—fresh and sun-laden—and looked down at her hands. She'd grasped some grass and pulled it out, and now it fluttered to the patchy ground below.

The Stallion had kept her from this, *all of this*, for eight long years. It was time to make sure it was his turn to not see daylight for a hell of a lot longer.

Jaime drove the Jeep toward where Cooper's map said there'd be a ranger station. Once they had access to a phone—The Stallion's laptop had been too encrypted to be of use—Jaime would call his superiors and Ranger Cooper's.

Things would be real soon enough, and he still wasn't back to Gabby.

Still, he answered Cooper's questions and only occasionally glanced at the woman sandwiched between him and the Texas Ranger.

She was slighter than Gabby, certainly softer, and yet she'd been the one to shoot The Stallion as though it had been nothing at all.

Jaime glanced at Cooper's crudely bandaged arm wound. It was bleeding through, though he'd looked over it himself and knew, at most, Cooper would need stitches.

There was an awkward silence between every one of Ranger Cooper's curt questions and every one of Jaime's succinct answers. Tension and stress seemed to stretch between all of them, no matter that The Stallion was apprehended in the back and would likely survive his injuries.

Unless Jaime slowed down. But it wasn't an option, not without news on Gabby and the raid. Too many unknowns, too many possibilities.

He finally found a road after driving through mountains and desert, and soon enough a ranger station came into view. Jaime brought the Jeep to a stop, trying to remember himself and his duty.

He pushed the Jeep into Park and looked at Cooper. "If you stay put, I'll have them call for an ambulance, as well as call your precinct. We'll see if there's any word on the raid to Callihan's house, where your sister was."

Ranger Cooper nodded stoically, putting his hand on his weapon, his glance falling to the back of the Jeep where Victor Callihan, The Stallion, Jaime's tormenter, lay still and tied up.

Bleeding.

Hopefully miserable.

Jaime glanced at Gabby's sister, but she only stared at him. She'd asked no questions about her sister. She'd said almost nothing at all. Jaime figured she was in shock.

"I don't know what to ask," she said, her voice weak and thready.

Jaime gave a sharp nod. "Let me see if I can go find out some basics." He left the Jeep and strode into the station.

A woman behind the counter squeaked, but Jaime held up his hands.

"I'm with the FBI and I need to use your phone." He realized he didn't have his badge, and he still had far too many weapons strapped to his body.

He needed to get his crap together and fast. He kept his hands raised and recited his FBI information. The woman shoved a phone at him, but she backed into a corner of her office and Jaime had no doubt she was radioing for help.

It didn't matter. He called through to his superior, trying to rein in his impatience.

"I'm in a ranger station in the Guadalupe Mountains National Park. I have Texas Ranger Vaughn Cooper and civilian Natalie Torres with me. The Stallion is hurt and disarmed. We need an ambulance for Callihan and Cooper, and I need an immediate debriefing on what's happening at The Stallion's compound in the west."

"Immediate," Agent Lucroy repeated, and though it had been years since Jaime had seen the man in charge of his undercover investigation, he could imagine clearly the man's raised eyebrow. "That's quite the demand."

"Sir," Jaime said, biting back a million things he wanted to yell. "There are four women in that compound, whom I left with armed and dangerous men. It is my duty and my utmost concern that they are safe."

There was a long silence on the line.

"Sir?" Jaime repeated, fearing the worst.

"The raid has been initiated per your message. Our agents are on the ground at the compound…"

"And Ga—the women?"

"Well… Let me get off the phone and contact the necessary authorities to get you out of there. We'll do a proper debriefing when you're back in San Antonio."

Jaime nearly doubled over, fear turning into a nauseating sickness in his gut. Oh, God, he hadn't saved her. She wasn't safe at all.

"What happened to the women?" he demanded. "One of the captives… Natalie Torres, the woman Ranger Cooper has been protecting, she's the sister of one of the captives. She deserves to know…" She deserved to know how horribly he'd failed.

Agent Lucroy sighed. "Let's just say there's a slight… situation at the El Paso compound."

Chapter 16

"Do you think we can carry a computer as far as we need to walk?" Gabby asked, looking dubiously down at the hard drive Alyssa was unhooking from a million monitors.

Alyssa shrugged. "We can get it as far as we need to. Then it's got just as much a chance of being found by whatever cops we can find as any Stallion idiots."

It was a good point. In fact, Alyssa had made quite a few. Though Gabby still didn't trust Alyssa not to go off and do something drastic or dangerous, the woman was very effective under pressure.

They hadn't found any bags or things they could haul evidence in, so they'd shoved any important-looking papers into their pockets. Gabby had come across a map with markings on it, and she thought with enough time she'd be able to figure it out. She'd taken a page out of Alyssa's book and shoved it into her bra.

Gabby went through a shelf of tech gadgets and picked up anything she thought might have memory on it. Anything that could make sure this was over for good.

It's not over until you're out of here.

She tried to ignore the panic beating in her chest and *focus.* "That should be good, don't you think?" When she turned to face Alyssa, the woman was staring at a shelf of dolls. They all looked like variations of the same. Dark hair, unseeing eyes, frilly dresses.

A heavy sense of unease settled over the adrenaline coursing through Gabby. She understood now, completely, why the dolls had weighed so heavily on Jaime. She tried to look away, but it felt as if the dolls were just…staring at—

The shot that rang out made Gabby scream, the doll's head exploding made her wince, but when she wildly looked over at Alyssa, the woman was simply holding the gun up, vaguely smiling.

"Think I have enough bullets to shoot all of them?" she asked conversationally.

"No," Gabby said emphatically. "Let's go. Let's get the hell out of here."

Alyssa nodded, grabbing the computer hard drive and hefting it underneath her arm. She kept the gun in her other hand, but before either of them could make another move, the door burst open.

Gabby dropped to the ground, trying to hide behind the desk that dominated the shed, but Alyssa only turned, gun aimed at the invasion of men.

Men in *uniform.*

"FBI. Put down your weapons," they yelled in chorus.

Gabby scrambled back to her feet, blinking a few

times, just to make sure… But there it was in big bold letters.

FBI.

Oh, *God.* She searched the men's faces, but none of them was Jaime.

"Drop your weapon, ma'am," one of them intoned, his voice flat and commanding.

Alyssa stared at the man and most decidedly did *not* drop her weapon.

"Alyssa," Gabby hissed.

"I'm not going to be a prisoner for another second," Alyssa said, her voice deadly calm.

"It's the *FBI.* Look at his uniform, Alyssa. Do what he *says.*" Gabby held up her hands, hoping that with her cooperating the men wouldn't shoot.

But Alyssa didn't move. She eyed the FBI agent, both with their weapons raised at each other.

"Ma'am, if you do not lower the weapon, I will be forced to shoot. You have to the count of three. One, two—"

"Ugh, fine," Alyssa relented, lowering her arm. She didn't drop the weapon and she stared at the men with nothing but a scowl.

"They're here to save us," Gabby said, feeling a bubble of hysteria try to break free. She wanted to cry. She wanted to throw herself at these men's feet. She wanted Jaime and to know for sure…

"It's over, isn't it?" she asked, a tear slipping down her cheek.

"Ma'am, you have to drop your weapon. We cannot escort you out of here until you do," he said to Alyssa, ignoring Gabby completely.

"There are two other women inside the house. Did

you—?" Gabby had started to step forward, but one of the men held up his hand and she stopped on a dime.

"We will not be discussing anything until she drops her damn weapon," the man said through gritted teeth.

There were four of them, three with their weapons trained on Alyssa, a fourth one behind the three on a phone, maybe relaying information to someone.

Alyssa had her grip on the gun so tight her knuckles were white and Gabby didn't know how to fix this.

"What are you doing?" Gabby demanded. She wanted to go over and shake Alyssa till some sense got through that hard head of hers, but she was afraid to move. They were finally free and Alyssa was going to get them both killed.

That made her a different kind of angry. "Why are you treating us like the criminals?" she demanded of the four men, soldier-stiff and stoic.

"Why won't you drop your weapon?" the agent retorted.

Gabby didn't know how long they stood there. It seemed like forever. Alyssa neither dropped her weapon, nor did the men lower theirs. Seconds ticked on, dolls watching from above, and all Gabby could do was stand there.

Stand there in limbo between prison and freedom. Stand there with the threat of this woman who'd become an ally and a friend dying when they'd come this far.

"Please, Alyssa. Please," Gabby whispered after she didn't know how long. Gabby had spent eight years trying to be strong. Beating any emotion out of herself, but all strength did in this moment was make this standoff continue.

She looked at Alyssa, letting the tears fall from her

eyes, letting the emotion shake her voice. "Please, put down the gun," she whispered. "I want you safe when we get out of here. I don't want to have to watch you get hurt. Please, Alyssa, put down the gun."

Alyssa swallowed. She didn't drop the gun, though her grip loosened incrementally.

"We all want this to be over," Gabby said, pushing her advantage as hard as she could. "We all want to go home."

"I don't," Alyssa muttered, but she dropped the gun all the same.

Jaime supposed that someday in the future it would be a point of pride that he'd yelled at his superior over the phone and had to be restrained by three fellow agents, and still retained his job.

But when Agent Lucroy had explained there'd been a standoff—a *standoff*—with two women who had been *captives*, no matter how dangerous he'd felt Alyssa could be, Jaime had lost it.

He'd sworn at his boss. He'd thrown the phone across the ranger station. The only thing that had kept his temper on a leash as they'd waited for the ambulance was the fact that Natalie was Gabby's sister.

She didn't need to be as sick with fear and as stuck as he was.

The being restrained by three fellow agents had come later. When they'd had to forcibly put him on a flight to the field office in San Antonio instead of to Austin with Ranger Cooper and Natalie.

There had been a *slight* altercation once getting off the plane when he'd demanded his car and been refused.

In the end, a guy he'd once counted as a friend had had to pull a gun on him.

He'd gotten himself together after that. Mostly. He'd met with his boss and had agreed to go through the mandatory debriefing, psych eval and the like. Sure, maybe only after Agent Lucroy had threatened to have him admitted to a psych ward if he didn't comply.

Semantics.

He was held overnight in the hospital, being poked and prodded and mentally evaluated. When he'd been released, he was supposed to go home. He was supposed to meet his superiors at noon and inform them of everything.

Instead he'd gotten in his car and driven in the opposite direction. He very possibly was risking his job and he didn't give a damn. He should go see his parents, his sister. They were in California, but if he was really going to take a break with reality, shouldn't it be to have them in his sight?

When he'd spoken to Mom on the phone, she'd begged him to come home, and when he'd said he couldn't, she'd said she'd be heading to San Antonio as soon as she could. He'd begged her off. Work. Debriefing.

The truth was... He wasn't ready to be Jaime Alessandro quite yet. He'd neither cut his hair nor shaved his beard. He was neither FBI agent nor Stallion lackey, he was something in between, and no amount of FBI shrinks poking at him would give him the key to step back into his old life.

Not until he saw Gabby. So he drove to Austin. Thanks to Ranger Cooper apparently being unaware that he wasn't supposed to know, Jaime had the information that Gabby was still in the hospital and had yet to be reunited with her family.

When Ranger Cooper had relayed that information, Jaime may have broken a few traffic laws to get to the hospital.

All he needed was to see her, to maybe touch her. Then he could breathe again. Maybe then he could find himself again.

Maybe then he'd forgive her for not getting out when he'd wanted her to.

He did some fast talking, but either the hospital staff was exceptionally good or they'd been forewarned. No amount of flashing his badge or trying to sneak around corners worked.

Eventually security had been called. When one security guard appeared, Jaime laughed. Then another had appeared behind him and he figured they were probably serious.

He wasn't armed, but there were ways he could easily incapacitate these men. He could imagine breaking the one in front's nose, the one in back's arm. This middle-aged, not-in-the-best-of-shape security guard *and* his burly partner. Bam, bam, quick and easy.

It was that uncomfortable realization—that he was pushing too hard, pressing against people who didn't deserve it—that had him softening.

So, when the guards grabbed him by the arms, he let them. He let them push him out the doors and into the waiting room.

"What the hell is your problem, man?" the one guy asked, clearly questioning the truth of his FBI claims.

That was a good enough question. He was acting like a lunatic. Not at all like the FBI agent who had been assigned and willfully taken on the deep under-cover operation that had just aided in busting a crime organization that had been hurting the people of this state—and others—for over a decade.

"You come through these doors again, the police will be taking your ass to jail. FBI agent or not."

Jaime inclined his head, straightening his shoulders and then his shirt. "I apologize," he managed to rasp, turning away from the guards only to come face-to-face with two women frowning at him.

"Why are you trying to see my daughter?" the mid-dle-aged woman demanded, her hands shaking, her eyes red as though she'd done nothing but cry for days.

If she was Gabby's mother, perhaps she had.

It was the thing that finally woke him up. Really and fully. Gabby's mother, and a woman who looked to be Gabby's grandmother. He'd assumed Natalie wasn't there, but then she walked in from the hallway carry-ing two paper cups of coffee.

"Agent Alessandro," she said, stopping short. "Did something hap—?"

"No, Ms. Torres. I merely came by to check on your sister, and I was informed, uh…" He glanced at the women who'd likely seen him get tossed out on his ass. "She wasn't seeing visitors."

Natalie handed off the drinks to the other two women, offering a small and weak smile. "She's asked not to see anyone for a bit longer yet, from what the doctor told me."

"And her, uh, health? It's…"

"As good as can be expected. Maybe better. They've had a psychiatrist talking to her a bit. Are you here to question her? I'm not sure—"

"The case we're building against The Stallion will take time, but your sister's contributions... Well, we'll certainly work with her comfort as much as we can."

He looked at the three women who'd been through their own kind of hell. He didn't know them. Maybe they'd spent eight years certain Gabby was dead. Maybe they'd hoped for her return every night for however many nights she'd been gone.

Gabby would know. She'd be able to figure out the math in a heartbeat, or maybe it was her heartbeat, every second away from her family.

A family who had loved her and taken care of her for twenty years. A family who had far more claim to her than the man who'd spent a week with her and left her behind.

He straightened his shirt again, clearing his throat. He pulled out his wallet, a strange sight. It held his ID with his real name. His badge. Things that belonged to Jaime Alessandro, not Rodriguez.

He blinked for a few seconds, forgetting what he was doing.

"Do you want me to call some—?"

He thrust his business card at Natalie, effectively cutting off her too kind offer. "If you need anything, anything at all, any of you, please don't hesitate to contact me. I'll be back in San Antonio for at least another day or two, but it's an easy enough drive."

Natalie looked at him with big brown eyes that looked too much like Gabby's for his shaky control.

"I want all three of you to know how strong Gab—Gabriella was during this whole ordeal," he forced himself to say, feeling stronger and more sure with every word. FBI agent to the last. "She saved herself, and those women, and did an amazing amount of work in allowing us to confidently press charges against a very dangerous man."

She'd been a warrior, a goddess, an immeasurable asset and ally. She was a *survivor* in every iteration of the word, and he wasn't worthy of her. Not like this.

That meant he had to face his responsibilities and figure out how to come back as just that.

Worthy of Gabby.

Chapter 17

Gabby sat in a sterile hospital room dreading the seconds that ticked by. Every second brought her closer to something she didn't know how to face.

Life.

Her family was in the waiting room. She'd been cleared by both the doctor and the psychiatrist to see them. To be released from the hospital. There'd be plenty of therapy and police interviews in the future, but for the most part she could go home.

What did that even mean? Eight years she'd been missing. Eight years for her family to change. Daddy was gone. Who knew where Mom and Grandma lived. Surely, Natalie had her own life.

Gabby sat on the hospital bed and tried not to hold on to it for dear life when the nurse arrived. Gabby didn't want to leave this room. She didn't want to face whatever waited for her out there.

She'd rather go back to the compound.

It was that thought, and the shuddering denial that went through her, that reminded her... Well, this would be hard, of course it would be. It would be painful, and a struggle, but it was better. So much better than being a prisoner.

"Your family is waiting," the nurse said kindly. "I've got your copy of the discharge papers and the referrals from the psychiatrist. Is there anything you'd like me to relay to your family for you?"

Gabby shook her head, forcing herself to climb off the bed and onto her own two feet. Her own two feet, which had gotten her this far.

She took a shaky breath and followed the nurse out of the safety of her hospital room. The corridor was quiet save for machine beeps and squeaky shoes on linoleum floors. Gabby thought she might throw up, and then they'd probably take her back to a room and she could...

But they reached the doors and the nurse paused, offering a comforting smile. "Whenever you're ready, sweetheart."

Gabby straightened. She'd never be ready, so taking a second was only delaying the inevitable. "Let's go."

The nurse opened the doors and stepped out, Gabby following by some sheer force of will that had gotten her through eight years of hell.

The nurse walked toward three women sitting huddled together. None of them looked *familiar* and yet Gabby knew exactly who they were. Grandma, Mom, Natalie. Older and different and yet *them*.

Natalie got to her feet, her face white and her eyes wide as though she were looking at a ghost.

Gabby felt like one. Natalie reached out, but it was almost blindly, as if she didn't know what she was reaching for. As if Gabby were really a vision Natalie's hand would simply move through.

Her little sister. A woman in her own right. Eight years lost between them, and she was reaching out for a ghost. But Gabby was no ghost.

"Nattie." It was out of her mouth before Gabby'd even thought it. She grabbed Natalie's hand and squeezed it. Real. Alive. Her sister. Flesh and bone and *soul*. They weren't the same women anymore, but they were still sisters. No matter what separated them.

Natalie didn't say anything, just gaped at her. Mom and Grandma were still sitting, sobbing openly and loudly. Two women she'd barely ever seen cry. The Torres family kept their *sadness* on the down low or hidden in anger, but never...

Never this.

"Say something," Gabby whispered to Natalie, desperate for something to break this tight bubble of pain inside her.

"I don't know..." Natalie sucked in a deep breath, looking up at Gabby who remained an inch or two taller. "I'm so sorr—"

Gabby shook her head and cupped Natalie's face with her hands. She would fall apart with apologies from innocent bystanders. "No, none of that."

Natalie let out a sob and her entire body leaned into Gabby. A hug. Tears over her. Gabby didn't sob, but her own tears slid down her cheeks as she held her sister back.

Real. Not a dream. Nothing but *real*. She glanced over Natalie's head at her mother and grandmother. She held an arm out to them. "Mama, Grandma." Her voice

was little more than a rasp, but she used as commanding a tone as she could muster. "Come here."

It only took a second before they were on their feet,
wrapping their arms around her, holding on too tightly,
struggling to breathe through tears and hugs.

Gabby shook, something echoing all the way through
her body so violently she couldn't fight it off. It was
relief. It was fear. It was her mother's arms wrapped
tight around her.

"Are you all right?" Natalie asked, clearly concerned
over Gabby's shaking. "Do you need a doctor? I'll go
get the nu—"

But Gabby held her close. "I'm all right, baby sister.
I just can't believe it's real. You're all here."

"They…told you about… Daddy?"

Gabby swallowed, her chin coming up, and she did
her best to harden her heart. She'd deal with the softer
side of that grief some other time. "The Stallion made
sure I knew."

"But…"

Gabby shook her head. She shouldn't have mentioned
that man, that evil. She was free, and she wasn't going
back to that place. "No. Not today. Maybe not ever."

"One of us needs to get it together so we can drive
home," Mama said, her hand shaking as she mopped up
tears. Her other hand was a death grip around Gabby's
elbow. Gabby didn't even try to escape it. It was like
an anchor. A truth.

"I'm all right," Natalie assured them. "I'll drive.
Right now. We're free to go. We're… Let's get out of
here. And go home."

"Home," Gabby echoed. What was home? She supposed she'd find out soon enough. But as they turned

to leave the waiting room, someone entered, blocking the way.

Gabby's heart felt as though it stopped beating for a good moment. She barely recognized him. He'd had a haircut and a shave and today looked every inch the FBI agent in his suit and sunglasses.

She stiffened, because she wasn't ready for this, because her first instinct was to throw herself at him.

Because an angry slash of hurt wound through her. He hadn't come to check on her, and no one had told her what had happened to him.

She'd been afraid to ask. Afraid he'd be dead. Afraid he'd been a figment of her imagination. So afraid of everything outside these walls.

Now he was just *here*, looking polished and perfect. Not Jaime, but the man he'd been before the compound. A man she didn't know and…

She didn't know how to do *all* of this today, so she threw her shoulders back and greeted him coolly, no matter how big a mess she must look from all the crying.

"Ms. Torres."

Even his voice was different, as though the man she'd known in the compound simply hadn't existed. That had been a beating fear inside her for days and now it was a reality.

She could only fight it with a strength she was faking.

His gaze took her in quickly then moved to her sister. "Ms.…well, Natalie, I've got a message for you."

Gabby's grip tightened on Natalie's arm, though she didn't dare show a hint of the fear beating against her chest.

"It's from the Texas Rangers' office."

It was Natalie's turn to grip, to stiffen. Jaime held

out a piece of paper and Natalie frowned at it. "They couldn't have called me? Sent an email?" she muttered.

Jaime's gaze was on Gabby and she just…had to look away.

"Agent Alessandro, would you be able to escort Gabby and my family home while I see to this?"

Gabby whipped her head to her sister, whose expression was…angry, Gabby thought. She thought she recognized that stubborn anger on her sister's face.

"I'd love to be of service," Jaime said. "But I doubt your sister…"

He was trying to beg off because of *her*? Oh, no. Hell, no. "Oh, no, please escort us, Mr. *Alessandro. I* don't have a problem with it in the least," Gabby replied, linking arms with Mama and Grandma.

He didn't get to run away anymore.

Gabby saw the uncertainty on Natalie's face, but Gabby wanted to be done. Done with law enforcement and the past eight years. "Tie up loose ends, sissy. I want this over, once and for all," she said, not bothering to even look at Jaime.

"It will be," Natalie promised before she stalked past Jaime.

When Gabby finally looked at Jaime, his eyebrows were drawn together, some emotion shuttered in his expression. She couldn't read it. She didn't want to.

He didn't want anything to do with her now. Couldn't even stand to be in her presence? Well, she'd prove that she didn't care about him at all, no matter that it was a lie.

Driving Gabby and her mother and grandmother home was very much not on Jaime's list of things to do today. It, in fact, went against everything he was *trying* to do.

The FBI psychiatrist he'd been forced to talk to had insisted that any relationship with Gabby had been born of the situation and not actual feeling.

Jaime didn't buy it. He was too seasoned an officer, had been in too many horrible situations. He knew for a fact Gabby was just *different*.

But the problem was that Gabby wasn't a seasoned officer. She was a woman who'd been a kidnapping victim for eight years, and no matter what he felt or what he was sure of, she had a whole slew of things to work through that had nothing to do with him.

He'd only meant to relay the message from Ranger Cooper to Natalie. Not...see Gabby. With her family. The same woman he'd shared a bed with only a few days ago, before the strange world they'd been living in imploded.

She'd been crying, it was clear. He'd had to stand there, forcing himself not to take another step, for fear he would grab her away from all of them.

He glanced over at her sitting in his passenger seat. She was in his car. *His* car. In the daylight. Real and breathing next to him.

Her eyes were on the road, her profile to him, chin raised as though the road before them was a sea of admirers she was deigning to acknowledge.

He wanted to stop the car and demand she tell him everything, forget the fact her mother and grandmother were in the back.

But those women remained a good reminder of what had knocked him out of the raging idiot who'd nearly gotten himself fired and ruined the rest of his life. Women who'd truly suffered, nearly as much as Gabby, in the loss of her.

She deserved the time and space to rebuild with her family first. He didn't have any place in that. He would drive her home and…

He had to grip the wheel tighter because if he thought about leaving her at her house and just driving away…

But he'd made his decision. He'd made the *right* choice. He would keep his distance. He would give her time to heal. If she… Well, if she eventually came to him… He had to give her the space to make the first move.

You know that's stupid.

He ground his teeth together. No matter how stupid he *thought* it was, he was trying to do the right thing for Gabby. That's what was important.

"Natalie tells us you were undercover with the evil man?" Gabby's grandmother asked from the back seat.

"Yes." He turned onto the street Gabby's mother had named when they'd started. He didn't realize he'd slowed down to almost a crawl until someone honked from behind.

"It's the blue one on the corner," the grandmother supplied.

Jaime nodded and hit the accelerator. No matter that he didn't want to let Gabby out of the car, it was his duty. More, it was what she needed. Her family. Her life.

It would be a difficult transition for her, and he didn't need to make that any more complicated for her. It was the right thing to do.

No matter how completely wrong it felt.

He pulled his car into the driveway of a small, squat,

one-story home. It looked well kept, if a little sagging around the edges.

Gabby blinked at it and it took every last ounce of control he had not to reach over and brush his mouth across the soft curve of her cheek. Not to touch her and comfort her.

She looked young and lost, and he wanted to protect her from all that swamp of emotion she'd be struggling with.

"I got written up," he blurted into the silence of the car.

What the hell are you doing?

He didn't know. He needed to stop.

"You..." Gabby blinked at him, cocking her head.

"I think they gave me a little leeway what with just being out of undercover and all, but they don't take kindly to ignoring orders."

Shut your mouth and let her go, idiot.

"You...ignored orders," she repeated, as though she didn't quite believe it.

"They told me not to come to the hospital. Or try to see you. I may have..." He cleared his throat and turned his attention to the house in front of them. "I may have caused a bit of a scene."

"He got kicked out by security guards that first morning you were in the hospital," Grandma offered from the back. "A little rougher around the edges that day."

Jaime flicked a silencing glance in the rearview at the grandma. She smiled sweetly. "Natalie said you must have spent some time together when you were both in that place. Did you take care of our Gabriella?"

Gabby stiffened.

"I tried," Jaime said, perhaps a little too much of his still simmering irritation bleeding through. *If* she had come with him, she wouldn't have been in that standoff with Alyssa. They would have had... They could have...

"Mama, Grandma, will you...give me a few minutes alone with Agent Alessandro?" Gabby asked, her voice soft if commanding.

"Gabriella..." Her mother reached over the seat and put a hand to Gabby's shoulder.

"Gabby, please. Only Gabby from now on," Gabby whispered, eyes wide and haunted and not looking back at her mother.

"Come inside, baby. We'll—"

"I just need a few minutes alone. I promise. Only a few." She looked back at her mother and offered a smile.

But he was supposed to be giving her space. Not... alone time. "You should go—"

Gabby sent him a glare that would have silenced pretty much anyone, Jaime was pretty sure.

"Come now, Rosa," the grandmother said, patting the mother's arm. "Let's let these two talk. We'll go make some tea for our Gabri—Gabby."

Gabby's mother brushed a hand over Gabby's hair, but reluctantly agreed. The two women slid out of the back of his car and walked up to the house with a few nervous glances back.

Gabby's gaze followed them, an unaccountable hurt anguishing in her dark brown eyes. He kept his hands on the wheel so he wouldn't be tempted to touch her.

"So..." Jaime said when Gabby just stared at him for long, ticking seconds. "How are you feeling?"

She didn't answer, just kept staring at him with that hauntingly unreadable gaze.

"Well, I, uh, have things to do," he forced himself to say, wrenching his gaze from searching her face for signs of things that were none of his business.

"Take off your sunglasses," she said in return.

"Gabby—"

She reached over and yanked them off his face with absolutely no finesse. "Hey!"

"You look different," she stated matter-of-factly.

"A haircut and a shave will do that to a man," he returned, still not meeting her shrewd gaze. He had a mission. A job. A duty. Not for him, but for her. For *her*.

"You look *scared*."

"Scared?" he scoffed, despite the overhard beating of his heart. "I hardly think—"

"Then look at me."

Scared? No. He wasn't scared. He was strong and capable of doing his duty. He was a reliable and excellent FBI agent. He could face down a man with guns and evil, he could certainly face a woman—

Aw, hell, the second he looked at her he had to touch. He had to pull her into his arms despite the console between them. He had to fit his mouth to hers and *feel* as much as know she was there, she was alive, she was safe.

He brushed his hands over her hair, her cheeks, her arms, assuring himself she was real. Her fingers traced his clean-shaved jaw, over the bristled ends of his hair, as she kissed him back with a sweetness and fervency he wasn't supposed to allow.

"I'm not supposed to be doing this," he murmured against her lips, managing to take his mouth from hers only to find his lips trailing down her neck.

"Why not?" she asked breathlessly, her hands smoothing across his back.

"Space and…healing stuff."

"I don't want space. And if I'm going to go through all the shit of healing, I at least want you."

He focused on the edge of the console currently digging into his thigh, because if he focused on that instead of kissing her in daylight, real and free, he might survive.

He managed to find her shoulders, pull her back enough that her hands rested on his forearms.

Flushed and tumbled. From him.

"I'm supposed to give you space," he said firmly, a reminder to himself far more than a response to her.

"I don't want it," she said, her fingers curling around his arms. "And I think I deserve what I want for a bit."

She deserved *everything*. But he wanted to make sure giving it to her was…right. Safe. "I've had to see a psychiatrist, and there's some…mandatory psychological things I'll have to do before I'm reinstated to active duty. I'm sure the doctor suggested the same thing to you."

"Therapy, yes."

"There's a chance…" He cleared his throat and smoothed his hands down her arms, eventually taking her hands in his.

That wasn't fair because how did he say anything he needed to when he was touching her? "You shouldn't feel *obligated* to continue what happened in there. You should have the space to find out if it's what you really want."

She cocked her head, some mix of irritation and un-

certainty in the move. "Do *you* feel obligated by wha
happened?" she asked.

"No, but—"

"Then shut up." Then her mouth was on his again
hot and maybe a little wild. But it didn't matter, did it

He didn't want it to matter. He wanted her. Thi
strong, resilient woman.

She pulled back a little, always his warrior, facin
whatever hard things were in her way. "I want you. Th
Jaime I met in there. And I want to get to know thi
you," she said, running her finger down the lapel o
his suit. "The thing is, awful things happened in there
but it was eight years of my life. I can't…erase it. It'
there. Forever. An indelible part of me. I don't nee
to pretend it never existed to heal. I don't think that'
how you heal."

"But I have this whole life to go back to, Gabby.
know you aren't starting over, but people knew I wa
coming back. I'm coming back to a job. It isn't the sam
space we're in. I don't want you to feel as though yo
need to make space for me. That…you need to love m
or any of it."

She studied him for the longest time, and the mar
velous thing about Gabby was that she thought abou
things. Thought them through, and gave everything th
kind of weight it deserved.

Who was he to tell her she needed space? Who wa
he to tell her much of anything?

"I will tell you when I need space. You'll tell m
when you need some. It's not complicated." She trace
a fingertip along his hairline, as though studying thi
new facet to him. Eventually her eyes met his.

"And I do love you," she said quietly, weighted. "If that changes, I'd hardly feel obligated to keep giving you something I didn't have."

"Such a pragmatist," he managed to say, his voice dusty in the face of her confession. "I was trying to be very noble, you know."

Her mouth curved and he wondered how many things she would file away in his memories as *first in daylight*. The first time he'd kissed her with the sun shining into the car. The first smile under a blue sky.

He wanted them to outnumber his memories of a cramped room more than he wanted his next breath.

"I don't want noble. I want Jaime." She swallowed. "That is, as long as you want me."

"I practically lost my life's work for wanting you, and I'd do it a million times over, if that's what you wanted. I'd give up anything. I'd fight anything. I hope you know, I'd do *anything*."

She rubbed her hands up and down his cheeks as if to make sure he was real, and hers, though he undoubtedly was. Always.

"Come inside. I want to tell my mother and grandmother about the man who saved me."

"I didn't—"

"You did. I'd stopped counting the days. I'd stopped hoping. You came in and gave me both."

His chest ached, a warm bloom of emotion. Touched that anything he'd done had mattered. Moved beyond measure. "We saved each other." Because he'd been falling, losing all those pieces of himself, and she'd brought it all back.

"A mutual saving. I like that." She smiled that beau-

tiful sun-drenched smile and then she got out of his ca
and so did he. They walked up the path to her hom
with a bright blue sky above them, free and ready fo
a future.

Together.

* * * * *

She's spent her life concealing her identity.

Now she must trust an undercover agent to survive.

Willa Zimmerman grew up as the daughter of spies, so she's always known her life could be in danger. That's why when North Star undercover operative Holden Parker follows her to her home, seeking a lead on a hit man, she captures him. But soon they learn they're actually on the same side— and they're being pursued by the same relentless foe. Together, can they stop a deadly hunter before they end up as the next victims?

Don't miss
Shot Through the Heart
by Nicole Helm.

Available now wherever books are sold.

SPECIAL EXCERPT FROM

⬡ **HARLEQUIN**

INTRIGUE

*Ford Cardwell is shocked when his college crush
calls him out of the blue—even more so when he hea
a gunshot. But when he joins forces with medical
examiner Henrietta "Hitch" Rogers, she makes him
wonder if he was set up to believe the woman was a
victim—not a murderer.*

Read on for a sneak preview of
Trouble in Big Timber
by New York Times *bestselling author B.J. Daniels.*

The narrow mountain road ended at the edge of a rock cl
It wasn't as if Ford Cardwell had forgotten that. No, wh
he saw where he was, he knew it was why he'd taken t
road and why he was going so fast as he approached t
sheer vertical drop to the rocks far below. It would ha
been so easy to keep going, to put everything behind hi
to no longer feel pain.

Pine trees blurred past as the pickup roared down t
dirt road to the nothingness ahead. All he could see w
sky and more mountains off in the distance. Welcome ba
to Montana. He'd thought coming home would help. He
thought he could forget everything and go back to being t
man he'd been.

His heart thundered as he saw the end of the road comi
up quickly. Too quickly. It was now or never.

The words sounded in his ears, his own when he w
young. He saw himself standing in the barn loft looking
at the long drop to the pile of hay below. Jump or not jum
It was now or never.

He was within yards of the cliff when his cell phone
[rang]. He slammed on his brakes. An impulsive reaction to
[the] ringing in his pocket? Or an instinctive desire to go on
[living]?

The pickup slid to a dust-boiling stop, his front tires
[inches] from the end of the road. Heart in his throat, he
[look]ed out at the plunging drop in front of him.

His heart pounded harder. Just a few more moments—a
[few] more inches—and he wouldn't have been able to stop
[in ti]me.

His phone rang again. A sign? Or just a coincidence?
[He] put the pickup in Reverse a little too hard and hit the
[gas] pedal. The front tires were so close to the edge that
[for] a moment he thought the tires wouldn't have purchase.
[Fish]tailing backward, the truck spun away from the
[pre]cipice.

[F]ord shifted into Park and, hands shaking, pulled out
[his] still-ringing phone. As he did, he had a stray thought.
[Ho]w rare it used to be to get cell phone coverage here in the
[Gal]latin Canyon of all places. Only a few years ago the call
[wou]ldn't have gone through.

[W]ithout checking to see who was calling, he answered
[it, h]is hand shaking as he did. He'd come so close to going
[ove]r the cliff. Until the call had saved him.

"Hello?" He could hear noises in the background.
"[H]ello?" He let out a bitter chuckle. A robocall had saved
[him] at the last moment, he thought, chuckling to himself.

[B]ut his laughter died as he heard a bloodcurdling scream
[com]ing from his phone.

Don't miss
Trouble in Big Timber *by B.J. Daniels,*
available June 2021 wherever
Harlequin Intrigue books and ebooks are sold.

Harlequin.com

Love Harlequin romance?

DISCOVER.

Be the first to find out about promotions,
news and exclusive content!

f Facebook.com/HarlequinBooks

🐦 Twitter.com/HarlequinBooks

📷 Instagram.com/HarlequinBooks

📌 Pinterest.com/HarlequinBooks

You Tube YouTube.com/HarlequinBooks

ReaderService.com

EXPLORE.

Sign up for the Harlequin e-newsletter and
download a free book from any series at
TryHarlequin.com

CONNECT.

Join our Harlequin community to
share your thoughts and connect
with other romance readers!
Facebook.com/groups/HarlequinConnection

HSOCIAL

HARLEQUIN

Heartfelt or thrilling, passionate or uplifting—Harlequin is more than just happily-ever-after.

With twelve different series to choose from and new books available every month, you are sure to find stories that will move you, uplift you, inspire and delight you.